Best Wishes
Mark Burch

To Joe Williams -
From your friend
Dr. Robert Allison
5-6-05
May all lifes discoveries
be wonderful.

The Battle of Dragons
Book 1

Merlin the Sorcerer

William P. Burch

A Taylor-Madison Publishing Book

Taylor-Madison Publishing, Inc.
P. O. Box 201236
Arlington, Texas 76006
www.taylor-madison.com
williampburch@taylor-madison.com
www.thebattleofdragons.com

ISBN 0-9744947-0-4
LCCN: 2003112181

Edited by Dorrie O'Brien, Aurora, CO

Cover design by William P. Burch and Gail Cross, Desert Isle Design, Mesa, AZ

Cover photo by Blauvelt Photography, Arlington, TX

Acknowledgments

There are way too many people who contributed to this book to list them all here. I would like to say a special thank you to my children, Jennifer with her corrections, Paul with his many intelligent ideas, Cheri for being Cheri; my companion Gizmo, who slept on my arm while I typed; my mother and stepfather, Pat and W.J. Turney; my fabulous editor, Dorrie O'Brien; and my many friends who assisted in various ways with this book.

This book is dedicated to
my loving wife, Jane.
Without her support,
it would not exist today.

Introduction

When I was first asked to write this introduction, I didn't quite know what to think.

Being an archaeologist and not having seen the book yet was like knowing about a new Stone Age find and not being in a position to go check it out.

My imagination ran wild, thinking of what I would write as Bill Burch stood before me, handing out small bits of information that teased my brain and made pictures of what the whole story would be like when I read it. Here I was once again putting together what something would look like when it was completed. A story, instead of a Stone Age camp. When Bill dropped off the manuscript I was *really* ready to excavate.

I have been involved in discovery by doing field work and studying bits and pieces of the past for over forty years. This book turned out to be a treasure on its own, and I didn't even have to leave my home to discover it! Knowing what I did from what Bill had told me, I began reading what turned out to be an exciting and dangerous archaeological excursion into the unknown. As I dug through the pages I could see the ideas unfolding in the characters' minds the way I had on many field trips before. But this time I knew there would be a conclusion and I wasn't worried about following another trail that would lead to only more questions.

I would like to thank Bill Burch for bringing so much detail and realism to this book, and for giving me back excitement I haven't experienced in reading for a very long time. I can hardly wait to read the next adventure.

–Dr. Robert Allison,
Archeologist,
Diamond Enterprises, Texas

Chapter One

The windows revealed the cold, gray sky outside. Dr. Merlin Lakin twitched his nose like a rabbit as he looked up from his worktable. He hated the city with its noise and pollution; it always wreaked havoc on his sinuses. To give his office at the Carnegie Institute more of an open feel, he'd insisted upon a double-pane glass wall being installed, but since he still needed his privacy at times, he'd had white vertical blinds put in. The open blinds revealed a large room divided into cubicles, busy with activity.

The door to his office opened and in walked a fifty-three-year-old gray-haired woman. "What's up?" she asked.

Merlin glanced over his shoulder and saw Dr. Annette Stewart standing in the doorway.

"Is Adrian coming?" he asked.

Annie looked at Merlin, with his suit coat off, sleeves rolled up, tie loosened, and his shirt halfway unbuttoned. "Merlin, can't you ever keep yourself together?"

"It's this city. I've gotta get out of here. So where's Adrian?" Merlin, the team leader at the young age of thirty-four, turned his attention to some photographs on his worktable.

"He's coming. Give him a minute. What are those photos of?"

"I'll tell you when Adrian gets here. I don't want to go over it but once."

"There's no need to be so snippy. Anyway, speak of the devil," Annie said as a burly, bearded man about Annie's age entered the office. Dressed in a tweed sport coat with a matching hat to cover his bald spot, Dr. Adrian Dupré somehow seemed out of place in the cosmopolitan atmosphere of Washington, D.C. He was only a couple of inches shorter than Merlin's six feet, but was a full seventy pounds heavier at two hundred-fifty pounds.

"What's up, my boy?" Adrian asked, still retaining a bit of his French/British accent even after all his years in America. He'd always sounded a bit peculiar as a result of his parents' union.

"Y'all come here. I've found our next project." Merlin handed some of the photographs to each of his co-workers. "These are some satellite photos taken with a special, high-powered lens. Look. Look right here." Merlin pointed at what appeared to be clusters of buildings hidden under thick covering. The buildings seemed to be camouflaged rather than overgrown.

A big smile appeared on Annie's face after she'd looked at several of the photos. "Well, Merlin, it seems like you might have found us a way out of DC."

Merlin's face lit up. "Yeah! We're all approved to go. Let's pack," he said, knowing full well it couldn't happen that fast, even if he wanted it to.

***

A few weeks later, Merlin, Annie, and Adrian arrived in Flores, Guatemala, which was to be their main base for receiving supplies–Flores provided the nearest airport to the team's ultimate destination. Flores is near Tayasal, where the Itza Maya were the last of the Maya to surrender to the Spanish.

They traveled north from Flores on a narrow road to Carmelita, near the center of the Maya Biosphere Reserve. They then continued west in a Hummer into the Petén Jungle along a rough and old dirt road.

Their guide, Chac Garcia, had a Mayan first name and a Spanish last name. At five feet, he was considered tall by local standards, but compared to the Americans, he was only about Annie's height. His round face and dark skin gave away his Mayan heritage. Although he worked as a guide, Chac was well educated and held a degree in Indian Studies from the University of Mexico. Unfortunately, he'd been heavily involved with the Mayan resistance movement in Guatemala and had lost his accreditation with the university. Merlin had known Chac for many years and had worked on other archeological digs with him. Chac was the first person outside the Carnegie Institute Merlin had enlisted for the new adventure.

The team followed an old trail that would take them almost two-thirds of the way to their destination. Merlin thought about how lucky he was to be away from the high-tech modern world as he watched the workers clear their way with machetes; he loved the relaxed pace of a dig. He would have given anything to have been born at a time when the pace was slower, which was what had first interested him in archeology.

Adrian sat beside Merlin in the Hummer and wished they could use a laser beam to clear the way. Instead he just sat there, sweating in the heat, fanning himself with a battery-powered, hand-held fan. Adrian loved technology and all it had done to advance the field of archeology. He'd been a member of the team that had developed the computer program to translate the Mayan language into English a few years before this trip. On another dig, he'd located and translated a Mayan book that talked about the disappearance of the rulers and scientist of the Maya Empire, though he'd been disappointed in that the book had only said they'd all departed at one time and from one place.

As a result of the discovery, Adrian was showered with recognition and given many opportunities to lead his own team. Adrian, however, never liked the publicity and preferred working with Merlin as a team member rather than being the team leader. Besides which, Annie usually worked on Merlin's team, and he rather liked Annie.

"I see that smile again," Annie said, as she watched Merlin. "It's nice to see you content again." Annie had been torn apart ten years before when her husband died after falling through the roof of a hidden chamber on another dig. Merlin and Adrian had helped her through this rough period and she would now do just about anything for her friends.

"Thanks. I think I'll go help the workers. Adrian, why don't you take the wheel for a while?" Merlin suggested as he inhaled the pollution-free air.

"Yeah, like we're going anywhere anytime soon," Adrian said, raising an eyebrow at the men slashing away at the tangled vines and undergrowth in front of them.

Merlin grabbed his machete and joined the workers in clearing the way for the vehicles. He could think much better while working with his hands than he could just sitting in the Hummer. Merlin knew the odds were against him that behind all of this foliage was the city where the Mayan rulers had disappeared around 850 AD, 1170 years before. The odds were even greater against his finding the answer to what had happened to them, but he liked to remain optimistic and looked at the worst-case scenario: the rare chance to locate an ancient city that was virtually intact. He'd been able to tell from the new satellite photos that this city appeared to be complete and his gut told him that the answer to the mystery lay here, and was of course what had gotten him out of Washington DC–always a bonus.

As the team moved deeper and deeper into the jungle, they got less and less sunlight penetrating through to the jungle floor. The Hummer and trucks provided some light, but the workers also put on headbands with lighting attached, and it was still almost as though they were working at dusk.

As the day grew long, Chac spotted a clearing where they could make camp for the night. The workers increased their speed in anticipation as they rapidly cleared the way for the trucks. Once they broke through, the drivers moved the trucks into position to be unloaded. The workers ran to the trucks and began hauling out the equipment and setting up the campsite. Fires were lit, tents sprang up, and a small village began to emerge in the clearing; people busily prepared for the evening. Soon the camp began to settle down as the cooks prepared the evening meals.

Merlin, Annie, and Adrian moved their folding chairs near one of the campfires so they might enjoy the symphony of the forest as they ate, and drank their coffee. Merlin looked up at the stars and sighed in his thick, Texas drawl, "It don't get much better than this."

Chac soon joined them just as the roar of a distant jaguar joined the music of the jungle. "Dr. Dupré," he said. "I'm very impressed with your findings regarding the rulers of the ancient Maya who disappeared."

"Why, thank you, Chac," Adrian said, stroking his beard.

Chac asked, "Is this the reason for our expedition?"

Merlin looked at his Mayan friend. "Perhaps. We've found what may be a unique city. It appears that the buildings are not in ruins."

"But haven't all the ancient sites been located?"

"We don't know that to be true. Years ago NASA mapped the entire world with the aid of satellites–"

"Yes. I know. I've seen the photos," Chac interrupted. "Close-up views of the area occupied by the Maya revealed more than fifty thousand sites. Many were previously unknown."

"That's true. And a few months ago I was looking at some of those photos and noticed an odd area that seemed out of place. I requested and received approval from NASA for photographs to be taken of the area we're going to, using a special filter on a satellite. These photos revealed a hidden city that's almost completely intact. I also had them take some infrared photos so I might get an idea of the age based on the heat given off from the decaying buildings. The odd thing about these photos is that the buildings give off virtuously no heat."

"So you think this may be the site where the ancient rulers disappeared?"

"Call it a gut feeling."

"Is that how you got the funding for the dig?"

"He didn't need that as a reason," Annie said. "The idea of finding a completely intact city was enough."

"Well, let's hope it's what you're looking for," Chac said.

The four of them retired to their tents, accompanied by the distant roar of another jaguar.

After fighting their way for over a week in the dense jungles, even Merlin had begun to grow weary of their difficult trek. They were about to return to the city for a break, when they stumbled into a wall of vines so thick that light couldn't penetrate it.

Merlin hesitated for a moment before shouting, "I think this is it!"

"You must be out of your mind, my boy," Adrian said.

"No, I think Merlin's right," Annie said.

"Chac, have your men bring out the power saws and let's see if we can cut through this," Merlin ordered.

Chac had his workers unload the saws from the trucks and they began the task of cutting a pathway through the vines. After tunneling through the vines for a few hours, the workers reached a rock wall.

"Merlin, come quick," Chac said, gesturing toward the wall.

"I knew it!" an enthusiastic Merlin yelled. "This has got to be it. Chac, take some of your men and work your way to the top."

Chac had his men begin unloading ladders, scaffolding equipment, a generator, and lights, which were strung through the vine tunnel while the men on the ladders continued to cut their way to the top of the wall. Merlin and Annie checked out the wall and noticed how cool it felt. Once the workers reached about twelve feet up, they began setting up the scaffolding equipment to reduce the risk of falling. Finally, after about four hours of work, they reached the top of the wall and peered over to the other side.

"I can see the other side," Chac shouted. "I don't think you're going to be happy though."

"Why? What do you see?" Merlin asked.

"You better come up."

Merlin worked his way to the top and what he found surprised him. "You're not going to believe this," he shouted back to his friends. "It's pitch-black in here and it's full of water. I think the wall was sealed with some type of compound that makes it watertight."

"What? Oh jeez, just what we need," Adrian moaned.

"I think it might be best to set up a base camp and work on this tomorrow," Merlin said.

"Where do you propose we set up this base camp? There's no clearing here," Adrian asked.

"Why don't we just use our last campsite?" Annie suggested.

"Good idea," Merlin agreed. "Chac, let's leave the ladders and lights, but grab the generator. Let's get to the campsite and set up before it gets too late."

The workers returned to their last campsite and began building it with an eye toward making it a more permanent location. The light was quickly fading to darkness, so only the most basic structures were set up to begin with. Over the next several days they would be able to establish more functional work and living areas. Over dinner, the team discussed how they should go about handling the problem with the water, and if this was even the correct location. Merlin concluded that the best way to solve the problem would be to go back to the Institute, apprise them of the situation and request professional divers be brought in to see just what was there, under all that water.

Merlin left Adrian and Chac in charge of the base camp while he and Annie traveled to Washington to discuss the situation with Dr. Bill Barnes, head of the Carnegie Institute. As Merlin and Annie drove to the headquarters, Merlin's nose began to twitch again. "You see?" he complained. "Every time I get in this city, my sinuses go crazy; it drives me nuts."

The two explorers drove up to the building and parked their car. Only a few hours before they'd been in the Petén Jungle, now they were in the asphalt jungle of Washington, DC. Despite needing baths and still dressed in their jungle clothes, they entered the modern building and headed straight for Dr. Barnes' office. The office workers all turned, some smiling, some not, as the two walked down the corridors.

Merlin turned to Annie. "They must think I look hot dressed like this."

"No, they think we stink."

The two entered Dr. Barnes' office and his young and pretty secretary asked them to have a seat while she let Dr. Barnes know they'd arrived. She made no attempt to hide her disapproval of their odor as she got up.

Dr. Bill Barnes was a distinguished-looking man of average height and was about Annie's age. Dr. Barnes welcomed the two explorers home and invited them into his office, where they immediately began their discussion on how to handle their jungle problem. Merlin was in a hurry to return to the site, not only out of concern for his discovery, but also because of his desire to breathe regularly again.

It took several days, but they all eventually came up with a plan they felt comfortable with, though it would require quite a lot of additional funding to make it work. Annie began lining up the additional equipment, and Merlin returned to Guatemala in an effort to convince the appropriate government officials to provide the divers and some of the equipment that would be needed, while Bill Barnes worked on getting the money.

Happily, things worked out: The Guatemalan government

officials volunteered to provide a team of divers and their equipment from the Guatemalan army, which Merlin quickly returned to Washington to report. Annie was able to secure the remaining equipment, much at bargain prices. Dr. Barnes raised so much money that they would actually have a large surplus. With all their work completed, Merlin and Annie did not hesitate to return quickly to Guatemala.

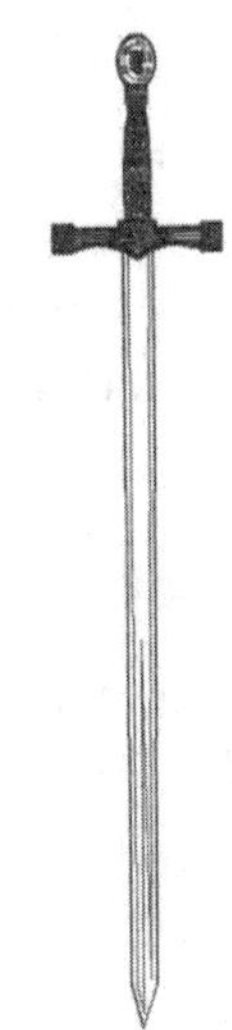

Chapter Two

Upon landing in Flores, Guatemala, they were met by Chac Garcia and a Guatemalan army officer. The officer was much taller than Chac and presented a strong, aristocratic appearance. "Dr. Lakin," he said, extending his hand. "I'm Captain Quetzal Coatl."

"Like the Toltec God?" Merlin asked, shaking Quetzal's hand.

"Well, yes. But it's purely coincidental," Quetzal answered with a laugh. "I got a lot of teasing as a youth about being named for a bird, and a last name meaning 'snake,' not to mention the reference to a Toltec God."

"I mean no offense, but you don't look Guatemalan," Merlin observed, looking the tall, light-skinned man up and down.

"No offense taken," Quetzal said. "Most of my bloodline is Spanish. I do have some Indian blood on my father's side. But, getting on with it, I have my men over by those trucks. Let me get them and they can unload the plane. I've made arrangements for rooms at the hotel in town for the two of you."

"Great," Annie said. "I can use the beauty sleep."

"Why don't you meet us for dinner tonight? We'll fill you in on what the mission is," Merlin said.

"That's fine. I'll see you tonight then," Quetzal said.

Merlin and Annie went to the hotel while Chac stayed behind to help with the equipment and supplies.

After checking into the hotel and getting their belongings put away, they went downstairs where they found Chac waiting for them in the lobby. Merlin said, "Hi, Chac. You ready to eat?"

"Yes, but I must speak to you privately for a minute." He took Merlin's arm and directed him to an empty corner of the lobby. Then, in a low voice while looking nervously at the floor, Chac said, "I don't trust this man Coatl. There's something about him that doesn't feel right."

"Are you sure it's not because of your past problems?"

"Maybe." Chac shrugged his shoulders and looked up and into Merlin's eyes. "But I think it's more than that. I don't think you should tell him too much about why we're here."

Annie, who had a habit of stroking her chin when thinking about serious matters said, "That's a prudent idea."

Merlin said, "Well, I don't think there's anything to worry about, but I'll keep to a need-to-know basis. Okay?"

"Great. Here he comes," Chac said in a hushed tone.

Captain Coatl walked toward them with a friendly, but somehow plastic smile. He extended his hand to Merlin. "It's a pleasure to see you again. Will your worker be joining us?"

Merlin shot him an offended look. "Chac is not a worker, he's a friend. Oh, and yes, he'll be joining us."

"I'm sorry. I meant no offense," Quetzal said, maintaining his erect, aristocratic posture.

"None taken," Merlin said with a smile. "Let's go eat."

The four of them entered the restaurant and were seated at a table near the center of the room. The odd mixture of a Mayan, a Guatemalan army officer, an American in a safari outfit, and a woman who looked like everybody's grandmother, drew curious looks from the other diners.

After giving their waiter their orders, Quetzal turned to Merlin. "Now tell me, please, about this mission."

"We believe we've located an undiscovered Mayan city that's completely intact," Merlin said.

"Ah. Interesting. But why do you need my team?"

Merlin hesitated for a moment as he thought about his answer, then he leaned forward and said softly, "We've literally run into a wall. In fact, a twenty-foot-high wall, that we think surrounds the whole city. We don't know how far down the wall goes on the other side."

"Yes, but where do I come in?"

"There is nothing behind the wall but water; we think an entire city lies beneath it. That's where you come in."

"So you want me to explore this city for you. Is that all? You could've hired any group of divers for that rather than tying up my country's military."

Annie stroked her chin as she watched and listened to Merlin and Quetzal. She reached over and placed her grandmotherly hand on Quetzal's. "The decision to use you wasn't ours. It was made, no, insisted upon, by your government."

"I just can't imagine my government being behind this waste of time," Quetzal said angrily. "There must be more to this than you're telling me. What's supposed to be in this city?"

"We won't know what's in the city until we get there," Merlin said as Chac looked on. Remembering Chac's earlier warning, Merlin tried to change the subject by saying, "About

Chac here. You should know that he's a graduate of the University of Mexico and majored in Indian Studies."

"Wonderful. So why's he working as your guide?" Quetzal asked rudely.

Merlin hadn't expected the question. He turned and glanced quickly at Chac. "Let's just say he's suffering under a cloud of disfavor from some of the members of your government."

As he took another bite of food, Quetzal asked, "What did he do to draw the attention of members of my government?"

"I wanted freedom for my people," Chac said. He looked at Quetzal with a steely stare and shouted, "Now I remember you! You're Coatl, the Snakeman."

Quetzal raised one eyebrow and looked at Chac as if for the first time. "I've been referred to by many names; only my enemies used that one."

Suddenly Chac lurched across the table, but Merlin grabbed him. "Whoa, wait a minute. What goes on here?"

"He's a butcher," Chac said.

"I'm a patriot," Quetzal said.

"Hold it now. Hang on," Merlin said. "Chac, you first. What's the story?"

"He's the one who conducted the 'interrogations' of my people. He tortured them. Many disappeared."

"Is this true?" Annie asked, horrified.

"Part of it," Quetzal said. "I was in Army Intelligence. But I don't know anything about these torture charges."

"You liar," Chac shouted.

"Hold on now," Merlin said. "Let's hear the man out."

"Well, I did interrogate some of the prisoners. And maybe we were a little rougher than we intended to be," Quetzal admitted.

"'Rougher' than you intended to be!" Chac yelled. "You *killed* people and you *enjoyed* it."

Obviously caught off guard, Quetzal wasn't prepared to defend himself. Yet he held his aristocratic pose as he said, "I transferred out of Intelligence. I wanted no part of hurting people and I certainly didn't enjoy it."

"So why did you do it?" Chac asked.

"It was my job."

"Hey guys, that's in the past," Merlin interrupted. "I've got a job to do, too. I need both of you to get it done."

"You don't need me if he's going to be part of it," Chac declared.

"Look, Chac. You're my friend. You know more about what's going on than he does. This project's important to you and your people," Merlin said.

"Okay, okay. I'll stay. But he goes when his part is done."

"Agreed."

There wasn't much talking during the rest of their meal. When they finished, Merlin quickly paid and they left for their rooms. Merlin and Annie were on the fourth floor while Chac and Quetzal were on the second floor.

Just after Chac and Quetzal got off the elevator, Quetzal grabbed Chac and slammed him against the wall. "Look, you little piece of shit. I'll gut you in a minute if you give me any more trouble. You hear me?"

"I hear you. But you put your hands on me again and I'll do more than gut you."

"You keep thinking that," Quetzal said as he turned and walked to his room.

They loaded into the trucks in front of the hotel the next morning for the ride to the base camp. There wasn't a lot of talking on the way, but something told Merlin the story didn't end at the dinner table.

Because of the work done already, they reached the base camp by early the next day. The divers quickly began setting up their tents in the space Chac provided them. Merlin looked around the campsite and noticed that the whole area had been vastly improved. Latrines had been put in place, a mess tent established, and chemicals set out to ward off the mosquitoes. It was almost homey. In fact, it might have been a little too homey for Merlin.

The team, the workers, and the divers headed to the site after breakfast. The tunnel through the vines and area immediately in front of the wall had been widened and more lights had been added. Quetzal and his men climbed the steps that had been built to the top of the wall. They looked over the wall into the dark water before them. The divers all wore yellow dive suits to help to be seen through the water's darkness; they also each had a camera and lights attached to the top of their dive helmets, which resembled motorcycle helmets. Inside each helmet was a voice transmitter and receiver as well as a video screen that allowed them to see what the other divers saw. They could keep in voice contact with each other, as well as with Adrian, Annie, and Chac, who had stayed on land. Adrian, Annie and Chac could see what was going on by watching monitors that had been set up in a cleared area.

Once underwater, Merlin looked around, but could see nothing other than the lights of the other divers. The water was dark brown from decaying plant life, which gave everything an eerie look as the lights shined through it. The swimmers followed the wall to the bottom where they found a rock walkway that extended out for about six feet and continued along the wall as far as they could see. From there, the ground appeared to be level for several more feet where it began a gradual descent. Quetzal told the divers to level out when they were fifty feet down; he didn't want to go any deeper with the first dive into unknown waters.

Merlin looked around and thought he spotted a building in the distance. "Adrian, zoom in with my camera and see if you can make out if that's a building ahead of me."

Adrian used the joystick to focus the camera on the distant object. As he brought the image closer, he said, "I can see it, but it's still rather blurry."

"Is it a building?"

"I can't tell for sure. It's still out of focus, but it could be," Adrian said.

"Let's get closer," Merlin ordered the divers as he took off in the direction of the building.

"Dr. Lakin," Quetzal said, "I advise against this. We should take it more slowly."

"Nonsense," Merlin said. "Are you coming?"

"Merlin, it's starting to look more like a building now," Adrian said.

"Come on, guys, let's take a look," Merlin said.

The divers moved cautiously toward the building. Merlin was the first to arrive at what appeared to be the upper level of a large building. "This *is* it. I knew it," he exclaimed.

"Don't go in it," Quetzal ordered. "We have no idea what might be in there. Let's go back and plan it out so we can enter it more safely."

"Fine, but I want to swim around it first. Adrian, are you getting all this?" Merlin asked.

"Yeah, it's coming through great."

Merlin and the divers swam around the exterior of the building, and noticed how well preserved it was; they could even tell that some of the building had been painted light blue. Merlin ran his fingers over the beautiful carvings and wondered what it must have been like when it was occupied and standing in the light.

"Dr. Lakin, it's time to go," Quetzal said. "We're about out of air."

Merlin and the divers reluctantly surfaced and returned to the wall where Adrian and Annie were waiting.

"Fabulous, my boy. Simply fabulous," Adrian said as he shook Merlin by the shoulders enthusiastically.

They were anxious for another dive, but decided it would be best to break for lunch since they had to prepare the Zodiac boats anyway. Upon returning to the base camp, the divers began their preparations while Merlin, Adrian, Quetzal, and Annie discussed their findings.

"We need to get the water out of the way so we can excavate the area," Annie said.

"I agree," Merlin said. "But first we should test the structures to make sure they'll stay together once we expose them to the air."

"And we should try to remove the vines that cover the area," Adrian said.

"We've gotta be careful doing that," Annie advised. "The whole growth might cave in and destroy the buildings."

"I could try to get my army's engineering department to provide us with helicopters to assist in the removal of the vines," an enthusiastic Quetzal said just as Chac joined them.

Chac frowned at Quetzal, wondering about Quetzal's motives. "You need more men to do this. You should consider cutting the vines from around the wall. You need to know how large an area you're talking about before you consider removing the vines."

"It's 'we,' Chac," Merlin said. "You're part of this too, you know. We also need to survey the city and see how many buildings are actually there."

They laid out a plan: Chac would cut around the circumference of the wall using his workers and some soldiers provided by the Guatemalan army. Adrian would monitor the dives from land, while Annie tried to determine if the structures would hold up once exposed to air. Merlin, Quetzal, and the divers would survey the underwater city and draw a map of the site. An engineering team would be called in to work with Annie to see how the city could be drained and if it were, whether the structures would remain standing.

As the days progressed, Merlin and Quetzal were able to locate all the buildings and draw a rough map of the area, but they stayed away from the inside of the buildings due to the potential risks.

Adrian brought in a draftsman and the two used the computers to make drawings of each building. The function of most of the buildings was clear, though they were stumped by one large one. Also, they found no pyramids, which was unusual for a city of this size.

Chac's work showed that the city covered a much larger area than expected and was in a valley. He also found that a stream had once run down the mountain and through the complex, providing it with fresh water. However, at some point in time, the stream's exit had been blocked. The divers discovered it had been sealed on purpose; they located where the stream had actually been diverted back into the town on no set course. Chac, working on the outside, and the divers, working on the inside, discovered that the entrance of the stream was sealed through an intricate device that worked like a toilet flusher. As the water rose to the level of the stream, a large ball pushed a wooden rod up. This rod lowered another rod, which released a stone tablet that sealed the wall. The tablet was designed so that it also divided the stream, causing it to flow equally in different directions. As the tablet dropped, it raised two wooden gates, releasing the water into two trenches. Chac discovered that, because of where the vines were planted, the stream provided them with irrigation. Pieces of rope were found that indicated the vines had been planted and laid out to grow up and over the city on purpose.

Some evidence indicated that the city had been flooded while the residents still lived in it.

Annie and the engineers found that the structures should hold together if the water was drained, but they had deep concerns about removing the vine cover. They again considered cutting the vines and lifting them by helicopter, but it wasn't feasible because it would take precision timing that couldn't be obtained with the helicopters. If one should fall, it might cause a domino effect. They considered some type of floatation device, but it was also rejected as too dangerous. Many other ideas were tossed around which included lasers, support platforms, fire, and chemicals, but all were put on hold or rejected as too dangerous.

Merlin called the team together, including Quetzal, the rest of the divers, the engineers, and the draftsmen. Adrian began the meeting by showing a three-dimensional rendition of the site. It showed beautiful paved streets with colorful buildings on either side. The buildings were painted in various shades of blue, red, yellow, and green and blends of all four. Statues had been placed at various locations, depicting leaders of various Mayan tribes rather than just one tribe, as was the norm. Everyone noticed that the city was without pyramids or ball courts, which made it look oddly unfinished.

The large, beautiful, multistoried building attracted everyone's attention.

Merlin asked for everyone's thoughts about entering the structures while they were still submerged. Annie and Quetzal were strongly against it. Adrian wanted to see what was in the big building. One of the engineers came up with the solution they went with: They'd bring in a remote-controlled submersible robot camera to view the interior of the building. If everything looked safe, then the divers would enter the building and check it out.

After a few days of preparation and waiting, the submersible, remote-controlled camera arrived. The divers loaded it onto one of the Zodiac boats and took it to a spot above the "mystery" building, as the group had begun to call it. As the submersible was carefully lowered into the water, the team back on shore viewed the camera shots on a monitor while Quetzal used the remote control to maneuver it.

Quetzal moved the camera through the entrance of the building on the first floor. The walls looked orange in the camera lights and were lacking the painted figures that normally decorated the interior walls of Mayan structures. Adrian noticed an opening in the ceiling and directed Quetzal to it. The submersible popped through the opening and into an air pocket. It looked like there were more rooms and a hallway in the air pocket, along with what appeared to be artifacts in the room.

They brought back the submersible and sat down to discuss the new situation they found themselves in.

Quetzal sounded excited as a kid. "We've got air here! We'll be able to walk around without air tanks–breathing ancient Mayan air!–and explore this area."

"Wait a minute," Merlin said. "That air is probably too stale to breathe."

"What do you mean?" Quetzal asked, disappointment clear in his tone.

"The air may be too stale and you won't be able to breathe it."

"What we can do is bring some smaller tanks in that will allow us to walk around and breathe safe air."

"That'll work," Merlin agreed.

"Wait a minute," Annie said.

"What now?" Merlin asked.

"What's the potential of the floor collapsing?"

Adrian stroked his beard while watching the monitor. He looked up. "I don't think the floor is what we have to worry about. I'd be more concerned about the ceiling caving in and the water crushing you. Remember, you're going to be down about a hundred feet."

"I agree," Quetzal said. "If there's any kind of hairline fracture or other weakness in the ceiling, the vibrations from our being there could cause it to give way. We could be in big trouble really quick."

"Is there any way to shore it up as we go?" Merlin asked. "Like they do in rescues or mining?"

"Maybe, but you'd need a secure base for the support or you'd just be compounding your problems," Adrian answered. "Remember that you'll be on the second floor of a seven-story structure. You'll have a lot of potential for disaster from both above and below you."

"Well, this floor has to have been sealed off somehow or the water would have flowed in from the sides or above," Merlin argued. "That leads me to believe that this is some kind of chamber. It could also mean that it has some kind of special support on the sides and maybe above it."

"Makes sense," Adrian agreed, "but it looks like an awful big risk."

"I think it's worth it," Merlin said. "We can go in and shore up the first floor before entering the chamber. We can then add support in the chamber as we go along. I think that if we're cautious and take our time, we can greatly reduce our risk."

"Well, I'm willing, provided we use the caution you just described," Quetzal agreed. "But just so you know, if the bubble tilts and starts to move out, it could destroy the building and everyone in it."

The team made the plan for the exploration of the building. The engineers worked with the divers in planning the support. Merlin sent copies of their findings to Dr. Barnes back at the Carnegie Institute, while Quetzal reported to his government. Within a matter of days, the campsite more than doubled in size as reporters, Guatemalan government officials, Carnegie Institute officials, and curiosity-seekers came to watch.

The entire team soon found their faces on magazine covers, newspapers, and worldwide television. Mayan protesters showed up, demonstrating against the disturbance of a perceived burial site. The crowds grew to the point where the team could no longer get their work done. Merlin had to ask for troops from the Guatemalan army to help keep people out of the area.

The Guatemalan government saw a tremendous opportunity for recognition and money as a result of the discovery. They began charging the news media and individuals for access to the site. They also began widening the road from Flores to Carmelita and built an asphalt road from Carmelita to the site.

It wasn't long before the Mayan protests became violent. Merlin and Chac decided to speak to them. Chac was well known and respected by the protesters, so they listened attentively to what the two men had to say. Chac and Merlin described the city and showed the people photographs and film clips of it, as well as the model Adrian and the engineers had built. They then explained how this city was of extreme importance to the Mayan people because it might answer the question of what happened to their ancient leaders. The two men also pointed out how this site couldn't possibly be a burial site, though it could've been the site of a mass suicide. After the meeting the protests continued, though without the violence. The protests did have the effect of intensifying the world's interest in the discovery.

Finally, everything was ready for the exploration of the air-pocket chamber. The engineers had reinforced the first floor and the team was given the green light to go.

The day before the dive, Merlin met with Quetzal and the divers to go over last minute instructions. Merlin said, "Gentlemen, as a precaution, do not shave tonight or tomorrow morning."

The divers looked at each other, then at Merlin, wondering about the odd order.

Quetzal was the first to speak. "I don't understand. Why shouldn't we shave?"

"Past archeologists have discovered that ancient air usually contains deadly micro-organisms that can penetrate the skin through small cuts. We believe that this is the reason so many archeologists in the past died after opening tombs. So, let's be careful."

The divers had placed cameras on nearby buildings and the exterior of their target building, which they now called the "Science Building." Special monitors were set up for the media. Television stations from around the world were giving hourly updates with many nightly news programs devoted partially or entirely to the exploration.

Merlin was the second man to enter the chamber and immediately shed his diving gear for the freedom of the smaller tank. The rest of the divers joined him as the first diver set up a camera inside the room. Quetzal directed some of the divers to begin shoring up the chamber while Merlin used a couple of the divers to test the air–they reported that it wasn't safe to breathe, so they kept their masks on.

Outside, Adrian, Annie, and the rest of the world watched as the divers went about their tasks. Suddenly Annie gasped as dust fell from the ceiling where one of the divers was working.

"Be careful," Merlin instructed the diver who had tightened the support too tight.

Merlin spotted some artifacts in a pile of what looked like books. He directed his men to place the artifacts in sealed containers while he did the same with the books. Merlin then instructed two of the divers to take the books and artifacts to the surface.

As Quetzal and his men moved farther into the chamber, they found a hallway and stairs leading to another level of the building. Quetzal's men had not completed supporting and testing the floor they were on, but Quetzal still climbed cautiously up the stairs, then shined his light around the third floor as he entered it from the stairway. Merlin heard Quetzal say he was moving onto the floor of the third level. One of the divers called out a warning that the second level wasn't secure yet and suddenly there was dust all around, followed by a loud scream and Quetzal fell through the floor. When he hit, it caused a small crack in the second level floor.

Merlin and the divers ran to Quetzal to help him. Quetzal lost his oxygen tank in the fall and took a couple of breaths of the poisonous air of the chamber. One diver grabbed Quetzal's scuba tanks and got him breathing again, though shallowly.

Merlin told the base what had happened, though there was no need given that practically the entire world was watching the event on television. Merlin sent two divers to wait at the boat so they could help with Quetzal, and the other divers helped Merlin get Quetzal into the water. Merlin told the divers who stayed behind to finish shoring up the second level, then to come to the surface.

Merlin and another diver grabbed Quetzal and helped him swim through the first level. Just as they were about to exit the building there was a loud noise behind them. Merlin looked toward the sound and saw a large wall of water and debris heading toward him. The other diver took off, leaving Merlin and Quetzal a few feet from the exit of the building. Merlin grabbed Quetzal's arm and pulled him along. There was a lot of screaming and shouting in his ear set and someone began telling Merlin to leave Quetzal and save himself.

Merlin hesitated briefly, remembering Chac's comments about Quetzal's actions as "the Snakeman." A piece of debris hit Merlin's air tank and he lunged forward, pulling Quetzal with him. As they exited the building, Merlin saw that the top floors had collapsed onto what were the second and third floors. The entire world gasped as they watched the entire building fall toward Merlin, held back by helping Quetzal.

Adrian grabbed a Zodiac and headed to the other boat with Chac. As they reached the boat, Annie told him that the building was collapsing on top of Merlin. Adrian grabbed one of the divers and told him to go help Merlin. The diver grabbed his partner and the two of them took off. Adrian glanced inside the diver's Zodiac and saw the ancient books in their waterproof containers. He grabbed the books and headed back to shore, leaving Chac to help with the rescue.

As the divers reached the bottom, they spotted Merlin

and Quetzal trapped under a large slab from the building. They rushed to them and managed to get the two men free. Quetzal was barely breathing as they broke the surface of the water. Chac helped the divers haul Merlin and Quetzal into the boat just as another Zodiac arrived with four more divers. Chac told them to go down and try to locate the other divers as he took Merlin and Quetzal back to the wall.

At the wall, Merlin and Quetzal were slowly carried down to the bottom where a doctor waited to check them out. The doctor motioned for stretchers. "They must be moved to a hospital fast. We'll send them by helicopter to Guatemala City."

"How are they?" Annie asked.

"Not good," the doctor said, shaking his head.

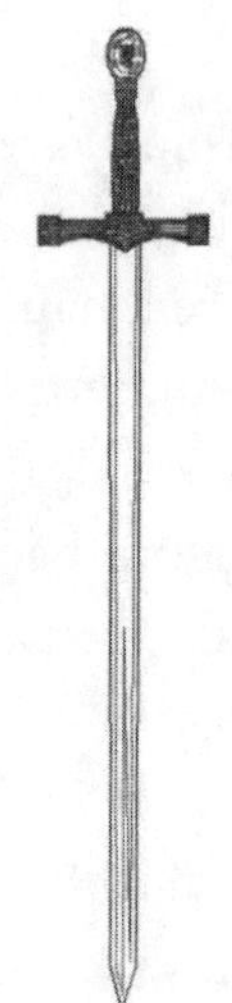

Chapter Three

A month after the disaster the site had changed considerably. Adrian had left the project and flown home the day after. From time to time he checked in on Merlin, who was hospitalized in Guatemala City.

Annie had been temporarily placed in charge of the project. She and Chac weren't allowed to enter the sunken city, and the Guatemalan government placed guards around the perimeter, so Annie worked primarily around the outlying area to learn what she could about the ancient city.

Officials in the Guatemalan Department of Antiquities were concerned about some of the material that had been found in the Science Building before it collapsed. The surviving divers said they'd brought up some artifacts and books, but the books were missing. Chac told the representative of the Guatemalan government that he'd seen them in the Zodiac boat, but they weren't there when the boat reached the wall.

Quetzal had been rushed to the hospital in Guatemala

City where he stayed in intensive care for several weeks. The stale air had burned his lungs and there was the lingering possibility of brain damage due to his lack of oxygen. (Chac told Annie that he thought Quetzal was brain damaged before the accident.) All but two of the divers died who had been in the building at the time it collapsed. In a review of the disaster, Guatemalan government officials placed the blame for the accident on Quetzal for not following procedures, but the information was unofficially removed from Quetzal's military file for unknown reasons.

Annie received permission from the Guatemalan government to leave her confinement at the project so she could accompany Merlin to Washington, DC upon his release from the hospital. Chac was required to remain behind–something like a hostage–since the Mayan books were still missing and the whole team was under suspicion for theft. Annie rushed to the hospital with her ticket out of the country. She was not normally so anxious to leave a dig, but the past month had felt much like forced confinement. She quickly gathered up Merlin and the two of them left Guatemala and their dream project.

When they arrived in Washington, a strangely excited Adrian met them. Instead of taking them to the Carnegie Institute's headquarters, he took them to his townhouse in Georgetown. Merlin leaned on his cane to walk up to the two-story brick home. This was the first time Merlin had ever been to Adrian's home. Adrian sat his friends in his Victorian-style living room, filled with beautiful antique furniture. Merlin particularly liked the foxhunt-scene wallpaper.

Adrian brewed a pot of freshly ground Kona coffee, which he served to his friends in elegant china coffee cups. Merlin thought it odd that such a big man had such dainty coffee cups. After they settled in, Adrian said, "I've got one hell of a story to tell you. I don't know how true it is, but it does explain a lot."

"What are you talking about?" Annie asked.

"Let's get on with it; my leg hurts like hell," Merlin said.

Adrian gave an upward gesture with his big hands, stood up and stroked his neatly cropped beard and began to pace, organizing his thoughts. He finally said, "I know what happened to the Maya leaders."

"What?!" Merlin exclaimed.

"How would you know?" Annie asked. "You left right after the disaster."

"I took the Mayan books and translated them," said Adrian.

Annie jumped to her feet and lunged at the big man. "You son of a bitch!" she said. "I was held a prisoner in that hell hole because of you!"

Adrian held her away with his big arms. "Calm down, little one. I think you'll forgive me after you hear what I have to say."

"Come on, Annie," Merlin said. "Let's hear him out."

"This had better be good. Right now I'm ready to kill you," Annie said.

"Oh, it's good all right. Let me begin by saying this involves many of the legendary characters of the Maya, including the High-King Hunac-Cel, the God Kukulkán, the Sorcerer Priest Lakin Chan, and even the Toltec God Quetzalcoatl."

"It already sounds like a fairy tale," Annie grumbled, thinking about the trouble she'd been through because of the missing Mayan books.

"Listen to me," Adrian said patiently. "According to the books, Kukulkán united all the smaller Mayan kingdoms. The other kings offered to make Kukulkán the High-King of this new empire, but he turned them down. The sub-kings then elected Hunac-Cel to be their High-King. In order for the administration of the new United Mayan Empire to be able to work smoothly, they created a new city as their capital and named it Mayapan."

"Adrian. Hello-o-o-o-o," Merlin said, squirming uncomfortably in pain. "We're all considered experts in Mayan history. So what's with the history lesson?"

"Well, let me finish."

"Yeah, let him finish," Annie said, "otherwise we'll be here all day."

"Okay," Adrian said. "It seems that Hunac-Cel grew tired of serving at the pleasure of the other kings. He knew the other kings would be in attendance at a wedding in Ucyabnal of Chac-Xib-Chac. Under the pretense of wanting the bride for himself, he attacked the city during the ceremony. He was repelled when the Sorcerer Priest Lakin stood by a well and directed a beam of light at the attacking forces. This caused the attackers to scatter and the Itza Maya won the battle. In honor of what Lakin had done, the city changed its name to 'Sorcerer of the Well' or *Chichén Itzá,* in the Mayan language."

"Okay. Well, thanks for the history lesson." Merlin rose to leave. "You have yet to reveal anything new. Everyone who works with Maya archeology knows that story."

"What they don't know is that Hunac-Cel enlisted Quetzalcoatl's aid. I believe this was the catalyst that caused the kings to leave and how the Toltec came to influence the Maya."

"And you have proof of this?" Merlin asked as he stopped in his tracks.

"Yes, and that's not even the good part," Adrian said, baiting Merlin.

Merlin turned and looked into his friend's eyes. Then he smiled and returned to his seat, walking like an old man crippled with arthritis. "All right. Let's hear some more."

"The Maya leaders heard about the alliance. The kings knew they would have trouble individually defending their kingdoms against the well-trained army of Hunac-Cel combined with Quetzalcoatl's army. Their only hope would be to stand together and combine their military forces." The big man began to pace and stroke his beard, giving the impression that he was one of the leaders trying to figure out how to defend their cities against such a powerful force. Adrian stopped pacing for a moment. "What they needed was time; time to get word to their kingdoms about the threat; time to build and train a united military force; time to develop military plans. Time. Something they didn't have much of."

Adrian went quiet and paced some more, this time with his hands behind his back. "The Maya thought they had a way to accomplish what they needed to do. They thought they had found the time needed by using the results of the research from a secret scientific center that had been funded by the combined kingdoms."

"And what was this research?" asked a skeptical Annie.

Again the big man hesitated as he resumed his pacing.

Merlin said, "You're going to wear a hole in that carpet if you keep it up. Just tell us what they were researching."

"All right, my boy," Adrian said, staring into Merlin's eyes. "They were researching time travel."

"Okay. It's a historic fact that the first people to do research into time travel were the Maya," Annie said. "So what're you trying to tell us? That they succeeded?"

"Yes. That's exactly what I'm trying to tell you." Adrian nodded. "They invented time travel."

"Whoa. Wait a minute," Annie cried. "You don't expect us to *believe* they invented time travel?"

"Adrian, there are a lot of things you can come up with that we would buy," Merlin said as he once again rose to leave.

"This just happens to not be one of them. Come on, Annie. Let's get out of here."

Adrian grabbed some papers on the table and ran after his two friends. "No. No. Please. Just look at these."

Merlin took a few more steps before he looked up at his old friend standing before him with papers in his hands and a look of desperation on his face. He then looked at Annie, who had a sad look in her eyes. Annie was thinking that her friend had lost his mind and she felt bad for him. Merlin turned back to Adrian and said with pity, "Let me see what you have."

Adrian practically leapt to where Merlin was standing. He was desperately trying to get the correct paper in Merlin's hand when he suddenly stopped and stood straight as an arrow. He slowly handed to Merlin a page of paper, which was a copy of one of the pages in one of the Mayan books, and with a smile said, "My boy, what we have here is the means for time travel."

Merlin forgot his pain as he looked through the copies from the books and the translations Adrian had done. He felt his knees grow weak and returned to where he'd been sitting, still holding some of the pages.

"Merlin," Annie insisted, "close your mouth and tell me what you've got."

"I'm not a physicist, but if any of this is true . . ."

"If any of what is true, then what?"

"If it's true, we have the means to travel through time," Merlin said, not looking up from the papers.

Annie was clearly skeptical as she picked up some of the pages Merlin has let slip from his hands, and began looking at them. Then, "Oh my God," she said.

Adrian bent over and said with a smile, "Well. Didn't I tell you?"

"Yes, you did. And who else did you tell?" Annie asked.

"No one. Only the three of us know about this."

"Do you realize what we can do with this?" Merlin exclaimed. "We can go back to when the cities were actually occupied and see firsthand what they were like."

"Are you kidding?" Annie said. "We can meet the great leaders of history!"

"Yes, my friends," Adrian said as he put his big arms around the shoulders of his two friends and said with an equally big smile, "We can become 'Time Travel Archeologists.'"

"We've got a long way to go before that happens," Merlin said. "You need to get Dr. Barnes involved with this."

"Not a chance," Adrian declared. "You're the salesman among us. I think I'll let you have the honor."

Merlin called and told Dr. Barnes that he and Annie had arrived back in town. Dr. Barnes wanted to know if their flight had been delayed since Merlin had just now checked in. Merlin explained that they had gone to Adrian's home first and that he hadn't had a chance to call before then. He told Dr. Barnes that there were some important matters they needed to discuss and they arranged to meet later that afternoon. Adrian took his two friends to their homes so they could unpack and get ready for the meeting with Dr. Barnes.

That afternoon, the three explorers arrived at the Carnegie Institute and went straight to Dr. Bill Barnes' office. The team was quickly ushered into the office by Bill's secretary. Merlin was still in a great deal of pain and sat on the couch rather than one of the chairs in front of the desk.

Bill moved from around his desk to shake hands with the team members. "You still look bad, Merlin."

"Yeah, I know," Merlin said, shaking Bill's hand. With a

twitch of his nose, he said, "As much as I hate to admit it, it's good to be home."

Bill placed his hands on his knees as sat down. He leaned forward. "It's good to have you home. Now tell me: What's up?"

"I guess you've heard about the missing Mayan books," Merlin started.

"Yeah. That's too bad. It's caused us a great deal of trouble. The sad thing is, *we* have more interest in finding the books than the Guatemalan government does."

"Well, I know where they are," Merlin said, glancing over at Adrian.

"You do?! Well, tell me, so we can get them back. We need to turn them over to the Guatemalan Department of Antiquities so we can get them off our back."

"Not so fast," Adrian said.

"What do you mean?"

"It's better that you not know where they are. The less you know, the less you can say about them," Annie said.

"The three of you have the books, don't you?" Bill said sternly. "I want those books in my office immediately. You three are playing a dangerous game here. You've jeopardized all this Institute stands for."

Merlin loosened his tie and unbuttoned the top button of his shirt. He looked at Bill in hope of sizing up the situation. "The books go way beyond traditional archeology. They tell us about the disappearance of the Mayan rulers and scientists and how to find them."

"So why do you want to keep this a secret?"

"Well, there's a lot more to these Mayan books than we can understand at this time. We need to do some extensive experiments in physics, nanotechnology, engineering, and botany to fully understand the information in them."

Bill looked as though he was a deer caught in headlights.

"Whoa. Hold up a minute. Two questions: Where do you plan to get the money to pay for this and second, why is this going to involve so many disciplines outside the field of archeology?"

"Oh. Thanks for reminding me," Merlin said, waving off Bill's questions. Merlin was becoming more and more excited as the discussion proceeded. He used his cane to stand up and began gesturing with his hands. "We need a large building with housing for the staff. This should be in a fairly secure area."

"Damn, Merlin. You know I can't come up with that," Bill said.

Merlin grabbed Bill's arm and looked him in the eye for a moment. With as sincere a look in his eyes as he could muster he said, "Bill, you've trusted me in the past and I've never let you down, have I? I need you to trust me on this too."

"Okay," said Bill said, after some thought. "I'll agree to the following. I have a friend who heads the Nanotechnology Department at the University of Texas at Arlington. I'll call him and see if he can lend us someone. If not, he can probably get us someone from the European Organization for Nuclear Research to help out–"

"You mean CERN," Annie said.

"Yeah, CERN." Bill nodded, scratching his head. "Now as far as the botanist goes. We have one on staff, so that shouldn't be a problem. I also have access to a former army base. But I should warn you: They say it's haunted. Not that I believe that sort of thing." Bill smiled as he looked around the room, trying to discern a reaction from the team to his mention of the haunted base, hoping for discouragement.

It apparently went right over their heads, so concentrated were they on their needs.

"Thanks. I knew you could do it," Merlin said.

"I hope you realize the risk you're asking me to take," Bill said, writing a note. "It better be worth it. Now you three get out of here; I've got work to do. Here's the address to the place you'll be working out of. That is, if the ghosts don't scare you away." Bill still saw no apparent alarm, but he could still hope. He wanted the team back to work and the Mayan books back in Guatemala. As a bureaucrat, Bill wanted a return to normal and the return of the books to Guatemala might accomplish that.

"Yeah, right," said Annie with a smirk. "Ghosts."

Bill smiled. "I'll call and get all of you clearance to get in there. Let me know how you like it."

The team immediately left Bill's office, walking on air like school kids who'd just won a big prize at the science fair.

Annie looked at Adrian and then at Merlin. "I bet this is the first time you've ever seen a fat man fly."

Merlin laughed. "He is walking a little lighter, isn't he?"

"Ah, my boy. I'm in heaven. After all, we've got the deal and are on our way to becoming the first Time Travel Archeologists in the whole history of the world!"

Merlin didn't want to dampen his friends' enthusiasm, but he felt he needed to put a little pragmatism in their thoughts. "Don't get too carried away yet. We have a lot of work ahead of us and we don't have the funding yet, either."

The three of them raced to the car for their trip to inspect what could be their new working environment. Merlin turned on his GPS and got driving directions. The location, outside Warrenton, Virginia, had once been an old-horse farm. It had later been bought by the U.S. Army and converted into an Intelligence base known as Vint Hill Farms Station.

They saw a highway sign directing them to the exit for Vint Hill Farms Station. They turned in and drove down a narrow road, past beautiful horse farms with magnificent thoroughbred horses on each side. Merlin loved the wide-open space and the deep green grass of the area. Finally they came to a turn-off for the base. Since the base was not currently in use, it was staffed by only a few MPs whose job was to keep out trespassers. Annie pulled the car up to the red brick guard shack where an Army Military Policeman came out to greet them.

The MP requested their IDs and, as Merlin showed his, he said, "I understand this place in haunted."

"Well, sir," the MP answered, "I don't know if it's haunted or not, but there have sure been some odd things happen around here."

"Oh really?" Annie asked, raising an eyebrow and looking over the rims of her glasses.

"Yeah. Things seem to appear from nowhere. We even had a man appear out of the blue."

"Where's the man now?" asked Merlin.

"I don't know. He ran outside the old Operations Building, dug a hole and disappeared again."

"Sounds rather spooky to me," Adrian said.

"You folks are cleared to go. I've been instructed to direct you to the commander's office. He's the one in charge here."

The team drove to the post commander's office, as instructed. The post commander assigned Lieutenant Lance Wilfred to show them around.

Lieutenant Wilfred was a handsome young man with dark hair and an engaging smile. He showed them the old horse barns that had been converted to Intelligence use when the Army Security Agency had first started using the farm. He then took them to a large, windowless building that at one time had been the Operations Building; a chain-link fence with barbed wire on top surrounded it. The entrance had an old wooden guardhouse that they passed before entering the building through two huge metal doors.

"This is the center of the spooky events you may have heard about," the lieutenant said.

"We heard something about paranormal events happening here," Merlin said as they walked down a cold corridor. "But we figure they're just folk tales, so we aren't too concerned."

"Well, these paranormal events, as you call them, are real. That's the reason we have a Company of Military Police here rather than security guards from the General Services Administration. It's also why no other agency wants to convert this property," said Lance.

"You sound as though you believe these events are real," Annie said, voice more highly pitched than usual.

"Believe them," Lance said. "Let me show you."

"Wait a minute," Merlin said, grabbing the lieutenant's arm. "You have pictures of these things?"

"We do," Lance said, pulling away from Merlin's grip. Lance knew from experience that he had the team's full attention. "In fact, we have a room over here where we store the objects that appear that aren't alive."

"What do you mean when you say that 'aren't alive'?" Adrian asked.

"Some are just objects like balls or cubes and stuff, while others are living, breathing dogs, cats, even a few monkeys, and a chimp showed up once. We've got videotape of a man and a woman who have appeared from time to time. Funny thing though, it seems to be the same man and women over and over again. Kind of like ghosts, I guess. Come on. I'll show you the room where we keep the stuff."

The three archeologists huddled for a minute before following the lieutenant, quickly agreeing that this all sounded like more than paranormal events.

Lance led them to a room where dishes, paper, plastic and cardboard boxes, articles of clothing, and metal cylinders were displayed on several tables around the room.

Lance pointed to one of them. "You'll notice there are some messages on the ones on this table."

The team looked at the balls, cubes, and other objects on the table. There were notes such as Weird, isn't it?, Say hello to Mama!, What a fox! and more.

Annie held up a rubber ball and whispered to Merlin, "Dr. Lakin, come here for a minute."

"What's this 'Dr. Lakin' bullshit?" he whispered to Annie as he moved beside her.

Annie handed him the ball. "Read it."

Written on the ball was: Hi, Merlin. What took you so long? Now go view the tapes and CDs on the people who've appeared here. Check out the woman. She's a real fox, isn't she?

Annie looked at Merlin and said quietly, "Any other questions?"

Merlin looked at Lance. "We'd like to see those tapes and CDs, if you don't mind. Particularly the ones showing the people appearing."

Lance wondered for a second how they had known there were tapes and CDs; he'd only mentioned the tapes. He put it out of his mind and motioned for the team to follow him and led them to a room that contained a couple of monitors and CD players. He arranged the chairs for his guests and went to a cabinet where he pulled out a couple of tapes. He put the first one in. "If you need to see more, we have them in the cabinet over there. I'm going to get a cup of coffee. Would any of you like me to bring you back some?"

"No, we're fine," Merlin answered.

As Lance left the room, an image popped up on the monitor of a man—who looked much like Merlin—carrying a long pole with some type of round glass object on the end. The man looked around the room for a second and then moved to stand against the wall. A few moments later a large bag appeared exactly where the man had been standing. The man grabbed the bag and left the room.

Lance returned to the room as the team was watching another appearance of the stranger. Merlin turned to him. "How is it that this man could show up like this and your people never confronted him?"

"Well, he always appears when we're changing shifts or out of the room for some reason. Anytime someone left the room for any reason, it was written into the log here. When we changed, the new guard would usually be getting a cup of coffee. By the time he returned, everything would be back to normal. The only reason we were able to catch him on tape is that we always have someone fast forward through the tapes to see if we missed anything. That's when we see him."

"Did anyone think of requiring the guards to get their coffee before they started working?" Annie asked.

"Sure. But they'd go to the bathroom and the guy pops in while the guard's away. We even increased the number of guards. That stopped the activity for a while, but once we returned to one guard during leaves or holidays, it happened again. It's as though they had inside information on our activities. But we can't explain how they knew when our guards went to the bathroom."

"Can you get a close-up of this?" Merlin asked.

"Sure," Lance said. He moved to the controls. "Use this control pad. You can get as close as you want."

Adrian moved in front of the control pad and pushed a

button that paused the tape. Then he made a frame around the head of the man in the film and brought it up as a close up. He then focused the picture and cleared up the image.

As the image cleared up, Adrian gasped, Annie sat up straight and Lance dropped his coffee cup.

The young lieutenant turned to Merlin and stuttered, "Tha-that- that's you!"

"So it would appear," Merlin said, looking closely at the image on the monitor screen.

"You look a little pale, Lieutenant," Annie said, laughing.

"Yeah, I think this base will do just fine," Merlin said. "Let's see if we can find this mystery woman."

"Here she is," Adrian said. "Want a close-up?"

"Yeah. Let's see who she is."

"How's this?" Adrian asked as the image of a stunningly beautiful young woman appeared on the screen. "She's quite attractive. You know her?"

"Never seen her before in my life."

"Well, the two of you are on tape together in a couple of the shots," Lance told them.

"Guys, let's get back to Washington and cut a deal on this place," Merlin said. "Okay if we borrow this tape?"

"Sure, go for it," said the stunned lieutenant.

"Looks like you're going to have a new tenant," Annie said.

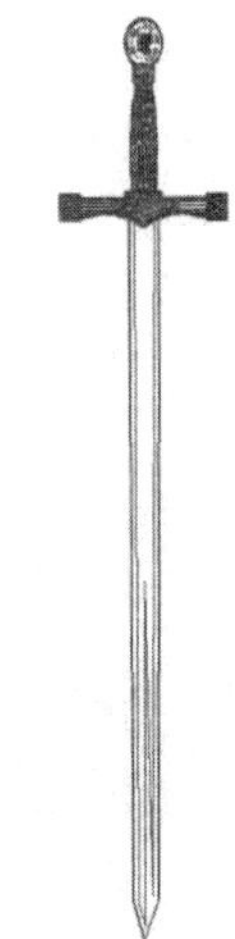

Chapter Four

The next day Merlin, Adrian, and Annie went to Bill's office, carrying the ball with the message about Merlin, which Annie had conveniently dropped into her purse, and the videotape.

After they'd settled into their seats, Bill said, "I hear something oddball took place with you at Vint Hill Farms Station yesterday. Why don't you tell me about it?"

"Well," Merlin said, handing the ball to Bill, "we'd rather show you."

"Is this a hoax?" Bill asked, looking over the ball.

"If it is, it's a good one," Adrian said, sliding the tape into Bill's video player. "Watch this."

Bill read the message and watched the video with total disbelief. Merlin touched Bill on the arm in a consoling way "The one thing we don't know is who this woman is."

Bill scratched behind his ear as he looked at Merlin. "I was hoping you'd go over there and figure it wasn't worth it to work in a haunted place. Now you bring me this."

"Were you trying to get rid of us?" asked a decidedly angry Annie.

"That's right. I was. But now I have a bigger problem."

"Really," Merlin growled. "And what might that be?"

"The woman in the video. I know who she is."

"What?!" Adrian gasped.

"She's a physicist from CERN," Bill said. He moved over to his desk where he removed a piece of paper with a photo on it and handed it to Merlin. "This was e-mailed to me today in response to my request. Her name is Dr. Vivian Weatherall. She'll be here in a few days. I wanted you to talk to her just in case we were to go ahead with this project. Now tell me. What's going on? What is this project?"

Merlin stood up and began to pace the same way Adrian had the day before, except that he limped. "Bill," he asked, twitching his nose, "what do you think is going on here?"

"I hesitate to guess," Bill said, throwing his hands into the air. "How can a woman who none of us know be on a video tape with you, taken at a site none of us had been to?"

Merlin looked at Bill with a sly smile. "Well. The only answer I can come up with is time travel. How about you, Adrian?"

"Yeah." Adrian nodded, joining in the joke. "Sounds right to me. What about you, Annie?"

Annie laughed and nodded. "Yeah, that's all it can be."

"Okay. Now stop with the jokes. This is serious," Bill said. "The three of you are involved in the theft of Guatemalan antiquities. You have your reputations and that of the Institute's on the line. Tell me what's going on here."

So they told him the whole story. He was irritated at Merlin for the deception, but quickly saw the value of the project. They began by discussing Adrian's findings in the Mayan books and used the videos and the ball to show that they would be successful in the project. They looked at how they would be able to solve the great mysteries of history that have lingered over time. Adrian brought up his idea of a title for their new profession, Time Travel Archeologists. The excitement and potential overwhelmed them all. Bill decided that they should keep the project a secret for now. Once they reached the point where they could demonstrate the viability of time travel, the appropriate officials in the United States government would have to be notified. They didn't want to notify anybody beforehand out of fear that they'd lose control of it.

Another potential problem was that the plant that acted as the catalyst for the time travel wormhole was available only in the Petén Jungle in Guatemala.

Bill enlisted the aid of Dr. Adelina Perez to work on obtaining the plant. Adelina was from Belize and had worked for the Institute for several years, specializing in plants grown, eaten or otherwise used by the ancient civilizations of South and Central America. She joined the team while they were in process of moving into their new quarters at Vint Hill Farms Station. She was familiar with Mayan history and was excited about what this could mean to everyone everywhere. The olive-skinned beauty with long, straight black hair fit in well with the other members of the team right from the start.

After a few days another potential new member of the team, Dr. Vivian Weatherall of CERN, the European Organization for Nuclear Research, joined them. Vivian was a physicist who was making quite a name for herself at a rather young age. Adrian was the one assigned to pick up the young physicist at the airport, a duty he fully appreciated when he met her: she was personable, enthusiastic, and beautiful.

Adrian drove Vivian to the Operations Building at Vint

Hill Farms Station so she could be introduced to the other members of the team before settling into her quarters. As Adrian was introducing her to Annie and Adelina, Merlin and Lance walked in. Merlin couldn't believe his eyes: Vivian was even more beautiful than she had appeared on the videos.

Annie couldn't help but laugh as she nudged Adelina before saying, "Merlin, put your tongue back in your mouth. Dr. Weatherall, this is our fearless leader, Dr. Merlin Lakin."

"The famous Dr. Lakin; it's a pleasure to meet you in person. You're quite the TV star," she said, referring to Merlin's Guatemalan adventure.

"I don't know about the TV-star part. Please call me Merlin," he said, shaking her hand. "We try to stay informal here."

"Thank you, Merlin. And how are your injuries healing?"

"Oh, I'm doing just fine, thank you."

The rest of the team watched Merlin check out the new recruit, all of them enjoying the show.

For her part, Vivian found herself unusually attracted to the handsome man in front of her. Her life had been so filled with her research that she'd never allowed herself to think of men in a social or romantic way; she simply hadn't the time for it. Her boss back at CERN felt she needed to slow down some, which was one of the reasons she'd been sent to see about working on this project. "When may I be briefed on the project?"

"We'll get you settled in, then we can get together after dinner and discuss it," Merlin promised. "This is Lieutenant Lance Wilfred. He'll see you to your quarters."

The team got ready to make a presentation to the young woman. When the time came, they all got together at Merlin's house for dinner, which had been the Post commander's place. It was a large, Georgian red brick mansion. The team enjoyed a nice meal, prepared for them by the base's head cook. After they finished eating, they adjourned to the living room, which had been rearranged for the presentation.

Merlin began the presentation by telling Vivian about the expedition into Guatemala's Petén Jungle. Vivian, and the rest of the world, had followed the story on television and in the newspapers and magazines. She'd been as fascinated with the story as everyone else. She listened closely to what Merlin had to say, particularly about what had not been reported at the time. This was the first time Lance and Adelina had heard the full story and they were drawn in just as Vivian was.

Merlin brought the audience up to the point of the disappearance of the Mayan books. Having been responsible for the translation of the Mayan books, Adrian took over at this point to explain his findings. He rose and then fell silent for a few moments while stroking his beard, thinking. "The books tell us that the Mayans built all their pyramids to the exact same height from sea level and at the top of each pyramid was a large round gem, which had been built into a holder and placed on top of a pole. Each pole was built to the exact same length and sent to the cities involved. Then these poles were set up in a manner that allowed them to capture a beam of light and send it on to the next pyramid, the light becoming more concentrated at each stop. The light's final destination was a scientific research center in what is now called the Petén Jungle. Once there, it would strike a pool filled with the liquefied remnants of a special plant and caused an instantaneous rotation of the material within the pool. Within the rotation was a pathway to another point in time. The Mayans were able to regulate how far back to travel using the placement of the beam of light."

Dr. Adelina Perez began the next portion of the story. "We have a problem with the plant described by the Maya. At the time the Mayan books were written, the plant grew only in the vicinity of their research center. At that time they had no means of synthesizing the plant. This placed a limit on how often they could travel back in time. Also, this plant is not one that has been identified in modern times. Annie and Merlin believe they saw it growing in the vicinity of the Mayan city, but the Guatemalan government isn't very receptive to anyone from the Carnegie Institute and may not grant us access to the area again."

Annie took over by saying, "It's a documented fact that the Maya were the first people to conduct research into time travel, but this is the first evidence we've ever had that they were successful. It seems that they built a large laser that shot a beam over hundreds of miles. At each juncture the beam tightened or condensed. It also appears that the beam increased in speed as it moved. The laser beam turned to a greenish color before merging with the solution within the pool. This created a reaction in the pool that caused the formation of a spinning black hole, hole probably a wormhole. They were able to travel back and forth only at this one location simply because they had no means of duplicating the device for a return elsewhere."

Merlin said, "We believe the Mayan rulers used their time travel machine to travel backward in time to avoid being killed by Hunac-Cel. We believe they evacuated the city through the time portal they created. They left behind a means of flooding the city and hiding it so Hunac-Cel or his followers couldn't use it. We also believe these Maya are the ones responsible for the Mayan Classic Period, though we can't prove it at this time.

"Now, Vivian," Merlin continued with uncommon nervousness, "you may find what we've said to be interesting. You may have found it to be crazy. Particularly coming from a group of archeologists and a botanist rather than someone of your background. But I would like you to consider the following as perhaps the most compelling evidence I can present. Vint Hill Farms Station has been here as a farm or a military base for more than a hundred years. During this period, there have been more than one hundred documented events of objects or people appearing out of nowhere within and without the buildings."

Vivian jerked back. "What? I've enjoyed your presentation so far, but aren't you getting a little farfetched now?"

Merlin sighed. "Well, we'll let you be the judge of that. The army has placed the objects in a room in the Operations Building. They include a variety of objects such as dishes, balls, boxes, and many other articles. Of particular interest to you at this time would be the videos. I've selected one that you should find really special."

Merlin played the video showing him and Vivian appearing in the room together, as well as her appearing by herself. He looked at Vivian. "Unless you have another explanation for the two of us appearing in a room together, I'd say that we're about to rediscover time travel."

Shocked, Vivian fell silent for a couple of minutes, then she looked at Merlin and the rest of the team. "I guess we're in the time travel business."

The team surrounded her, shook her hand and patted her on the back, delighted to have her join the group.

They immediately went to work organizing their research approach. Vivian had been working with nanotechnology in developing a palm-size particle accelerator and requested approval from CERN for key members of her staff to be lent to the project. Adelina and Merlin went to Guatemala on a mission to obtain permission from the Guatemalan government to search for the plant and to try to obtain Chac's release. Adrian began searching the computer files and the internet for any information he could gather regarding the Maya and time travel or anything that would further explain various subjects in the Mayan books. Annie began organizing the base with the help of the new base commander, the newly promoted Captain Lance Wilfred.

Vivian was the first to obtain results. She flew to CERN Headquarters and met with her boss. Vivian got him to commit to total secrecy regarding the project and had him sign documentation to that effect. She explained the project to him and, when rebuffed by his skepticism, Vivian played one of the videotapes for him. This was enough to gain his approval, though he held back full endorsement for the project. He did agree to provide the loan of the personnel Vivian requested, along with paying for their salaries. She was even successful in getting him to loan the project certain pieces of equipment that was not obtainable elsewhere. The staff and equipment were quickly assembled and flown to their new home in Virginia.

After studying the files concerning the Maya, Adrian formulated a theory on where the Maya leadership may have gone. He felt there was strong evidence that they reappeared at the beginning of the Mayan Classic Period, about 200 AD. There was also evidence that, if Kukulkán was with the leaders when they disappeared, they may have made their way south and either begun a new civilization or taken over an existing one. Adrian felt certain that the best way to find out would be to go back and check it out firsthand.

Merlin and Adelina had much more difficulty in working with the Guatemalan government. The Guatemalan army divers had been unsuccessful in locating the Mayan books. They had removed the stones and thoroughly searched the site, but to no avail. Thus the government strongly suspected that Adrian was the thief and, though they stopped short of directly accusing him, they wanted the Mayan books back. After finally tiring of his efforts, Merlin went to Bill Barnes for help.

Bill called a friend of his, who was a high-ranking bureaucrat with the U.S. State Department and another friend, who was with the State Department of the United Mexican States. During the negotiations with the Guatemalan government it came out that the United States was in possession of the Mayan books but that they would not be returned to Guatemala for any reason.

The Guatemalan official responded by saying they would not release Chac because he was one of their citizens. They were under no obligation to negotiate with a foreign government regarding a citizen who had not broken any laws in the United States but might have been involved in a conspiracy within Guatemala regarding the missing Mayan books. They also expressed no interest in exporting a valuable resource without full disclosure as to why the United States wanted the plant so badly. The officials also declared that no archeologist from the United States would be allowed to work within the borders of Guatemala due to the lack of support from the United States in protecting Guatemalan antiquities.

At that point Bill began to feel betrayed in what appeared to be an obviously dumb move in the negotiations on the part of his friend.

The Mexican officials gave the appearance that they were exasperated by the direction of the negotiations, but Bill detected an odd smile from his friend with the U.S. State Department. The negotiations took an odd turn when the Mexican negotiators took the lead and worked out a compromise. The Mayan books would remain in the United States on a loan until the project was completed. However, the Guatemalans would be allowed to assign one of their Intelligence officers to the project to insure that the Mayan books would not be given to anyone else. The Guatemalan government would also allow a limited harvesting of the plant the team needed and would "lend" Chac to the project so as to protect other interests the Guatemalan government might have as a result of the findings from the research.

Ecstatic, Merlin and Adelina made their first stop in Carmelita, Guatemala, where Chac was waiting for them. Merlin gave Chac a bear hug, then turned to introduce Chac to Adelina by saying, "Dr. Adelina Perez, I would like you to meet a very good friend of mine, Mr. Chac Garcia. Chac, this is my botany specialist, Dr. Adelina Perez." Chac looked at the beautiful Adelina and bowed, kissing her hand. Merlin laughed. "Rather Continental of you, don't you think?"

"Ah, my friend," Chac replied, "but this is a true princess."

Adelina smiled. "Then you know."

"Yes," Chac said with a knowing nod and a smile.

"Know what?" Merlin asked, confused. He was answered only by smiles from his coworkers.

Merlin and Adelina left for the Mayan city to find some of the plants while Chac remained in Carmelita. By the end of the day they had found the plant and obtained all the samples they needed. Merlin felt very uncomfortable around the ancient city that had claimed the lives of the Guatemalan army divers, so they quickly returned to Carmelita to pick up Chac and a quick helicopter flight back to Guatemala City. They checked into the Hilton Hotel for a good night's sleep before getting an early start the next day.

After an early breakfast, Merlin, Adelina, and Chac were picked up by a military escort and taken to the hospital to see Quetzal. At the hospital, they saw that Quetzal had still not fully recovered from his injuries. His face was swollen and he had a mild cough.

Quetzal smiled as wide as he could when he saw Merlin. "My friend," he said, "I've not had a chance to thank you for saving my life."

"No thanks are needed," Merlin said, examining the cast on Quetzal's leg.

"I understand that we'll be working together again."

"Oh really?" Merlin replied, surprised. "I thought they were going to provide us with someone in your Army Intelligence Department."

"They are, uh, they did," Quetzal stuttered. "That is, they felt I'd be the best one to be assigned to you since we know each other and I'm familiar with your team. And, since I was once a part of the Army Intelligence, all they needed to do was to transfer me back to Intelligence. Besides, I can't be of much help diving anymore."

"Do you know anything about this project?" Merlin asked.

"I know something about it. I was given a briefing by someone in my State Department and someone from your State Department," Quetzal said. "It sounds like a very interesting project. Is what they say about the project true?"

Merlin knew that no one in either the United States government or the Guatemalan government knew what the team was researching. "It depends. What did they tell you?"

"They told me there's a plant that grows only in the Petén Jungle. My understanding is the plant may be able to cure many diseases in the world. They say you're attempting to make a synthetic version of this plant. Is this true?"

"Oh yes, it's true," Merlin said, relieved. He knew he'd soon have to inform both Chac and Quetzal about the real project, but now was not the right time or place for that discussion. "I'd like to introduce you to our chief botanist, Dr. Adelina Perez. And of course you already know Chac."

Chac looked at Quetzal with an obvious frown.

"Hello, my dear lady," said a suave Quetzal as he looked over Adelina. "An angel sent to watch over me."

"Thank you," Adelina said, suddenly self-conscious as she looked back at the handsome officer.

Merlin watched the three and saw that there was going to be trouble ahead. Merlin helped Quetzal get his things from the hospital together and then the four of them were escorted to Quetzal's bachelor's quarters to get his personal effects together for the move to Virginia. Quetzal's larger items were set aside either for storage or for shipment to his new base in the United States. After taking care of the arrangements for his personal items, Quetzal signed Off Post and the four were on their way to the airport and their flight to Vint Hill Farms Station.

Chapter Five

Annie and Lance immediately struck up a strong working relationship. Lance loved to talk to her about her work in archeology. His mother had been the one who first introduced him to history and he became an avid history buff. His two areas of greatest interest were the Roman Empire and, perhaps because of his current proximity to the Battles of Bull Run, the American Civil War. He was swept away by how Annie, who was old enough to be his mother, would still work the archeological digs, uncovering the past one layer at a time. Annie pointed out that police work, particularly that of a detective, was close in many respects to her work. Lance told Annie that he enjoyed his MP work, and hoped to be a detective for a large city one day.

Lance did whatever he could to help the team and they began to think of him as a member. He arranged to have all the office furniture and equipment they would need loaned to the team. He was also able to have some clerical personnel assigned to the Post to assist the team as well as to get some basic supplies like pencils, pens and paper.

Merlin called Annie prior to his departure from Guatemala City and asked that she make arrangements for a party to celebrate having finally brought together everyone who would be needed for the project. Upon their arrival, Merlin helped Quetzal and Chac get set up in their quarters in the old enlisted men's barracks while Adelina attended to the plants. Annie and Lance set up the party at the old NCO Club.

Quetzal told Merlin that he would find his way to the party on his own, so Merlin left to change clothes and returned to pick up Chac and drive him to the party. As they entered the club, Chac spotted Adelina and turned to Merlin. "I'm glad Snakeman's not here. I kind of like Adelina and I think she likes me."

"I don't know," Merlin mumbled as he spotted Quetzal slowly making his way toward Adelina, "look over there." Merlin noticed a beautiful woman with long hair he'd not seen before. Looking closer, he realized that it was Vivian Weatherall. Merlin looked at Chac with a sly smile. "While you work on Adelina, I think I'll get to know Vivian a little better."

Chac made a beeline to Adelina in an effort to keep her away from Quetzal while Merlin decided to see if there was more to Vivian than her being a top-rated physicist. As he slowly made his way closer to her, Merlin felt a tinge of nervousness creep up on him; he had always been shy and awkward with women outside the work environment and now was no exception.

Vivian was with a group of her staff from CERN and seemed to be having fun as Merlin inched his way toward her. The conversation stopped when Merlin reached their tables. He looked around and noticed the smiles and stares of Vivian's staff. Merlin hesitated, his stomach knotting up, before he finally leaned toward Vivian and asked, "Would you care to dance?"

Vivian turned without smiling and looked him over. Though she wasn't nervous, she was unaccustomed to being approached by a man in a social situation. She had devoted so much time and effort to developing her skills as a top physicist that she had never taken the time or interest to develop social skills. She finally said, "I'd be delighted."

The two distinguished scientists worked their way through the crowd to the center of the dance floor. The hum of the club turned silent and the other dancers moved to the sidelines as the two project leaders began to dance. Merlin and Vivian both noticed the change in the room, but soon blocked out everything in their surroundings but each other. The two danced through the night. The dance floor became packed after their first dance, but neither of them was aware of it. Eventually, they were alone on the floor again as the rest of the people left for home. Without saying a word, the two suddenly woke up from their spell to discover that they were the only ones left in the club. The bartender called out to them and asked if they were going to be there much longer. They both laughed as Merlin called back to him, "No, I think we'll be leaving now."

Merlin drove Vivian to her house and wanted the night to never end. Vivian felt the strength of Merlin's arms pulling her toward him. She wanted him so bad she felt a tingle go up her spine. But, as right as it felt to them at the moment, they knew that now was not the time, so they reluctantly said goodnight.

As much as Merlin had enjoyed the evening, Chac was frustrated by it. Quetzal had successfully used his injuries to gain Adelina's sympathy. Chac wanted to warn her about the

Snakeman's past, but wisely decided to wait until another time. All Chac could do was imagine sticking a knife between Quetzal's ribs. Unfortunately, he had made a promise to Merlin.

The next day, Merlin brought the primary team members together so they could explain the project to Chac and Quetzal. After discussing the project and showing the videos to the two newest members, Quetzal told them that the Guatemalan army divers had found some more of the old Mayan books. Merlin divided his team into different groups, each with a specific task to perform. Because of the new information from Quetzal, Merlin assigned Adrian and Quetzal the task of obtaining the original or copies of the Mayan books that were in the hands of the Guatemalan Department of Antiquities. If they got their hands on them, Adrian could translate these to determine if they would be of any value to the project.

The plant was still a key ingredient to the success of the project; it was important that Adelina break down its composition as soon as possible. Once she did, Vivian would be called in to further the breakdown to its atomic level. Merlin decided to assign Chac to help Adelina under the pretense that his knowledge of the area where the plants grew would be helpful; the real reason for the assignment was so his friend could be around the woman he was interested in.

Vivian had a huge task ahead of her. Not only would her staff need to work on the plants, but they also needed to figure out how and why the Maya used their light assembly as a catalyst. She quickly determined that the light-rays were converted into a highly concentrated laser beam, so now she needed to develop a miniature version, using nanotechnology, that could be used in the project.

Lance provided security for the project and oversaw the

military personnel on base. Annie acted as their supply chief, finding whatever equipment the other team leaders needed. Lance and Annie continued to build upon their friendship as Annie taught Lance about archeology.

As the days passed, Merlin began to feel a little confined in what amounted to an administrative role as the head of the project. Even with his friends around him, he longed for the open arena provided by the excavation of a site. But Merlin really cared for his friends and enjoyed watching the relationship between Adelina and Chac mature while Quetzal was gone. Occasionally Merlin caught a glimpse of them staring at each other or holding hands as he passed the botany research area. As Chac and Adelina's love for each other grew, Merlin daydreamed of walking in the moonlight with Vivian.

Merlin and Vivian had been too busy to spend any time together since the dance. One day Merlin went to the nanotechnology lab to discuss Vivian's progress. As he entered the lab, Merlin waited a few moments as he watched the researchers, busy at their tasks. Vivian walked up behind him and tapped him on the shoulder, making him jump. He turned and smiled at the beautiful lady in front of him. She had her hair up in a bun and was wearing safety glasses and had a pencil behind one ear. Her lab coat covered her figure, which made Merlin wish they were elsewhere so he could see more of her.

After a brief silence he asked, "May I see you in your office?"

"Sure, why not?" she said as she turned toward her office.

Merlin looked at her after her abrupt response and wondered why she was so terse. He followed her to her office and after sitting down said, "Is there a problem?"

"Why do you say that?"

"Your tone of voice."

"Well. Whatever. I'm busy, what do you want?"

Merlin hesitated for a moment before he said, "You. I was hoping we could see more of each other."

"Whatever gave you that idea? I don't have time for such foolishness right now."

"Wait a minute. Don't be so snippy."

"Why shouldn't I be?"

"Aren't you happy here?"

"No. Not really."

Merlin was totally unprepared for her response. He had come by wanting to see Vivian again on a personal basis and instead was confronted with her possible resignation or, even more horrifying, her termination. He looked at her and with a weak voice said, "What can I do?"

"Step aside and allow me to be the Project Director."

"What?! So the night at the club was just a front? You were just using me? Toying with me?" Merlin practically yelled while he rose from his chair.

"No, no, not at all," Vivian said, gathering her thoughts. She liked Merlin, but she felt that it was totally unfair for him to be the Project Director. She wasn't smiling as she got up too and put her hand on his shoulder. "I actually enjoyed that evening."

"Well then, what's the problem?"

"I'm the one who's making the project happen and you're the one who'll get all the credit."

"Hey. Wait just a minute here. You're looking at only one aspect of the project and not the big picture. First, you forget that Adrian is the one who translated the Mayan books and discovered the Maya's secret. Second, you forget that it's the Carnegie Institute that's funding this project. Third, when the means of time travel is perfected, someone with knowledge of ancient societies will be needed to travel back in time. And don't forget that we have a mission to try to find out what happened to the ancient Maya leaders."

"You can do none of it without me, but we *can* get someone else who knows about the Maya."

"Let's face it. We're both important to the project. But you should realize that we can both be replaced."

"You'll go nowhere fast without me."

Merlin grew increasingly furious. Here she was giving him attitude like a spoiled prima donna and he wasn't impressed. In an effort to try to calm her down he said, "You're right. So let's put our differences aside and work together for the good of the project."

"Not a chance," Vivian pronounced, still acting as though a great wrong had been committed against her. "I'll stay with the project for now, but I'll be talking to Dr. Barnes about putting me in charge. I'm sure that with CERN's influence behind me, he'll see the light."

"I wouldn't be too sure about that," Merlin threatened as he turned and stomped out of her office, bewildered and angry about the inexplicable change in her personality.

Their first really big breakthrough came as a result of Adelina's efforts with the plant; she and her staff were able to break down the composition of the plant, which was now being called "Adrian's Dreamer" because of Adrian's initial discovery.

Vivian also had success with the plant. She found that when the plant was liquefied and mixed with water, it had a chemical reaction with the water that created a new substance. When a small amount of this new substance was hit with a solid state green laser and certain wavelengths, it changed again, but this time into a miniature wormhole. Where it led, and how stable it was, nobody knew, but it created tremendous excitement within the team.

Adrian and Quetzal finally returned from Guatemala with copies of the Mayan manuscripts. Adrian immediately started working on the translation while Quetzal attempted to renew his romance with Adelina. Unfortunately for Quetzal, Merlin's interference on Chac's behalf had worked. They were far too close for Quetzal to have any chance at romance with Adelina. Quetzal looked down on the simple Chac, enraged at the thought that he'd lost out to someone he felt was far inferior to himself. Quetzal swore revenge against Chac, a situation Merlin could live without.

Development continued as Vivian's nanotechnology researchers began writing the software that would be used to produce the products needed for the project. All the work on the plant was completed, as was the work on the laser. They now only needed to learn how to determine the settings for travel back to a selected time and how to return from that time period to the present. Fortunately, the MPs had recorded the date and time of retrieval for each item that had appeared. This gave the team a basis to work from in that they could check the calibrations for an object they sent back and compare it to the calibrations of similar objects that were retrieved at different times. They also tested the effects of a variety of sizes, shapes, and materials to determine what, if any, effect the molecular makeup of an object would have on the calibration settings. Eventually they were ready to send animals back in time. They had the same success with animals as they'd with the other objects.

Vivian met with Dr. Bill Barnes on several occasions in an

effort to convince him that she should be the Project Director because she, in her mind, had made a greater contribution to the effort than Merlin and was irreplaceable to the project, whereas Merlin wasn't.

Her arguments fell through when it came time for a human to take the trip back in time. Vivian had just completed the testing on a nanofactory that was capable of producing the solution that was needed for the return trip. Merlin and Bill made the decision to send a test human subject back in time. Merlin insisted that he be first to take the trip because of his background in archeology. Vivian argued that she should be first because of her physics background. Bill pointed out to Vivian that, in her own words, she was the most valuable member of the project, therefore she needed to remain safely tucked away in the present.

Merlin and the team gathered for what everyone believed was to be a successful first trip. Everyone, especially Merlin, was excited about the trip and Merlin went to Vivian. "Let's talk."

"What do you want?" Vivian asked rudely, pouting like a spoiled brat.

"What I want is for you to be with me. To be part of this. I need you to be part of this. Without you, I don't know where we'd be."

"You would be nowhere, that's where."

Merlin grabbed Vivian's arms and looked straight into her eyes. He longed to have her as his friend and lover. He said, "Look. I don't want to argue with you. I care about you. I want to share this with you, and I will. Soon."

"Yeah, right," Vivian snapped as she tried to avoid Merlin's eyes. She was afraid. Afraid that if she looked into his eyes her resistance would melt away, something she wasn't ready to let it do. She would do anything she had to do to maintain the control she felt she needed to have.

"I will. Just hang in there," Merlin said, trying hard to look her in the eyes. "I know from the videotapes that I'll make it. But I must do this myself because there might be some internal damage that we're unaware of and I don't want to put you at risk."

Those eyes. If I could just avoid those eyes, she kept saying to herself. It was too much for her. She suddenly looked up and pulled Merlin's face next to hers and whispered, "Good luck." Her lips touched his in a long, passionate kiss. Then she turned and walked away without another word.

Merlin was stunned as he watched Vivian walk to her lab. After a long pause he shook his head and went to the Time Travel "Jump" Room, as it was now being called. It was a large, windowless room with people in front of computers and monitors of various types. They were laid out in three rows facing what resembled a slightly smaller than Olympic-sized swimming pool. The room was constructed in the space that had been occupied by several rooms before, so the outline of where the old walls had been were clearly marked within the pool so the time travelers wouldn't get into space occupied by a wall.

The solution was ready, the lasers were turned on, and into the pool he stepped, holding his laser wand in his hand. The solution began soaking into Merlin's clothes as he stood waist-deep in the pool. Motion was all around him, and it appeared to him that he was standing still while everything else moved. It was an odd sensation, not at all what he expected it to be.

Suddenly the motion stopped and the solution around him disappeared. He stood in a much smaller room in the building with none of the equipment or people around him. He felt his pants and surprisingly found that they were dry.

He moved out of the way and stood next to the wall in anticipation of the next arrival. As if by magic, a small backpack appeared right where he'd been standing.

Merlin grabbed the backpack and left the room. He carefully worked his way down the corridor to the exit doors, quickly moved through them and ran to the back of the building. He reached into the backpack and pulled out a special shovel that had the ability to pulverize the dirt and rock. He began to dig. He felt the perspiration pouring out of him as he worked feverishly to create his way home. After spending a couple of hours digging out the hole, he took out the nanofactory and gave it voice instructions regarding the size of the hole and the solution to make. Shortly the solution began pouring out of the factory, filling the hole. Merlin made the necessary adjustments to his laser wand and turned it on. The laser's green light struck the solution and the wormhole formed up. Merlin turned as he heard men shouting behind him. He saw several MPs running toward him; one of them was Lance. Without further hesitation, he threw in his backpack and quickly followed it into the wormhole.

Within seconds, Merlin found himself back on solid ground outside the operations building surrounded by all the members of the team. Applause and shouts of congratulations were coming from all directions but all he really cared about was finding Vivian. He felt a hand on his shoulder that pulled him out of his trance. Merlin turned and found Dr. Barnes' smiling face looking at him. He could see Bill's lips moving but he couldn't understand what Bill was saying.

Merlin smiled at his boss and then pushed his way through the crowd, with plenty of back-slapping, hand-shaking, and hugs to go around. As he broke free of the crowd, he saw Vivian near the far corner of the building. He began walking faster and faster until he was at a full run. As he got near her, he could see her standing before him, expressionless.

Merlin stopped and Vivian looked away. She said, “I was just curious to see if you were alive.”

He held her arms, but she pulled away and ran inside. Confused, he could only watch her go.

There was still a lot of work to do in order for them to perfect their time travel operations.

Merlin wanted to know why his clothes were dry when he “landed” and a team was assigned to find out. He had a problem with the shovel–it took far too long to dig the hole and fill it with the solution for the return home. Merlin realized that he could never make an instantaneous jump, but if the process could be speeded up it would help, particularly in an emergency. Another problem was dizziness; there’d been a moment at the end of the jump when he’d been momentarily dizzy and disoriented. He felt no other ill effects, but that one worried him and he wanted to see if it could be eliminated.

One of their biggest problems was finding out how to figure out the correct arrival day and time of a jump. The researchers had their calibrations down for the jumps that were within the period when the MPs on the base had retrieved the objects, but they had no idea about how it would work on extended jumps. The biggest difficulty was that they had no consistent way of knowing what the correct time of day was because time as we know it was not invented until 1884. Before that the time of day depended on what city you were in; even the various railroads kept time differently, resulting in many train wrecks between trains of two different companies. They needed a device that could withstand the journey, and tell the time and date based upon the position of the sun or moon, and be small enough to fit into Merlin’s pocket.

The research team was busy for the next few weeks tackling the various issues. Vivian's staff did most of the work, but Annie was given the task of searching outside the team for products that were currently on the market that could be used as is or altered for their purposes.

Merlin had not given up on Vivian, despite the wide swings in their relationship. Vivian was fighting against her own emotions, resulting in her erratic behavior to Merlin. Finding time to spend with each other was a problem, but there was an attraction that kept them both wanting each other.

They solved the dizziness problem first; Annie gave him a seasickness patch, which worked like a charm. The next problem solved was the determination of time of day. Quetzal suggested a piece of equipment that he'd heard of, but never seen, for use by divers that could pinpoint the correct time and day. Lance and Annie located the equipment and Vivian was able to duplicate it in a miniature form that Merlin could wear like a wristwatch and was unaffected by the plant/wormhole solution. The thing couldn't tell them what year it was, though.

Then they discovered that the solution had an extraordinary evaporation rate once the wormhole was created. This explained why Merlin was dry after completing a jump.

They couldn't find a solution for the shovel itself, but Annie came up with a novel idea. Why not bring back an inflatable pool? The only negative was that they needed to find a way to destroy the pool after it was used and leave no evidence behind. Vivian, Lance, and Quetzal worked together on solving that problem. They tested various incendiary devices and came up with one that left little residue and made almost no noise. Vivian then worked on breaking it down to the atomic level and writing a program so that the nanofactory could duplicate it.

***

With all the known problems solved, though not tested, Merlin felt it was time for him to come through on his promise to Vivian to take her back with him. He was not prepared for the excitement she displayed as Merlin told her of the mission. The pair made several short trips back, working with the new equipment and working out the bugs to where Merlin felt they could try something further back in time. He went to Vivian one day after a meeting with Dr. Barnes. "Are you ready for a period jump?"

"Period jump?"

"Yeah. You know. Let's go back one or two hundred years. To a time period where we can't prove the results in advance."

"Are you saying that you're okay with me taking the risk with you?"

"Sure. Besides, this is a jump that should be taken by two people in case there's trouble. You're the only other person with the experience for this."

"Fine with me."

Merlin brought the team leaders together. "Adrian, you pick the time and put the information together. Annie, you get with Adrian for the date and put together the proper clothing. Chac, you're in charge of making sure we have the correct provisioning for the trip, and Quetzal, you see to it that we have the correct weapons and know how to use them."

Adrian came up with a date just prior to the Civil War. He felt this would be a good testing ground and one of the safer time periods to work with while giving the time travelers an easy period to blend into the local population. They decided that Vivian and Merlin would take on the identities of a farmer and his wife. They worked together in studying the habits, customs, mannerisms, and speech of an 1850s farmer and wife. Time that brought them a bit closer together, something Vivian would never admit to but that delighted Merlin.

Quetzal and Lance found the weapons they thought Merlin and Vivian might need in a collection at a local museum. They worked with Merlin and Vivian in training them to clean, load, and fire the weapons. Although Merlin would carry the guns, Vivian was actually better at using them.

Annie had a local seamstress make the clothes for the time travelers. She told the seamstress that the costumes were for a couple of friends of hers who'd be using them in an upcoming re-enactment event, which was kind of true. The seamstress made three changes of clothes for the pair, including undergarments, stockings, and everything but a hat for Merlin, and shoes. Annie found a hat that would work from a garage sale and had the shoes made by a local shoemaker. She brought the outfits to the Operations Building for a dress rehearsal once they were completed. Vivian complained loudly about wearing so much clothing at one time; all of it was damned uncomfortable, too. Merlin was excited about his new costume. The thought that he would soon assume the role of a person living in the 1850s created a level of excitement within him that Annie hadn't seen in a long time.

The day finally arrived and to say that Merlin had butterflies in his stomach would be an understatement. This would be the first jump back in time without the security of knowing the outcome from the army tapes. Merlin and Vivian put on their outfits with Vivian pulling and scratching at her garments with every step. The weather was dreary and gray, with a constant mist outside. Merlin had hoped for a bright, sunny day, which he told himself he might yet get on the other end of the jump. Merlin took some medicine to calm his stomach and the two adventurers entered the pool and prepared themselves.

The weather had taken a turn for the worse and the lights started flickering as the time came for their jump.

As the wormhole dissolved around them, they saw that they were standing on dirt. They had arrived at a time prior to when the Operations Building had existed. They both laughed and high-fived one another, but stopped when they moved a few feet away and Merlin saw a group of Confederate cavalrymen heading toward them.

He looked at Vivian. "I think we've got a problem."

"No kidding. I hope they didn't see us appear out of nowhere."

The bags appeared and, as Merlin reached down to grab one, he said, "Grab the other bag and let's get moving."

The two explorers started heading toward where the future Interstate highway would be as the cavalry closed in on them. They could hear loud bangs, some rapidly or together, others at a lower pitch and more spaced out. They saw smoke in the distance as the horses pounded up behind them.

The cavalry troop pulled to a halt, surrounding Merlin and Vivian. The leader of the troop was a distinguished-looking young man with a black feather in his hat. He looked at the time travelers and said in an aristocratic, Southern accent, "Sir, I suggest you head in another direction. There's a battle in progress where you're going." The leader then motioned for his troopers to move forward without a single word from Merlin or Vivian.

Merlin felt goose bumps form on his arms as he heard the cavalry leader speak. Many years ago as a student he'd worked on a Civil War dig, which he'd found fascinating. Now he was actually back where it was happening in real time. He thought about Adrian's name for their new profession, Time Travel Archeology, and his enthusiasm and excitement soared.

Vivian woke Merlin out of his trance by saying, "Do you have any idea what date this could be?"

"Got me. I would guess that it's during one of the Battles of Bull Run."

"'One of'? How many were there?"

"Two."

"Two! What are we going to do? We need the year to get home."

"I suggest we find out what the year is."

"Duh," Vivian snarled. "Fine time for you to get a sense of humor."

"Ah, come on. We know there're people in that direction," Merlin said, pointing toward the battle.

"Hey, remember? We have no records regarding this trip. For all we know, we get killed here."

Merlin looked around. The sun was beating down on him; sweat poured down his back. He was concerned about the battle, but even more concerned about the possibility of being lost in time. As much as he liked working on the Civil War dig while in college, he didn't want to be stranded and live out his life there. "So we've gotta be careful here. Let's go ahead and set up for the return."

"What about the date?"

"We'll get it before we leave. But if something happens to this equipment, we'll never get back."

"Okay, but what about the plastic pools? We can't set them up yet."

"We'll have to hide them here. We may need to dig the entire hole rather than take the risk of being discovered."

"Don't you think people will think it a little odd for two travelers to be digging a hole during a battle?"

"Over there are some trees. Why don't we stash our packs

over there and then we can find out where we are? Come on, let's get going."

Merlin ran for the grove of trees. Once there, he and Vivian covered their wands with plastic and then took out their shovels and dug a hole for their equipment. By the time they finished, they were both hot and thirsty.

Merlin looked up and asked, "Does that nanofactory of yours happen to make water?"

"It could, but we didn't put in a program for that. Besides, you just buried it. Don't tell me you forgot the food and water?"

"I brought food, but no water. We're supposed to be able to find water here, remember?"

"Oh great."

"We'll just deal with it, okay? I'm going to the battle and find someone who can tell me what year it is. You coming?"

Merlin was about fed up with Vivian as the two explorers began their walk toward the sound of guns. As they reached the top of a small hill, they looked out over a panoramic view of a battle in full swing. There were lines of soldiers in gray firing on other soldiers in gray and soldiers in blue firing on soldiers in blue. There were soldiers in red, cavalry in gray, with plumes in their hats and capes on their backs in a confusing canvas of colors.

Vivian and Merlin stood dumbfounded by the screams of the wounded and shouts of the attacking soldiers from each side. Neither of them had ever witnessed a battle before, but even if they had, a modern-day battle would be nothing like this. Smoke from the hundreds of guns and cannon below floated up the hill and irritated their nostrils, causing Merlin's nose to twitch and both their eyes to water.

Based on Merlin's knowledge of the Civil War, he felt sure

this was the first Battle of Bull Run. He knew that in the beginning there had been no standard uniforms for the troops on either side and the various militias frequently wore customized uniforms of their own design and color. This made it difficult to know if you were fighting your friend or foe. One result of the battle was the standardization of the uniforms and colors for the two sides, blue for the United States forces and gray for the Confederate States forces.

Despite this knowledge, Merlin couldn't risk being wrong. They had to make sure of the date, so the two time travelers worked their way toward the fringe of the battle zone to get the information they needed. Merlin and Vivian found themselves stooping by instinct as they got closer to the battle. They found a group of soldiers in gray uniforms and approached the end of the line. Merlin cautiously approached one of the soldiers and asked, "Sorry to bother you, but what's today's date?"

The soldier looked at him and, in a strong Southern drawl, said, "Y'all crazy? Get outta here."

Vivian pulled Merlin back. "Real subtle, stupid. Let me handle this." Vivian went back to the line and began talking to another soldier. "Excuse me, but my husband and I have been traveling for some time."

The soldier looked at the pretty woman before him. "Ma'am, I suppose y'all should be traveling away from here and quick."

"We have to be somewhere by a certain date and would–"

An officer walked up to them "Ma'am, you and your friend need to get out of here now." He motioned with his sword and the soldiers rose and began moving into the battle.

"Come on, let's get closer," Merlin said.

"Are you nuts?"

"Let's just get the date and get out of here."

The two explorers moved closer to the battle lines.

Vivian found another soldier who was running back from the battle. "Sir, please help us."

"Ma'am, you better get outta here. I've got to get me more minie balls."

"No, please. I have to know today's date. Please help me."

"Ma'am, y'all are crazy. It's the twenty-first."

Just then Merlin yelled out in pain and fell to the ground. Vivian grabbed the soldier's arm. "The year, please." Vivian looked at the soldier with pleading eyes.

The soldier gave her an odd look. "You better help your friend, ma'am. I gotta go."

"Please. The year."

The soldier pulled away as Merlin lay in a pool of his own blood. Vivian dropped to her knees and began looking at Merlin's wounded shoulder. As the young soldier ran off, he looked back. "'Sixty-one."

"Merlin, can you move?"

"I don't know. How bad is it?"

"It's bad. We've got to get out of here." Vivian tore off a piece of her petticoat and used it as a bandage to try to slow the bleeding. "Let me help you up. You're losing a lot of blood. If we don't get you out of here, you could die."

Vivian helped Merlin up, but after a few steps he fell again. She saw a riderless horse nearby and went to it. She grabbed the reins and led it back to where Merlin lay. With her help and his last ounce of strength, he was able to get himself onto the saddle. Vivian climbed behind him and the two headed to where their equipment and supplies were hidden. Vivian pulled out the inflatable pool and started the pump to blow it up. She then took out the nanofactory and filled the pool with the solution. The barely conscious Merlin moaned as Vivian put away the supplies and prepared the charges to disintegrate the pool upon their leaving. Merlin turned pale from the loss of blood as Vivian got him into the pool. She pulled out the laser wand and set the coordinates for what she hoped would be a successful return home.

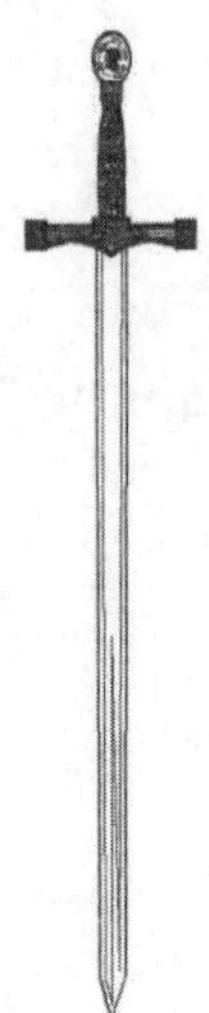

Chapter Six

Adrian sat in his office, worrying about Merlin and Vivian. The time calibration on the time machine had been destroyed when lightning struck the building. They'd all worked frantically fixing the damage so they could determine what effect it might have had on Merlin and Vivian's jump. Lance and Chac had volunteered to take a trip back to search for them, but since nobody really knew what time the first two had landed in, it seemed futile for the next two to make a jump.

Adrian heard a commotion in the hallway and got up from his chair to see what was going on. He opened the door and saw a crowd of people gathered in the hallway and walked toward them. He made his way through the crowd and found Vivian trying to say something, but was getting drowned out by the crowd. Adrian grabbed Vivian's arm and pulled her through the crowd. He gave her a bear hug, and then held her at arm's length. "Where's Merlin?"

Vivian was breathless and spacey as she looked up at the

burly archeologist with tears running down her dirt-and-gun-powder-stained face. “Please, Adrian. Merlin needs help.”

Adrian tried to calm Vivian down by slowly asking again, “Where’s Merlin?”

Vivian pulled Adrian’s big hand from her shoulder and led him through the crowd. “We must hurry. Come on.”

“Where is he, and is he hurt?” demanded Adrian.

“Yes he’s hurt. He’s not far from here. We’ve got to help him,” she said, showing an uncommon concern for Merlin.

“Wait a second.” Adrian grabbed the receiver from a phone on a wall near the entrance doors and called for a medical team to meet him outside. He then ran back to Vivian. “Okay, take me to him.”

Adrian grabbed a couple of nearby people and told them to follow him. The two team leaders ran out the door to the back of the building. Adrian instructed one of the people to wait for the medical team and to send them in the direction he was going. Adrian was having a tough time making his large frame move at the speed he wanted it to go. As they reached the back of the building, Vivian pointed to a spot several hundred yards past the fenced perimeter. Adrian instructed the remaining person to send the medical team in that direction.

Vivian and Adrian worked their way through the hole Vivian had cut in the chain-link fence and ran to where Merlin lay. Adrian paled at the sight of his bloodied friend. He bent down and checked Merlin’s pulse. He looked up at a still breathless Vivian. “He’s still alive, but just barely.”

Vivian dropped to her knees and held Merlin’s head in her lap. The blood from Merlin’s wound began to soak Vivian’s clothes as she cradled him. Her weird, frigid exterior began to thaw and her tears dampened Merlin’s cheeks.

Researchers began to crowd around the time travelers as sirens pierced the air. Adrian yelled for everyone to move back to allow the medics some room. An ambulance pulled to a stop in the parking lot and the attendants got out and removed their equipment.

Lance walked out the front doors of the Operations Building just as the medics were directed to the back of the building. He followed them to the rear of the building where they were pointed to where Merlin was lying. Lance rushed ahead of them, clearing the way for the medics.

One of the medics cut the clothing from around Merlin's wound and began assessing the situation while the other set up their equipment. Once the equipment was set up, one medic called the base medical clinic for instructions while the other asked Vivian how Merlin could have gotten this much damage from a shot.

Vivian could barely speak but managed to whisper, "Minie ball."

The medic looked at Merlin's clothing and then at Vivian's. She then looked at her partner with a "What the hell?" expression.

Lance saw the questions on their faces. "They're in a reenactment play. A musket accidentally went off."

The female medic looked around at the people dressed in lab coats and standard work clothes. She turned toward Lance as if to say "Yeah, right, and I'm the Queen of Sheba."

Her partner finished putting up the equipment. "Let's roll."

Lance grabbed the female medic's arm. "What's your security clearance level?"

The woman looked down at Lance's hand on her arm and pulled it off before saying, "Secret."

Lance looked at Adrian. "We need someone with a higher

clearance to be with him. I'll ride along and keep you updated."

Merlin was taken to the small base medical clinic where a doctor began working on him. The team sat in the waiting room while Adrian paced the hallways, bugging the nurses for news.

Lance scrubbed up and was in the operating room to observe the operation for security reasons. Lance's Executive Officer met with the two medics, informing them of the need to maintain secrecy regarding what they had seen.

After several hours, the doctor, accompanied by Lance, entered the waiting room. "Your friend required extensive repair and lost a great deal of blood. He'll require some therapy, but I believe he'll be fine."

Relief filled the air as the team hugged each other. Their leader had survived again. Annie gave Vivian a hug and, as Annie released Vivian, she saw Merlin's blood all over Vivian's clothes. "Dear, we need to get you home so you can get cleaned up. Are you okay?"

"Yeah, I'm fine. I just need a little rest."

Annie held Vivian at arm's length and smiled. "You love him, don't you?"

"No. I couldn't possibly. I'm way too busy for that." Vivian made a hasty effort to wipe the tears, dirt, and gunpowder from her face. She looked down at her bloody clothes. "Annie, let's not talk about this anymore. Can you run me home so I can get cleaned up?"

"Sure, let's go."

The next day, Vivian called a meeting of the team leaders, minus the recovering Merlin. She wanted to brief them about the last jump and attempt to figure out what happened and how they might avoid it in the future. Vivian told them about the trip, when and where they'd landed, and the problems they'd run into trying to find out the exact year.

Adrian told her about how the lightning had hit the building, destroying the mirrors that brought the sunlight into the laser.They developed a list of problem areas to address and each was assigned a task to work on. Chac and Adelina worked on developing a small, hand-held computer and loading it with topographical and weather information for as far back as the data could be obtained. Lance had a lot to do in running the base, but he took on the task of having the security clearances of all the base personnel, including the medical staff, upgraded to Top Secret Crypto and transferring all personnel who couldn't pass the background test for the upgrade. Annie and Quetzal worked on putting together a better backpack to include an extensive medical kit, bolt-cutters, and a small, battery-operated digital video camera so that future jumps could be recorded. Adrian and Vivian began working on better protection for the equipment and tried to understand why the landing date had been off so far.

Each member of the team went by the clinic every day at various times to check in on Merlin. Vivian was especially attentive, always coming to Merlin's physical therapy sessions. Vivian found herself being drawn closer and closer to him, and although she continued to fight it with all her resolve, she just couldn't help herself. It was as though she'd become addicted to him as someone would to a drug. She didn't want a relationship, but she couldn't resist him either.

Dr. Barnes arrived at the base a month after the accident. His first stop was the Operations Building, where everyone was concerned that Bill might shut the project down as being too dangerous. After being briefed on the trip and the aftermath, he was brought up to date on how the team was progressing on the recommended changes. Vivian told him that they were ready to try out the changes and Vivian requested approval to make a jump on her own. Bill seemed to like what he'd heard, but he also seemed a bit distracted, as if something else was on his mind.

After the meeting, Bill asked Adrian to drive him to the medical clinic so he might check in on Merlin. Outside Merlin's room Adrian said, "I'll wait out here so the two of you can visit."

"No," Bill said. "I asked you to come with me to talk with Merlin about our new plan."

The two men entered the room. Merlin was lying on the hospital bed, almost asleep. Bill said, "I'm sorry I haven't been by sooner. How are you holding up?"

"That's okay. I'm doing fine," Merlin assured him.

"I met with your team before coming over here to see you. They gave me a briefing on your last jump and the progress they've made since then in solving some of the problems that you ran into. I must say that I'm quite impressed with them. It's my understanding that they're planning a jump without you."

"Oh really?" Merlin sat up in bed. "This is the first I've heard of it. Adrian, why didn't you tell me about it?"

"I would've, but it's somewhat of a new development."

"So I take it this was Vivian's idea," Merlin said.

"Well, yes, but . . ." Adrian began, searching for the right words.

"I knew it," Merlin yelled. He got out of bed. "I was just beginning to get to where I could trust her. Now this."

"Wait a minute, Merlin," Bill said. "I haven't given the

okay on this yet, but . . ." He hesitated for a moment just like Adrian had, to allow himself time to get just the right words together. "I've been working with Adrian on something since you've been in here. You might find it more interesting than what's happening with Vivian."

Merlin sat back down on his hospital bed. "Okay. I'm game. What's up?"

"My thinking is that perhaps we should let Vivian go ahead and finish working out the kinks for a while."

"You're nuts. Why should we do that?"

"Well, actually I'm thinking we should let her take over as Project Director here for a while," Bill said with a sly smile.

"Why that conniving bitch," Merlin said.

"Wait a minute, my boy. Hear him out. I think you're going to like this."

"What could I possibly like about this? I get injured during a jump and suddenly I lose my job?" Merlin said, stomping around the small room.

"Merlin, calm down for a minute," Bill said. "You're not really losing your job. It's just going to change a bit."

Merlin stopped and looked at his boss curiously. "Why don't you just tell me what's going on instead of beating around the bush?"

Bill laughed. "Okay, okay. Adrian and I have been working on a mission for you and your team. You feel up to it?"

"Mission? What kind of mission?" Merlin returned to his bed, his interest piqued.

"To continue your research into the Maya as a Time Travel Archeologist."

Merlin smiled. "Well, I'll have to think about it. Adrian, could you hand me my pants and we can talk about it on the way to the plane? I assume you have it gassed up for the trip?"

"So I can take that as a yes?" Bill asked.

"I think so. Where do we start?"

"I've talked with Adrian and he feels you should start with a site in Mexico. Probably in the Yucatan Peninsula."

"Great. Let's go."

"Wait a minute. You've got to get well first," Bill said.

Merlin's head was beginning to swirl with hundreds of images and questions. He had dreamed for years of going back to see the ancient Maya at their grandest stage. He looked at Bill. "There's so much to do. I've got to get started."

"No, no. You get well. Adrian and Annie can handle everything for now. Besides, if you're to lead a team to the past you have to be in shape for it."

"Okay. I understand. Now, about Vivian . . ."

"Don't worry about her. She's not trying to undermine you."

"That's fine. But I don't want her going back on these test jumps alone. Lance seems to be in good shape. Why not send him back as an added level of protection?"

"Sounds like a good idea. Incidentally, Vivian will still report to you. Your new title will be Director of Extended Research."

"Director of Extended Research? What's that supposed to mean?"

"We couldn't very well make you Director of Time Travel Archeology, could we? Besides, it means the same." Bill gave a shrug of his shoulders.

Bill worked with his friend in the State Department to arrange a high-level meeting with the President and those members of his Cabinet who were the heads of agencies that needed to know about the time travel program. These people agreed that there was a great amount of risk in time travel, but if it were limited to the new profession of Time Travel Archeology the benefits might outweigh the safety risks. They all further agreed that they would keep the research on a need-to-know basis when it came to other governments and they'd take a position of "plausible deniability" when it came to the inevitable press leaks. They also worked out a way for the National Security Agency to set up a special section whose job would be to keep abreast of developments throughout the world, to specifically look for volatile situations that might be diffused through research conducted by Merlin's team.

The highest officials of the Mexican government were informed of the program and permission was granted for the Maya Project. The Mexicans were excited about the prospect of solving the Mayan mystery and perhaps redirecting the unrest within the modern-day Mayan communities, although there was a faction that felt only negative results could come from empowering the Maya with this new information.

Adrian, Annie, and Chac went to work to find the best location to build a facility, but to do this, they needed to know the time period they wanted to investigate. It was decided that the most significant would be the period related to the legendary Mayan god called Kukulkán. The site they selected was near the ancient capital of Mayapan.

Chac, Adelina, and Quetzal moved to the new site, along with a few members of the support staff and several researchers. The team initially worked out of trailers and lived in tents while the research center was being constructed. Adrian was put in temporary charge of the project and proved to be a fine leader, which came as a surprise to everyone, including Adrian. Quetzal was put in charge of security, a job Lance would have been given if he had not stayed at Vint Hill Farms Station. Chac and Adelina surveyed the area, looking for old Mayan roads or pathways that might prove useful to the time travelers. Chac loved working with Adelina, which gave him a chance to show her what he was good at. Annie again assumed the duties of obtaining the supplies and equipment needed to run the operation, only this time she had additional funding from both the American and Mexican governments. Soon a true research facility began to take shape.

Vivian was told of her promotion, but in a strange way she didn't get the satisfaction from the announcement she thought she would. It wasn't that she no longer wanted the increased responsibility, nor did it bother her that Merlin also was promoted. In fact, she was sincerely happy for Merlin. She was becoming truly confused by her own emotions.

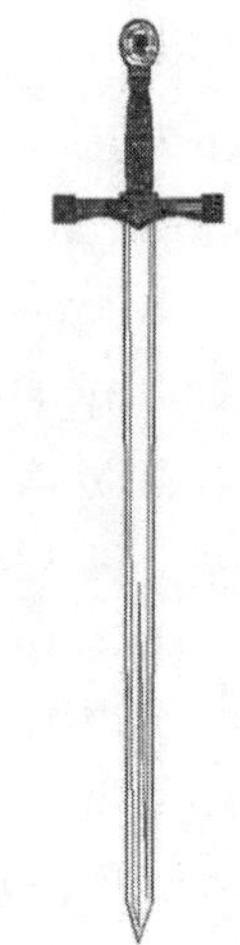

Chapter Seven

The day arrived for Vivian's first jump without Merlin and Lance's first jump ever. The mission was to jump to May 12, 1880. There was no particular reason for picking that date, other than there were no known hostilities in the area during that time. Once they arrived, they were to proceed to Warrenton, Virginia, and confirm the date and return back to the present. They would be spending several days in the past, but they were to calibrate the return for one day after the day they left. They also prepared a return location just outside the Operations Building. The area would be placed under guard and the guards would remain outside a wide perimeter that had been created to prevent any accidents when the two returned.

Merlin was driven to the Operations Building to observe the jump and to be there for his two friends.

Even though Vivian and Lance had been well coached for their jump, they were still quite nervous about it, as was Merlin. Special provisions, including water, were prepared. The weather was perfect. The two time travelers went to Merlin to say goodbye with Vivian embracing Merlin and Lance giving him a firm handshake. Merlin told Lance to take care of Vivian and the two explorers began their journey to test the new equipment and procedures.

As the wormhole formed, Lance looked at it and began to get second thoughts. Vivian grabbed his arm. "Too late to back out."

Together, they jumped back in time.

Lance began to stomp his feet. "I can't believe it! I can't believe it! It's real! Oh my God, this is really happening."

Vivian grabbed Lance's arm and pulled him away from the landing site before saying, "You idiot. The supplies are coming and they'll tear you up if you don't get out of the way. I think you're supposed to be the one who protects me, not the other way around."

"I gotta pee," Lance declared. "Where's the restroom around here?"

"Lance, get hold of yourself. Have you totally lost it? Go over to that tree and hurry up. We've got work to do."

The supplies arrived and Vivian began sorting through them, setting aside those that needed to be stowed from those they would take with them. Lance returned from his tree and began taking the supplies that were to be stowed to a nearby copse of trees. It wasn't long before the two were on their way.

The walk to Warrenton took them the rest of the day. Once there, they went to a small hotel and got two rooms. Lance could barely contain his excitement as he met and talked to people from a different time period. They confirmed the arrival day and year as correct and spent the rest of their time observing the activities of the small town.

Everything was fine until their final full day in the past—they both became ill. They were running a mild fever and had diarrhea, which was even less fun without modern bathroom facilities or toilet paper. Vivian made the decision to leave then rather than waiting to get better, or worse, as the case might be. Though weak, Lance managed to rent them a couple of horses and they rode back to their jump site. Once back, they let the horses go free, set up the return pool, gathered their supplies and made their jump home.

They arrived at the time they were suppose to and had a crowd to greet them, including Merlin, who was very relieved to see them. Vivian held up her hand and yelled for them to stay back. She was afraid she and Lance might be contagious and asked the guards to call an ambulance. Once the medics arrived, the two explorers were whisked away to a special decontamination room at the medical clinic. Fortunately, it was only a strain of flu that neither of them had been exposed to before. Though they couldn't have done much to prevent this from occurring, it brought to light the need to check for diseases of the period they were to visit and have the time travelers inoculated against those diseases, if possible. Furthermore, it was apparent that simple medicines would be needed in the future medical kits to cover potential medical problems like colds.

Vivian and Lance spent the next two weeks in isolation as a precaution. Merlin checked out of the clinic and returned home for the duration of his rehabilitation but returned daily to check on his friends.

Dr. Barnes called Adrian away from the project in Mexico and Annie was given the task of finishing the facility herself. Annie found things tougher as she assumed Adrian's duties in his absence while continuing her own work. She was delighted to report to Merlin that there was a new development in the relationship between Chac and Adelina. Chac proposed marriage to Adelina and she accepted. They had not set a wedding date yet, but they hoped to be able to get married as soon as everyone with the Virginia team was well.

As Merlin's physical therapy neared completion, his excitement grew as he thought about the idea of going back in time and meeting the actual Mayans he'd studied for so long. Soon he would be on his way to Mexico and a new adventure. His only regret was that he would have to leave Vivian behind.

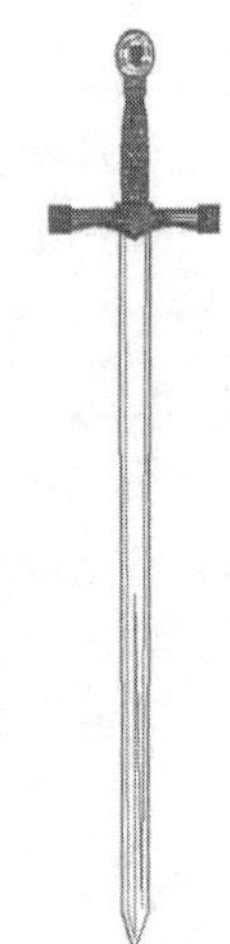

Chapter Eight

Vivian had been released from the hospital and was sitting with Merlin on his couch enjoying a glass of wine and contemplating their future when the doorbell rang. Merlin excused himself and went to the door. He opened it and found, standing before him, a sullen-faced Bill Barnes and the missing Adrian. Merlin's happiness turned to concern as he looked at his two friends. All he could think of was that something must have happened to Annie or Chac for these two men to come all the way out to see him without calling first.

"Come in," he said, trying to maintain his composure.

The two men entered the house and went to the living room where Vivian was sitting. Without saying a word, they each sat in the wingback chairs located across from the sofa. Bill looked at Merlin. "We've got a problem."

More worried than before, Merlin looked at Adrian in an attempt to read something in his face that might let him know what was going on. "What?" he asked, not sure he really wanted to hear the answer.

"Have you been watching the news lately?" Bill asked.

"No," Merlin said with a sly smile as he looked at Vivian. "I've had other things on my mind."

"There's been a dramatic increase in rioting in London, Birmingham, and other cities in Great Britain," Bill said. "They want to do away with the monarchy. King Charles just abdicated his throne in favor of his son, Prince William."

"They've been wanting to do away with the monarchy for decades. What's that got to do with us?" Vivian asked.

Adrian looked at his two friends and asked, "Do you know Prince William's full name?"

"No. Can't say that I really cared," Merlin said.

"His full name is William Arthur Philip Louis Windsor," Adrian told them.

"So?" Merlin scratched his healing shoulder.

Bill started to explain but Adrian stopped him with a wave of his arm. Adrian stroked his beard and paced around Merlin's living room. "My boy, Prince William has the option of being crowned using any of his names. In a move to enhance Great Britain's position in the European Union and quash troubles at home, he's chosen to be crowned King Arthur II."

"What's that got to do with us?" Vivian asked.

"King Arthur II desires to institute a new 'Age of Camelot.' He's of the opinion that for him to have any chance of success, he must prove the existence of the old 'Age of Camelot' and the Windsor family's direct lineage back to King Arthur of legend," Bill explained.

Adrian broke in with, "They can show a link to Cerdac, but that's where it leaves off. Some believe Cerdac was the illegitimate son of King Arthur."

Merlin looked at his two friends standing before him and shook his head. "Gentlemen, I can see where this is headed.

But haven't you forgotten that we already have a mission in Mexico?"

"The Department of State has asked for our help," Bill said, scratching the back of his ear.

"How did this all come about? How did we get involved?" Vivian asked.

"As you know, the NSA set up a special group assigned to monitor news reports with an eye toward finding situations where our team can be useful in solving a problem," Bill answered. "With the increased friction within our closest ally's country, and because our team can find the answer, the NSA thinks that our group can provide the perfect solution to the problem. I was asked to look into the matter. That's when I called in Adrian, because he's a citizen of Great Britain. After checking it out, we figured that this was as perfect a use for our group as we can get. You might say it's textbook perfect."

"Okay. So where do we go from here?" Merlin asked.

"As you know, I've been gone for awhile," Adrian said. "I've set up a small research center in a barn outside Gloucester, England, which is in southwest England on the River Severn. I've arranged for housing for all the people we'll be bringing with us, though it's a bit spread out. I'll need to get with you and Vivian to go over the list of supplies and equipment that I have there so we can see what else we need to bring with us. Bill arranged transportation for our people and equipment, which is standing by at Andrews Air Force Base waiting for us."

Merlin looked at Vivian and scratched his head before he said, "Uh, wait a minute. You said they 'are' waiting for us. When do you think we're going to be leaving?"

"Tomorrow," said Bill.

"Wait a minute. We can't leave just like that. Who's going to take care of things here? And what about the team in Mexico?"

Bill was aware of the time and effort that had been put into the Mayan project and the importance to Merlin of that mission. But if they could succeed in the King Arthur mission, it would open up funding and they could really accomplish some great things. Another benefit would be that they might be able to go public if the outcome was successful, which would bring the Institute and himself a great deal of fame. Bill stared at Merlin for a moment before he said, "Don't worry about it, Merlin. We'll shut down the actual jumps from this location and leave some of the researchers here to carry on and coordinate activities between the King Arthur project and the Mayan project. Vivian, you can pick someone you trust to take over for you here. We'll leave everyone in place in Mexico. Besides, Chac, Quetzal, and Adelina would look out of place in old Briton."

"What about security at both places?" Vivian asked.

"We have Quetzal handling security in Mexico and he's doing fine. I've arranged for Lance and a platoon of his MPs to take care of security in England. His Executive Officer will take over here while he's gone."

"And what will the Brits say about having American troops handle security in their country?" Merlin asked.

"They're okay with it. This will mean fewer people will know about what we do. They'll just have to wear civilian clothes."

Goose bumps formed on Merlin's arms and the hair stood up on his back as his excitement grew at the thought of meeting the legendary King Arthur. He saw the same excitement growing inside Vivian. "One problem. I'm an expert on the Maya, but I have little knowledge of King Arthur, Briton, or even the language. How can I pull this off?"

"I'll teach you," Adrian replied. "But you'll have to forget about most of the legend. The real Arthur, if he existed, lived in the late fifth to early sixth century rather than the Middle Ages. I've updated a handheld computer with the legend, the perceived truth and the known truth. This should help you."

"Well, that's fine, but what about the language?"

"You're pretty good with Latin, but I've programmed a universal translator with the various dialects of the Celtic language, so you should be okay."

Merlin looked at Vivian and watched a smile creep up her face. He fought the same reaction, but couldn't hold back any longer as he too produced an uncontrollable grin. "I must be nuts. But okay, we're in."

The team immediately went to work. They compared the current supplies and equipment at the Gloucester site with what would be needed to conduct the new mission. They packed what they could of their personal items and left the rest for when they returned or for later shipment. Lance and his platoon of MPs would remain in Virginia for a few days to get the supplies and equipment together that would be needed in Gloucester.

The next day, Bill and the team leaders, along with a few of the researchers, left Vint Hill Farms Station for Andrews Air Force Base and the trip to Gloucester. Bill would be staying behind to help coordinate the move and to inform Annie that she would stay in charge of the Mexican project for a while. Lance and his MPs, the other researchers who would be needed, the supplies and equipment, and the rest of the personal items the lead group wanted would follow in a few days.

Once the lead team arrived in London, they transferred planes for the short trip to Gloucester. In Gloucester, they picked up their luggage and the rental cars that were waiting for them and drove to their new quarters. Adrian arranged for maps to be provided to the various members of the lead group, along with the description, address, and keys to their individual quarters. Adrian drove Vivian and Merlin into the countryside, past the cows and horses, small farms, and huge estates, to a quaint cottage.

"Welcome to your new home, Merlin," Adrian said as he pulled to a stop in front of a cottage.

Merlin looked around outside as Adrian unloaded the luggage. "Are we all staying here?"

"I've got an apartment in Gloucester. This is a two-bedroom cottage and each bedroom is equal in size. This will be home for you and Vivian, that is, if Vivian has no objections."

Vivian smiled as she wrapped her arm around Merlin's. "I'm fine with it if it's okay with Merlin."

"I'll let you two settle in and we'll get together tomorrow. There's plenty of food in the kitchen. I had it stocked with your favorites. You feel well enough for a short trip tomorrow to test things out?"

Surprised by the question Merlin said, "So soon? We're not fully set up yet."

"Just kidding." Adrian smiled. "But we'll want to be prepared to go once everything we need arrives in the next few days. I'll see you tomorrow."

Merlin and Vivian opened the door to the cottage and carried their luggage in. They looked around at the country interior design of the cottage. "Merlin, I can't believe this is happening. How's your Celtic and Latin?"

"Wrong question. What you should ask is how good am I at working the translator?"

Vivian picked the bedroom she wanted and Merlin took the other one. They unpacked and put away their belongings and then prepared a meal. This was the closest they'd ever been together. The thought of sleeping under the same roof with Merlin gave Vivian a nervous stomach.

That evening over dinner Merlin talked about how he wished Annie could be there with them. He'd always thought of her as his anchor. Now he was about to embark on the most exciting mission of his life without her being part of it.

Vivian knew Merlin would go on the first mission or two on his own, but she fully expected to be joining him on some of the missions soon. Now that Lance also had experience, they discussed having multiple missions going at the same time at some point in the future in order to expedite things. A lot would depend on what happened from the standpoint of safety. There had been incidents that occurred on each of the missions that they'd taken deep into the past, and these new missions would be the deepest of all. They talked about the excitement of meeting King Arthur, the Knights of the Round Table, seeing Camelot, and Merlin's opportunity to possibly meet his namesake, Merlin the Magician.

Adrian had left some audiotapes and some books on fifth century Briton and the legends of King Arthur so Merlin could brush up. He thought he'd scan through the legends first and compare them to what was believed to be the truth. He wasn't going to have enough time for an in-depth review of the material so he just hit the highlights. Most of the modern tales of Arthur had to do with the Middle Ages, but the true Arthur could only have existed in the late fifth to early sixth century, if he existed at all. This was a very dangerous era because Briton was in the midst of great change. The Britons had led a very rustic life prior to the Roman takeover, but for over four hundred years they had learned the refined ways of the Romans. Arthur and his brethren were on the cusp of the change from Roman to Saxon life when he'd lived and ruled.

The next morning, a tired Merlin woke to the smell of bacon and eggs. Vivian walked into his bedroom, dressed in a red satin robe. This was the first time Merlin had ever seen Vivian in a robe, and he liked what he saw. She sat next to him on the bed and pushed his hair away from his eyes.

"Are you awake?" she asked.

"Yeah, I couldn't sleep last night."

"Thinking about me?"

Merlin laughed as he reached over and pulled her down next to him on the bed. "No, I was thinking about the mission. About whether we're prepared enough to go."

"We will be." Not understanding why she did it, she laid her head on his chest. She was worried because of his injury during their jump back to the Civil War. She'd made only a couple of jumps herself since then, both with Lance. The first of those she got sick and the second was a turnaround jump just to make sure everything was okay. Vivian was concerned about what she was feeling for Merlin; she was convinced it was a bad idea for them to be sharing the cottage together because of her feelings. She lifted her head from his chest and without a smile said, "Come on. Let's get up. I've fixed us some breakfast."

Merlin ate his breakfast slowly, trying to prolong every minute with Vivian. Merlin wished he could've talked with Annie about his strange relationship with Vivian, but understood the need for confidentiality for the mission. The two of them finished dressing just as Adrian arrived to take them to the Gloucester Research Center.

Adrian stopped the car near six doublewide trailers set in a rectangle formation near the barn. There was a clear plastic roof that covered the area between the trailers and a pond nearby that had some type of platform built on it.

Merlin looked at Vivian in confusion but asked Adrian, "Is this it?"

"Yeah," Adrian said, embarrassed. "Nothing like home, is it? But it's the best I could do with such short notice. We needed to be operational immediately. Let's go in and I'll show you around before everyone else gets here."

The three team leaders went inside and Adrian showed them around the small facility. Merlin felt uncomfortable with the size of the area after working at Vint Hill Farms Station, but acknowledged that everything, except the supplies and equipment Lance was bringing, was in place for a trip.

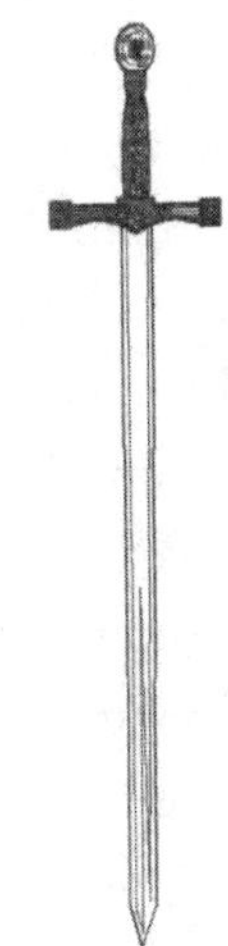

Chapter Nine

Merlin went into the wardrobe room and found a long, brown cloak with a hood, some knee-high brown boots, a loose-fitting shirt that pulled over his head and laced up the front with leather laces from about the chest up, and a loose pair of blue pants. He was letting his hair and beard grow for the mission, but they still had a long way to go. Fortunately, Adrian had thought of that too, and had provided several wigs and beards that could take care of the situation until Merlin's own growth was long and thick enough for him to work without them.

Adrian came in as Merlin was looking over the clothes and took him by the arm and led him to the equipment room. There, he showed Merlin some of his proudest accomplishments. The first was a laser that had been camouflaged to look like a walking stick. He then directed Merlin's attention to a small cart covered with a natural brown leather hide. Adrian pulled back the hide, revealing two nanofactories, a small solar battery-powered hand-held computer, a shovel with an improved laser attachment, a carrying bag, and containers for food, small supplies, and a large medical kit.

"How am I suppose to pull all this around?" Merlin asked.

"I would suggest you get a horse while you're there," Adrian said, tugging at his beard. "Everyone's arriving. I need to show them around real quick. You and Vivian might want to work out their assignments and maybe give them a little introductory speech on what we're doing here."

"Why is there a platform built into the pond?"

"I assume you think there's water in the pond."

"Well, yeah," Merlin said, nodding.

"It's filled with the solution. That's where you'll be making the jump."

"You've got to be kidding."

"No. During the time period you'll be jumping to, there actually was a small lake there. It's been gone for centuries, but it'll provide you with some degree of cover for your jumps."

Merlin and Vivian prepared the initial work assignments. They met with the team members and told them about the mission. Excitement exploded throughout the room as it dawned on the researchers what they'd be working on.

The rest of the team arrived a few days later. Vivian and Merlin met Lance as he drove up, followed by a busload of MPs and researchers. The bus would be used to ferry everyone around except for the few with cars at their disposal. There were also two trucks full of equipment and supplies. Adrian had prepared an area in the barn to store everything until it could be sorted and put to use.

Merlin met with the new arrivals to explain the mission, which was greeted with the same enthusiasm as the other researchers had greeted it. That was, with the exception of the

MPs, who had never been informed as to what was going on at Vint Hill Farms Station or Gloucester until this meeting. They had heard unconfirmed rumors, but to have them confirmed was initially met with disbelief, then anger at not being trusted in the past, then interest, curiosity, and even a bit of pride for being a part of it.

Merlin had been preparing himself for the trip by studying the facts, legends, history, habits, food, language, clothing, and everything else he could think of that was even remotely related to the area and time period he was going to travel to. There were numerous books and debates on the possibility that Ambrosius–Merlin's first target–was Uther Pendragon's brother, or King Arthur, or Merlin the Magician, or just a great general. Merlin secretly hoped that Ambrosius was Merlin the Magician, thus relieving Merlin of that burden. If Ambrosius turned out in fact to be King Arthur himself, then this would be a short mission and they would be on their way to Mexico.

Merlin also prepared himself by studying the old and new maps of the area. His computer was loaded with information about it, but he liked having as much direct knowledge of the country's names as possible. He'd already become familiar with many of the current city and town names, but they were different in the time period he was traveling to, for instance, the town of Gloucester was known as Glevum, London was Londinium, Wroxeter in Wales was Vircontim, and England was Briton.

Everything was finally in order and the team was ready for a small test jump. Merlin and Vivian arrived early at the research center so they could make sure everything was set up like they wanted it and Merlin could change into his clothes for the trip back. Merlin was surprised to find Adrian already there and hard at work. Despite the early hour, the center was teeming with activity. The cart had been loaded and covered with a waterproof cover to protect the contents.

Annie had recently thought of a potential problem with jumps that she'd voiced to Bill on his recent trip to Mexico to check on the construction of the Mexican Research Center. What if the terrain was significantly different in the past? By simply adding a tree where they were jumping to, it could mean the jumpers would be jumping to their deaths. Annie worked with Quetzal on a simple solution: Send back a video camera to film the landing area first. For the return, attach a small platform that would deploy a small, inflatable pool on arrival. The pool would fill up with solution, and a small, preset laser would send out a beam that would return the camera to the present. They built the device and Bill had it sent to Vint Hill Farms Station and then to Gloucester for use in Merlin's jump. Annie, however, was still kept in the dark about where Merlin was and what he was doing.

Everyone involved with the jump left the trailers and went to the jump pond. The pond was surrounded by Lance's MPs and covered by a white canvas tent. Adrian and two of the research assistants put Annie's small camera in the middle of the pond while Vivian, Merlin, and Lance watched from the side. Once everyone was clear of the solution in the pond, one of the researchers hit the remote button, sending the camera back more than sixteen centuries.

A few moments later, the camera reappeared a few feet from where it had left. Two attendants quickly retrieved it and brought it to the side. The videodisc was removed and the four team leaders ran to the trailers to check it out. What they saw was a bit different than the way it was in the present, but there was no specific danger awaiting Merlin at the other end of the jump.

Merlin hurried to his office to get ready while the rest of the team prepared for his jump. It wasn't long before he emerged from his office and walked down the well-lit corridor. Busy workers in their white lab coats stared and smiled at him as he made his way to the time pool. How odd he looked in his outfit, which was in stark contrast to those around him. As he walked through the Center's main door, Lance and Vivian joined him. The two walked with Merlin to the platform at the time pool. Adrian was waiting there with the cart that had everything in it Merlin thought he could ever possibly need, which would follow him a few minutes after he jumped.

Vivian looked up at the long-haired, bearded Merlin and pulled his face down to hers. She gave him a long, passionate kiss. "I didn't want you to forget me," she said, dusting off imaginary dirt from his coat. She turned her moist eyes up to meet his and wrapped her arms around his neck.

"Maybe we should postpone this trip for another day," Merlin said with a smile and a wink.

"Come on, my boy," Adrian called. "No time like the present. Let's get you going." Adrian shook Merlin's hand as Merlin began to walk up the platform stairs. Technicians had already placed the parts he would need to build a ramp at the edge of the lake for the removal of the cart. A technician asked Merlin to pull up his sleeve while in his right hand he held a menacing-looking gun to inoculate Merlin against any potential medical problems that might come up. At the top of the stairs still another techie handed Merlin a package of dry clothes he could change into and a few supplies he would need prior to the arrival of the cart.

Merlin twitched his nose, turned and waved to his team as he walked across the platform and then descended the stairs into the pond. This was the part Merlin hated most about the job: He was concerned about the arrival of the cart, someone seeing him arrive in the past, in fact, every detail of the trip. Suddenly, with a burst of green light from his camouflaged laser, he disappeared into the wormhole.

Chapter Ten

Suddenly, he found himself submerged and gasping for breath in the murky water of a lake. He raised his head above the surface of the water and saw that he was no longer in the clear solution of the time pool. He looked around the colorful autumn setting and saw the parts he needed for the ramp floating nearby. He made his way to the ramp package and pulled it and his other package to the shore. He walked out of the lake and felt a chill as the cool autumn air hit his wet clothing. He put the watertight package down and returned to the lake to assemble the ramp. The ramp was made so that Merlin could raise or lower it, thus allowing him to conceal it within the murky water.

The cart had still not arrived by the time he'd finished the ramp, which began to worry him because the cart had his way back packed aboard it. To take his mind off the missing cart, he decided to go ahead and change clothes and build a fire; the wind was light and the sun was out on this cloudless fall day, so stripping was not as troublesome as it could have been.

Standing naked to the elements, Merlin quickly put on the dry clothes and gathered some wood. After getting the fire going, he built a drying rack and put his wet clothes on it. Merlin checked his fake beard and wig and was pleasantly surprised to find them still firmly attached.

He searched his bag further and found a sandwich, some chips, a Dr. Pepper, and a cup designed from the era. He made himself comfortable while he waited for the rest of his supplies. As he finished his meal, he heard some twigs break behind him. He turned and saw a short, slim man, dressed more like a Roman than a Briton, coming toward him. Damn, Merlin thought as he looked at the plastic wrapping for his sandwich. He quickly hid the remnants of his lunch as the man approached closer. He didn't seem threatening, but Merlin stood and prepared himself just in case, a new problem running through his mind: He and his fellow time travelers would need to be trained in the martial arts as an added layer of self-defense. They'd also need to be careful about what they brought back in time for meals. Nothing but the cup could be explained; even the sandwich hadn't been invented yet.

Merlin turned away from the man and quickly attached his universal translator to his belt under his coat and tried to get the ear piece into his ear, his heart racing when the man spoke while Merlin fumbled with his equipment.

"*Durdathawee!*" the man said.

What in the world does that mean? Merlin thought as he finally got the translator set up. All he could think of to say was good day. He whispered it into the translator, which responded with "*Deth da.*" He turned back to face the man. "*Deth da.*"

Merlin raised his hood just as the man said something else. Merlin waited for the translation, which was, "What have you to hide? Is your face that well known?"

Again Merlin whispered his answer so the translator could convert it into Celtic. Within a split second he received his translation. With a heavy accent, Merlin said nervously, "I'm a traveler. I have learned to be cautious."

The sandy-haired man walked up to Merlin. "You have nothing to fear from me. I'm the caretaker of the estate of Lord Cadwellon. You speak in a curious manner, stranger. Who are you and from whence do you come?"

Merlin extended his hand to shake the hand of the caretaker. "I'm known as Merlin. I'm–" He stopped short when the caretaker jumped away as though Merlin were a leper.

"Why are you trying to grab me?" the caretaker asked.

Merlin had forgotten that people of this time period didn't shake hands. This was going to be much tougher than he'd originally considered. He had to be careful with his every action if he was going to be successful. Merlin thought for a moment before he said, "I'm sorry. In my land we clasp hands as a show of welcome." The caretaker calmed down. "As I was saying, I'm from a land far from here."

"I see. Your land has customs I find rather strange. Perhaps you would care to join me at the estate of Lord Cadwellon?"

Merlin spoke quietly into the translator but learned that it wouldn't give him all the words he needed. He kept trying to get a translation for "okay," but the translator remained quiet. Evidently Adrian didn't have time to get all the words entered into the translator. "Yes, that would be nice. If you'll give me the directions, I'll meet you there soon."

"Please, we can walk th–" The caretaker stopped in midsentence as he heard a sudden splash in the lake. He turned in the direction of the sound and saw Merlin's cart floating in the lake. "What is that?"

Merlin looked at the cart, held up by a bubble in its protective wrapping. He made a mental note to devise some sort of signal for the future to show when he was ready for his supplies to come through. "It's my cart. I had it hidden under the water in case of bandits."

"I don't know about bandits, though we do have Saxon soldiers who raid in this area at times."

"Saxon? That's good to know. Would you help me get my cart?" Merlin used the end of his staff to hold the cart and float it to the shoreline where the two men pulled it ashore. Merlin thought about how he'd wasted time building the ramp, but it would probably be needed in the future. "Incidentally, I told you by what name I am known, may I inquire as to what name you are known by?"

"Uh, yes. I'm known as Thomas." Thomas looked at the plastic cover. "What manner of cover is this?"

"It's a waterproof wrapping we use in my land."

"It could bring a lot in trade here."

The two men unwrapped Merlin's cart and left for Lord Cadwellon's estate. Walking with a cart wasn't something Merlin had practiced, and it was far more difficult than he'd thought it would be. Thankfully, the Romans had built a network of small brick and stone roads, connecting villas, farms, and villages to larger roads. As they walked, Merlin looked out over the fields and saw the various farming equipment in use. He pointed to one and asked Thomas about its use. Thomas told him about the reaper: it was pushed by a mule and had a wheel on each side. There was a long handle that went from the reaper, around the mule, and extended several feet beyond the mule. Two men worked with the reaper, one in back guiding it while the other cleared the cut grain from the reaper's teeth.

As they rounded a turn in the road, Merlin saw a beautiful Roman-styled villa. Merlin's thoughts turned to Vivian and how she would love to see this beautiful building. He quickened his pace as they neared the villa. The only Roman villas he had seen were those from excavations. The most complete were those he'd seen in Pompeii, Italy. This villa was a bit different from that one in that the bottom half had white stucco walls with a green, ornamental trim. The top half was made from rough timber that blended beautifully with the bottom half.

A lovely young servant woman dressed in a short white tunic of a Roman style met the two men at the entrance. Thomas asked her to bring some refreshments. While waiting, Thomas began to show Merlin the magnificent mansion. They entered the atrium and proceeded to a study, which overlooked an open garden. The garden was rectangular, with a fountain in the center and rooms on three sides. The one room that stuck out in Merlin's mind was the toilet room. He'd heard about Roman plumbing, but this was the first time he'd actually seen it in action. Near the toilet room was a bathroom, something Thomas invited Merlin to enjoy after their refreshments. In the study, there was a round table of about four feet in diameter with elegantly carved chairs around it. There were no paintings on the light-blue walls, but there were several statues placed throughout the villa. Most of the statues appeared to be of Roman soldiers, but there were a few statues of beautiful women.

Thomas gestured toward the chairs. "Please, have a seat."

"Thank you. Thomas, the cart I have is a real burden. Might you have a horse I could trade for?"

Merlin was becoming increasingly frustrated by the inability of the translator to give him the words he needed. Adrian was going to have to make this his top priority when he returned home.

"We have many horses, but Lord Cadwellon has not granted me permission to conduct a trade on my own."

"Where might I locate Lord Cadwellon so I might be able to make a trade?"

"Lord Cadwellon is in Glevum, but I don't believe he'll trade with you. He takes great pride in his horses. The kings pay much for them. So tell me, Merlin, where is this land you're from which gives you such a curious sound?"

"I'm from a land far to the west," Merlin said, suddenly realizing his Texas accent might create some problems for him in this ancient time.

"From the west," Thomas repeated with a hint of alarm. "Are you saying you're a Scot?"

"A Scot? No, I'm from the west, not the north."

The bewildered caretaker said, "You obviously know nothing of this land. The Picts are to the north. And a barbaric people they are. Why are you here?"

Again a blooper by Merlin; he was learning that there was more to fitting in during a time travel jump than could be learned in a few days of preparation. In the future, he'd have to study the time period more thoroughly than he had for this trip. Looking at the confused caretaker he said, "My mission is to visit your land and learn about its people. But I am also interested in finding a man named Ambrosius. Have you heard of him?"

The young woman entered the study with a bowl of fruits and some wine. Thomas poured Merlin and himself a glass of wine. "I've heard of a young boy of that name. He's said to be bewitched. But I don't know where he is. I've heard that King Vortigern is also searching for this boy, as are the Saxons. I wonder, are you a Saxon spy?"

Merlin was obviously at the right time, but if the search

was already in process for Ambrosius then he would have to work fast. "No, I'm not a Saxon spy, but please, tell me about this King Vortigern."

"Vortigern is the High-King of the Island of the Mighty, but he does not rule over most of the land. His treachery has helped put the Saxons and other barbarians in control of large portions of our land while he sits in Wales. My master has met this Vortigern and has told me of the wrong he's brought to us. We fear that the Saxons will destroy what's left of our Roman civility. A time of dread is coming for all Britons."

Thomas proved to be a great resource for Merlin in his quest for information. Thomas explained how the Romans had abandoned Briton sixteen years before and how the kings decided to elect Constantine III High-King to coordinate the military forces and protect Briton from the raids of the Picts and the Irish. King Constantine was strongly in favor of the lifestyle he and his fellow Britons had enjoyed as part of the Roman Empire, but this had made the Britons weak and unable to effectively counter the raids by the Picts and the Irish now that the Roman legions had left Briton. Constantine's top advisor, Vortigern, was in favor of returning to the old Celtic lifestyle, thus forming a division between supporters of the pro-Roman ways and pro-Celtic ways. Vortigern saw an opportunity to assassinate High-King Constantine III and take the title of High-King by force. The Britons under Vortigern, though, were still not prepared to properly defend themselves, so Vortigern had hired the German Saxon, Anglo, and Jute tribes to protect the Britons. Merlin knew this move would eventually lead to the downfall of Briton.

Merlin stayed the night and asked permission to leave his cart at the villa while he located Lord Cadwellon. Thomas agreed and Merlin thanked him with a small, golden necklace as a gift.

***

Early the next morning, Merlin packed a large bag with batteries, a change of clothes, some food and water, and a few toiletry items for his trip and left for Glevum.

Thomas directed Merlin to a nearby road, which had been constructed by the Roman army many years before. The caretaker said it would be easy for Merlin to follow and it would take Merlin directly to his destination. Merlin found the road and discovered it to be paved with iron slag in a manner that was unexpectedly smooth.

The main road to Glevum was about forty feet wide for most of its length and remarkably straight. The road was built up, thus allowing water to drain into the ditches on either side. The total width of the road, including the ditches, was about eighty-five feet, about a third of a modern football field.

Merlin recorded into his hand-held computer the things he'd learned from Thomas and saw as he walked. He consulted his computer to get the date, based on the information Thomas had provided; the computer calculated it to be 428 AD, which put him toward the end of Vortigern's reign, and about twenty-six years prior to Arthur's estimated reign. Historically, this was a very dangerous time for Merlin to be in Briton. He knew that he must take extreme care to survive during his explorations into the time of old Briton.

As he walked, he noticed how sweet the air smelled and how bright the colors were. It seemed much had changed with the aging of the world. Merlin came upon other people who, judging from their clothing, were probably of the peasant class. An oddity that came to light was that while some of the people were dressed as he would've expected a Roman peasant to dress, others were dressed in colorful plaid outfits similar to how a Scotsman of Irishman might dress. The clothing in itself showed Merlin the internal conflict within Briton between what Merlin thought of as the pro-Constantine or Roman faction, and the pro-Vortigern or Celtic faction.

He noticed how they all stared at him. He checked his fake beard and his wig, which felt to be on correctly, though they were beginning to itch. He was at a loss to explain it until an older man came up to him and asked if he were a sorcerer.

"A sorcerer?!" said Merlin. "No. Why do you ask?"

"Your staff," the man said, pointing to Merlin's laser rod. "It glows at times."

Oh my God, Merlin thought. Another screw-up. Will it never end? I'm going to get myself killed before this is all over with. He looked at the old man, searching for words as he said hesitantly, "I see. Well, it's simply a walking stick. There's nothing special about it. Maybe it's just the way the light is striking it at times."

"You're not from here," the old man said as a statement of fact. "You're a Druid, are you not?"

Merlin remembered the history of the Druid religion, or as much of it as he could without consulting his computer. The man was probably thinking he was some sort of Druid sorcerer because of his accent and staff. Merlin said, "No, I'm not a Druid, either. I'm known as Merlin and I'm a visitor to your land."

This didn't seem to satisfy the old man, who looked at Merlin through the corner of his eyes. The travelers began to keep pace with Merlin. As others joined them, it began to look like Merlin was leading a small parade. The people weren't in the least menacing, just curious about this stranger named Merlin.

A few miles from his destination, a band of Saxon soldiers converged on the group of peasants following Merlin. The

Saxon leader demanded, "Who's in charge of this flock of beggars?"

"Sir," Merlin said, "we're not beggars. We're merely travelers on our way to Glevum."

"A likely story coming from you Britons. I'm more apt to believe you're on your way to join the futile efforts of Vortigern. Maybe we should fight you now, rather than wait for you to become armed," the Saxon mused. Turning to his men he yelled, "What do you think? Shall we kill them now or later?"

His men responded with shouts of "Now, now, now!"

Merlin was not a fighter and as he looked around he knew that those with him were not fighters either. Even if they were, he could see no weapons on any of them. The only thing he had was his mouth and now seemed like a good time to use it. "Sir, these people are merely farmers and shopkeepers; there are no soldiers here. We have no special allegiance to Vortigern or anyone else. Please leave us in peace. We mean you and your people no harm."

"And who might you be?" the Saxon asked as his troops begin to draw their swords.

Merlin glanced around and saw that the peasants were frightened by what was happening. "I'm known as Merlin. And by what name are you known?"

"I am the gatekeeper and you'll pay a toll to go through the gate. I believe that all of your possessions should be enough to pass."

"There is no gate here," Merlin said.

"You may not be able to see it, but I can and that's all that matters," replied the Saxon as his men began to circle round the peasants and grab their bundles.

Merlin couldn't let the Saxons take his bag because it contained a nanofactory and other equipment from the future, but he'd never been in any kind of physical fight in his life. The leader made a move for Merlin's bag, which dropped to the ground. Merlin swung his laser staff, striking the leader in the stomach, doubling him over. Questions raced through Merlin's mind that he didn't have time to consider the answers for: What would happen if he broke his laser? How would he get home? Why did he hit this man, he wasn't a fighter. But then without another thought, he directed the laser toward several of the attackers and shot a beam at them. The Saxons stopped in their tracks in shock, and dropped the bundles they'd stolen. Merlin thought, Oh God, what have I done now?

Holding the laser on the Saxon leader, he said with an inner strength he didn't know he had, "I demand that you and your men drop your weapons and belongings now or I'll turn the energy of the sun on you."

The Saxons, terrified of Merlin, began to throw down their weapons and belongings.

The Saxon leader asked, "What kind of wizard are you?"

"A good one, if you ask me," said the old man as he laughed at the Saxons. He then looked at Merlin with a raised eyebrow and commented, "Not a sorcerer?"

The peasants crowded around Merlin, thanking him for saving them. Merlin directed them to divide up the Saxons' weapons and other belongings. The peasants grabbed all they could carry while the Saxons looked on in despair.

The Saxon leader said, "We've not heard of you in the past. In the future, we'll be prepared. Beware our next encounter, Wizard Merlin." The defeated Saxons turned and hurriedly departed to the cheers of the crowd, leaving one horse behind per Merlin's instruction.

The old man walked up to Merlin after the Saxons departure and handed Merlin a sword. "This is the sword of the Saxon leader. It belongs to you now, Merlin the Sorcerer."

Merlin looked at the barbarian's sword with its jagged blade and then at the old man, wondering if he should accept it. Then he said, "Thank you," and took the sword.

Merlin stood for a moment more thinking about how he had suddenly become his namesake. He'd found one of the legendary figures he was seeking and the person was himself, Merlin the Sorcerer.

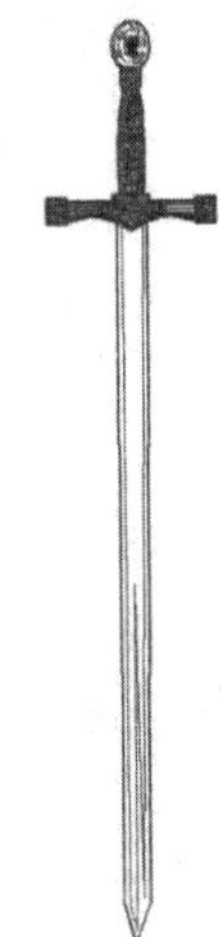

Chapter Eleven

Merlin and his little group continued on with their walk to Glevum. A few of the travelers went ahead and told their friends about what they'd witnessed and how Merlin the Sorcerer was nearing town. Soon all the residents had turned out and the town assumed a carnival-like mood with dancing in the streets and ale for everyone. Merlin and the remaining travelers soon entered the town and the crowds separated to allow the procession, led by Merlin, to pass through.

Near the center of the town, an aristocratic-looking man waited in the middle of the road for Merlin to reach him. The man was of a stocky build and dressed in fine clothing. Merlin stopped a few feet from him and looked at the man's scowling face.

The man suddenly moved forward with both hands stretched out, palms up. He grabbed Merlin and gave him a big hug. Merlin was at a loss for what to say or do. The man then said, "Merlin the Sorcerer, I presume?"

"Yes, and you are known as?"

"I'm Lord Cadwellon. I'm the patriarch of this village." Pointing to the public baths with his left hand, Lord Cadwellon said, "Please, I know you must feel weary from your journey. Let me invite you to enjoy a bath and some ale and food. Perhaps a bit of conversation will be enjoyable, as well. I'll take you to the inn later."

Merlin entered the public bathhouse and was amazed at what he saw. He was an expert on the Mayan culture and had always been amazed by their advances. He'd read a little about the Roman baths, but seeing the exercise rooms, the sauna, the steam rooms, the showers, and the large baths made this a truly remarkable experience. Lord Cadwellon led Merlin to an area where they disrobed and then into the bath, which looked to Merlin like a large swimming pool full of naked men. Fortunately for Merlin, he remembered most of the few words the unfinished translator gave him during his prior conversations; so being without it in the bath should not cause him to get in too much trouble.

Merlin began the conversation by saying, "It's a pleasure to meet you. I was told good things about you by your caretaker, Thomas."

"You know Thomas?"

"Yes. We met yesterday. He was kind enough to allow me to stay as a guest at your estate last night."

"Yes. Thomas is a good man. It's so hard to find that quality of a man to work for you nowadays."

"I have reason to believe that will always be the case."

The two men laughed at Merlin's words and Cadwellon said, "On hearing of your exploits on the road, I have to say that I'm humbled to be in the presence of such an accomplished sorcerer. Tell me, what brings you to our village?"

"I'm looking for a man or boy by the name of Ambrosius."

Cadwellon sprayed ale from his mouth at Merlin's statement. "Sir, have you not heard? Ambrosius is bewitched."

Merlin noted that Cadwellon's words didn't quite match his reaction. "I doubt that. Do you know him?"

"Yes."

"Where might I find him?"

Cadwellon gave Merlin a curious look. "Riothomus Vortigern's soldiers took him earlier today."

"Where are they headed?" Merlin asked urgently, remembering that in Latin, *Riothomus* meant High-King.

"They are headed toward Wales where Vortigern sits in hiding. Why do you want this boy?"

"He'll be a great warrior one day. I'm here to help him."

Cadwellon stared straight ahead and a tear formed in his eye. "He'll not be a warrior if Vortigern has his way. He wants to make him part of his walls."

"What?!" Merlin was appalled at the thought of losing a potential King Arthur. He looked at his new friend and wondered why Cadwellon was reacting the way he was.

"If you really want to help Ambrosius, you may have to fight the king and his men. We tried and failed in our efforts."

"I must do what I must do."

Cadwellon slapped Merlin on the arm. "Very well, my new friend. Tonight you eat and drink. I'll see to it that you're provided with a room at the inn and tomorrow you may begin your quest well rested. Now, enjoy."

Merlin rested in a room in the inn that night and headed out after a hearty breakfast the next morning. He wondered why Cadwellon took the extra trouble of helping him, but the explanation would need to come another time.

Merlin encountered a group of soldiers outside the town

of Vircontim. The soldiers stopped Merlin and asked him who he was and what the nature of his business was.

"I'm known as Merlin. I'm but a poor traveler," he replied, noticing a muscular young dark-haired boy of about fifteen sitting on the ground with his hands and feet bound by chains. The soldier continued to eye Merlin with a suspicious eye as Merlin asked, "Who's the boy?"

"The boy is none of your concern. He's being taken to Riothomus Vortigern."

"I see. Uh, I'm going the same direction as you and these roads are teeming with Saxons. Would you be so kind as to allow me to join you for protection?"

"You may, but stay away from the boy."

Merlin joined the soldiers on their journey to Wales. During the trip, Merlin made friends with some of them, who confirmed that the young boy's name was Ambrosius and that he was to be sacrificed: It seemed that Vortigern was building a fortress and the walls kept falling down, so to solve the problem, Vortigern's advisors had told him to locate a young boy with an immortal father. Vortigern was to then sacrifice the boy and drain his blood. The blood was to be mixed with the mortar and used to build the walls. The walls would thus become strengthened to the point that they would remain in place forever.

Merlin thought this was the biggest crock of bull he'd ever heard. He knew it wouldn't work and wondered what the originator of the idea had to gain. It seemed to Merlin that the art of "Cover Your Ass" had begun much further back than he'd ever imagined.

On a more positive note, Merlin had located Ambrosius. If the boy was *the* Ambrosius he was looking for, and Ambrosius was the King Arthur of legend, then this could be the beginning of the end of his mission and he could begin working on the Maya mission as soon as he got back. Merlin had researched Ambrosius before beginning his jump and found that there wasn't much written about him. He was variously Uther Pendragon's brother and rightful High-King of the Britons. Some legends had Ambrosius as King Arthur. He was also rumored to be Merlin the Magician, or the General of Briton's army in the late fifth century. There had also been a reference to an Ambrosius who was almost sacrificed under the conditions the soldiers had laid out. There were many questions, but no answers to this point. Merlin knew he'd have to follow along and see what happened.

Sometimes at night, Merlin broke away from the group so he could consult his computer about Vortigern's history. What he learned was that Vortigern had been a vicious and unwise leader. He'd been responsible for the assassination of King Constantine III, which resulted in his being elected Riothomus, or High-King, of Briton. He'd made a mistake in judgment by hiring Hengist, leader of the Saxons, to protect Briton from raiders–this had had the long-term ramification of the Anglos and the Saxons ultimately becoming rulers of Briton and changing its name to England, but Vortigern had hardly had that in mind at the time. To solidify his relationship with Hengist, Vortigern married Hengist's daughter, Rowena. Despite the protection afforded the Britons by the Saxons, the Britons hated the Saxons and their barbaric ways. Prince Voltimer, the son of Vortigern and his first wife, united a large group of followers who banished Vortigern and expelled the Saxons. But Rowena and her father persuaded the weak-minded Vortigern to have his own son poisoned and reclaim the throne. After the murder, Vortigern invited Hengist and his Saxons back to Briton. Hengist prepared a great feast with all the noblemen of Briton in attendance. At the height of the feast, the unarmed noblemen were all killed by the Saxons, sparing only Vortigern.

He also learned that the Welsh coastline had numerous dormant volcanoes, which could have something to do with why the walls of Vortigern's fortress kept falling down once they reached a certain weight. If there were caverns below the building site and the ground between the top of the cavern and the surface was thin enough, this would prevent any large structure from being built on the surface. Included in his search on volcanoes was a newspaper story regarding the island of St. Martinique and two battling dragons. In 1902, 30,000 residents had been killed when the Mt. Pelée volcano erupted, leaving only one survivor, a man in the local jail.

As the trip wore on, Merlin's face and head began turning red and itchy. The dirt and sweat were reacting to the glue in his fake hair, and he knew he'd have to be do something about it quickly. The next time they came near a pond, Merlin excused himself from the group so he could bathe and get rid of the fake beard and wig–unfortunately the weather was beginning to turn cooler, but there was nothing to be done about it, he had to get in the water. He took a salve from his bag and put it on his face and scalp in hopes of making the itch go away. He felt much better and rode to catch up with the slow-moving soldiers. As he got close, Merlin thought about the value of deodorant when he smelled his fellow travelers' repugnant body odor. He explained to the troops that he trimmed his beard and hair and they seemed to buy the story.

Word reached the soldiers about a great sorcerer who'd come to the land and was known as Merlin. They also discovered that this great sorcerer was the humble traveler they'd befriended. Word was sent to Vortigern of Merlin's presence and his destination. Vortigern sent back a request to meet this great sorcerer at Vortigern's camp on the southern slopes of Yr Aran.

As their journey continued, Merlin exercised his mind by comparing Time Travel Archeology with traditional archeology. It seemed that there was a great deal of detective work involved with each. What was said to be one thing was frequently something else.

He also spent as much time as he could with Ambrosius—these visits went unchallenged by the soldiers due to the stories they were hearing about the exploits of the great Merlin the Sorcerer. Merlin was amused by the embellishments and fabrications but did nothing to correct them; they were working to his advantage. Merlin and Ambrosius became very close as a result of the time they spent together. They each had their own motives: Merlin wanted to find out who Ambrosius was and the lonely and frightened Ambrosius needed a friend.

Indeed, over time, Merlin was able to pull the story out of Ambrosius as to why he so neatly fit the bill as Vortigern's sacrificial offering: Ambrosius' mother, Aldan, had told people she was raped by an immortal, which resulted in her pregnancy. The truth was that Lord Cadwellon had fallen in love with Aldan and the two of them had had an affair. It was not acceptable at the time for a peasant to marry a nobleman, nor was it acceptable to have a child out of wedlock. The only option for Aldan was for her to invent the rape story. The story took care of her problem, but then the unforeseen happened: Ambrosius met the requirements Vortigern was looking for. Merlin figured that the Druid priest who made the recommendation didn't know the story or existence of Ambrosius, thus letting him off the hook.

After a long journey, the travelers crested a small hill and could see their destination nearby. Merlin saw a construction site on the side of a small mountain overlooking the bleak Welsh coastline. The camp consisted of numerous leather tents, with two large tents in the center, as well as several shelters built of wood and straw that probably housed the workers and soldiers.

The group made their way down the rough road to where the tents were. The road in the Welsh part of their journey had not been a good one, which was further evidence of the future decline of the region. As they entered the camp, Merlin and Ambrosius were brought into a large leather-covered tent. The captain who had led the troops opened the flap of the tent and waved them in. Inside, Merlin saw a large, unfinished table with foodstains covered by maps. Merlin reasoned that this must be both the king's dining table as well as his desk. There was a bearskin rumpled in one corner with some pillows and wool blankets that was probably the sleeping area. Next to some bedding in the sleeping area was another small table with a flask and some beautifully decorated brass drinking cups. A tall man with long black-and-gray hair rose from a stool behind the table and approached Merlin. He had a purple cape over his green-and-brown-plaid wool clothing that made it apparent he was emphasizing his Celtic heritage. He also had the strongest body odor Merlin had ever smelled.

The man had hideously brown teeth that showed when he smiled. He said, "You must be this Merlin the Sorcerer I've been hearing about. I'm Riothomus Vortigern. It pleases me that you join me."

"The pleasure is mine," Merlin said. "I hear you intend to kill this young man?"

"Kill? Sacrifice is not 'killing.' The Druid priest has assued me that the young lad here will live on as Bran the Blessed did once we sever his head from his body. What concern is it of yours anyway?"

Merlin looked closely at Vortigern and the thought crossed his mind that he was actually speaking to a historic figure, though a pathetic one. "Sacrifice *is* killing, it's just a fancy name for it. Do you really believe that it's necessary?"

"I am a Christian and I have prayed for help, all for nothing. It is time to try the old ways: I need an army to defend our land from the Saxons and a place to fight from. We've been driven to this forsaken area as a result of my trusting Hengist. Now we must have walls to protect us and give us time to rebuild. Unfortunately, the walls fall as fast as we build them."

"Can you not go elsewhere?"

"We would if we could. My Druid advisor says I should sacrifice this young boy. I'm to use his blood in the mortar. This will make the walls stand forever, protected by the evil from within him."

"And you really think that's true?"

Vortigern shrugged. "Nothing else has worked."

Merlin stopped for a moment and looked over at Ambrosius. He was still not certain which of the four figures Ambrosius actually was. Merlin felt quite certain that Ambrosius wasn't Merlin the Magician because he himself seemed to be creating the legend as he breathed. That left Ambrosius to be King Arthur's uncle, King Arthur himself, or the great General of the Army of Briton. Whichever one Ambrosius was, Merlin felt that the boy's fate rested on his shoulders. So he said, "I have a proposal for you."

"A proposal from anyone else would be a waste of time. But coming from the great Merlin the Sorcerer, I'm willing to listen."

"I noticed the cliffs over there when we arrived. I would

like to go to the bottom of the cliffs, to where the sea greets the land. As a sorcerer, I can talk to the sea and the land; I will ask them to tell me what can be done to save your walls."

"You speak with much wisdom, Sorcerer. But I'm already aware of all that pertains to this area. I bought it on the advice of the local Druid priest. He's particularly knowledgeable of this location because his brother owned the land."

Merlin shook his head at the thought of a fifth century land scam. It seemed that the more things changed, the more they remained the same. Merlin had to fight off a snicker. "And is this the same Druid priest who advised you to make the sacrifice?"

"Why yes. I was concerned about my purchase and told him so. That was when the priest told me about the boy. He says that a curse lay upon me because of the deaths of the noblemen. He says that no matter where I build, the same thing will happen. This is the only way to resolve it once and for all."

Merlin didn't know whether to be mad or sad. Vortigern was too stupid to be the leader of Briton. Yet he couldn't really tell Vortigern his thoughts, as tempting as it may have been. "I believe I can solve the problem with my magic. If your advisors have any magic at all, let them use it. If not, allow me to help you."

"I know the Druid has no magic that he can demonstrate to me, but I understand that you do. If you'll show me some of your magic, and I agree that it's powerful, then I'll give you the chance to save the young boy and my army."

"Fine, shall we go outside?"

Merlin became alarmed when he stepped outside the tent with Vortigern–dusk had fallen and there was not enough sunlight remaining for his laser to work. Once again he was in trouble because of lack of foresight: No one had considered the possibility of using the laser at night, much less as a weapon. Merlin looked around the area again and, thinking fast, he said, "I'll do my demonstration over there in that clearing. We should do this after the sun rises tomorrow so there will be enough light for you and your advisors to see. Now, if you'll direct me to a tent where I can rest the night, we can continue this tomorrow. Oh, I would also like the boy to stay with me, if that is acceptable to you."

Vortigern looked at Merlin. "I like you, Merlin. It seems that everyone I seek advice from tells me what they think I want to hear rather than what I need to hear. I hope you're successful tomorrow. Tonight we'll feast as though this will be your last, which sadly it will be if you fail me. Regarding the boy, surely you don't take me for a fool. He'll be kept safe and under guard. But you'll not be the guard."

The king smiled and ordered his orderlies to bring forth a feast for him and his guest. Vortigern pulled out his dagger and began stabbing at the sliced pork while Merlin looked on. Not wanting to seem rude, though, he followed Vortigern's lead. The lack of refinement of Vortigern's Celtic table manners was in stark contrast to Lord Cadwellon's refined Roman table manners.

The next morning, an orderly sent by Vortigern wakened Merlin. He dressed and then followed the waiting boy to a table where Vortigern was waiting.

"My friend," Vortigern said as he clasped both hands around Merlin's shoulders. "My cooks prepared a wonderful breakfast for us. Please be seated." Vortigern sat in the center of the rectangular table while Merlin sat on the same side of the table but to the far right of Vortigern. "Merlin, I do hope you're prepared. Your survival depends upon it."

Merlin thought about how odd it was that he was not

afraid of what might happen. He didn't even question whether or not he would be successful. He knew with every fiber of his being that he'd succeed despite the treacherous nature of the weather in Wales during the fall. He asked, "Where is Ambrosius?"

"Why? Are you worried that I may not be a man of my word? That I might have him killed before you've had a chance to save him? Oh no, my friend. He's alive and well. At least for now. What kind of magic do you have for us today?"

"It is such that no one of this land shall understand it."

The two men finished their meal before withdrawing to the cleared area Merlin had picked out the night before. Ambrosius was brought out and told to stand near Merlin. Merlin was told that the boy would be killed if Merlin was unable to show his magic.

Merlin was ready just as a dark cloud moved overhead. The Druid priest began yelling that it was a sign caused by the sorcerer's evil. Merlin opened the laser in his walking stick and was ready to go. He had the soldiers place a small bench in the clearing, then he aimed his laser and yelled a command. As he pulled the trigger button, panic swept through him–nothing happened. Merlin looked around and saw that it was getting dark. He reached inside his cloak to one of the small bags tied inside that passed for pockets and grabbed a lighter in the hope that there would be enough light to start the laser. Just as he lit it, the crowd began shouting. It appeared from the angle people were viewing Merlin that the fire came from his hand.

Vortigern watched as Merlin produced fire from his hands. Many of the soldiers ran for cover while others stared in amazement, unable to move.

Vortigern said, "I must admit, I wasn't sure you'd be able

to convince me that you were a true wizard. What will you try next?"

"I must now go to the sea and the land and speak to them about your problem. This I must do alone. When I return, I'll tell you what they say."

Vortigern laughed at Merlin. "You are a clever man, Merlin. Perhaps a bit too clever. I'll post men at the beginning of the pathway as well as in two boats off the coast, but within sight of you."

"It seems that you too are clever." The two men smiled a knowing smile at each other. They were beginning to form an unlikely and unexpected bond. Merlin wondered how much of the stories he'd read about the king were true, then he remembered his own conversation with Vortigern just the night before. He decided that the stories were the result of the king's lack of intelligence and his being taken advantage of by unscrupulous people.

The morning held a heavy mist as Merlin left with a small contingent of soldiers. As instructed, the soldiers posted themselves at the top of the pathway. He looked out to sea and observed two small boats in the water near the location he was going to. He went down the steep, jagged path to the water's edge and found an opening in the side of the cliff that led to a deep cavern. In examining the cavern, Merlin could see it was created by a combination of erosion by the sea and volcanic activity.

Merlin reached into his bag which he always kept close to him so no prying eyes could examine the contents, and pulled out a flashlight. He shined the flashlight around the cavern and found what appeared to be red lava rock from a long dormant volcano. He then retrieved some of the rocks for a closer look. He pulled out his computer and consulted records on ancient Welsh volcanoes, then he looked at the crevices and examined the rocks he picked up. He soon discovered the cause of the walls falling and how the problem could be solved. After verifying his solution on the computer he turned around and headed to the top.

Merlin returned to the campsite and found Vortigern and suggested they go somewhere private to discuss his findings. Vortigern led the way to his tent, where he posted guards with instructions that they were not to be disturbed.

Merlin made himself comfortable. "I know what's causing the problem and can solve it for you. However, I'll require some sort of payment if I'm successful."

"Certainly," said a suddenly cocky Vortigern. "I'll pay you with the most valuable possession I have. I'll let you live."

"Riothomus Vortigern, I have heard of the Celtic games of boasting, but I really don't want to play. What I'll ask of you is of small cost to you. Yet what I'll do for you is of great value to you and your country. Besides, you can't harm me. Not now, and not before. I have never been in any kind of danger from you," he said, feeling pretty cocky himself.

"Your boast shall not go unrewarded. I think I'll have your little friend killed now. Maybe this will cause you to be more respectful of your king."

"It would seem that religion is not your only return to the ways of the Celtic past. Vortigern, let me remind you that you're not my king. I answer to no king. Second, should you or your men attempt to harm the lad, you'll feel the full force of Merlin the Sorcerer. I'm offering you a solution to your problem. For once in your life, be wise enough to take it."

"Why . . . you fool!" Vortigern smiled like a Celtic in an ancient boasting match and pulled out his sword. "Your head shall be my payment for your boastfulness."

Merlin looked at the king as he readied his laser and

thought, You've got to be kidding. He quickly looked around and saw that there was enough light for the laser to work. He didn't have time to worry about his lack of fighting skills as he pointed his staff at Vortigern's hand and shot off a laser beam. Vortigern let out a scream, attracting the guards from outside. The guards drew their swords but Merlin immediately cut them down with his laser.

Three more guards appeared at the entrance of the tent, swords in hand, prepared to attack Merlin when Vortigern shouted, "Stop. Sheath your swords. I can take care of this. Return to your posts and take these two with you." Vortigern held his hand in pain as he looked over Merlin. "You are truly a great wizard. I must admit that I didn't really believe the stories told of you. I'm humbled in your presence." Silence lingered in the air for a moment before Vortigern added, "Tell me. What kind of wizard are you?"

The adrenaline still flowed through Merlin as he slowly lowered his laser. As his heart rate began to slow, he smiled, remembering the words of the old man he'd met on the road. "A good one, wouldn't you agree?"

"This much I can see. I'm in hopes that we can put what just happened behind us. Let us move forward as friends and equals, shall we?"

Merlin wasn't too happy about what had just taken place. He knew he'd come very close to being killed. He was, after all, an archeologist, not a warrior. He looked at the pathetic king with disgust, but he knew that history required him to play his part and save Ambrosius. His mission was far from complete. "Vortigern," he said at long last, "I accept your offer. Now, as to my requests . . ."

"Anything within my power is yours. Now please tell me about the walls."

"Near my homeland is an island called Martinique. On

the island is a mountain named Pelée, which is said to contain a red dragon. One day the red dragon came down from the mountain. At the base of the mountain is the city of Saint Pierre. The red dragon used its fire to destroy the city. The red dragon then claimed domain over the city, which it ruled for some time. One day a great white dragon appeared from the surf. A fierce battle took place with the white dragon using the power of the ocean to extinguish the fire of the red dragon. Finally, after a long battle, the white dragon succeeded in defeating the red dragon and forcing it back into the mountain from where it had come. The white dragon stayed to protect the land and allowed its inhabitants to live in peace. This story is a metaphor. The red dragon represents a volcano and the white dragon represents the waves of the ocean. The same thing happened here. This battle created massive caverns beneath the surface, leaving the earth too weak to support your walls. The damage from this battle must be repaired before your walls will stand."

Vortigern looked at Merlin with a newfound respect, if not outright fear. He said, "Tell me, great wizard, what prophesy can you take from what has occurred here?"

Merlin's nose twitched because of the affect on his sinuses Vortigern's odor was having. His eyes instinctively squeezed shut in an effort to find some relief as his head began to pound. All he could really think about was getting home, something he knew wasn't going to happen soon. He also knew he wasn't a prophet; of course, he didn't have to be one because he knew what was going to happen. But despite, or because of, his growing dislike of the Celtic part of Vortigern's personality, he decided to give the man a prophecy based on history and legend.

He turned to the king. "The Britons, who have ruled this

land for a long time, are represented by the red dragon. The white dragon represents the Saxons, who have pushed you to the very edge of the sea. One day a great king will come to Briton. He'll defeat the white dragon and rule this land in a noble and just manner while returning honor to the Britons."

"And just who is this great king?" Vortigern looked at Merlin, expecting the answer any of his advisors would give him. But Merlin remained silent. Vortigern, pushing for an answer, said, "And I am to be this great king you refer to."

Merlin turned to exit the tent and looked back at Vortigern before he said, "No."

Vortigern ran up to Merlin and grabbed him by the arm. Merlin turned and looked into Vortigern's eyes. Vortigern said, "Merlin, you're a great sorcerer. What can I do to become this great king?"

"Nothing. You've already made your place in history. Neither of us can change that."

Vortigern knew the truth in Merlin's words as he dropped his head into his hands. Merlin almost felt sorry for the king as he turned and exited the tent. History could not be changed and too many potentially great men learned their lessons too late and ended up living in mediocrity or worse.

Merlin grabbed one of the guards. "I'm releasing Ambrosius." Vortigern nodded his approval. Much had changed in Merlin's relationship with Vortigern, but he hadn't told Vortigern what payment he would ask for his services. That could wait until dinner. Merlin and the guard walked to the tent where Ambrosius was and Merlin told Ambrosius of his release.

That night, Ambrosius and Merlin dined with King Vortigern. Ambrosius immediately noticed a change in the king's demeanor to that of one of great respect, a change he suspected Merlin had somehow caused.

As the food was served, Merlin broke the silence by saying, "I will now request my payment."

"Yes, yes," said Vortigern. "What is it you desire for payment?"

"I have designed a pool that I want built within the walls of the fort. The pool will not be large, but it must be dug before the fort is completed."

"Why do you want a pool?" Vortigern asked.

"It shall allow me to come and go as I please. Second, I want Ambrosius to receive training to be an officer in your army. Furthermore, no harm, save in battle, shall befall him."

"Agreed. What else would you want?"

"I'll need a troop of your cavalry to accompany me to get my cart. I want Ambrosius and the captain who accompanied me before to go with me. We'll need fast horses as I desire to return swiftly."

"Granted. What else do you desire?"

"Nothing but your good health."

And with the agreement concluded, the three raised their wine in a salute to each other.

Merlin and Ambrosius rose early for their trip the next morning. Vortigern had a surprise for Ambrosius; he presented the young lad with the position of *Tribunus Laticlavius*, which was a position used in the Roman army for a political appointee. He was also given the equipment and clothing for a man of this position. Vortigern further promised Merlin that Ambrosius would receive the best military training possible.

Before leaving, Merlin showed Vortigern and his officers the problem area in the cavern and suggested that the engineers determine how they might shore up the cavern to allow for the construction of the fort's walls about it. He also suggested that if the fortifications were built there, that they be built on a much smaller scale. Merlin, Ambrosius, and the cavalry unit–or *ala* as the Romans called them–headed out to retrieve Merlin's supplies. The return trip was much faster than it had been before with all the men mounted and no prisoner to slow them down.

They spent several days in Glevum to allow Ambrosius time to see his mother, Aldan, and father, Lord Cadwellon. While in Glevum, Merlin and his escorts partook in the pleasures of the Roman baths at the public bathhouse. Merlin couldn't help but think that this was a pleasure many archeologists would kill for. To actually see a working Roman bathhouse during the period of its actual use was exciting. After the bath, Merlin felt remarkably better; his load of dirt and sweat was gone and he could actually feel his skin tingling. Added to that was the realization of just how bad he must have smelled before the bath.

Within a couple of weeks they had returned to Vortigern's fort, Dinas Emrys. The fort was coming together, though it was never to become a castle as Vortigern had wanted.

Because of the fraud perpetrated upon him by the Druid priest and his brother, Vortigern had had them killed while Merlin was gone. But of more importance to Merlin was the construction of the pool, which appeared to be finished. Merlin liked the idea of having a permanent escape route to the future available to him and thought it might be a good idea to have others built on his return. Vortigern mentioned to Merlin that, because of the construction problems, the fort was not going to be large enough to meet his long-term needs, and said that he would probably garrison a training unit there and leave Ambrosius there for his training, but he'd move his main forces to Tre'r Ceiri in Yr Eifl–Merlin's translator called this "the Rivals"–in Lleyn. He also planned to refurbish the old hill Fort of Caer-Guorthigirn–"Little Doward"–above Ganarew.

After a couple of days' rest, Merlin removed one of the nanofactories and began filling the pool with the solution. Several soldiers gathered around and watched in awe as the pool began to fill, Merlin covering the actual event with lots of hocus-pocus arm movements and babbled words, and not incidentally building up his reputation even though he was but a few hours away from his departure home. Merlin went to Vortigern and received permission to have the soldiers who'd accompanied him to retrieve his supplies, be assigned as Ambrosius' personal escorts. Merlin then had the men of the troop swear allegiance to Ambrosius.

Merlin packed his belongings and dressed with a hooded, leather coat that covered his clothing. He instructed some of the soldiers to place his cart on the edge of a ramp that'd been built to go down into the pool. Merlin then charged the pool with his laser and watched as the solution in the pool began to swirl until a wormhole formed. As a mist began to form over the wormhole, Merlin pushed the cart in while the entire garrison watched.

Merlin turned toward Ambrosius, who looked on in awe, and winked. Ambrosius stood next to an equally impressed Vortigern as Merlin raised his staff into the air. Merlin shouted to his audience, "I, Merlin the Sorcerer, shall depart this world for now. But, be warned, for I shall return. Let no harm come to Ambrosius while I am gone or you shall have to deal with me." Merlin sent a burst from his laser into the sky, bringing fear into the hearts of his audience. Then he recharged the solution in the pool, creating another wormhole a few feet from the last one so he wouldn't land on his cart. He looked with a bit of regret into the wormhole. Soon he'd be home. He looked once more upon his new friends, and then jumped into the highway home.

Chapter Twelve

Merlin shook his head as he fell against his cart. The air was a bit cool and dirty as he looked around. Merlin looked at the ancient ruins of Dinas Emrys. Little was left of Vortigern's last fortress. It was time for Merlin to get home. He looked in the cart and pulled out his wireless phone and called the research center. Merlin asked to speak to the team leader who was on duty and was connected to Annie. After a brief hesitation Merlin said, "Annie? What are you doing here?"

"Hey! You're back?! Uh, where exactly are you?"

"I'm in Wales. What are you doing here?"

"I came over with the rest of the crew to help out. You were supposed to have been back weeks ago."

"Yeah, I know. I'll tell you all about it. But right now I need someone to pick me up. It's damn cold out here. I'm sitting here on a rock in an ancient Briton outfit looking stupid. I'm at an old fort in Wales known as Dinas Emrys. Do you know where that is?"

"I don't, but let me check and see if I can find it. You say it's in Wales, right?"

"Yeah, and hurry up before I freeze to death."

"Okay, I think I have it here. We'll send a helicopter to pick you up. Sit tight. We're on our way."

Merlin was checking himself, his clothing, and his equipment for foreign substances that he might have inadvertently brought back from the past when the helicopter arrived. Two people got off the helicopter wearing white biological hazard suits. One was carrying another suit and the second was carrying a large steel case. They walked up to Merlin and one of them said, "Dr. Lakin, we're from the research center. We need you to put on this suit so we can keep you safe until you're checked out at the center."

Merlin nodded okay and took off his coat before he began putting on the suit. The two attendants took a covering out of the case and began to cover the cart after putting in Merlin's coat. As they finished, another helicopter arrived and two more people got out. They joined the first two attendants in loading the cart on the first helicopter. Once that was completed, the first two attendants boarded the first helicopter and took off.

The remaining two walked to where Merlin was standing and one of them said in a familiar voice, "Welcome home, my boy. We were just about to send a team back to find you."

"Adrian," shouted a happy Merlin as he attempted to give his old friend a hug. Unfortunately, the bulkiness of the suits prevented him from doing so. "God, it's great to see you again."

"I'm pleased to hear that. But it's only been three weeks."

"That's three weeks for you. But almost two months for me."

"We've got a lot to talk about, don't we?"

"You wouldn't believe."

They boarded the helicopter and took off for the research center. As they flew over Gloucester, Merlin thought about the changes between the Glevum of old and the Gloucester of today. As soon as they reached the Gloucester Research Center, Merlin jumped from the helicopter and saw that his cart was being unloaded in a roped-off area near the barn and the contents were being prepared for decontamination. He was quickly hustled inside, where attendants had him remove his suit and clothes and put on a hospital gown. His clothes were taken out for examination along with the items in his cart, while the doctors checked him for any contaminate he might have brought back with him.

It took several exhausting and boring hours for the tests to be completed and Merlin to be given the okay to leave. Adrian brought Merlin a robe to cover the hospital gown. "My boy, you need a hot shower. You're rather ripe, if I do say so myself. I left a change of clothes for you in your office. Why don't you go in there and get cleaned up? Then we can talk for a few minutes over a hot cup of coffee."

"God, I think I could sleep for a week. But you're right. I'll feel much better after a hot shower. Did I tell you about the Roman baths?"

"You can tell me about that later," Adrian said as he tried to mask Merlin's odor with a handkerchief. "Right now you need to get going, and quick."

"Incidentally, I could have gotten killed because of the translator."

"Really? Why?"

"The damn thing wouldn't give me half the words I asked for."

"Give me a few examples."

"How about 'okay'?"

Adrian began to laugh so hard that he lost his breath. "My boy, that word didn't exist in the fifth century. I'll bet that was the reason you had your problem. But I'll check it out anyway."

Merlin put on the robe and walked to his office. When he got there he went straight to the bathroom, where he opened the glass door of the shower and turned on the water to allow it to warm up. He hadn't really appreciated having a shower in his office before, but now felt that it was a well-deserved luxury. He removed his clothes and brushed his teeth, another luxury he'd forgotten about. His gums had turned red from the lack of attention, but he believed he could get them back into shape within a few days–one more problem that needed to be addressed before the next mission. He then walked into the spray of the hot water and felt his muscles relax as the water ran over his head and face, then down his body. He closed his eyes as the sweat and dirt melted from his body. Suddenly he felt a pleasant shiver go up his spine as a firm brush moved slowly up and down it. Startled, he turned and, looking through his water-filled eyes, found a nude woman standing in the shower with him.

"Relax," Merlin heard the woman say in a voice that sounded exactly like Vivian's. "Let me help you get rid of that awful smell. Then maybe I can show you how much I missed you."

Merlin was totally confused. This couldn't possibly be Vivian. She would never let her guard down this much. Instead of fighting it, though, Merlin smiled and turned back around. He felt her small hand move through his hair, gently massaging his head. She then returned to his back and arms. He felt her slowly work her way around to his chest, pressing her breasts against his back as she gently cleaned his chest and stomach. Merlin was in heaven as she finished his buttocks and slowly turned him to face her. As she began to clean his genitals, he brought her lips to his and they began a passionate kiss that seemed to linger forever. As she went down on her knees to clean his legs, Merlin's mind began to move light years away from the shower as he fought off exhaustion.

Soon the shower was complete and they began to dry each other off. Merlin could see that Vivian had thought ahead because the sleeper sofa in his office had been pulled out and the covers were pulled back waiting for the two of them. Merlin took another few wipes with the towel to dry his hair some more, then he walked to the bed and got under the covers. He turned and got a glimpse of Vivian, his first full look at her perfect body. As she finished towel-drying her hair, he closed his eyes for a moment, just until she joined him.

Merlin popped opened his eyes when someone knocked at the door. He looked over and saw Vivian fast asleep with her head on his arm and her naked body next to his. All he could think was Oh damn, I went to sleep. He gently pulled his arm from under her head so as not to wake her, when he heard the knock again. As he rose from the bed, he said, "Just a minute." He grabbed his robe and put it on and then reached over to cover Vivian. He stole one more look at the woman he wanted to make love to so badly, but had yet to do so. He opened the door a small portion of the way and, with his eyes still trying to focus, asked, "What's up?"

Annie looked at him with a smirk on her face. "Come on, lover boy, it's time to eat."

"Annie, it's not what you think," Merlin said as Annie turned and walked off down the hall.

Merlin hated to wake Vivian, but knew he must. The two got dressed, with Merlin still unshaven and his hair a bit longer than it was when he left. After dressing, they met Annie, Adrian, and Lance in the hall.

Adrian said, "Come, my boy, it's time for a feast."

At the mention of food, hunger pangs flamed in Merlin's stomach. He'd forgotten how good a nice steak with fries, or even a hamburger, tasted. The team ran through the rain and piled into a van and headed for a restaurant.

Adrian looked back at Merlin. "We feel you've probably become accustomed to the food of the past, so we had the local restaurant prepare us a meal straight out of the fifth century."

"Oh no," Merlin said as his stomach churned and his eyes rolled back in his head.

Annie laughed. Adrian patted Merlin on the leg. "Just kidding, old boy."

They arrived at the restaurant and were seated in a private room. Merlin ordered a steak, lobster, corn, and a baked potato. The waitress looked at Merlin, with his shaggy beard and uncut hair as though he were a vagabond.

Adrian looked at the waitress's expression and said with a laugh, "Not to fear my dear, he is our boss."

Vivian rubbed Merlin's stomach. "Are you sure you have room for all that? You've lost a little weight."

Annie laughed. "Merlin, tell us what it was like in the past."

Merlin thought for a moment. "Well, it's the things we take for granted that makes life today so different from that of the past. Things like toilet paper, toothpaste, cars, and electricity. Hell, they didn't have a decent Burger King anywhere."

Vivian had dreams of castles and princes in her head. "What about the people? Did you meet any kings or princes? What about Ambrosius and Merlin the Magician?"

"The people? Well, in many ways they're just like we are.

They have dreams, ambitions, flaws, and laughter, just like us. There are dangers of a different kind than we have, such as the Saxons, but many of the dangers we face today didn't even exist for them."

Annie stopped Merlin. "Saxons! You had contact with the Saxons?"

"Yes. And I'm proud to say I defeated them."

Lance looked up, drawn into the conversation. "You mean you beat them as in a fight, not defeated them as in battle, right?"

Merlin smiled. "No, defeated. Yeah, that's the right word. But more on that later. You mentioned kings. I met King Vortigern."

"You met an actual king!" Vivian screamed, excitement in her voice.

"Whoa, back to the Saxons. You were in a battle?" Lance interrupted.

"One thing at a time. One thing at a time, okay? Now, about Vortigern, I was talking to him, trying to save Ambrosius' life–"

"Hold on, my boy," Adrian said. "Now I must interrupt. You actually talked to Vortigern and you met Ambrosius?"

"Well. Yes."

"So, is Ambrosius King Arthur, or Merlin the Magician, or who?" Annie asked.

"Well, I don't know if Ambrosius is King Arthur, but I can assure you he's not Merlin the Magician."

"Are you trying to say you actually met Merlin?!" Vivian was almost teenage-giddy in her excitement.

"I came, I saw, and he is I," Merlin said with an almost evil grin just as the waitress began serving the food. "Oh great, the food's here. I'm famished."

"You're not going to leave us hanging there, are you?" Lance asked.

Merlin looked up "Yes. That's exactly what I'm going to do."

Annie looked at Merlin and began to smile. "Wait a minute. I think he just told us that he, Merlin, is in fact, Merlin."

Silence hung over the table for a moment and then, as if on cue, the entire table looked at Merlin and simultaneously said, "No way."

Merlin looked up and laughed. "Uh yeah, way."

Merlin summarized his two-month-long journey during the rest of the meal. He told his fascinated listeners all about his adventures, the problems he encountered, and what new stuff he'd need before he could go back again. He was exhausted before the meal, and by the time he was finished with his feast and the adrenaline rush from telling his tale, he had only one thought left–he looked over at the beautiful Vivian, and was sad, or frustrated, that all he wanted to do was sleep.

Which was all he did for the next two days. No matter how much he wanted to make love to Vivian, he just didn't have the energy to do it. As it turned out, that was fine with Vivian because she and the rest of the researchers were busy working on solutions to the problems Merlin found.

Merlin had hoped to be able to return to old Briton within a few days, but it didn't work out that way and the days turned into weeks. He grew more and more impatient with the wait, unhelped by the fact that his relationship with Vivian remained unconsummated because of her tireless work on making the jump safer.

Finally all the problems were solved but one, and it would take a jump to find out how that would work out. Merlin convinced the staff that he should make the jump from the ruins of Dinas Emrys. Ambrosius was in charge of the training post and Merlin's horse was stabled there. He felt he could get more done in a shorter period of time by jumping directly to the fort, thus allowing him an opportunity to return home and pursue Vivian more aggressively.

The day for his jump arrived. Merlin looked at Vivian and managed to get a kiss, the first since he'd arrived back from his last jump. Merlin looked again and noticed a tear forming in Vivian's eye. Merlin fought to hold back his own tears as Vivian whispered, "Come home safe."

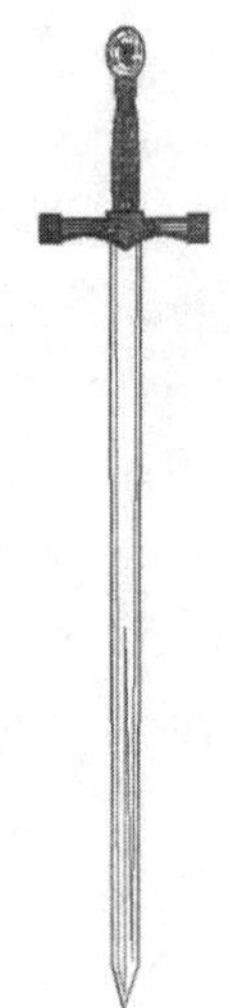

Chapter Thirteen

Merlin jumped into the wormhole and found himself once again in the same place he'd been in a few months before. It looked like springtime when he walked out of the pool. A nearby guard saw Merlin and shouted, "Halt! You can't be in Merlin's pool. No one but Merlin is allowed in there."

Just as his cart arrived, Merlin looked at the soldier, who had drawn his sword. "Shut up, you fool. I am Merlin. Now go get Ambrosius. I want to make sure he's still safe."

Merlin watched the man run off and noticed that there were many more troops at the fort than there should have been. Merlin adjusted the Saxon sword he'd been given by the old man on the road, then motioned for a couple of the soldiers to help him remove his cart from the pond. Ambrosius and one of his officers ran up just as they were removing the camouflaged plastic cover.

"Merlin!" an exuberant Ambrosius shouted. He gave Merlin a bear hug. They each examined the other and Ambrosius said, "My you've grown sturdy."

Merlin laughed. "Yes, and you've just grown."

"Well, it's been more than three years since you were last here. I was beginning to wonder if you were ever going to return."

Merlin's face dropped at the realization that he'd missed his target date by almost two years. He shrugged. "Tell me everything that's happened since I left."

"There's much unrest in the land. Vortigern's suspicious of everyone. He even sent soldiers to kill *me*, and I have offered him no harm."

"Where did all these soldiers come from?"

"In a manner of speaking, from you. Each time Vortigern sends his soldiers to kill me, they join up with me instead. It seems they remember your parting words and decide it's safer to stand against Vortigern than stand against you."

"If Vortigern's no longer supporting you, how are you able to pay and provision these soldiers?"

"I don't. The people from the area are providing most of the provisions. We also raise some crops ourselves. My father is also providing some financial support. But I'm worried."

"You're worried? Worried about what?"

"About how confused in spirit King Vortigern has become. I'm afraid he might do something to my father."

"Where is Vortigern?"

"He's still at Tre'r Ceiri in Yr Eifl in Lleyn. Prince Amris Pendreic and Prince Uther Pendragon, the sons of King Constantine III, are on the march to take the crown."

"How long before they get here?"

"They will not arrive before the first snow."

"Who's in command here?"

"I have that honor."

"Interesting." Merlin scratched his beard for a moment while contemplating his next step. This was supposed to be a short trip back, but it was already looking like another long stay. Merlin thought about the condition things were in when he left and how events had turned in a new direction. He kept telling himself that he was an archeologist, not an advisor to the past leaders of Briton; he was supposed to investigate the events, not participate. His arguments to himself made sense, but, unfortunately, despite what he told himself, he knew what he had to do. Merlin looked at his protégé. "Get your troops assembled. It's time for us to pay Vortigern a visit."

Ambrosius assembled his troops on Merlin's command. Merlin was given his old horse, which had been well cared for in his absence. Merlin and Ambrosius rode to the front of the assembly, which was not close to the Roman formations he'd studied about in the time since his last jump. He quickly realized that many of the Roman ranks and titles had been done away with and the troop formations had vanished entirely. Merlin realized that if Ambrosius was to be the historic leader he was destined to be, Merlin would have to help him get organized.

Merlin told Ambrosius to have the men break formation and gather the supplies and equipment they would need for a long march and battle. Merlin also told Ambrosius to have the officers gather in their headquarters for instructions. Merlin knew that this army would probably be no match for Vortigern's fortified forces at Tre'r Ceiri, but he had an idea of a way they might be able to win anyway.

Merlin counted the men and their functions during the meeting. He had two hundred archers, three hundred cavalrymen of various grades, and nine hundred infantry. He drew out a basic formation for the army, putting the infantry in two lines of four hundred men each with a small reserve force of one hundred men; these would make up the center of the army. The archers would stand behind the infantry, but were to move to the front line to begin the assault. The cavalry was divided in half, with each half to line up on one of the flanks of the formation. There was no siege equipment, but Merlin didn't think he would actually have to fight a battle anyway.

Merlin dispatched a rider to meet the army of the two princes coming from the east to inform them of Ambrosius' intention of deposing King Vortigern. He dispatched another rider to Tre'r Ceiri to inform the defenders of the coming arrival of Merlin and the army of Ambrosius and to offer amnesty to any soldier who deserted Vortigern and joined Ambrosius.

Merlin wasn't concerned with the fighting ability and discipline of Ambrosius' army as much as he was interested in their lining up properly at Tre'r Ceiri. Merlin's main desire was to trick the defenders into thinking that it was in their best interest to defect and join with Ambrosius, thus avoiding a battle Merlin and Ambrosius might not be able to win with the troops on hand.

While everything was being prepared, Merlin was pleased to see that at least part of the Roman past was still being used at Dinas Emrys. The layout of the fort was similar to that of Roman-built forts. There was a small bathhouse and barracks for the troops. There were some storage rooms for food, though these walls were very thin and not very tall since the ground would not support much weight.

Once everything was prepared, the men rested for the night so they could have a fresh start early the next morning. There was much excitement in the camp at the thought of the upcoming battle. The soldiers reasoned that with Merlin on their side, victory was assured. Merlin took the opportunity to talk with Ambrosius and explain to the young General some of the things he would need to do once the fighting with Vortigern was over.

With the coming of Uther Pendragon, Merlin reasoned that Ambrosius was not going to turn out to be King Arthur, because Uther was the legendary Arthur's father. It also seemed reasonable that if Amris Pendreic accompanied Uther, then Amris, not Ambrosius, was Uther's brother and Arthur's uncle. It didn't mean the legends were wrong, just mixed up somewhat, which time tended to do.

The next morning, the troops rose to an already prepared breakfast. After breakfast, the soldiers gathered their equipment, pulled their cloaks tight around themselves and marched into the cold Welsh springtime wind toward their objective, Tre'r Ceiri. Within a couple of days, the messenger sent ahead to announce Merlin's arrival met them on the road. The messenger delivered the news that Vortigern had abandoned Tre'r Ceiri, but a large number of soldiers had elected to stay behind and join Ambrosius and Merlin. This added almost three thousand soldiers to Ambrosius' army, but Vortigern still had more than two thousand troops under his command, which would be more than enough to put up a strong defense of the old hill fort of Caer-Guorthigirn, which was where Vortigern was headed.

Merlin, Ambrosius, and sixty heavy cavalry–knights, as they were soon to be called–rode ahead to meet up with the soldiers who'd not gone with Vortigern. Merlin and Ambrosius were welcomed at Tre'r Ceiri with loud cheers from the defectors as they entered the fort. Fort Tre'r Ceiri sat atop a summit of the eastern peak of the three peaks of Yr Eifl. The front of the fort had an irregular wall about thirteen feet high, with the longest ramparts a little less than one thousand feet and the width at about one-third of the length. There were more than one hundred stone and brick buildings inside the fort and an even larger number outside the walls toward the valley. Merlin and Ambrosius climbed to the top of the ramparts and were greeted by a spectacular view of islands and water and the land leading to the fort. Merlin thought that the whole place was a fine capture.

As the rest of the army arrived, Merlin and Ambrosius met with both the old and new officers, with the idea of reorganizing the army for the attack on Caer-Guorthigirn. The addition of the new soldiers brought the number of men under Ambrosius' command to almost four thousand five hundred men, which was about the size of a full Roman legion; the new soldiers included some four hundred mounted archers.

Still, the problem remained that the soldiers were poorly trained and equipped. Merlin laid out a new formation as four rows of infantry with five hundred men in each row to form the center. There were now six hundred archers, who would take up the rear. Five hundred infantry would be held in reserve and there would be seven hundred cavalrymen on each flank, of which two hundred were now mounted archers.

Merlin called for the provisioning of the men for a march early the next day to Caer-Guorthigirn and an end for Vortigern. As night befell the fort, Ambrosius and Merlin stood on the walls overlooking the sea below. Their faces were cold from the autumn wind as the sea below crashed into the cliffs. They talked about the past and where the end of Vortigern's reign might lead them. Merlin was tempted to tell Ambrosius about who he really was, but he stayed silent.

Merlin rose early the next day and grabbed himself a quick bite of breakfast. He walked to the wall overlooking the road they'd soon be using to get Ambrosius' army to Caer-Guorthigirn. Ambrosius joined Merlin at the wall just as the sun was giving light to the rainbow of colors below them. They talked about the upcoming battle and how the rogue king needed to be deposed. Neither man had been in battle before and it was not Merlin's desire to be in one now. Ambrosius mentioned that Vortigern's wife, Rowena, had given birth to a daughter whom they'd named Morgause. Merlin asked Ambrosius to agree not to harm Vortigern's wife and daughter, a request Ambrosius could not refuse.

Soon the army was off to fight a battle with Merlin and Ambrosius at the lead, two virgins to the art of war. Merlin could only hope he found a way around the learning curve.

A few days passed before the soldiers found Caer-Guorthigirn before them. Merlin sent a rider to the fort to ask Vortigern to meet with him. Vortigern informed the rider that he would meet Merlin, as long as he could remain on the ramparts of the fort and Merlin stayed outside the walls.

Merlin rode to just outside the gate of the fort and told the guards to inform Vortigern of his presence. Vortigern had gone almost completely mad in Merlin's absence. He feared that everyone was out to get him, the Romans, the Picts, the Irish, the Germans, and the sons of King Constantine III.

Merlin requested that the soldiers' wives and children, Vortigern's included, be given safe passage outside the fort. Merlin wanted them to go to a location that would keep them out of danger, to which Vortigern agreed. Merlin also suggested that if any of the soldiers wanted to leave and escort the women and children, they would also be given safe passage.

Vortigern was given the opportunity to leave, though he would no longer be allowed to remain High-King. Vortigern refused to surrender and would only allow an escort of fifty soldiers for the women and children, though everyone suspected that many more of his soldiers would have left if allowed to do so. Merlin suspected that Vortigern wanted to die; unfortunately, he would be taking many good men with him.

Merlin, Ambrosius, and their highest-ranking officers

watched the procession of escorts, women, and children file out of the fortress. Merlin thought about how it reminded him of a scene in a movie when the women and children of the Alamo left. He reasoned that this time there would be no heroes of Caer-Guorthigirn, because, unknown to anyone but himself, there would be no battle, only death.

Merlin made one last plea for Vortigern to surrender, which was promptly refused. Merlin then rode to Ambrosius and asked him to have his infantry men lay down their weapons and encircle the fort, then have the mounted soldiers surround the fortress, too, but remain armed. Merlin told the curious Ambrosius to have the men grab blankets from the supply wagons and prepare to save as many of the defenders as they could–their mission would soon become one of mercy.

Ambrosius did as he was instructed and the bewildered soldiers obeyed their General. The troops deployed under a clear blue sky and a light, but pleasant breeze. The defenders looked out at the attackers and began to laugh; they might even have attacked but for the deployment of the armed cavalry. The defenders were taunting the attackers about their feeble blanket-weapons when suddenly lightning bolts began striking the fort. The fortress was made of wood and fires began breaking out all over. The taunting defenders began screaming as many of them plunged to their death trying to escape the fire. Ambrosius' army watched in horror as their enemies and brothers burned before their eyes.

Merlin adjusted himself a bit in his saddle as he covered the laser in his walking stick. He turned to Ambrosius and, with a tear in his eye, said, "You may send your men in now. Have them save all they can. The battle is over and you have won."

Ambrosius gave the order to his officers, who relayed it to their soldiers. The soldiers responded immediately and ran toward the fortress to save their enemies who had once been their friends. Vortigern, in his madness, had surrounded himself with half of his troops. All of these, including Vortigern, perished. Of the remainder, some died, but most were injured or burned. There were only about four hundred soldiers from Vortigern's command who survived unharmed. Only those around Merlin knew that it was he who had caused the destruction. Most assumed it was an act of god upon the evil king. The fires burned through the night and into the next day.

Merlin instructed Ambrosius to move the army back to Tre'r Ceiri. Merlin also had Ambrosius send riders to intercept the women and children, and have them rerouted to Tre'r Ceiri.

Once the army arrived at Tre'r Ceiri and was properly housed, the women and children of the defenders were attended to. They were all treated with respect, and those whose husbands died were sent to their homes or those of relatives. Those with wounded husbands were allowed to attend to the them and were joined by many others.

Merlin, Ambrosius, and the officers went about the business of organizing, training, and establishing discipline within the army. They had to prepare to march out and meet the army of the two princes, ready to do battle if necessary.

The training went well. The troops learned how to form the tortoise, wedge, saw, skirmishing, repel cavalry, and orb formations. The tortoise was a formation where the men in a front line hold their shields in front of themselves while the rows behind them hold their shields above their heads, thus giving them protection against arrows. In the wedge formation, the soldiers form a V so as to penetrate the lines of the enemy; the saw was just the opposite. Skirmishing resembled a checkerboard layout, while the repel cavalry formation had the men in the front line put their shields together, forming a wall with their spears angled upward, and the second line was designated to attack the riders with their spears. The orb formation was a defensive formation where the officers and archers stood in the center of a circle, surrounded by shield-bearing soldiers.

As the training got underway, the rider sent to find the two princes and their army finally returned. The princes were interested in helping in the battle against Vortigern, but were tied up fighting the Saxons, Anglos, and Jutes. Merlin had the rider draw a map showing where the princes' army was and sent out a fresh rider to meet them and tell them about Ambrosius' victory. In the message, the rider was to convey that Vortigern had lost more than three thousand soldiers to defections, more than one thousand had been killed, and more than six hundred wounded. The messenger was instructed not to tell them any of the details about how it had happened; he was to give them statistics only and say that the details would be given to them when Ambrosius arrived–which might be a matter of months.

It took several weeks for the troops to be trained and properly equipped. Merlin looked at the time he'd spent on this trip and thought about how this was supposed to be a short test trip, not a full mission. With the lull in activity, Merlin once again became homesick. He missed his family of friends and his way of life, yet he was excited about his new life also. He had developed a strong bond with Ambrosius and found it intellectually stimulating to be able to study the past while living it. He was comfortable enough with himself to accept that his ego was stimulated by the realization that he was one of the greatest legendary figures of all times, Merlin the Sorcerer.

At last, Merlin and Ambrosius agreed that the army was trained enough to be able to make a good showing of themselves should the situation arise. Besides, if necessary, they would have Merlin as a backup. Merlin wanted people to believe that

God and Ambrosius were responsible for the ultimate defeat and death of Vortigern. That way, when Merlin wasn't around, potential enemies would be less likely to want to bring harm to Ambrosius the way Vortigern had tried to do.

As the army prepared to move out, Merlin called for Vortigern's wife and daughter, Rowena and Morgause, to meet with him. In the meeting, Merlin swore he'd provide protection and a place for both of them to live. Rowena had never been particularly close to Vortigern, as their marriage had been a political alliance, not a love match. Rowena was not a happy woman; she'd been used by her father and her husband as an object rather than a person, and heartily resented it. She actually felt closer to Merlin than to the others because of his kindness toward her and her daughter. She wasn't in love with Merlin, but felt a special friendship for him that made her feel at peace when around him.

The next day the army marched off to meet the army of the two princes at Glevum. Ambrosius left three hundred soldiers behind to guard the fort and the inhabitants of the area. After a week of marching, the front units finally reached Glevum and were met by the rider Merlin had dispatched to meet the two princes. He informed Merlin that Prince Amris Pendreic and Prince Uther Pendragon would be in Glevum soon.

Merlin and Ambrosius decided that it would be best to have Ambrosius' army camp out on Lord Cadwellon's estate. Ambrosius gave his officers directions to the estate and then broke off from the army, accompanied by his guards and Merlin. They entered the town with cheers ringing through the streets because of the death of Vortigern and Ambrosius' part in it.

They rode to the inn, where they met Aldan and Lord Cadwellon. Lord Cadwellon clasped General Ambrosius about the shoulders and gave him a warm hug to welcome home his son, the hero. This was followed by a kiss from Aldan. Inside the inn, the newly united family and their friend, Merlin, began to sound more like a family of Merlin's time than what Merlin would think a fifth century family would sound like. Good news was presented in that Lord Cadwellon had asked Aldan to marry him, which she agreed to do.

While waiting for the two princes to arrive, Merlin and Ambrosius used and enjoyed the Roman baths and Glevum's luxuries. Both of them spent much of their time at Lord Cadwellon's estate where they got to know Thomas and Lord Cadwellon better. When the weather turned colder, Merlin welcomed the villa's central heating, a vast improvement to the harsh conditions he'd endured in Wales.

A few weeks later, Merlin was relaxing at the baths when a rider announcing the imminent arrival of the two princes broke him out of his semi-state of consciousness. Merlin instructed the rider to meet again with the princes and ask them to wait at a location a league from town. He then dispatched a rider to alert Ambrosius and have him form up his army at the same location.

Everyone had been instructed on what to do and was prepared for the arrival of the army of the two princes. Ambrosius arrived to join Merlin at the head of his army just as the army of the two princes arrived. The two armies faced each other across an open, snow-covered field; over ten thousand men were dressed and ready to do battle.

The fur-covered Merlin, Ambrosius, Lord Cadwellon, their guards and highest-ranking officers, were the first to move by walking their horses slowly toward the two princes. Upon seeing Ambrosius and Merlin ride toward them, Prince Amris and Prince Uther, and their highest-ranking officers, began an equally slow ride to meet them. The leaders of the two sides met at a spot about midway between the two armies.

Prince Amris was a tall, stately-looking young man in his late twenties of muscular build with long, dark brown hair under his helmet. Prince Uther was a handsome but portly young man in his mid-twenties of about the same height as his brother, but with sandy brown hair and slightly more fat than muscle.

With the winter winds beginning to pick up, Prince Amris sat high in his saddle as he shouted for all to hear, "I am Prince Amris Pendreic, son of Riothomus Constantine III, High-King of The Island of The Mighty and his rightful heir. This is my brother, Prince Uther Pendragon, and we are here to claim the crown that our father's murderer stole."

As the oldest member of the delegation, Lord Cadwellon was the first to speak from the opposing army. He said in a much softer voice, "I'm Lord Cadwellon. This is my son, General Ambrosius. He is the man who defeated Vortigern, the murderer of your father. And this is his mentor, Merlin the Sorcerer. We are honored to meet you at long last."

Prince Uther looked back at his army and then rose in his saddle to look at the men of Ambrosius' army. Then he looked first at Merlin and then at Ambrosius before saying, "Gentlemen, between us we have the largest and perhaps strongest army in Briton. Combined, we can make a formidable force. General, I have heard about your recent heroics and I must say that I am honored to know you. Merlin, if half of what they say about you is true, then I'm truly humbled in your presence. How may we work together for the benefit of the people of Briton?"

Merlin was trying to read the two men using his recently acquired training in how to read a person's body language when he said in a loud, booming voice, "I'm not of this land, but I have a proposal that should be acceptable to all. With Vortigern gone, there is no one but General Ambrosius strong enough to oppose you for the crown you so rightly seek. I propose that General Ambrosius be placed in command of all the armies of Briton. I propose that Lord Cadwellon, and his soon-to-be-wife, Aldan, be crowned Early-King and Queen of Glevum and all the land west through Wales, with his son, Ambrosius, as his true heir. I also propose that Prince Amris Pendreic be crowned Riothomus of Briton, High-King of The Island of The Mighty. Furthermore, should Prince Amris not father a son, Prince Uther Pendragon shall be declared Prince Amris' first and rightful heir. I also propose that General Ambrosius be given the order to clear Briton of the Picts, Irish, Saxons, Jutes, Anglos, and any other enemies of this land that might come forth in the future."

There wasn't much to discuss at that point. The men of both armies began to cheer. An agreement was at hand and it appeared that Merlin would soon be on his way home. He did agree to attend the wedding as well as the coronations of the two kings before his departure.

The night before the wedding and coronations, Amris, Uther, General Ambrosius, Merlin, and Lord Cadwellon bathed in the public baths and were later joined by Lady Aldan at the amphitheater for entertainment. As soon as the wedding and coronations were concluded, Merlin said goodbye and set up a return pool at a location that would return him directly to the Gloucester Research Center. Then, with a flash from his laser, he jumped into the wormhole and was on his way home.

Chapter Fourteen

A tired and hungry Merlin emerged from the pool at the Gloucester Research Center, startling the MPs standing guard. A large board had been built next to the platform at the pool that had the current date on it. Passersby and visitors probably wondered why the current date was displayed so prominently next to what appeared to be a pond, as if wanting to give the date to the nonexistent fish in the water. But Merlin knew: It told him that he had arrived almost one month from the day he left.

The MPs ran to Merlin in the pouring rain to see if they could help him. Merlin asked them to get his cart and bring it to the main building for him. He entered the building and passed a couple of the research assistants on his way to his office.

At least he wouldn't have to go into quarantine like he'd done before. The research team in Mexico, led by Adelina, had discovered that microorganisms were neutralized by the plant solution used in creating the wormhole. This discovery soon proved to be a valuable product that helped with much of the funding for the project. At the beginning of the program, Adrian had made the comment that the discoveries and inventions from the project could well equal or exceed those of the space programs. As time went by, Adrian would be proven correct.

A new problem the researchers would need to work on was to find some way to make a solid state laser that would not rely on the sun and still be light enough to carry and small enough to fit within the confines of a walking stick.

Once Merlin was in his office, he called the operations room and spoke to Adrian, letting Adrian know he'd returned. He asked Adrian to wait a few minutes to allow him time to change clothes before they all got together for a debriefing.

Merlin took a quick shower and just as he finished, he heard a knock on his door. He grabbed a towel and wrapped it around himself before opening it and when he did he found Vivian staring at him.

Smiling a wicked smile she said, "You'd have a lot more fun if you'd leave your door unlocked."

Despite Merlin's desire to grab her and make passionate love to her, he held back. "Why is it that you only seem to be in these moods after I've been gone for a while?"

"I don't know." Vivian pushed her way inside Merlin's office and closed the door behind her. She wrapped her arms around him and began to kiss him passionately, at the same time removing his towel. She then took off her lab coat and looked over Merlin's body. She kept up her striptease by slowly unbuttoning and then removing her blouse and pants, revealing her Venus-like figure.

Just as Merlin pulled her close and began to rediscover her body and mouth, the phone rang.

Annie was on the line. "I didn't want to embarrass you the way I did last time, particularly since I can't seem to locate Vivian. You should know that Bill's here and wants to see you immediately. We're in the main conference room, so grab Vivian and the two of you get in here ASAP, okay?"

Merlin sighed in disappointment. "Yeah, okay, we'll be right there."

Merlin and Vivian grudgingly got dressed and went to the main conference room to meet with the rest of the team leaders. It'd been months since Merlin had last seen Dr. Bill Barnes and he sort of wanted the ego-lift that only a good boss can provide. As Merlin and Vivian rounded the corner to the hall where the conference room was, he noticed there were several men in civilian clothes with automatic rifles in their hands; two of them were part of Lance's squad of MPs. Merlin and Vivian opened the door to the conference room and saw that it was full of their co-workers and a special visitor, King Arthur II.

The king was dressed in an expensive, dark brown suit and was meticulously well-groomed, which highlighted the handsome aristocrat's best qualities. The king turned to face Merlin as Merlin entered the room, presenting a stark contrast to Merlin's shabby long hair and beard. Merlin looked totally out of place in his blue corduroy shirt and blue slacks covered by a lab coat.

King Arthur smiled a charming smile and extended his hand to the homeless-looking Merlin, who immediately shook the king's hand.

King Arthur said, "I've read the report of your last jump and I must say that it's an honor to actually meet Merlin the Magician. I've admired you since I was a child."

Merlin, who had actually met some of the kings who were largely responsible for setting Briton on the course to what it was today, men who'd led armies and fought battles–something today's royalty had no firsthand experience with–replied politely to the king by saying, "Your Majesty, I'm the one who's honored."

The king gestured toward a chair at the head of the conference table. "Please be seated. I know you must be tired but I'd like to hear about your latest exploits."

Merlin took the seat. "I was in Briton about six months this time and there were many things I witnessed and was a part of, which included the deaths by my hand of more than a thousand Britons and a High-King named Vortigern."

"You personally killed those people? Why is there no record of this in history?" the king asked.

"Unfortunately, there is. Vortigern retreated to the wooden fortress of Caer-Guorthigirn. The day was clear, the sky was blue and, according to history, lightning struck the fortress, setting it on fire. The lightning was from my laser," Merlin explained.

The king thought for a moment before saying, "Yes, I recall the story. But in the story, Ambrosius, son of High-King Constantine III, and his brother Uther pursued Vortigern. They were seeking the crown of High-King of Briton." The king attempted to comfort Merlin about his involvement in the deaths by reminding Merlin that all these people were dead anyway from the perspective of the current time period.

Merlin was still not at ease with what he'd done and bringing up the memory was very painful. He was close to tears when he said, "Ambrosius wasn't the son of King Constantine III. He was the son of Lord Cadwellon, who was made Early-King by High-King Amris Pendreic. King Amris is the son of King Constantine III and brother of Prince Uther Pendragon. Ambrosius was given command of all the Armies of Briton and was General Ambrosius, not King Ambrosius, though Ambrosius was the heir of Early-King Cadwellon, so he could eventually become a king."

"That's interesting. It does clear up some mixed-up issues with our history. Did you meet King Amris and Prince Uther?"

"Yes." Merlin found it interesting how much the king knew about the history of Briton and his heritage. He'd always felt it was a shame that most of the people he'd met knew little about either.

Merlin spent the next three hours talking with the king and the research staff, answering their questions about all aspects of life during that era. There was a great deal of interest in the rapidly declining infrastructure and quality of life as a result of the Roman departure. Adrian had food brought in for those in attendance, with special attention given to Merlin's wish for American pizza.

The king was excited about the results thus far and was anxious for Merlin to conduct further research. The king felt there was a need for Merlin to be accompanied on future trips by someone, anyone, but Merlin explained that it wouldn't be wise at this time because they still hadn't worked out the bugs regarding the arrival time in either direction.

After the king's departure, Merlin and Vivian left for their home. They'd shared it for many months now but, despite Merlin and Vivian's desire for each other, they had yet to make love. Unfortunately, this would be another of those nights as Merlin was way too tired to do anything but sleep.

With the king's instructions, this was going to be a quick turnaround for Merlin. The king wanted information on Uther Pendragon, the perceived father of King Arthur I. There was much to do to get ready for the trip, part of which was to allow Merlin to catch up on his rest. Vivian was once again tied up, preparing a special piece of equipment that could create a mask of someone's face and allow the wearer to assume the identity of that person. There was equipment that had been around for years to do that, but they needed to miniaturize it as much as possible and write a program for the nanofactory that would allow it to produce the material needed for the mask.

Within two weeks everything was ready and Merlin was rested. An approximate date was selected for his third arrival, supplies were loaded into his trusty cart and the research center was put on alert for a jump the next day.

Merlin prepared a fire in the fireplace after he and Vivian finished a fine steak dinner. Merlin sat on a rug in front of the fire and Vivian joined him with a glass of red wine for each of them. They began talking about what Merlin expected to encounter on this trip, when Vivian moved close to Merlin and gave him another of her long, passionate kisses. Merlin pulled her close to him, his heart racing, and then gently laid her down on the rug. His heart began beating so hard it hurt. Merlin slowly ran his hand along Vivian's pants between her thighs, then moved his hand up Vivian's blouse to her breast, cupping it in his hand while she held their embrace. He began unbuttoning her blouse while she began pulling at his shirt, unbuttoning it just as he was doing to hers, exposing the shine of her passion-soaked skin. Merlin reached the front clasp of Vivian's bra and began to open it just as the doorbell rang.

A breathless Vivian said, "Let's pretend we're not here."

"Good idea," Merlin agreed, out of breath, as the doorbell rang again.

Again the doorbell rang, but this time it was followed by knocking and a voice saying, "Merlin, it's us. Let us in."

Merlin shrugged his shoulders and, with a disappointed

look, got up and went to answer the door while Vivian buttoned her blouse. Merlin called out, "Who is it?"

"Merlin, come on and open the door," shouted the voice on the other side of the door.

Merlin opened the door and found his so-called friends waiting to get in. They stood there for a second, looking at a rumpled Merlin. Annie said, as she pushed her way in, "At it again, I see. You two are like rabbits."

"But I've never–" Merlin began before Annie brushed past him.

Merlin and Vivian enjoyed the farewell party, or at least as much as they could, all things considered. It was then that Adrian told Merlin about Bill's plan to expand the research center at the suggestion, and funding, of King Arthur II. One condition was that others on the team accompany Merlin on a mission in the near future to verify Merlin's story–which sent the message that the king wasn't sure Merlin was telling the truth about his trips back in time, which the gang found unsettling. Adrian had also to admit that it was he and Annie who had been designated as the two to accompany Merlin. The king and Bill seemed to feel that Vivian's judgment might be a bit clouded due to her relationship with Merlin, something that didn't sit too well with Vivian. A little later Annie and Vivian entered the room with Vivian carrying a tri-colored collie. Vivian told Merlin it was a gift to the two of them from King Arthur II. The collie's name was Shadow because it would become Vivian's shadow when Merlin was gone.

The party didn't last too late because no one wanted Merlin to begin his trip exhausted. Unfortunately for Merlin and Vivian, they were too dedicated to the project to pick up where they'd left off, knowing it could put Merlin at risk if he didn't get enough sleep before the jump.

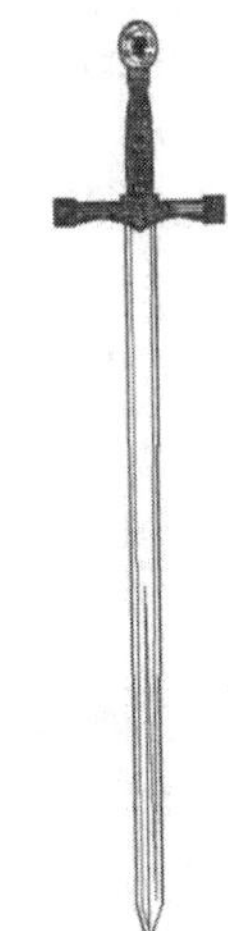

Chapter Fifteen

All was prepared for Merlin's new adventure the next morning and a sudden regret worked its way into Merlin's thoughts: regret at having to again leave his friends for what could be months. The wormhole was activated and the cart was sent ahead. Merlin followed within a few minutes and soon found himself once again in the lake near Early-King Cadwellon's estate.

Merlin pulled the cart out of the lake and quickly took off his waterproof coveralls and water-protective coverings for his shoes, thinking that the cart was going to have to go. This was a new innovation from Annie, and which Merlin was grateful for. He pulled out his cape and his laser wand and moved the cart to an area surrounded by trees where it would be hidden. Merlin covered what was still showing with some branches. Unsure of what lay ahead, Merlin set off in the direction of King Cadwellon's estate.

When Merlin arrived, he saw immediately that it was in a state of extreme disrepair and there were several people loading up three carts with statues and other items from the villa. As Merlin got closer, he saw that Thomas was the one directing the other workers.

Merlin called out as he got closer to the villa. "Thomas, it's Merlin. What's going on?"

Thomas put down a tool he was holding and walked toward Merlin. "Good day, Merlin. I haven't seen you for years. How are you?"

Merlin waved at Thomas. "I am fine, and you?"

"I too do well. Why don't you come join me inside? Much has happened since you've been gone."

Merlin looked around and noticed small piles of trash here and there as well as dirt and mold on the walls. The fountain no longer worked and there were no servants about to care for them. Thomas grabbed a chair for himself and one for Merlin and motioned for Merlin to have a seat.

Thomas began by saying, "We've missed you, Merlin. Much has happened in your absence."

Merlin leaned forward in his seat. "Really. I want to hear about all that's taken place, but first, what are you doing with the villa?"

Thomas smiled. "Ah, yes. I can see your lack of knowledge. King Cadwellon has built a castle nearby and we're moving the last of his furnishings that have remained here to the new one."

"Ah, I see. Now tell me of the events since my last visit."

Thomas sighed. "You should be proud of King Cadwellon's son. General Ambrosius brought a great degree of peace to the land by defeating most of the barbarians."

"That's good to hear. When I left, he had a large army to command, but I was concerned about their training and level of discipline."

"He took care of that by bringing in some retired Roman officers and paying them a large number of coins to oversee the training and discipline of the army. His army is now one of the best. But even with this success, if not partially because of it, we've seen an increase in the number of poor citizens."

"Well, I'm saddened to hear that. I know Vortigern rejected many of the luxuries associated with Roman civilization because of his marriage to Rowena."

"It's much more than that. King Amris and King Uther were both of the political view that embraced the Roman civilization and all the conveniences that came with it. But there are many Britons who came to agree with Vortigern's beliefs. Of course, the biggest problem is the destruction of some of our cities by the barbarians. In particular, the destruction of our aqueducts. There are few *plumbum* workers in our cities, as most went to Rome. Many of those who stayed were prevented from doing their work by Vortigern, as well as the Germanic tribes, the Saxons being the worst."

Merlin had never really given much thought to the value of plumbers before. "I see from what you're describing that civilization as I know it would fall into a terrible state without the *plumbum* workers. Wait a minute: You mentioned King Amris, who was the Riothomus of Britain when I left. And you said King Uther, who was a prince when I left. Has something changed there?"

"Yes. The right and noble King Amris was murdered. We don't know for sure who was behind it. Some suspect the Picts. Others think it was one of the Germanic tribes. Many, including King Uther, suspect one or several of the Early-Kings. Many of the Early-Kings suspect Riothomus Uther, who took the title upon his brother's death."

"Why would they suspect Uther?"

"The High-King, Riothomus Amris Pendreic, gained his power as a result of your support and his military might. King Amris appeared to be a good king, but the destruction was wide and there has not been enough time, silver, or people, to restore things to the way they were. There has been unrest among the southern Early-Kings. They've seen their land taxed to pay for Briton's army led by General Ambrosius and the extensive training of the soldiers. Many of the southern Early-Kings consider this a waste of silver, not understanding or seeing the benefit of the army and wanting faster reconstruction of the aqueducts. The northern Early-Kings are disturbed because they've seen their lands taxed and most of the reconstruction of the aqueducts has been done in the south. They demand that the army should station soldiers at the deserted Roman forts along Hadrian's Wall, as well as protect the coastlines from attack. They insist that, as large as the army is, it must be larger to keep the barbarians that General Ambrosius ran off from returning. King Uther doesn't remember that he rules as the elected representative of all the kings."

"Well, it seems I need to pay a visit to King Uther and try to straighten this mess out. Where might I find the good king?"

"My understanding is he's in Londinium. Would you like me to accompany you there?"

"No, that's fine. I'll find my way there."

"No, I insist. It won't take long to finish loading and I can send the workers to the castle and come with you."

"What about your master?"

"He'll be good with it. After all, I'm no longer his caretaker; King Amris began a system called 'knighthood' wherein the Early-Kings could select men with leadership qualities and knight them and give them a title. I'm now known as Sir Thomas," said Thomas with obvious pride.

Merlin scratched his chin. "Well, that's good. Yes, as soon as you're finished here, we'll leave."

It wasn't long before the packing had been completed and the two men were off to Londinium. Along the way they heard many stories about Merlin's return and how he was going to straighten out the king. Merlin was amused as he thought about how rumors, even in the fifth century, seemed to fly faster than a phone call. He also found it fun that he wasn't recognized by anyone and he wouldn't allow Sir Thomas to tell anyone who he was. Another odd thought Merlin had was whether or not he remembered to put back the carton of milk he'd left out on the kitchen table before he'd jumped back in time.

As the two men approached the outskirts of Londinium, twelve soldiers approached them and said they were of the King's Guard. They asked if it were Merlin they were speaking with and when Merlin confirmed it, they said they'd been sent out by King Uther to escort Merlin to the palace.

Merlin was unsure of these so-called escorts and knew that if there were one person in the kingdom who didn't need a bodyguard, it was he. Merlin became more alarmed as a result of the rough treatment they seemed to be giving Sir Thomas. One of the guards attempted to grab Merlin's laser–which Merlin certainly couldn't allow. Using some of the techniques he'd been taught during his last layover in his own time, Merlin struck the man in the stomach, then between the legs, behind the knee, and finally laid him flat on his back.

Merlin looked at the captain of the guards. "It appears that you may be in more need of bodyguards than am I."

Sir Thomas couldn't hold back an approving laugh as the guards backed off with Merlin holding them at bay with his laser. With all the commotion, no one took notice of a tall, distinguished, and handsome young man who came up behind Merlin. The man said, "These men are an escort to honor you, not detain you."

Merlin stood straight up and slowly turned toward the man. "Ambrosius? Ambrosius, is that you?"

The two men embraced. "Merlin, it has been a long time. I've missed your advice and help. I could have used your magic a few times, too. Come, let us make attendance to King Uther. He is waiting."

The two men, followed by Sir Thomas and the twelve escorts, mounted their horses and rode over the bridge and into Londinium. Once in the city, the road continued to the Forum, but they turned to the left to the palace where King Uther was staying. They dismounted and three of the guards took the horses' reins while two others carried the travelers' bags, and the rest stationed themselves outside the palace.

The three men entered the palace and went down a short hallway to a large, sparsely furnished room. Merlin saw King Uther lying on a long bench, eating grapes. Merlin noticed that Uther had gained considerable weight since he last saw him; his short hair and clean-shaven face, gave him the appearance of a poor imitation of a Caesar.

King Uther looked at the three men and in an arrogant tone said, "What have we here? Please, move into the light so I might see you better."

Merlin was astonished at what he saw. No wonder the man had brought such distrust upon himself. Merlin's two companions moved into the light as commanded, but Merlin held back, refusing to be ordered about by this man. He said, "Uther. Get up. Who do you think you are?"

Surprised by such a statement, Uther reacted immediately. "Guards! Guards, come quick."

"Sire," Ambrosius said. "I wouldn't do that if I were you. Have you forgotten who this is?"

Several guards burst into the room with their swords drawn. Uther raised his hand, motioning them to stop. Uther thought about the potential consequences of his actions and decided that it might be prudent to let this one slide. Uther looked at the rumpled-looking man with the long beard and long hair and began to laugh. "Merlin, it's good to see you again."

"There's much we need to discuss, Uther. There are problems in this land that could lead to your assassination, or to war. I'll not tolerate your allowing the situation to continue. We must talk."

King Uther was surprised by Merlin's announcement. He knew there were problems within Briton, but he felt they were being dealt with in the best possible manner. Merlin, though, knew that the Early-Kings were furious that King Uther was trying to rule by dictate rather than consensus. Merlin told King Uther that he would have a large, round table built and installed in the Basilica that was connected to the Forum. The table would seat all forty-two Early-Kings plus King Uther and General Ambrosius. In this manner, they would all feel they were equals in discussing the needs of Briton.

Merlin had the table built and, upon completion, gave it to Uther during a great ceremony. All the lesser kings had been invited to attend the ceremony and all were present. Along with the Round Table, Merlin unveiled another new idea for the kings: Each Early-King would henceforth be known as an Earl and would swear allegiance to the High-King or Riothomus. Upon doing so, they would each be knighted and go by the title of "Sir." Each Earl would retain all their prior powers, including the power to vote on the policies of the government of Briton.

The Early-Kings agreed to this arrangement simply because no one wanted to risk angering the wizard. King Uther drew Caliburn, the mighty and beautiful Roman-styled Sword of Briton from its sheath. The pummel and hand guard of the former sword of Maximus shined as the light reflected off its polished brass and gold. The mighty silver-plated iron blade was a truly beautiful and powerful sword. The first to be knighted was King Ector of Caer Gar, followed by King Cadwellon, and then the rest of the Early-Kings. King Uther touched each man once on each shoulder with his mighty sword, thus beginning the tradition of "knighting."

During the knighting ceremonies, King Uther noticed a beautiful young woman and sent one of his men to find out who she was. Her name was Ygerna, the wife of the just-knighted Sir Gorlois of Cornwall in the southwest corner of Briton. Sir Gorlois was a muscular man in his late twenties with strong, handsome features.

At the end of the festivities, King Uther, still thinking about Ygerna, called the earls into council so their grievances could be heard. As they were about to conclude the meeting, a messenger entered with troubling news: There was a new invasion by the Anglos and Jutes at Damen. The news effectively ended the southern earls' argument about reducing spending on the army, though they were obviously suspicious about the fortuitous timing of the message. To waylay their fears, King Uther invited them to join him in pushing the German invaders into the sea.

Chapter Sixteen

King Uther commanded General Ambrosius to gather his troops, but only about a fourth of them were immediately available. Uther didn't want to wait; he told Ambrosius that he'd take command of those who were ready to go and that Ambrosius should catch up with him when the rest were assembled. Merlin, Sir Thomas, Sir Cadwellon, and Sir Ector accompanied General Ambrosius in bringing in the rest of the army, leaving only a skeleton force at each of the earls' fortresses.

Within a week, the main Army of Briton had gathered and was ready to do battle. As they marched out of Londinium, word came to them that King Uther had been defeated at Damen and was retreating north toward Eboracum—Merlin's computer told him that was York on the River Ouse in North Yorkshire in the 5th century. Fortunately, the Roman-built roads were still in good shape leading to Eboracum, which allowed for faster movement of the army. General Ambrosius laid out a plan to meet up with King Uther and the remainder of the king's army at Eboracum. Ambrosius sent a messenger with his plans to Uther and a suggestion that King Uther should not leave Eboracum, but should try to hold out as long as possible until he could arrive.

Merlin, Sir Ector, and Sir Thomas rode ahead to analyze the situation and bring back intelligence to General Ambrosius so Ambrosius could draw up a battle plan. Sir Cadwellon decided to remain with his son and the main body of the army in order to spend as much time with his son as possible.

After two days of hard riding, the three men stopped at a high rise in the land that gave them the opportunity to view the city and fortress and the combined armies of the Jutes and the Anglos and their camps in the distance. It was a sight that sent chills down the spines of all three men. King Uther's army was outnumbered at least two to one, but the worst part was that it appeared that the German armies possessed large numbers of archers and cavalry while Uther's army was mainly infantry. Fortunately, the forces being brought up by General Ambrosius would reverse the numbers and throw the advantage in every area to King Uther–if he made it in time.

Merlin knew he might have to use his special equipment to help Uther, though he hated the thought. He still hadn't gotten over his sorrow at killing more than a thousand men under Vortigern at Caer-Guorthigirn.

Sir Thomas made a swing around the invaders in an effort to gather as much intelligence about them as possible.

Merlin and Sir Ector turned their steeds for a ground-eating gallop to the entrance to the fort to avoid the German arrows that were sure to fly as they neared the front gates. Merlin heard the arrows pass close over his head and felt some of them hit his cloak, but without the velocity needed to penetrate the tough leather. Suddenly he heard a horse scream behind him. He turned his head and saw Sir Ector's steed stumble and roll on the ground. With Anglos running toward their prey and arrows flying all around, Merlin turned his horse around and headed for the fallen Sir Ector.

Ector pulled himself from beneath his mortally wounded horse and began running toward Merlin. As the two men got close, Merlin leaned down and forward on his horse and reached out his arm for Ector to grab onto. Ector responded and grabbed Merlin's arm at almost the same instant that an arrow pierced Merlin's shoulder. The two men fell to the ground with Ector's body cushioning Merlin's fall.

Merlin's horse stopped and began to return to where the two men lay when another storm of arrows felled him. Merlin looked around for his laser, their last remaining hope. With the Anglos closing in, he spied his laser and ran to retrieve it as Ector lay on the ground in pain. Merlin picked up the laser stick and found that it'd been broken in half. He could but pray that it would work. He removed the camouflaged cover and aimed his laser at the closest Anglos and fired. There wasn't much intensity, but it was enough to stop the Anglos in their tracks.

Merlin held the attackers at bay by slowly swinging his laser from side to side. Merlin walked to where the fallen Sir Ector lay, keeping an eye on the wary attackers, who nevertheless continued to look for an opening to bypass his weapon as Merlin used his injured arm to help Ector to his feet.

Ector's leg was badly injured and he was forced to use Merlin as a prop as the two men backed toward the gate. One of the attackers lunged at Merlin just as the main gate opened. Merlin fired a blast from his laser with deadly results while ten of King Uther's knights came barreling toward them. The knights brought two horses for the fallen warriors and Merlin helped Ector onto one.

Merlin ran to the other horse just as the Germans began to charge. The archers inside the fort fired their arrows while the knights fought with the first of the enemy to reach them. Merlin grimaced as he broke off the arrow protruding from his shoulder. He held the laser in one hand and managed to pull himself up onto the saddle with the other.

The knights and the two wounded warriors fought their way to the gates as the arrows from the men of the fort continued their deadly flow. Several hundred infantrymen ran through the gates, clearing a path for the returning knights. The men finally made it through, with the infantry retreating behind them. As the gates closed, the barbarians stopped their pursuit and returned to their lines.

King Uther had been watching the skirmish from the ramparts and ran down the stairs to check on the condition of the wounded. Sir Ector was pulled from his horse and taken to the infirmary. Though Merlin was in great pain, he fought to maintain consciousness so he could tell King Uther to get a message to General Ambrosius with as much information as possible on the state of his men and that of the enemy's.

King Uther had his personal physician look after Merlin and Sir Ector, while he prepared the information to be sent to Ambrosius. The messenger left the fort just as Ector cried out in pain from the physician setting his leg.

The physician gave Merlin some opium for pain and then removed the arrowhead from Merlin's shoulder. Just as the physician was bandaging him up, a soldier burst through the door with the announcement that the Anglos and Jutes were preparing another assault.

While still under the influence of the opium, the two warriors slowly pulled themselves from their cots. Ector grabbed a crude crutch to help him walk and began to hobble out the door. Merlin grabbed the laser and his sword and followed Ector. The two wounded soldiers slowly made their way to the top of the ramparts and looked over the wall at the enemy massing for the attack.

King Uther, surrounded by his top officers, was barking out orders with a newfound confidence. He ordered his knights to prepare themselves for General Ambrosius' army to get there. He commanded the archers to prepare for the enemy's assault. The remaining soldiers were to man the defenses of the wall with about two hundred held in reserve should a breech occur.

Suddenly a shrill yell filled the air as the combined forces of the Jutes and Anglos propelled themselves forward in a sea of humanity. As they drew close to the walls, they were met by a hail of arrows from the meager group of archers supporting King Uther's forces. The Germans lost some men to the archers, but not enough to slow them down. The enemy archers unleashed their own onslaught of arrows in such force as to almost blot out the sun. The only advantage King Uther enjoyed was that the enemy's infantry barely outnumbered his own, and Uther's were behind walls.

Merlin was startled to see the top of a ladder appear on the outside of the wall in front of him. Sir Ector grabbed a few men who helped him push the ladder away from the wall. Despite the heroics of Uther's men, it was obvious to Merlin that they were soon to be overrun.

Ladders appeared faster than the defenders could push them down and the barbarians started entering the rampart. Both defenders and attackers were falling into the courtyard; some were injured and some were dead. Merlin looked to see if Ambrosius had arrived. Suddenly, in the distance, he saw the standards of Ambrosius' army. Within seconds of spotting the huge mass of men that was encircling the enemy, he began to hear their trumpets. He looked down at the outer limits of the enemies' lines and noticed they were beginning to pull back from the fort.

General Ambrosius launched his men into the battle, quickly overrunning the Jutes' campsite, destroying everything and everyone in sight. As flames began to heat up the sky from the Jutes' camp, the same was happening in the Anglos' camp. Ambrosius sent half of his cavalry to each of the enemy's flanks and had his archers form up between the two flanks. As the first arrows found their mark, the Jutes and Anglos on the walls of the fort began joining their fellow soldiers in an effort to retreat from the battlefield.

As the main gates became clear of attackers, Uther commanded that the gates be open and that his knights chase the fleeing enemy. With the order, the knights on horses burst through the gates and began struggling to get over the dead bodies, their hooves suddenly painted red by the blood of the fallen invaders.

Ambrosius' cavalry was having a much easier time of it in that they had few obstacles in the way as they plowed into the panicked Germans. The cavalry easily overwhelmed the archers and made short work of the opposing cavalry. By now, it was almost every man for himself in the destroyed Jute and Anglo armies. Cheers exploded from the fort as Merlin looked on, observing the first battle in which he had done little to influence the outcome.

General Ambrosius recalled his troops, leaving a small force of cavalry to herd the surviving invaders back to their ships, anchored several hours away. Few of the survivors made any attempt to fight, so there was little likelihood that more troops would be needed. Ambrosius commanded his reserve troops to begin the chore of clearing the battlefield of the dead. They began by piling them onto funeral pyres. The sight of Ambrosius' men killing the wounded and captured enemy sickened Merlin. There would be no prisoners.

Merlin and Ector turned away from the battlefield and faced Uther. King Uther called for his knights and officers to meet him at the bathhouse for an evening of relaxation and food. The rest of the soldiers were to use the fort's bathhouse as soon as everything was put back in order.

Merlin and Ector, as well as several of the other wounded, were invited to attend the victory celebration. The two heroes were assisted into the bathhouse. As they lay on the massage tables, Ector conveyed his thanks to Merlin for saving his life and swore that, should Merlin ever need anything of him, he would comply without question.

Within a couple of days, the battlefield was completely cleared, the wounded cared for, and the army well rested. Ambrosius gave the command for the units to return to their postings. King Uther had messengers sent to each of the earls' home castles with invitations for the earls' ladies and their families to join in a festival to be held in Londinium upon King Uther and his army's triumphant return.

Merlin informed the king that he would not accompany him on the journey to Londinium, but would meet him there in time for the festival. Merlin knew he needed to return to his own time so he could be properly treated for his wound. This Time Travel Archeology was not important enough for him to die for. Fortunately, General Ambrosius had brought Merlin's supplies to Eboracum along with all the rest of the supplies for the army.

Merlin said his goodbyes amid promises to return. He then headed for the nearby woods and set up a pool that could be used for his return and pulled out the extra laser wand that Vivian had fortunately insisted he take with him. Once everything was ready and his cart sent back, Merlin rode back to the fort and requested one of the light cavalrymen to follow him. Once Merlin was within a few yards of his pool, but with the pool out of sight, he gave the cavalryman the reins of his horse and asked the cavalryman to take the horse to General Ambrosius. Merlin also asked the cavalryman to tell the General that Merlin would retrieve it in Londinium.

Merlin watched as the cavalryman rode toward Ambrosius. Once the soldier was gone, Merlin returned to his pool and put his sword safely into the cart. He checked the charges to make sure they would go off and destroy the pool after he was gone. Merlin sighed at last and started the wormhole and entered it for his jump to his own time.

Chapter Seventeen

Merlin felt the ground become solid again and he thought he heard screams as the swirling wormhole came to a stop. He was shaking from the jump because he hadn't had time to put on the patch that countered the dizziness. He was having a hard time focusing as he staggered around like a drunk, and could barely make out a figure standing a few yards away. As he regained his senses, he saw that he was in somebody's back yard. He peered through the misty morning and saw his cart nearby. He put up his laser want and was looking through the cart for his cell phone when two police officers came toward him, batons in their hands.

The first officer looked at the dirty bum with old clothes stained with blood. "Hold it right there, sir. We don't want to hurt you. You'll be coming with us now."

Merlin looked at the officer as he grabbed Merlin's arm. Merlin was still a bit shaky as he pulled his arm back, causing him to lose his balance. The two officers each grabbed an arm, which made Merlin scream out in pain, and began to drag Merlin to their car.

As they reached their car, one of the officers said, "It looks like this man's injured. Perhaps we should call an ambulance."

The second officer, a constable, said, "He's just a drunken old bum. Come on, let's get him back to the stationhouse. We'll have to have the car cleaned out after we drop him into lockup."

"Whatever you say, but I think we're making a mistake," said the first officer, a probationary constable.

Merlin cried out again as the constable pulled his arms back to put handcuffs on him. The probationary constable said, "There's fresh blood on him. This man's been hurt."

The constable said, "Look, I'm not waiting around for any ambulance. Our shift will be over by the time we get the paperwork done on this bum. Let's get going. Mary's going to have supper ready and I'm plenty hungry."

The probationary constable went back to check on Merlin's cart while the constable radioed in to let the dispatcher know they were on their way in. The probationary constable came running back to the car. "There must be thousands of dollars' worth of stuff in the cart. This guy must be a burglar."

"And here I thought you were a drunken bum," the constable said, looking back at the bewildered Merlin. "I've got to call it in. This guy better not make me late tonight." The constable radioed the change in status to the dispatcher and requested another car to take care of the loot in the cart. Within a few minutes another police car showed up and Merlin found himself on the way to the police station.

It had only been an hour since Merlin had been a hero to Briton. Now he found himself being treated as a drunken bum and burglar. He struggled to get his words out. "Please, officers. I must call my office."

The constable laughed. "Oh, look what we have now; a regular dandy. Your office wouldn't be in a cardboard box now, would it?"

Merlin shook his head. "If you won't call my office, then call Windsor Castle and ask for King Arthur. Tell him that Merlin needs to speak to him."

The probationary constable began to laugh at Merlin's words. "Maybe you're right. King Arthur and Merlin. A bit delusional, I guess."

"All right now, Merlin the Magician, is it? Now, Mr. Merlin, if you need to talk to the king so badly, why don't you just wave your magic wand and pop yourself right over to him? In the meantime, keep quiet back there," the constable said.

Merlin felt himself grow weaker as the blood slowly oozed from his wound. By the time the police car pulled into the stationhouse, Merlin was barely conscious. As the two officers pulled Merlin from the car, the probationary constable said, "You know, I think he may actually be hurt."

The constable looked at Merlin before saying, "You may be right. Let's get him inside and we can check him out in there."

The two men dragged Merlin into the police station and the constable said to the desk sergeant, "We picked up this bum nosing around a lady's back yard. He's drunk and he resisted arrest. He may also be some sort of burglar. He has all sorts of expensive equipment in a cart we saw him with. I think he may be hurt, though. What do you want us to do with him?"

"Does he have a name?" the sergeant asked.

"He says he's Merlin the Magician. Wants to talk to King Arthur, don't you know."

Merlin could barely talk. He managed to mumble, "My name is Dr. Merlin Lakin of the Carnegie Institute. Please, call my office. They will verify it for you."

The sergeant looked at Merlin for a moment and let out a grunt as he pulled back his chair from the front desk. "Right, give me the number and I'll check it out."

The probationary constable said, "Hey, isn't that the name of that archeologist? You know, the one on TV in that Mayan City."

The sergeant then turned to the constable. "Yeah, probably just a coincidence. Take him upstairs and get the paperwork started. One of you needs to check out that wound. We wouldn't want to lose His Majesty here too quick, now would we, him being a famous archeologist and magician and all?"

As the sergeant was making the call, the two officers took Merlin inside the squad room. The constable started doing the paperwork while the probationary constable began looking at Merlin's wound. He turned to the constable. "This looks really bad."

The sergeant came running in and interrupted the two men. "Get him cleaned up quick! I just hung up from King Arthur himself! He's sending a helicopter to pick up this guy."

Eyes popping out of their heads, the policemen scrambled around in a sudden hurry to get some help for Merlin and to get him cleaned up. Merlin was barely awake while all this was going on, but he did hear one of the officers say, "He really is Merlin, then."

Merlin smiled but said nothing.

A helicopter landed in a few minutes and a handful of British soldiers entered the police station to retrieve Merlin and his cart. While four soldiers handled the cart, two medics worked on Merlin. It was obvious that Merlin had lost a great deal of blood, so they decided to take him to the hospital. Orders were given for two of the soldiers to stand guard over Merlin at all times. After dropping him off, the helicopter continued to the Gloucester Research Center with the cart.

Adrian, Annie, and Vivian boarded a helicopter at the research center and rushed to meet up with Merlin. Lance stayed behind to take care of the cart and make sure all the equipment was still there. By the time the trio reached the hospital in York, Merlin was already looking better.

Annie looked at Merlin and his wound. "Looks like you lost a couple of quarts. You feeling better yet?"

Although Merlin was still a bit weak, he managed a smile for Annie. He grimaced a bit, more for dramatic affect than pain. "How long have I been gone this time?"

Merlin's semi-pretend suffering had the effect he'd hoped for. Vivian squirmed and wrapped her arms around him. Merlin wasn't pretending though as the pain shot throughout his entire body as she grabbed him. "Oh, I'm sorry. I didn't mean to hurt you," she said, jerking her arms away from him.

Merlin stayed in the hospital for almost a week, with heavy, round-the-clock security. No one at the hospital was allowed to ask him any questions about anything without someone from the research center and a representative of the king present. They couldn't even ask him what he wanted to eat. The security drove Merlin crazy, particularly when Vivian was present.

Vivian couldn't spend the time she wanted with Merlin because she had a new task to perform. Because his recent return had almost had tragic results, everybody agreed that Vivian's team should build a global positioning system receiver small enough to fit into Merlin's laser walking stick. Once the location was received, the information would be sent to a transmitter and from there to the research center. The transmitter needed to be miniaturized and put into the stick. All of this needed to be activated at the same time the wormhole was created so Merlin wouldn't need to worry about activating it when he arrived in the future. This would take care of any future situations similar to what happened when he last came home and it would also allow him to carry an emergency device that would let the research staff know there was an emergency at Merlin's location back in time. To fully accomplish the latter, they needed to be able to determine the time and date the device was sent from, as well as a digital recording device that would allow a message to be sent with the laser stick. A similar device needed to be prepared that would work independently of the laser stick for emergencies when the sender did not or could not accompany the device.

While Vivian worked on the GPS receiver project, Annie and Adrian got ready for their upcoming trip. There hadn't been any formal plan for the two explorers to go on the next mission with Merlin, but they were needed now more than at any other time.

Finally Merlin was well enough to be taken home, a mission Vivian was happy to volunteer for. Lance would accompany her and they would both be followed in a separate car by two of Lance's MPs. Two British soldiers, a doctor, a nurse, and a representative of the king would then follow the MPs.

The drive back to Gloucester through the dreary gray skies along the mist-dampened road was uneventful after picking him up. When they reached the cottage, Vivian ran to the front door and let Shadow out. Even though Merlin had only been gone a few weeks, Shadow had grown like a weed. The dog ran to Merlin, who bent down painfully to pick up the puppy that had doubled in size since the last time Merlin had seen him.

He spent the next few days at the cottage resting and bonding with Shadow. The exercise was proving to be of great benefit to Merlin as he rebuilt his stamina; he and Shadow went out every morning and evening for a walk around the neighborhood. Merlin got to know all his neighbors and Shadow made many dog friends along the way. In the afternoon, Merlin always took Shadow out to play fetch in the backyard and do a little roughhousing.

Vivian came home and smiled as she watched the two play together.

Vivian wanted to make love to Merlin so much that it made her body ache anytime she thought about him. Unfortunately, it was more important to make the equipment modifications so Merlin would stay alive.

The time came for Merlin to return to the days of King Uther. Since he was going to be meeting Uther in London, the team decided that Merlin, and his team, would go to London for his next jump. For security reasons, they needed a place where a crowd wouldn't gather and the most logical was Windsor Castle.

The king was only too eager to help, especially now, having realized that these jumps were dangerous. A pool was prepared on the grounds with provisions made for security and secrecy. The team leaders were accompanied by four of Lance's MPs, who would assist the king's security force around the pools.

They were escorted down a long, wide and well-lit hallway named St. George's Hall when they got to Windsor Castle. Merlin looked up to see full-size suits of armor standing poised on pedestals halfway up the wall. Each was different and each held a sword and lance. Below the suits of armor was a row of coat of arms and below that was medium-brown paneling cut in a rectangular design. There were gold-framed, red-velvet-covered chairs along one wall and similarly colored benches along the other. Statues on pedestals were spaced evenly along both walls. In the tall, dark wood ceiling were more of the colorful coat of arms.

Soon they arrived at a lavishly decorated waiting room. The king came out to personally welcome his guests and invited them on a personal tour of the grounds, which they quickly accepted. After the tour, the king asked them to stay for dinner. He also suggested they spend the night and get an early start the next morning, an offer none of them dared or desired to turn down.

As great as it was for the team leaders, the MPs were experiencing something nobody back home would ever believe—enlisted men dining with the king! It was beyond belief and they couldn't wait to tell everybody they knew as soon as they were allowed.

The team had a wonderful time and was treated like royalty. Unfortunately, it ended far too soon. They rose early the next morning and had a hearty breakfast. Adrian and Annie barely slept the night before, partly out of the realization of where they were, partly out of the realization of where they would soon be.

After breakfast, the trio of archeologists prepared to jump into the wormhole for their first adventure together since this all began in Guatemala. There had only been time enough for two laser sticks to be built; Merlin and Adrian claimed them. They all decided at the last minute that they would travel lighter and not take the cart with them this time. Everything they would actually need was divided between them and put in carrying bags. The king put his arm around Vivian to comfort her as he, Vivian, and Lance watched the trio vanish.

Chapter Eighteen

The three explorers found themselves next to a wooded area. From there, they could follow the Thames River all the way to Londinium to King Uther's festivities. Annie and Adrian looked around at their surroundings, totally amazed. No longer were they on the grounds of Windsor Castle, in fact, the castle didn't even exist yet. Where there had been streets filled with cars and sidewalks full of pedestrians, there were now fields with grain ready to be harvested. As much as Merlin wanted to let them linger and enjoy the beginning of their first jump, they had to get going. The two time-travel novices pulled their cloaks tight and were grateful that Merlin had suggested they wear light-weight long johns for more comfort.

It took them until early evening to reach Londinium; they were totally exhausted as they crossed the bridge. Adrian complained throughout the walk about how uncomfortable his wool clothing was. Annie had to keep nudging him forward or they never would have made it to their destination.

After crossing the bridge, the trio stood for a few moments so Annie and Adrian could get a look at the city and its people. Just the sight of a person walking down the street was enough to get them excited. They were really back in time.

Merlin talked to some of the people and discovered that the main body of the army returning to Londinium was not expected until the afternoon of the next day, but King Uther and some of his knights had arrived a few hours before. Word had already spread about the great victory and plans had been set in motion for a great festival that was to be held once the main force arrived.

Merlin, Annie and Adrian went to the palace to see Uther. They were escorted to a room where King Uther sat at a large table with several of his knights, including Sir Ector.

Merlin walked up to the king. "Well, I see you made it back to Londinium without my help."

"Merlin!" the king shouted, rising to greet him. He grabbed Merlin by the shoulders. "My, you've healed fast. Who are these who travel with you?"

"These are two of my friends, Adrian and Annette."

"Well, your friends are welcome."

"Sir Ector," Merlin asked. "How does your leg?"

"It has not healed as fast as your shoulder, but it will be fine," Sir Ector told him.

"Merlin," said the king. "I'll have my servant show you to your rooms so you can put away your belongings and join us for dinner. Adrian will have to share accommodations with you. We have a great gathering and I did not know you'd be bringing someone with you. Annette will also have to share her room."

Merlin, Adrian, and Annie were shown to their sleeping spaces and put away their gear. The three of them went to the dining hall where Merlin said, “Sir Ector, I’ve brought some medicines from my homeland to use on your leg.”

“If it cures me as quickly as it did you, then I’m willing and thankful,” Sir Ector said.

After the meal, Merlin, Annie, Adrian, and Sir Ector retired to Merlin and Adrian’s quarters where they went to work on Sir Ector’s leg. After setting the leg, they made a cast for it so it would heal better. Merlin didn’t think it was the best job that could be done, but he knew it was many times better than anything the doctors of the time could do.

Merlin spent the time before the festival showing Annie and Adrian everything he could about life in fifth-century Briton. The plumbing was the subject that most interested Merlin’s two friends. Annie was most intrigued with the toilets and sewage system and golden faucets, while Adrian’s interest lay with the bathhouses, central heating and the hot and cold running water.

The trio had a special task they wanted to perform on this mission. They wanted to get an image of each of the earls, so latex masks could be made of them. They wanted something that would tie the earls’ lineages together in an effort to better understand how King Arthur could be related to them. Annie and Adrian each carried the pencil-sized scanners in their hands and were able to scan their subjects’ faces without creating any concern by having them close their eyes. As the trio completed a scan, they downloaded the image into a small computer Merlin had brought.

The two were to gather—as surreptitiously as possible—DNA samples of each of the earls and their wives, so evidence could be collected that might give them a clue as to who was going to be King Arthur’s ancient great-grandparents, and who might be directly related to King Arthur II.

Soon the day of the festival arrived and the entire town, as well as many visitors from other parts of Briton, filled the streets. The army, led by King Uther, General Ambrosius, Merlin, and all the earls, marched through the streets, banners waving in the breeze. Many of the onlookers had seen parades of this type when the Romans were in charge, but this was their first from their fellow countrymen defending Briton. National pride was high that day. Adrian and Annie had gotten caught up in all that was going on around them, but this topped everything.

Room was made around the Round Table, at the Basilica, so Adrian, Annie and the earls' wives could join them in the feast. King Uther had the crowded seating arranged so that Ygerna, wife of Sir Gorlois, would be sitting to the king's left and Merlin would be sitting to the king's right. He seated Sir Gorlois at the farthest point across the table from himself.

As the night progressed, Uther became more and more bold in his attentions to Ygerna, all within sight of Sir Gorlois. Merlin was certainly aware of what was happening and was unhappy about it. The king placed his right hand on Ygerna's thigh and began to work his way between her legs. Ygerna tried to push him away, but the king was too strong. Seeing this, Sir Gorlois sprang from his chair and made a mad dash around the table, pulled his wife away and swore vengeance upon King Uther. Sir Gorlois, his wife, his servant, Britachis, and Jordan, his castellan, left the feast and went straight to the palace where they prepared for their return home.

Drunk, King Uther rose to his feet and demanded silence. He told the earls that Briton had been insulted and a traitor had been discovered within the palace. Each man looked at the one nearest to him and then around the room in an effort to discover who this traitor might be. The drunken king, stumbling and weaving even as he spoke, told them the traitor was Sir Gorlois, Earl of Cromwell, and he had to be punished.

Merlin tried to dissuade the king from taking this action, but his words fell on deaf ears. The king demanded that the army be reassembled for a march on Gorlois. Having recently witnessed the power of the army under General Ambrosius, none of the earls dared challenge King Uther. The consequences could prove devastating to their own lands.

Uther told Ambrosius to send the earls home to return with their infantry and archers for the battle and leave their cavalry behind for defense. General Ambrosius was also to call in the Army of Briton. All the soldiers were to meet at Sir Cadwellon's castle in Glevum. King Uther went to Merlin and asked him to use his magic to make him look like Sir Gorlois so he could have his way with Ygerna, a right that, as the High-King of Briton, he felt was his.

This request troubled Merlin deeply–it went against every value he held dear. To rape a woman was morally wrong. Unfortunately, Dr. Merlin Lakin, familiar with the legend of King Arthur, knew that he, Merlin the Sorcerer, had to play a part in the evil scheme. Merlin took Annie and Adrian into his room and explained the disgusting situation to them. To his surprise, his two friends were excited rather than disgusted. They were looking at the situation with the detachment of scientists rather than the perspective of a friend seeing another friend turn to evil for sexual pleasure.

The question was, now that they had to do it, how to do it? Adrian figured they could use the image of Gorlois they'd made and produce a latex mask from the kit Merlin had brought. The mask they produced this way was a perfect image of Gorlois, but there was one more problem: How would they be able to get Uther in to see Ygerna without arousing suspicion? Annie remembered that she had the images of Gorlois' servant, Britachis, and his castellan, Jordan. So the team made two more masks.

To pull the deception off, they would have to insure that the masks fit correctly and, if there was some sort of trouble with the mask, that it could be corrected. The only way for that to happen would be for one of the team to accompany Uther on his trip. Annie couldn't go because she was a woman, and Adrian was much larger than either of the two servants. So they decided that Merlin would accompany Uther and Adrian would accompany General Ambrosius. Annie would stay behind at Sir Cadwellon's castle in case something happened to one of the other team members so she could help them.

King Uther sent two of General Ambrosius' officers as spies to determine where Gorlois and Ygerna were hiding. Within a few days, the spies returned with news that Gorlois had hidden Ygerna in Tintagel Castle while he waited with his forces at Dimilioc.

General Ambrosius took his army to Glevum and Sir Cadwellon's castle to meet the rest of the forces. King Uther, Sir Cadwellon, Merlin, Adrian, Annie, and King Uther's knights headed out in advance so they would be well rested by the time the rest of the army had arrived.

Merlin had the opportunity to check on Vortigern's wife, Rowena, at Sir Cadwellon's castle. He had been able to find a safe haven for her and her daughter and they'd been able to keep a low profile up to that time. Uther was not at all pleased to see Rowena, but there was little he could do about it since Merlin had given her sanctuary.

Within a few days, soldiers from all over the island filled the castle grounds. General Ambrosius, King Uther, and Merlin sat down to plan the battle. Early the next morning, everyone had a good breakfast and then General Ambrosius' forces, with Adrian dressed to look like the king, began their march on Dimilioc, while King Uther, Merlin, and Sir Ulfius–Uther's closest friend–set out for Tintagel Castle and Ygerna. As part of the deception, Ambrosius was to place Adrian, dressed to resemble King Uther, near the edge of the battlefield with three hundred defenders. He made a promise to Merlin that he would keep Adrian safe.

Fortunately for all, the weather, while still a bit cool, was sunny without a hint of a cloud in the sky.

The first to reach their destination was General Ambrosius. Ambrosius felt that the right thing to do would be to give Sir Gorlois the opportunity to surrender, which was promptly refused. Ambrosius had his men surround Dimilioc Castle while he prepared the battle plan for the next day, which was a simple one: his archers would ignite their arrows and send them blazing into the castle.

As the arrows landed, the Gorlois soldiers sought cover wherever they could find it. Occasionally an arrow found one of the soldiers and he'd run from their cover, screaming, as the flames grew bigger and bigger. Others ran out and tried to save whoever was hit, sometimes with tragic results. Hiding places were sometimes set ablaze, sending men scattering. The arrows struck repeatedly until finally the whole castle was on fire. Panic grew steadily among the defenders.

Sir Gorlois knew that something had to be done or all his men would eventually be burned alive. He had some of his troops douse the fire while he prepared the rest to fight Ambrosius outside the walls. He had most of his men form up in the tortoise formation to handle the main part of the battle while the leading troops were put in the wedge formation. His cavalry would follow from the rear to protect the flanks. The plan was brilliant in that it would allow them to cut through the main line of Ambrosius' army and still be protected from the massive onslaught of Ambrosius' archers. The highly mobile cavalry would rapidly move to wherever they were needed.

Sir Gorlois commanded his troops to begin their attack. The doors to the castle swung open and his fighters plunged out. They reached Ambrosius' leading edge of soldiers within a few yards, who were in skirmish formation. Gorlois' superior numbers at the point of attack scrambled Ambrosius' lines, allowing Gorlois to push forward with strong results, undoubtedly spurred forward with the knowledge that if they didn't overpower their enemy they had nowhere to go but back to the flaming castle behind them.

Gorlois saw an orb formation in the distance of about three hundred soldiers formed in four rows circling a tall man and about twenty archers. The soldiers in the formation had knelt to the ground, allowing the man in the center a view of the battle. Gorlois assumed the man was probably Uther, afraid to do battle with him. Gorlois looked to his rear and saw that Ambrosius' men, in tortoise formation, had cut off any return to his castle. Sir Gorlois looked around at the dead and mangled bodies of his soldiers. He changed his direction of attack toward the man he thought was Uther.

Gorlois reasoned that if he was going to die, so would Uther.

While Gorlois was changing direction, Merlin, King Uther, and Sir Ulfius arrived at the bottom of the cliffs of Tintagel Castle on Tintagel Island. Before preparing the king and Sir Ulfius, Merlin let Uther know the conditions of the farce: If successful, King Uther would give Merlin any child conceived as a result of this deed, to which King Uther, engulfed with his lust, readily agreed.

Merlin gave Uther one warning: Do not kiss Ygerna or the spell would be broken. The three men put on their masks, with a lot of help from Merlin, and walked toward the gates at Tintagel. As the men moved through the velvet darkness of the night with the only other sounds coming from the insects and an occasional owl, they could see the torches that lit the front of the castle. At the gate, the main guard recognized Sir Gorlois and his two companions, Britachis and Jordan, and let them in. The men made their way through the stone hallways and up the wide stairways to the fourth floor of the castle where Ygerna was asleep.

Merlin's thoughts turned for a moment to Adrian. The excitement of seeing a historical battle and being able to record all that was happening was a dream come true for an archeologist. Of course there was also the gore, the dismembered arms, legs, and heads, and men screaming in pain. The more Merlin thought about it, the more he suspected that Adrian would probably not want to ever return to the past.

As the men reached Ygerna and Gorlois' private quarters, Merlin grabbed King Uther's arm. "Uther," he pleaded, "it's not too late to stop this. Why don't we leave here and let this woman lie in peace?"

"Nonsense. This is my right." King Uther quietly opened the door and slid in while Merlin and Sir Ulfius stood guard outside Ygerna's door.

King Uther looked at the sleeping Ygerna as she lay in bed. There was a sheer white fabric covering the three sides of the bed and blue velvet covered the back wall. The cloth hung from four tall bedposts, each carved in an intricate design. Ygerna lay motionless before the lustful Uther. Her long brown hair spread over her pillows in a manner that framed the beauty of her face. Uther's heart pounded with excitement as he quickly removed his clothing.

Merlin partially opened the door to the bedroom and saw Uther. The High-King of the Island of the Mighty was standing totally nude, about to commit the sins of rape and adultery. What a pathetic little man, Merlin thought as he looked at the king.

Uther pulled the cover away from Ygerna and slid under it and alongside her. Uther could feel Ygerna's body heat already warming his side. He reached over and placed his hand on her chin and turned her face toward his. He looked into her eyes when she opened them. Suddenly she jumped up and started to scream, but Uther quickly put his hand over her mouth and muffled the sound. Uther whispered in such a low voice that Ygerna could not tell this was not Gorlois. "My flower, it is I, Gorlois. I have won and now we shall celebrate my love for you."

"You are safe," she cried as she flung her arms around Uther. She melted in his arms as tears of joy dropped down her cheeks. "Oh my love, how I feared the worst. Tonight we shall make love in celebration 'til the sun rises."

Merlin listened as Ygerna spoke to Uther and felt tears swell up in his eyes. This woman was truly in love with her husband. Merlin was guilt-stricken. Here he was, helping Ygerna's husband's enemy rape this beautiful lady by using his trickery. Merlin knew this was part of his mission and that Briton needed him to play his role, but it didn't make him feel any better about himself. When he couldn't listen anymore, he walked away to check the corridors for people, leaving Uther to have his way with Ygerna while her husband was fighting Ambrosious and could already be lying wounded or dead.

Uther whispered to Ygerna, "As much as my lips desire yours, tonight they must not touch. The taste of battle is something that I will not share with you."

He slowly moved his hand under her gown and moved it up her body until he could gently lift it off her. He lifted the covers, revealing the smooth, white flesh of this beautiful woman. She was undeniably more beautiful without her clothes on. She was a goddess lying there and he was about to take her. Uther caressed her as he slowly kissed his way down her body. Tenderly he moved her legs apart to make love to her.

Gorlois felt strange, Ygerna thought, as they moved passionately together. This was unlike anything she had experienced before with him. My, how the war had changed him. Her breathing intensified as every nerve in her body came alive. Maybe she could finally conceive a child from this evening of love. Suddenly she cried out as her body reached a peak of passion. She was not yet ready for Uther to leave her and was saddened when he rolled over, finished. She pushed it out of her mind as sweat poured from her body.

She turned to her loving husband and put her arms around his neck and pulled him to her for a kiss. Looking deep into his eyes while feeling the latex against her mouth, she suddenly screamed in panic, "My God, what have I done? How–? What are you doing here?"

Uther put his hand over her mouth as he heard the sound of swords clashing in the background. Merlin ran into the room and saw Uther jump out of bed. Ygerna tore Uther's mask with her fingernails and then knew that it was Uther she had made love to, not Gorlois. The thought of her husband's enemy being with her drove Ygerna mad as she screamed, "And who are you? Merlin. It has to be. Only you could have done this. You are the devil." She looked at Uther and cried, "What have you done to my husband? You've had me. Now please let him live. I'll do anything you want. Please, please let him live. I have done this. I'm no longer worthy of my husband. Please."

Ygerna, crying, begging for her husband's life, not caring about her nakedness, clung to the robe of the devil who had just raped her.

Merlin felt terrible for this noble woman. Nobility Uther could never match. This was worse than Merlin had imagined. "Uther, let's go. We have company coming," he said, hearing men running down the hall.

Uther looked down at the flower he had just plucked. As Ygerna begged for the life of her husband, he said callously, "My flower, the head of your husband shall be displayed on the spear of one of my warriors by the break of day. There's nothing anyone can do to save your husband from the destiny he brought upon himself."

Uther turned to Merlin and motioned that it was time to go. The men left the bedchamber with the sound of Ygerna's cries trailing them.

They made their way down to where Sir Ulfius was fighting with Ygerna's guards. Uther, Ulfius, and Merlin fought their way down the corridor. By the time they reached the stairs, the guards were dead. They rushed down the four flights of stairs and heard Ygerna's haunting cries following them as she cried out her husband's name . . . "Gorlois, Gorlois" . . . over and over again. The men burst through the front doors of the castle and ran as fast as they could to their waiting horses. They mounted and rode hard to join the battle that was in progress.

Chapter Nineteen

On the battlefield, General Ambrosius ordered his infantry into tortoise formation on each of Gorlois' flanks. He put his heavy cavalry–a small but effective unit–to the rear, and his skirmishers to the front. The trumpets began to play their battle tunes and all banners and flags were set out, flying in the breeze.

Gorlois' army reminded Adrian of a tube of toothpaste as he watched the battle play out before him. Ambrosius squeezed Gorlois from both sides, while his cavalry rolled up the back. And when the men were squeezed out the front, the skirmishers slaughtered them. The screams of the wounded almost drowned out the sounds of the trumpets as Ambrosius' cavalry continued squeezing Gorlois' army from the rear. The infantry doubled the pace of their attack even as they tripped over the dead and dying.

It was with deep regret that Ambrosius looked out upon the destruction of his fellow Britons.

Gorlois knew it would only be a matter of time before his

army would be destroyed. His heart ached for his beloved Ygerna, but then turned cold at the thought of Uther, cutting him off from the sounds of his wounded and terrified men, screaming in pain and fear. Sir Gorlois blinded himself from the sight of his dead and wounded friends who lay all around him, men with whom he had fought side by side in so many battles before. Only now he was fighting fellow Britons rather than outside invaders.

Gorlois focused on King Uther and his personal guards. What a coward, he thought. King Uther has surrounded himself with a special force so he won't be harmed. Jealousy stirred within him as he thought about Uther taking his wife after he'd been slain on the battlefield. Gorlois was determined that that would not happen—he might die on the battlefield, but he would take Uther with him. Gorlois had less than half his men left. He gathered together all that remained of his tattered army and ordered an all-out charge on the small force Gorlois believed surrounded Uther.

Gorlois charged like a mad man, waving sword and shield. He fought like a demon as he began to penetrate deeper and deeper into Adrian's defenses. Gorlois' soldiers were outnumbered on the battlefield overall, but they far outnumbered the force between him and the man he assumed was Uther.

General Ambrosius saw Gorlois and his men swing toward the forces guarding Adrian and realized what was happening: Gorlois had mistaken Adrian for Uther. Ambrosius remembered his promise to protect Adrian, a promise he held especially close due to his many debts to Merlin. He called out to his cavalry reserves to follow him as he led a charge in a desperate attempt to save Adrian.

Adrian saw that his guards were taking the main thrust of the counterattack from Gorlois and knew that unless help came soon, his guards would be overrun and he'd be killed or wounded. This was not supposed to happen in the relatively safe world of archeology. He didn't have a weapon other than his laser walking stick and his guards were too close for him to effectively use it without hurting one of them. He'd begun looking around for a weapon when one of the attackers broke through. Adrian's instinct for self-preservation made him put up his stick to protect himself. The attacker's sword came down on the walking stick and broke it in half. The sparks from the broken laser distracted the attacker long enough for Adrian to grab a sword from one of his fallen guards and thrust it between his attacker's ribs. Adrian spotted a shield and seized it to protect himself as the battle heaved and roiled around him.

He had had military training from his days in the Royal Army as well as the training Merlin had set up as a result of his time-travel experiences, but it was for a different kind of fight. The training for this type of warfare had not been established yet. Adrian swore that if he lived, the first thing he'd do when he got home would be to set up a training program to cover this era of combat.

Suddenly, another one of Gorlois men broke through and ran toward Adrian. Adrian put up his shield to take the main thrust of the attacker's sword and countered with a slice at the man's stomach. Adrian was lucky and slit the man's stomach with a clean stroke, spilling the unlucky soldier's insides upon the battlefield. The man looked down with his mouth open and then into Adrian's eyes. Adrian hesitated as his own tears welled up, but then he thrust his sword into his victim's heart, putting the man out of his misery as you would a dying dog.

Gorlois and ten of his men charged directly for Adrian. Sir Gorlois was determined to have Uther's head on his spear, held high for all to see. And maybe, just maybe, if he could kill Uther, he might be able to stop this battle and win. He might even be elected High-King. *That* would teach Uther. He now fought not as a man wrapped in imminent death but rather as a man who had a chance to save himself and his army by killing just one man. He watched as the first of his men reached the nobleman and were cut down, but this nobleman didn't fight like Uther–it was as though he'd never been in a battle before, Gorlois thought. How can everyone have been fooled so badly? How had Uther gotten away with his lies about beating back the Saxons? Yet, this man *was* a fighter; Gorlois watched as the man cut down another of his men, standing his ground.

Ambrosius moved as fast as he could toward Adrian, but the battle around him was slowing him down. He fought off the assaults of Gorlois' men as they tried to pull him from his horse. Ambrosius saw his reserve forces moving rapidly to the aid of Adrian's guards, but he also saw Adrian, and what he saw frightened him. Ambrosius was not going to be able to reach Adrian in time. Ambrosius was not frightened so much about what Merlin would do to him when Merlin saw the body of Adrian, lying dead on the ground. What terrified Ambrosius was the thought of letting his friend and mentor down the only time Merlin had called on him. Ambrosius knew that the only way he could save his honor would be to commit suicide if he let Adrian die.

Adrian swung his sword at another attacker and scored a direct hit. His luck was holding out thus far, but he saw several attackers breaking through and heading straight for him. Why were they out to get him? he wondered. He stood frozen in place for a moment, even though he knew it was idiotic and Gorlois' men must think they had a real fool in their sights for him to just stand there waiting for them. If he could just get his legs to move, he could get out of there and let the real fighting men take care of the battle. After all, he was just an observer, not a soldier. And besides *that*, this wasn't his fight.

Gorlois and his men finally made it to Adrian. Gorlois called out to his men to stand clear. This one was his. Through the smoke of the battlefield and with his adrenaline flowing at full speed, Gorlois had failed to recognize that his target wasn't Uther.

Ambrosius was pushing his way through the throng of men, keeping Adrian in his sight. He watched the reserves hacking away at the remnants of Gorlois' army. He suddenly spied Gorlois standing near Adrian. Gorlois had his men to his side, protecting the engagement, and his sword drawn high. Desperately urging his horse over the dead and wounded until he reached the outer circle of guards, Ambrosius shouted, "Gorlois, stop this madness. Your army's in ruins and we shall have your head if you continue."

Gorlois had but one thought in his mind as he snarled, "Victory is within my reach with the head of Uther. And now I shall have it."

Gorlois slammed his sword toward Adrian's head, but Adrian protected himself with his shield, but still felt a searing pain in his side–the more experienced warrior had been ready for the opening and had jabbed a dagger into Adrian.

Ambrosius screamed out in anguish as Adrian began to slump to the ground.

First one, then two, then three, then four of the archers protecting Adrian took aim. Ambrosius slid from his horse and ran full speed toward Gorlois, holding his sword high with both hands. Six of Gorlois' men surrounded Gorlois and the fallen Adrian with their shields held high. Gorlois slammed down his sword with both hands, aiming at Adrian's neck so he could sever Adrian's head from his shoulders.

***

Covered in sweat and dirt from their hard ride, Merlin, King Uther, and Sir Ulfius saw the fires from the funeral pyres in the distance. As they got closer, the breeze carried the smell of burning flesh to their nostrils. Soon they approached the battlefield and asked the first group of soldiers they met where General Ambrosius and his captains might be. One of the soldiers pointed to a small rise just a short distance away.

Merlin looked around at the soldiers as they went about the gruesome task of picking over the bodies of the dead, removing their equipment and valuables, then bringing them to one of the funeral pyres. Other soldiers were looking for the wounded and giving them assistance. At least they weren't putting the sword to them as they did the Germans, Merlin thought. The battlefield smell seemed worse then normal to Merlin as the men made their way around the dead and wounded and the busy soldiers on the field.

As the three got close to where Ambrosius and Adrian should be, Merlin saw the most disgusting sight he'd ever seen. Highlighted by the glow of the many battlefield fires was the head of a man on a stake. The severed head reminded Merlin of the traditions of the Celtic warriors he'd learned about, a tradition he thought had vanished with the Romans' more civilized behavior. Suddenly he recognized the face and dread spread throughout his body. Merlin looked at Uther and then at Ulfius as they all urged their horses to move faster. Merlin wiped the sweat from his brow as he moved closer and closer to the stake. Beside the stake was the lifeless, arrow-filled body of the beheaded man. Next to that was another body that Merlin recognized. His heart began to throb as he jumped from his horse and ran the last thirty feet. My God! he thought, no longer able to hold back his tears. What kind of death was this? He looked again at the head on the stake, then fell to his knees beside the wounded man.

King Uther slowly walked up behind Merlin and placed his hand on Merlin's shoulder to comfort his friend, a bit of remorse finding its way into Uther's heart. Sir Thomas and Sir Cadwellon were nearby to provide further comfort to their friend. Merlin looked up and asked if someone could get a litter so he could carry Adrian back to the lake. Merlin turned and gently held Adrian's head in his lap, relieved that his friend was still alive. Merlin examined Adrian's wounds in the light of the nearby fires and he was terribly afraid that if they didn't move soon, Adrian would join Gorlois in death. Merlin asked Sir Ambrosius to have Sir Thomas ride ahead and get Annie and their belongings to the lake. Sir Thomas and a small detachment took off across the battlefield with great speed on fresh horses.

King Uther congratulated his soldiers on their victory and offered a pardon to any of Gorlois' soldiers who swore allegiance to him. He then ordered Sir Ulfius to take the head of Sir Gorlois to the gates of Tintagel Castle and leave it there, displayed as a warning to all who would dare defy him.

Merlin overheard the king's orders and felt disgusted. Merlin knew he could never feel the same toward King Uther again. Merlin reminded King Uther that he would return in nine months for his payment. The king laughed at the thought that Merlin would know whether or not Ygerna was pregnant. Merlin gathered the earls around him and told them what had transpired. They demanded that Uther take Ygerna as his wife. The king agreed without hesitation.

Merlin and General Ambrosius prepared for the trip back to the lake. Ambrosius had grown into quite a man since he first met Merlin. He grabbed Merlin's arms. "I'm sorry about your friend. I hope you can forgive me."

"Forgive you? I just hope you can forgive me for helping that madman," Merlin said as he looked at King Uther.

The first light of morning was just beginning to shine over the desolate field as Merlin, Sir Cadwellon, General Ambrosius, and a detachment of twenty cavalrymen rode out with Adrian. The lingering smell of death followed them as the knights lined the road in honor of their leader, General Ambrosius, and the sorcerer, Merlin.

This would be one time Merlin was ready to leave.

Sir Thomas could barely keep his eyes open as the sun began to climb above the horizon. He took a small, dirty cloth from his tunic and wiped some of the sweat from his brow. This unseasonably hot day had come from nowhere. His face was almost black from the fires of the funeral pyres and the dirt and smoke of the battlefield. His horse was dragging almost as much as he was, but Sir Thomas had made a promise to Merlin, one he dare not break. Sometimes, on days like this, Sir Thomas longed for the old days as caretaker. Sir Thomas looked back at his men and saw that as bad as he was, they were in even worse shape. He kept telling himself that if he could just make it to the castle, he could take a nice bath and sleep for a few days. It was about all that kept him going.

With the sun's rise, Sir Thomas could finally see Sir Cadwellon's castle in the distance. He turned to his soldiers and pointed to it, which raised their spirits. He could feel the surge of energy as they urged their mounts to pick up the pace. Soon they reached the front gates to the castle where they all sat up in their saddles, entering the walls as conquering heroes.

Once through the gates and into the courtyard, they dismounted and handed their horse's reins to the waiting stable hands. Sir Thomas could barely walk as he struggled to find his remaining strength. He forced himself to move so he could find Annie and tell her about Adrian.

It was still early in the morning when the attendant went in to wake Annie; she certainly wasn't ready to get up yet. The attendant urged Annie to get up and get dressed. Annie was a bit startled but did as she was asked. The attendant added even more urgency by saying something had happened and she was needed downstairs immediately. Annie, now alarmed, grabbed her clothes and threw them on, missing a fastener here and there. The attendant came up behind her and started redoing her fasteners. As soon as she was dressed, Annie ran down the stairs, where she saw a filthy Sir Thomas looking like he was about to fall over.

Sir Thomas looked down at the floor and then at Annie. He told her about Adrian and that Merlin wanted her to get their things together and get to the lake as fast as she could.

Annie turned to Sir Thomas and asked him to prepare some horses and an escort to take them to the lake. Although Sir Thomas was about to drop, he told Annie that he would accompany her as soon as he could get some fresh horses. He would also get a couple of the guards from the castle to go along with them. He didn't want to take his men who had accompanied him back to the castle because they were totally exhausted.

By the time Annie had gathered all their meager belongings, Sir Thomas had the horses and escorts ready to go. Everyone mounted their horses and rode as fast as they could. Annie was in a near panic as she said to Sir Thomas, "Will Adrian live, do you think?"

Sir Thomas looked at Annie and replied, "I do not know, but we need to be prepared for your departure by the time Merlin arrives."

***

The sun beat down on Merlin's back as he neared the lake. With the sudden change in temperature, Merlin wished he hadn't had the brilliant idea of wearing long-johns. He had never been this tired in his life. He looked at Ambrosius and saw that as tired as he was, it was nothing compared to what Ambrosius was feeling. Merlin looked down at Adrian, wishing they could somehow hurry up but knowing it would hurt Adrian even more.

Ambrosius told Merlin about what happened to Adrian. He told Merlin about how Gorlois had changed the direction of his attack in an effort to get Adrian. Gorlois apparently thought Adrian was Uther, which was what they had wanted to happen, never contemplating an attack on Adrian's position. Adrian fought like a warrior but was knocked to the ground. Gorlois was coming down with his sword, aimed at Adrian's head when Adrian managed to use his feet–Merlin said a silent prayer of thanks for Adrian's martial arts training–to knock Gorlois off balance. Four archers fired their arrows at about that moment, hitting Gorlois with deadly accuracy just as Ambrosius made contact with Gorlois' neck, cutting his head off.

Merlin spotted the lake and pushed his horse forward. Annie had not yet arrived, so Merlin slid from his horse, content to just sit and rest a bit until she did. Merlin had ridden horses while growing up in Texas and just couldn't get accustom to saddles without stirrups. The rest of the troop practically fell from their horses, almost falling asleep where they landed.

Before Merlin could relax, he checked out Adrian. Adrian's litter was red and his face was pale from the loss of blood. Merlin cleaned the wound as best he could before he nodded off, which he thought was only for a second when he was drawn back to consciousness by familiar voices. He struggled to focus and when he did, he saw Sir Thomas helping Annie set up a pool in the lake. Merlin struggled to his feet and then he woke up Ambrosius and Cadwellon. Merlin saw that although Annie was trying to be strong, Adrian's injury was having a bad effect on her. He gathered all their belongings and put them in the three bags.

Merlin told Annie to go first and get some help. Annie leaned over and gave Adrian a passionate kiss, one he would never know of. Merlin took his laser and soon the wormhole was formed and Annie was gone.

Merlin said goodbye to his friends and told them he would return in a few months; he kept it to himself that he would be coming to claim Uther and Ygerna's child. He also warned them to stay back from the pool because it would vanish once he disappeared and could injure or kill them if they were too close. Sir Thomas and General Ambrosius wouldn't let anyone but themselves help Merlin with Adrian. Merlin told Ambrosius not to blame himself, and then he and Adrian vanished.

Chapter Twenty

Merlin and Adrian appeared in the pool just as the medics arrived. What a change in temperature . . . they had just left the unseasonably warm weather of the past and were met by a cold front as they emerged from the chilly pool. An emergency medical team was always standing by now; this time they would earn their pay.

Annie looked at her friend. “Merlin, you’re exhausted. You can’t do any more here. I’ve called Vivian; she’ll be here soon. Why don’t you go take a shower and get some rest? I’ll wake you as soon as we know something.”

Merlin agreed and hurried to his office to get cleaned up. As he was walking toward the trailer, it dawned on him that construction had begun on a large building next to the lake. In fact, it was almost halfway finished. He looked at the date and saw that he’d been gone for two months. Oh well, he thought, I’ll worry about it later.

Hours later, Vivian entered Merlin’s office and nudged him awake. She didn’t want sex this time. She had news about

Adrian. Merlin opened his eyes to see the one woman he truly loved. Vivian brushed back his scraggly hair and sat down beside him. "Adrian's still weak, but he's going to be okay."

Merlin slowly sat up in bed; he was still exhausted from his ordeal. "How's Annie?"

"She's okay. She's with Adrian now. I asked her about what happened, but she says she doesn't really know the whole story. What went on back there?"

Merlin rubbed his eyes to get the vestiges of sleep out. He got up and put away the folding bed in total silence. Vivian stayed quiet as Merlin looked for the words to describe what went on. Then he sat down and told Vivian all the details he knew about Uther and Adrian. "Vivian, with the risk we've taken, I see another problem we need to solve: We need some type of device that will let you know when we're in trouble."

"What do you mean?"

"Well, when Adrian had his laser destroyed in the battle, he could have been lost in time forever, or died of his wounds had we not brought him back here. Fortunately, I was there with my laser so we could return. But what if I wasn't there? What if there was only one of us back in time and something happened? Can you do it?"

"I don't know, but it's something I can work on. Off the top of my head I guess it needs to be a small device that can fit into your pocket-bags or into a piece of equipment. I'll work on it for you and see what I can come up with. But first, how do you feel about getting something to eat?"

"God, I thought you'd never ask."

"I'll go get everyone and be right back." Vivian left and came back a few minutes later with Annie, Lance, and a couple of other people. "You ready to go?"

Merlin stood up from the couch and turned to see Chac

and Quetzal standing in front of him with big smiles. Merlin hugged the two men he hadn't seen for so long.

Chac was the first to speak. He gave Merlin a big laugh. "It's great to see you, you look terrible."

"Well, thanks a lot. It's good to see you too," Merlin said, returning the laugh. "What are you guys doing here?"

"Let's talk over dinner," Annie said. "I'm starved."

The six team leaders piled into the Suburban and headed down the slick highway for the steakhouse. Merlin told them the story about Uther, then about Adrian. The team was impressed by how Adrian had handled himself in battle. Vivian told Merlin and Annie about how Bill decided to bring in Chac and Quetzal to handle things if she and Lance had gone to find Merlin, Annie, and Adrian. They talked about other problems beyond the one Merlin had already assigned to Vivian. The most important was a means to communicate over a long distance should a problem arise and more than one person was back in time and were separated from each other. Fortunately, Vivian had recently solved the problem of operating the laser without the use of sunlight, which would greatly advance the safety of the work.

After a long dinner, and even longer discussion, the team went back to the research center. They checked in on Adrian, then went their separate ways. Vivian and Merlin went back to their cottage where Shadow went nuts when he saw Merlin. Shadow was almost his full size now and practically knocked Merlin over. The two rolled around on the floor for a few minutes before Shadow finally settled down.

Vivian grabbed a bottle of wine while Merlin put some quiet music on. They sat down on the sofa and enjoyed their wine while they talked. Merlin said, "I need to go back pretty soon."

"Why? You just got home."

"I'm worried about something happening to Arthur. Uther's just too unstable. Besides, I've got to make sure he lives up to his word and marries Ygerna."

Vivian put her glass down as she leaned over to kiss Merlin. Vivian tilted her head and gave Merlin a sly smile. "We've still got tonight."

The two began to caress each other intensely. Their lips barely parted as they pulled their tops off. Merlin fumbled with Vivian's bra strap and they barely heard the dog barking. Suddenly the bells they were hearing were no longer in their minds as the doorbell ringing turned to loud knocking. The knocking turned to yelling. They recognized Annie's voice.

"Not again," Vivian said, sighing.

Merlin answered the door just as Vivian was pulling down her blouse. Annie shook her head and smiled. "I can't leave you two alone for a minute. Speaking of which, Chac, get in here."

Chac walked in with a suitcase in his hand. He shuffled his feet as Annie said, "Some idiot put Chac and Quetzal in the same apartment. The police called and asked me to pick this one up. Seems they're trying to kill each other."

Merlin looked at Chac and threw his arms in the air. "What the hell?"

"Yeah, well," said Annie. "Looks like you've got a roommate, Merlin."

"Great," said a disappointed Merlin. "Well, shut the door and get in here; you're letting the cold air in. You can put your stuff in there," he said, pointing to his bedroom.

Merlin took the next few days off to try to find Chac another place to live–he wanted a little privacy at home with Vivian–but none were available at the time.

Chac and Quetzal began their training and each was assigned duties within the research center. Quetzal became the number two man in charge of security while Chac went to work overseeing the construction.

Merlin wasn't going to be gone for long on his next trip, so he didn't take but two bags with him. He told himself that nothing could happen on this jump. Then he remembered that he'd thought the same thing on his past jumps, too. Shrugging, he grabbed the two bags, thankful to leave the cart behind and jumped back in time again.

Chapter Twenty-One

He looked around through the misty morning air and took off on foot toward Glevum and Sir Cadwellon's castle. Merlin had made this trip many times by now and looked forward to seeing Sir Thomas and Earl Cadwellon. Merlin thought about the first time he'd traveled this road and the apprehension he'd felt. Now he walked with total confidence as he hurried along the miles to the castle.

He was soon at the gates of the castle and the guards escorted him right in. Merlin saw his friends and he told Sir Cadwellon that he needed a horse for his trip to Londinium. Sir Thomas offered to accompany him on his journey, but this was one mission that Merlin was going to have to accomplish on his own.

He left early the next day, which proved to be a cool, spring day, and made great time in getting to Londinium. Two days later, he was crossing the bridge into the city and on his way to see King Uther. He entered the palace and told them who he was and was immediately escorted to see the king.

As Merlin entered the reception hall, King Uther rose and walked toward Merlin with his arms out. He gave Merlin a bear hug and kissed him lightly on both cheeks before saying, "Merlin, I wondered if I would ever see you again. I knew you were not pleased with me when you left. How is your friend? Adrian, isn't it?"

"He'll be fine. Did you and Ygerna get married?"

"Yes. She's upstairs. She'll be down in a minute. She's taking care of my son."

"Son?" said Merlin.

"Yes. I have an heir."

"Is your son in good health?"

The king slumped his shoulders. "Your presence here reminds me of the devilish deed I did."

Merlin looked at King Uther and wondered if there had been a real change in the king. "And so you should be reminded of your actions. I hope you're not asking for my forgiveness."

"No." The king sighed deeply. "No, only God can forgive me. And I believe that's too much to even ask him for. General Ambrosius told me about the prophecy you foretold to Vortigern. Perhaps you can grant me one."

Merlin looked at the king for a moment, rubbing his beard; his nose began to itch from the whiskers touching it. He moved his eyes closer together for a moment and said, "Uther, it's true that Vortigern asked for a prophecy. But what I told Vortigern was not a prophecy. It was a metaphor for the truth. It is also true that what I told Vortigern had not occurred at that time but would occur in the future. So I cannot give you a prophecy any more than I could Vortigern."

"I am confused. Are you telling me that you somehow know what the future holds? How is that not telling a prophecy?"

"I'm sure you would agree that things are what they are, based upon one's perspective. From my perspective, what I told Vortigern was the past. From Vortigern's perspective, what he heard was the future."

"I'm not sure I understand."

"It's not that you don't understand; it's that you don't comprehend. You have always thought that you are the red dragon from the story. Correct?"

"Yes. That's correct."

"Well, you're not. But the red dragon lives."

"Oh really. And just who might this red dragon be?"

"Your son. That's why I'm here. I must take your son so he will not be corrupted. This nation will rise and he will help your nation not once, but twice. My purpose in visiting your land has always been to help him in his quest."

"You're not really going to take my son, are you? You can't. I won't let you, Merlin. He's all I have with Ygerna. You simply can't do this."

"What you did with Ygerna served its purpose. Now I must move to the next step. But, do not fear, dear king. You would never have lived to see him grow anyway. Your suffering is soon to end."

"Do you mean to kill me?"

"No. I would never do that. You see, from my perspective, you died long ago."

"I do not understand."

"Nor will you ever. I did not want to help you commit your evil deed with Ygerna, but I had to help you so that your son would be born. You did what you were destined to do. I helped you achieve your destiny. Now I must take your son, so that he too may fulfill his destiny as the future King of Briton."

Merlin took Arthur from the arms of the grieving Ygerna.

Ygerna hated Merlin: He had helped Uther rape her and now he was taking her only child, the future King of The Island of The Mighty.

Merlin left Londinium and traveled with the baby Arthur to Caer Gai and Sir Ector's castle. This was Merlin's first visit to Sir Ector's castle and he was looking forward to it. He arrived at the castle in only a few days and was greeted at the gate by a guard who did not recognize the great Merlin the Sorcerer.

"I'm here to see Sir Ector," Merlin said.

The guard looked down at the scraggly-looking man with a baby in his arms and asked rudely, "And what makes you think that my lord desires an audience with the likes of you?"

"Perhaps if you will tell him that a friend awaits, he might take it upon himself to have this audience," Merlin said, impatient with this fool.

The guard was not impressed and raised his bow to show Merlin his authority. "I have no interest in disturbing Sir Ector at the request of a beggar."

"A beggar?" Merlin was growing tired of this little man. "I have no interest in bringing harm to you. If you will please get Sir Ector I'm certain he'll reward you."

The guard drew back on his bow and let go an arrow that landed in the dirt near the hooves of Merlin's horse. "Be off with you or the next one will find its mark."

"Are you really that big a fool?" Merlin removed the cover of his laser. He said under his breath, "I was hoping I wouldn't have to fight anyone for once." He aimed the laser near the guard and let go a short burst.

The guard jumped back from the laser shot and began to put another arrow in his bow. Sir Ector came running to the rampart to see what was going on, looked over the edge and then back at the guard. He gently put his hand on the man's arm and pushed the guard's bow down. Ector said, "I don't think that would be a wise move. Merlin could destroy this entire castle if he so desired."

"Merlin!" said the astonished guard. "No. It cannot be. Merlin is a giant. Merlin is a nobleman. This is a beggar."

Sir Ector smiled, knowing the danger had passed. "I don't think I'd be calling Merlin the Sorcerer a beggar. You might raise his ire."

Suddenly nervous, the guard ran from the ramparts to open the gate for Merlin. Sir Ector couldn't help but laugh at the sight. The guard opened the gate and ran to Merlin. "Oh please, great wizard. Please forgive my ignorance. It's just that–"

"That's enough groveling," Merlin said as he pushed the man aside and entered through the gate. Sir Ector was at the gate, still laughing. Merlin looked at his friend and found that he too could no longer hold back a laugh. He said, "Ector. We need to talk."

Ector looked at what Merlin was carrying. "Has it something to do with the bundle you hold?"

"It does. Now where are we going to talk?"

Sir Ector walked with a slight limp as he led Merlin inside his castle. The two men entered the drawing room and Sir Ector asked the servant for some refreshments for the two of them. As they were served, Merlin realized that he was very hungry. As he ate, Merlin asked, "How does your leg?"

"It is fine, thanks to you. And how is your friend?"

"Fine. I'm here to ask you to pay a debt you owe me."

"And what debt is that?"

"Your life." Merlin said in a matter-of-fact tone.

"I see. And what is it that you would have me do?"

"This child I have is important to Briton. I ask that you raise him as your own."

"Whose child is he?"

"He is the child of Briton. All will be revealed in time. Will you do it?"

"Merlin. As you say. I owe you my life. Whatever you ask of me, I will happily comply."

"I will promise you this: One day I will reveal to you who this child is. In the time between then and now, I ask that you treat him and raise him as you would your own. Oh yes, the boy's name is Arthur."

Merlin spent a few days with Sir Ector and his wife getting to know them a little better. Merlin liked them both and would have spent more time with them except for the need to get home. The castle grounds were full of wonders: He particularly loved the butterflies–"flutter-bys," as they were known as at the time, which seem far more apt to Merlin–that danced about the castle's colorful garden. This was the perfect time of year to be in Briton.

Merlin built a permanent pool that looked like a well in a nearby forest. This would allow him to come and go a little easier. He asked Sir Ector to keep people out of the immediate area of the pool, but he also said that the child should be allowed to play there so Merlin could talk with him from time to time.

Chapter Twenty-Two

After constructing the pool, Merlin used his laser to create a wormhole and once again he found himself in his own time. He marked the spot where he returned so he could have another pool built exactly there, thus allowing him easy access in both directions. Fortunately, he had researched Caer Gai's location prior to the jump and knew he would be in the vicinity of Cowbridge, Wales, when he came back to his own time. He activated his GPS program and received a call on his cell phone within a couple of minutes, confirming that he had returned.

Cowbridge wasn't far from the research center, so it wasn't long before the helicopter arrived to pick him up. The team leaders met Merlin when he landed and he told them that he had picked up Arthur and the boy was safe with Sir Ector. Then he assigned Chac the task of constructing a small jump pond with one small temporary building at the site in Cowbridge so Merlin could check up on Arthur as the boy grew up. It was Merlin's intent to give Arthur special instruction on how to be a good king in order that Merlin might prevent Arthur from acquiring the taste for rape from his father, King Uther.

Vivian wasn't in Gloucester to greet Merlin this time; she had returned to Vint Hill Farms Station to work on developing a device that could be thrown into a time travel pool and returned to the present with an alert. Vivian believed they needed this in case an emergency came up that could endanger her love.

Merlin wasn't as worn out as he had been on his past trips as this one had been relatively short, which gave him the chance to spend a lot of time with Shadow while Chac and Vivian were gone. Shadow loved the attention Merlin gave him, something the others didn't do much of. Merlin even took time to drive to Scotland for a few days with Shadow and run up and down the mountains there. The two loved playing fetch in the cool air of the Scottish Highlands.

The contrast between Merlin's world in the fifth century and his world in the twenty-first century was one that he couldn't help continually comparing. One day he would be in the midst of kings, advising them on their war plans or how to take care of the infrastructure of their kingdom and the next he was buying eggs at the grocery store or playing ball with Shadow.

Merlin was playing in his front yard with Shadow when Adrian drove up. Adrian almost jumped out of his car before it had come to a stop. He pushed the door open and ran to Merlin, holding up a large manila envelope. Merlin put his arms out to stop Adrian. "Hold up there. What's got your dander up?"

The big man tried to catch his breath for a moment before saying, "We've got a package from Vivian. It's software and you're not going to believe what it does."

"Okay. I give. What is it?"

"It's the software for the nano robots."

"Okay. So what's the big deal?"

Adrian was still trying to catch his breath as he said, "My boy, this is the software that will allow us to program nanorobots to weaken the molecular structure of rock. This makes the whole sword thing possible!"

Merlin put Shadow up and grabbed a few things for his trip to London. Adrian promised to take care of Shadow since both Chac and Vivian were gone. Early the next morning, Merlin found himself outside the gates of Windsor Castle. The king had been notified that a mission would be leaving from there and came down to wish Merlin well. This was the first time he had seen Merlin in a while and insisted upon the two of them having breakfast together before Merlin left.

After a nice breakfast and conversation, Merlin went to the time pool and his jump to the past. He had calculated a time that should get him there just after King Uther had died. But there was no way to insure that because the dates they had were just guesses and most of the events were legends that might–or might not–be true. The least likely legend was the one related to the sword in the stone, so Merlin didn't have a lot of faith in this jump.

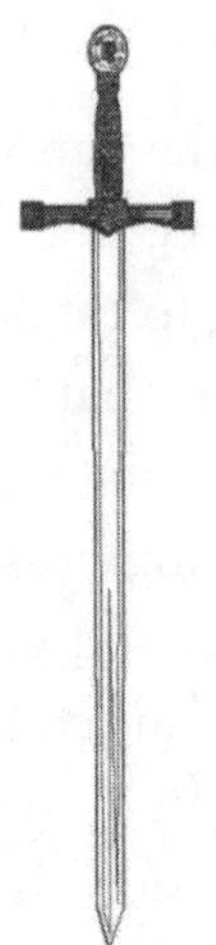

Chapter Twenty-Three

It wasn't long before Merlin found himself back in old Briton. He began walking the same route he took with Annie and Adrian to Londinium. The walk seemed much shorter than before, perhaps because his rubber-necking friends weren't there to hold him up. Soon he was walking across the bridge to Londinium and down the road to the palace. He noticed a lot of commotion outside the palace when he spotted Sir Thomas.

"What's going on?"

"Merlin! It is good to see you again," said an elated Sir Thomas. "We're getting ready for battle."

"Battle? What battle?"

"The Saxons are invading at Verulamium. Sir Lot led a small force to stop them but was turned back. It's now up to King Uther and General Ambrosius to get the job done."

Merlin remembered from his research that Verulamium had been a Roman fort near what was today St. Albans in Hertfordshire. "Uther's alive?"

"Why yes. Of course he is."

"Take me to him and I'll see if I can help him."

Sir Thomas took Merlin into the palace and to the drawing room where Uther was conferring with his battle captains. Uther spotted him and ran to embrace him. "It's good to see you. I believe we can win the battle without you, but with your help I know we will win." King Uther pulled Merlin away from the rest of the men in the room and whispered to Merlin, "My son. How is he?"

Merlin looked at the man before him with a bit of sadness. He knew his fate and wished he could tell him more about what was going to happen and about the current health of his son. Unfortunately, he could do neither. Merlin said, "I haven't seen your son for two years. But I know he'll be fine. I intend to provide him with some special instruction that I hope will make him a great king. How's your relationship with Ygerna progressing?"

"Sadly, it is not progressing at all. I do not hold it against her after what I did to her; I can't blame her. Other than the one time at Tintagel, we have never lain together in bed." The king's face suddenly lit up at a new thought. "Merlin, you told me the last time we were together that events that are to come are your past. Tell me please, am I to win this battle?"

"You may move forward with the knowledge that the battle will be won and your soldiers will never again be engaged in battle during your reign."

The king smiled as he stroked his beard. At first glance, the story brought great encouragement to the king, but this king was no dim-witted Vortigern. Uther looked at Merlin. "Are you telling me that this will halt the invasions of Briton or are you telling me that I am about to die in battle?"

Merlin didn't want to tell the king what was to happen because it could have the effect of changing history, yet he didn't want to lie to the king either. "You will not be killed in battle and one day your son will become the most loved king in history."

The king knew there was more to the story than Merlin was willing to tell but he satisfied himself with the knowledge that he was about to be victorious. General Ambrosius called the troops together and soon they were off to do battle with the Saxons. This was supposed to be a simple trip for Merlin, but he'd grown accustomed to the unexpected.

As the army neared Verulamium, General Ambrosius sent scouts ahead to determine as much as they could about the waiting Saxon army. The Saxons were feeling confident of victory after defeating Sir Lot's forces and were ill-prepared for King Uther's much larger army. The battle was a quick one with the archers making mincemeat out of the Saxons. The infantry moved forward in a wedge formation and the cavalry divided and covered the two flanks. The entire battle took only a few hours, which Merlin was grateful for, and the victory was total. The only problem was the heat; it was the hottest day Merlin had ever encountered while visiting the past.

As soon as the battle was over, the soldiers and officers plunged into the nearby streams to refresh themselves, leaving only Merlin, Sir Thomas, General Ambrosius, and a few hundred of the men who had been held in reserve to clean up the battlefield. As the funeral pyres were being lighted, one of the cavalry officers came riding hard to where Merlin, Sir Thomas, and General Ambrosius sat. The three men looked up at the panicked officer as he slid from his horse. The man bent over at the waist as he struggled to get to them. Sir Thomas and Merlin got up and ran to where the man struggled.

Sir Thomas asked, "What is it that would so panic you after such a great victory? Is there another Saxon army coming toward us?"

The man fell to the ground, with no apparent wounds. He began to vomit blood and could barely speak but managed to say as he gasped for air, "The water. The water. King."

The cavalryman fell silent. Merlin checked for a pulse: none. He looked at General Ambrosius. "He's dead. I think he was poisoned." Then he added under his breath, "And so it begins."

General Ambrosius ran to his horse and cried out, "The king; I must see the king. Sir Thomas, keep everyone away from the water."

Sir Thomas ran to his horse and quickly mounted. He rode to tell the remaining soldiers not to go near the water. Merlin knew what was going on and was well aware that there would be nothing he would be able to do to save the men at the stream, including King Uther.

Moments later, General Ambrosius returned with his head low, tears streaming down his cheeks. He slid from his horse and could barely walk as he shook his head over and over again saying, "They're dead. They're all dead."

"And the king?" Merlin knew the answer but felt he must hear it from Ambrosius.

"They're all dead. King Uther too," Ambrosius confirmed.

Merlin mounted his horse and the two of them gathered as many of the remaining soldiers as possible to clean up the dead from the water. Sir Thomas found King Uther and called Merlin over. Beside the king was his powerful sword, Caliburn, the Sword of Briton. Merlin retrieved the bloodied sword and called General Ambrosius over for a council. Merlin told his friend that it would be important for Ambrosius to rebuild the army as quickly as possible. The earls might begin fighting among themselves, as there was no apparent heir. Merlin would do what he could to keep things calm, but a strong army would be needed to prevent outsiders from interfering.

Merlin and Sir Thomas rode ahead to bring the news to Ygerna and to call the earls into council in hopes of heading off a civil war. They reached Londinium quickly and headed directly to the palace. Once inside, Ygerna at first refused to meet with Merlin due to her terrible dislike for him, but finally, after much effort, she agreed to grant an audience. Merlin told her of the death of her husband. She stood motionless for a moment without a tear forming in her eyes. Her greatest concern was for herself, as she had no love at all for Uther.

Merlin now had to do something to keep Briton whole until Arthur was ready to assume the role of Riothomus. He grabbed Sir Thomas and the two of them took off to a small church–which Merlin knew would one day be the site of the great Canterbury Cathedral–to pay a visit to its priest, Bishop Dyfrig. There was a large stone in front of the church. Merlin removed from his bag the vial of nano robots that had been programmed for this special mission. He poured some of them onto the stone and within a few minutes, the center of the stone became weak. Merlin inserted Caliburn into the stone until just the hilt and six inches of silver blade remained exposed as a speechless Sir Thomas looked on. Merlin removed another vial containing nano robots programmed to strengthen the stone and poured it around the area holding the sword.

The two men then entered the church and sought out Bishop Dyfrig. Upon spotting the Bishop, a rather plump man, Merlin called out to him saying, "Bishop Dyfrig, it's me, Merlin."

The good bishop turned to see the rugged-looking Merlin and Sir Thomas walking toward him. The bishop held up his hand upon recognizing them and walked slowly and steadily toward them. "Merlin. It's so nice to see you. What brings this honor to me?"

"King Uther has died and I'm here to attempt to prevent a civil war prior to a new king being named."

"The king is dead? Oh my Lord. And how do you propose to prevent a civil war?"

"I will invite all the earls to Londinium to sit in council with me at the Round Table."

Anguished, the Bishop wrung his hands. "I don't see how that will help. But what is more important, the Round Table is no longer in Londinium."

"What do you mean, it's not in Londinium? Where is it?"

Bishop Dyfrig shrugged his shoulders "The last I heard King Uther had given it to Sir Laodegan, Earl of Cameliard."

Merlin grew angry at the thought of Uther giving away a gift he'd had made for him and which served such a noble purpose. He squinted his eyes and frowned at the poor bishop. "Why in the world would Uther do some fool thing like that?"

"Merlin, calm yourself. There is nothing to be gained by focusing your anger upon a dead man. The reason King Uther gave away the table is that he believed there would be no challenges to him from anyone because of your support; the earls are afraid of you. King Uther also believed he could do anything he wanted to, so why have council with the earls?"

"Why that conceited–"

The good bishop interrupted again by saying, "Now Merlin. I insist that you calm down. This is the House of the Lord, you know."

"I'm sorry. You're right. But we've got to do something." Merlin frowned again as he thought for a minute.

"Why don't you invite the earls to Londinium and meet with them here? But what are you going to say that will halt a war?"

"I put Caliburn, King Uther's sword, into the rock outside your church. I'll just tell them that the one who can remove the sword from the stone will be the new and true Riothomus of Briton."

The surprised bishop said, "You did what?!"

Merlin waved his hand in a matter-of-fact way. "I put the sword in the stone that's outside your door."

"And how did you do that?" The bishop also waved his hands in the air, but not matter-of-factly. "No. I don't want to know. Please do not tell me about what must have involved sorcery."

Merlin sent word to all the earls notifying them of the death of King Uther and to inform them of the date of the council meeting regarding the selection of the new king. He asked Sir Laodegan to return the Round Table to Londinium.

Within a few days the city of Londinium was packed with noblemen and their entourages. Of special interest to Merlin were Sir Ector, Sir Cadwellon, and Sir Laodegan.

The first one Merlin saw was Sir Ector. He checked up on how Arthur was doing and asked that the relationship between them remain a secret. He then found Sir Cadwellon talking with Sir Thomas and General Ambrosius. After a bit of small talk he began looking for Sir Laodegan and learned that the man wasn't going to attend the council–he was afraid of what Merlin would do to him for accepting the Round Table from King Uther, a thought that had only briefly crossed Merlin's mind.

It came time for the meeting and each of the earls passed the sword in the stone on their way into the church. Merlin watched the earls as they stood around talking to each other. The scene reminded Merlin of old-fashion politics back home, only back home was about fifteen hundred years into the future.

Things began to settle down as Bishop Dyfrig asked the men to take their seats. Soon some of the earls began shouting for an election to be held while others began arguing about who should be the next Riothomus. A few threatened war and wanted the decision to be made at the end of a sword. The good bishop called the men to order once again and asked them to restrain themselves while in the house of the Lord. He turned the meeting over to Merlin, which immediately hushed the crowd.

Merlin rose and walked to the front of the sanctuary, holding his laser walking stick. He pulled his worn, brown leather hood back and began to speak. "Britons, I shall not allow this squabbling. You have lost your king in the defense of your nation–"

"Yes! We have lost *our* king, not *your* king. And we must get on with our business," said one of the earls in the back of the room who was careful not to reveal his identity.

Merlin's forehead wrinkled with his frown. He said, "I will tell you how you will determine the next king and you *will* go along with my wishes or I will take retribution upon you, your families, your castles, your lands, and anything else I can find. Do any of you have any doubts that I can do this?"

Silence.

Merlin explained that whosoever pulled the sword from the stone would be named High-King of Briton and would have Merlin's full support and protection. At once, all the earls lined up to take a turn with the sword, but no one prevailed. Many wondered if Sir Laodegan would be the one who would ultimately pull it out, since he was the only Earl not present. There was much quibbling among the earls about the fact that there was no High-King. They decided by majority vote that they would all return to their old title of Early-King until such time as a new High-King came forward. Merlin agreed to this and told the men that General Ambrosius would continue to handle invasions and patrols and that taxes would continue to be collected to support the defense and the administration of the central government.

The time finally arrived for Merlin to say goodbye to his friends in old Briton and return to his own time. This time he walked to the location that would return him to London and the current King Arthur.

Chapter Twenty-Four

The king was waiting for some news from Merlin and had placed a guard at the pool so he could be informed of Merlin's return. The guard greeted Merlin just as the fog was being cut away by the morning sun. They called King Arthur II to inform him that Merlin had arrived. The two men entered Windsor Castle, where King Arthur II met them and invited Merlin into the drawing room for refreshments and a bit of conversation.

Merlin wasn't in a mood for much conversation, though he always enjoyed his visits with the king. Despite his fatigue, he took the time to describe his last jump, including the battle that resulted in King Uther's death and his putting the sword in the stone. At the end of the conversation, the king provided Merlin with transportation to the Gloucester Research Center.

Merlin called Adrian to let him know he was back and then had the king's driver take him to his cottage. He could hear Shadow barking as he exited the limousine, which encouraged Merlin to hurry to the door so he could see his friend. When he opened the door, Shadow stood in the entryway wagging his big tail and smiling with his eyes. Merlin put his bag down and grabbed his big dog and gave Shadow a hug.

Merlin quickly changed into a jogging outfit so he could take Shadow for a walk. Merlin was stopped several doors down from his cottage by a neighbor who asked him what kind of work he did. Merlin asked why the neighbor wanted to know. The neighbor said–just only slightly embarrassed–that it seemed odd that a man groomed the way Merlin was, with long hair and a beard and at times dressed like a beggar, would be dropped off by the king's limousine driver.

It wasn't long before Chac had a temporary facility ready at Cowbridge for Merlin's jumps to help Arthur. The trips to Cowbridge were judged to be quite tame, thus a few of the other members of the team would be able to go on some of these trips to gain valuable experience for future jumps in both Briton and Mexico.

Merlin decided that his next jump should be by himself and at a time when Arthur would be old enough to understand what Merlin was talking about. The time selected was eight years after Merlin had dropped Arthur off at Sir Ector's castle. Everything was prepared and the security staff cordoned off the area so no outsiders would be able to see or interfere with the mission.

Merlin took out his laser stick and stepped into the wormhole and his ride to the past. After the swirling stopped, he looked around at his eerie-looking surroundings; the mist and fog covering the small clearing and nearby woods gave him the impression he was in the middle of an old B-movie. Of course, being Merlin the Sorcerer, he had nothing to fear. Right. Merlin set up a small tent in case the weather turned bad. He then put away his supplies and gathered wood for a fire. He dug a small pit and carefully arranged some stones around it. He took out a pot and filled it with water he had brought with him. He lit the fire and put some beans into the pot. Then he took out a coffee pot and filled it with water and coffee and put it on the fire. He found a large rock that would work perfectly as a seat and moved it close to the fire. He stood in front of the fire for a moment and admired his handiwork.

It wasn't long before Merlin heard the sound of someone's feet crushing the weeds as he walked. Merlin turned to find a small boy staring up at him. Merlin stroked his chin. "What have we here? You're a rather strange-looking deer. Oh well, I think you'll fit nicely into my pot."

The young boy seemed amused at Merlin's words and replied innocently, "I'm not a deer."

"Well, if you're not a deer, just what are you?"

"I'm a boy."

"And what is your name, boy?"

"My name is Arthur."

"Well, Arthur, why don't you join me over here by the fire and we can share some beans."

So at last Merlin was face to face with King Arthur, though the king didn't know his future as of yet. The two sat and talked for a couple of hours. Merlin told Arthur that he wanted to spend some time with him to teach him the ways of the world, how to fight, and how to deal with people. Arthur was a young boy at this time but still thought it odd that this stranger wanted to do so much for him.

Merlin spent a lot of time in the past over the next few months teaching and training Arthur. Even though he timed his arrivals one month apart, he was actually going back almost every other day. He managed to take back several of the team members so they could gain some experience in time travel. Of course the jumps made by Chac and Quetzal were their first.

After only a few months, Arthur had reached the age of twelve. He had grown accustomed to Merlin's visits, but on this one he found Merlin sitting on his rock by his campfire slicing an apple and eating it. "What's that you're eating?" Arthur asked.

"It's an apple. Would you like a taste?" Merlin cut off a slice and handed it to Arthur. As Arthur ate the slice of apple Merlin asked, "Is this the first apple you've had?"

"No, but I've never had one so delicious."

Merlin had a great interest in helping Arthur to be a different type of king than Vortigern or Uther. Merlin wanted Arthur to care about his people and for the people to care about Arthur. Merlin sat back on his rock. "Arthur, today I'd like to tell you a story of a man named John Chapman. John was a man in my land who entered the wilderness and cleared land for an orchard. He would plant apple seeds and as settlers entered the area he would sell these apple trees for a small amount of money or trade them for supplies. If they couldn't pay him, he would give them the trees with the idea that they would pay for them when they could. The settlers loved John, or Johnny Appleseed as he was called, and they would do anything they could for this kind man. I would like to see you become this type of man, one who cares about others, regardless of their station in life. If you do this, everyone in your nation will love you."

Arthur seemed to get the message Merlin gave him, but a question came to mind. "I will think on what you have said, but this place of apples you come from . . . this Avalon. Where is it?"

Merlin's mouth dropped open and his eyes grew wide. "What did you just say?"

"This Avalon. Where is it?"

Merlin sighed as he thought about how things just seemed to fit together at times. Rather than resist it, he said, "Across the sea."

"Is that where you go when you disappear in the well?"

"No."

"Do you ever return to Avalon?"

"At times."

"Where do you go when you leave here?"

"I go to another world."

"Please, tell me about your Otherworld. Do you have castles like we have here?"

"We have castles, but they're made of glass, which is a material not much thicker than cloth that one can see through. It's a beautiful world." Merlin looked to the sky and became a bit homesick. He knew he'd be home within a few hours, but his stays at home weren't long and Merlin longed for some time where he could just stay at home, with Vivian and Shadow.

"May I go with you and visit your land?"

"One day you may come with me. It'll be when you're in the most trouble. But you should know that people who visit my world from yours may never return."

He had something new and unusual to report when he got home after that visit: He had discovered the source of the terms "Avalon" and "Otherworld," and he was that source. Merlin also learned that Vivian was almost finished with her work at the Vint Hill Farms Station and she expected to be back in England within two months. By Merlin's calculation that would mean Vivian would arrive about the time he was finished with Arthur's lessons.

***

One day after Arthur turned fifteen years old he approached Merlin, who had been both his friend and mentor, in a considerable state of excitement. Merlin wanted to know what it was all about and Arthur said, "My brother, Prince Kay, and my father, King Ector, are taking me to Londinium. Kay is going to participate in a tournament there. Is there any way you can come?"

Merlin hung his head for a minute, realizing that the day had come for Arthur to become king.

Looking at him, Merlin could only hope Arthur was ready. He'd done everything he could to prepare Arthur for the job and Arthur was now about the same age as Ambrosius was when he'd become a General. Merlin would still play a part in Arthur's life, but things would be different. The day was also coming that Arthur would learn who Merlin was. In all the time they'd spent together, Arthur had never made the connection between Merlin his friend and Merlin the Sorcerer.

Merlin looked at the boy. "I'll be at the tournament watching over you. Thc day of the tournament shall be an important day in the history of Briton."

"I don't know about that," said Arthur. "But it'll be an important day for my brother."

Merlin looked at the young lad as the rays of the sun created an unusual outline around him. He said, "Arthur, come here and let's have a bite to eat." Arthur sat on a rock near Merlin who said, "This will be the last time we see each other in these woods."

Arthur looked at the bearded Merlin and asked, "Why? Did I do something wrong?"

Merlin slowly scratched the beard on his chin while staring into the forest. "No. You have done everything right. But you have reached an age where you will be taking the next step into manhood. I will still be with you, but it just won't be here."

A strange feeling came over Arthur as he contemplated his future, not knowing why or what was happening. He didn't want to leave Merlin this time, because he was afraid that when he left, he'd somehow be stepping into the unknown.

After Arthur left, Merlin looked around at his small encampment as if to say goodbye. He packed up his gear and opened the wormhole. Moments later, he was back in his own time. He stowed his equipment in the SUV he'd been using and grabbed his cell phone to make a quick call to Adrian. Merlin asked Adrian to set up a jump from Windsor Castle for early the next day. The excitement was obvious in Merlin's voice as he updated Adrian: He wanted to make a jump from the research center immediately.

Adrian got everything ready and as soon as Merlin arrived, he was on his way back in time. The sun was bright, making Merlin wish he could wear sunglasses. Merlin hurried as fast as he could to King Cadwellon's castle in Glevum. When he arrived, the gatekeeper allowed Merlin right in. Merlin found Sir Thomas and King Cadwellon together in the drawing room. Merlin hadn't seen his friends for months, but they hadn't seen him in many years.

King Cadwellon had grown old and weak over the years. Cadwellon rose to greet Merlin. "My, you look good. You don't appear to have aged one day."

"Why thank you, my friend," Merlin said.

Thomas looked at Merlin and made the same observation as the king. Then he asked, "Why have you returned after being away so long?"

"This is to be a historic time for Briton. I need your help for things to go as they should."

Sir Thomas was a bit put off by Merlin's enthusiasm after such a long absence. "And just what is it you want of us?"

"I need both of you to go to the tournament that's to be held in Londinium. But before that, I need you to get Ambrosius. He needs to bring as many soldiers as he can spare to Londinium. I also need you to get word to all the kings to be at this tournament."

King Cadwellon looked at Sir Thomas and then at Merlin before saying, "Just what is going on at this tournament that requires such attention?"

"I can't tell you, but you'll understand during the tournament. You must trust me."

The king and Sir Thomas agreed to Merlin's requests and King Cadwellon asked Merlin to spend the night at the castle. Merlin readily agreed to the king's request. He knew that he could adjust the laser so that he could arrive back at the research center just after his prior jump.

The next morning Merlin found himself anxious to return to his own time so he could get to London. He hurried through breakfast and said a quick goodbye before departing to the lake and home. Once home again, he hurried to his SUV without checking in and took off. He called Chac to make sure Shadow was taken care of and then called Adrian to give him an update. Adrian told him that everything was set up for him at Windsor Castle and he would meet Merlin there for the return.

Merlin was well rested, even though it was night in London. He was glad he'd stayed the night at King Cadwellon's castle before returning. Merlin drove his SUV to the gate, which was well lit by the lights and the full moon shined on the damp concert pavement. Merlin was greeted at the gate by a modern version of the gatekeeper and hustled in. He parked near the pool and told the guard that he was going to go ahead and make his jump but would be returning soon. Merlin also told the guard to give the king his apologies, but they could talk when Merlin returned the next morning.

Merlin was getting used to these jumps and had grown accustomed to taking only what he needed that wasn't available in the past. In making the jump to the past, Merlin arrived just as the fog lifted during the early morning hours, a stark contrast to the darkness he'd left behind. It wasn't long before he was once again on the path to Londinium. Merlin thought about how much better shape he was in than when he'd begun his adventures–a result of all the walking he had to do when back in the past.

Merlin arrived in Londinium in the early afternoon and soon crossed the bridge into the city. He walked until he got to the church, where he found Bishop Dyfrig. Merlin told the priest to prepare himself for a great event that was to occur at the tournament. He couldn't give away too much information, but Merlin's reappearance after being absent for so many years was enough to convince the bishop that something truly special was about to happen. After making arrangements for everything, Merlin returned to the spot where Windsor Castle would one day be and got ready for his return home to prepare for the tournament.

Merlin arrived back at Windsor Castle to find King Arthur II, Adrian, and Annie waiting for him. His jumps weren't timed to coordinate with the same time of day for both locations, which was having an effect on Merlin similar to jet lag. He left Londinium in the late afternoon and arrived in London in the early morning. So with his knees and stomach a bit weak, he accepted an invitation from the charming King Arthur II for breakfast.

The four entered the castle and went to the dining room where they were served a nice big American breakfast of ham, eggs, hash-brown potatoes, toast, and coffee. The king wanted a full update on events, which Merlin happily provided. Merlin sat in his fifth-century costume, looking like a homeless beggar, with his long hair and untrimmed beard. He eschewed his normal manners because he was starving. Although Adrian was a bit embarrassed, the king found it amusing. The king was also fond of talking about how interesting it must be for Merlin to be an advisor to Briton's kings at a time when being a king meant you had great powers. Annie's favorite observation was about how odd it appeared for Merlin, who looked like a beggar, to be having breakfast with the nicely dressed King Arthur II.

After updating the king, Merlin told him that he was going to get some rest and would return to the time travel pool at Windsor Castle in a couple of days. His next trip would make Arthur the king of Briton.

The king wanted to go with Merlin to witness this enormous event, but Merlin knew there were too many uncertainties in a jump and something usually went wrong. But Arthur was still a relatively young man in his forties with an adventurous spirit who longed to see the way things were in his country's past. Merlin did have a sneaky desire to take the king back with him; the king could see how important a person Merlin was in the past, which would certainly stroke his ego. But Merlin had a responsibility to protect both King Arthurs and he had to argue that the king had not gone through any of the necessary preparations to make the jump, thus avoiding a potentially tragic event.

***

Merlin and Chac spent the next couple of days relaxing and playing with Shadow. The neighbors' curiosity was about to boil over what with having a Mayan and a beggar man living in the cottage–both of whom were occasionally picked up by the king's men. Chac told Merlin that he caught a couple of them peeking through the windows one time, but he'd chased them away. The weirdness of living his two lives often struck Merlin too, especially when he was shopping at a local supermarket or other retail store, or when he was gathering stares from the people in the restaurants he and Chac ate in.

Adrian arrived to take Merlin to Windsor Castle and his jump back in time. Merlin assigned Adrian a new task that would require him to go back in time: Adrian must build a permanent pool within the lake near King Cadwellon's old estate. Merlin was going to need it in the near future and it should be completed right away.

Chac stayed behind to take care of Shadow. Shadow looked up at Merlin with an expression that clearly said he didn't want Merlin to leave him behind. Merlin bent down and wrapped his arms around Shadow, wishing he could take his friend with him. One day maybe he'd be able to let Shadow go where he could run free, without fear of being hit by a car or truck.

When they arrived at the castle, King Arthur greeted them dressed as a fifth century nobleman. Merlin looked at the king, shaking his head at the thought of the king's willingness to risk his life for the sake of an adventure. "I assume you're in costume to wish me well for this jump back in time?"

"No," the king said. "I'm going with you."

"And just where, sir, did you get the idea that I would allow that, even if I could?"

"I have every right to go; I'm the financial backer for this project."

"Well, first, there's the risk. As king of the United Kingdom you have an obligation to your people to keep yourself out of harm's way wherever possible. Second, if I went along with this I'd be probably be removed as head of the project at the very least, and may even get fired."

King Arthur gave Merlin a shy smile as he looked down and then moved his head slightly upward. "Look, I put myself at risk all the time. Simply moving from one point to another is a form of risk. And you must remember that I am a frequent snow skier. Many people die every year skiing and we have yet to have anyone die as a result of time travel."

Adrian looked at the king, not quite believing what he was hearing. His mouth was wide open and Merlin imagined steam coming out Adrian's ears and began to laugh. Adrian put his hands on his hips and bent slightly at the waist. "What the hell are you laughing at? This is King Arthur we're talking about." He turned toward Arthur. "And as for you, sir, you have no right to even consider it."

"Oh, I think I have every right to not only consider it but to do it," said King Arthur II.

Adrian said, "No you don't. Have you forgotten that I was almost killed on a jump? Have you forgotten all the scares from all the jumps Merlin's made? Hell, he gets wounded or injured on almost every jump he makes."

King Arthur put his hand on Adrian's shoulder. "Adrian, calm down now. It'll be okay. First, you should know that I'm trained in virtually all the martial arts. I am better trained in self-defense that either of the two of you. Also, you must consider the consequences of refusal. It would be very sad to have the funding for this project stopped when your team is so close to concluding its mission, wouldn't you agree?"

Adrian's frustration came to a head. "No, I would not

agree. Besides, we're doing this project for you, not for us. Our primary interest is with the Maya. So if you want to shut it down, go ahead. We'll just pack up and go to Mexico and begin our project there."

Merlin shrugged his shoulders. "Then again, what the hell. Let's do it." Merlin went over to the king, grabbed his arm and led him up the stairs to the pool.

Adrian ran after the pair, screaming, "No, no, no, no. Merlin, you can't do this. Not with the king."

Deep down, the king didn't really think Merlin was going to let him go. As the wormhole formed, the king began to have second thoughts, but then he reminded himself that Annie and Vivian had made the jump, so he slapped the patch on his neck and stepped into the past.

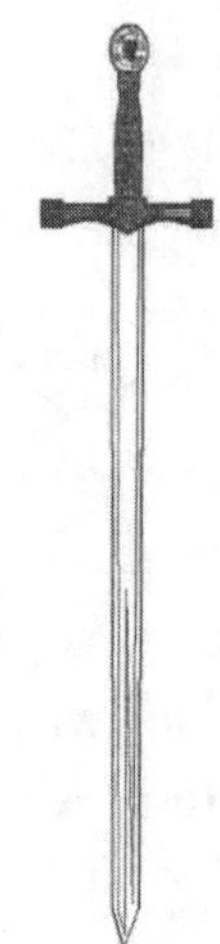

Chapter Twenty-Five

As the too men got their bearings, Merlin looked at the king and said, "I'll do all I can to look after you, but if you get in trouble, you may have to handle it on your own."

"Don't worry about it. I'll be fine. Is this where my castle lies?" The king looked around at the small hills and greenery, which seemed even brighter with the rays of the morning sun upon them, and tried to visualize the streets and buildings of the future in their place.

"Yep. This is it. We need to head off in that direction," Merlin said, pointing toward Londinium.

The two men made their way to a Roman road that led straight to Londinium. "I find it rather interesting how one day these trees and hills will be replaced by buildings and homes," the king said, looking over the landscape. The king pulled his coat tight as a cold wind suddenly whipped across the Thames River and cut right through the two travelers.

"I think you'll find the changes to be even more dramatic than what you see here. As we get into Londinium, you'll see a people and landscape that have little resemblance to what you're accustomed to," Merlin said, walking with the aid of his laser walking stick and looking straight ahead.

King Arthur asked, "Tell me Merlin, what is it like for the kings of this era?"

Merlin turned his head for a moment as he pondered the question. "To some extent, the kings of this period live a life that's more difficult than that of the common man of our era. At least in terms of creature comforts. But in terms of power, there is no doubt that they wield a power well beyond that of a modern king or any other leader of any nation, for that matter. But there are many things we assume a king could do in this era that wasn't as cut-and-dried as it might seem. For example, King Uther brought the military forces of Briton to bear against Sir Gorlois because he wanted Ygerna. But in order to do that, he had to convince the earls that Gorlois was a traitor. They would have never allowed Uther to go to war with Gorlois had they known the truth."

"Well, I must confess that their lives seem much more meaningful than the life I lead. I'm little more than a figure-head."

"I can't say that I feel too sorry for you. I'd think that any child of any ghetto in the world would trade places with you and not have to think twice about it."

"From that perspective, I guess you're right. I have much to be thankful for. But it's hard for me to not be a bit jealous of the kings of old in that they actually had something to do. I often feel more like an ornament than a person, sort of an oddity in the world."

"I think a lot of what you feel is due to what you're doing with your life. The monarchy is in trouble because of the jealousy of a few people. Your job has evolved over time to what it is today. In my opinion, what you do for your people in the form of charity work, education, and so many other areas, is far more significant than winning battles. I think that today is far closer to the Age of Camelot than the days of King Arthur the First could ever be."

The king stopped for a moment, pondering Merlin's words. He ran to catch up with Merlin. "I can see why the kings of legend held your wisdom in such high regard."

After a fairly long walk, the king and Merlin made it to the bridge leading into Londinium. King Arthur II wanted to stop for a minute and take in the sight of Londinium and the people as they crossed over the bridge.

Merlin looked at Arthur as the king observed the people of Londinium. "I must remind you of your obligation to say nothing about the future and to remain an observer rather than a participant in the events that will be taking place. I also caution you on speaking. Even though you know some Celtic and Latin, many of the modern words don't exist during this time period. I just wish you'd waited until I'd gotten a translator for you to use. Come on, let's get into town."

As the two men crossed the bridge into Londinium, Merlin couldn't help but worry some about the king. Merlin had taken on the awesome responsibility of keeping King Arthur II safe while also helping King Arthur I.

The two men entered the city, which was alive with activity. Soldiers, citizens, and kings were everywhere. With the streets so crowded, the task of watching after the king almost immediately became troublesome for Merlin–the king was so awestruck by what he was seeing that he tended to wander away from Merlin.

Merlin grabbed the king's arm. "Stay close."

The two men struggled through the crowds as they made their way to the church where they found Bishop Dyfrig. Merlin entered the bishop's oak-walled office, which contained a large, wooden writing table and several wooden benches on a wood floor. The bishop was dressed in white robes with gold trim. Merlin laughed as he shamefully mentally compared the bishop to a big white cruise ship. Bishop Dyfrig was absorbed in thought as Merlin approached him. Merlin said, “I noticed the sword is still here.”

The startled bishop looked up from his desk and regained his composure upon recognizing Merlin. In a high-pitched voice he said, “Yes. But I fear there will soon be a war over it as the kings are growing impatient with the Saxons and Anglos’ continued advances.”

“Today’s the day,” Merlin said with a knowing smile.

“The day for what, may I ask?”

“The beginning of a new age. A new king. The wait will end today.”

“I suppose you’re to be the new king? I’ve heard all this before from others.”

“Not I, you old fool. I’m the one who put the sword into the rock in the first place.”

“Well, that’s true. But if not you, then who? Who is this new king?”

“Uther’s son will remove the sword.”

“King Uther’s son is alive? How do you know this?”

“Do you really want to know or is this one of those times when you start covering your ears when I begin to answer your question?”

Bishop Dyfrig sighed. “You’re right. I don’t think I want to know. You know me much too well.” The bishop looked at the king. “Who is your friend?”

Merlin just smiled. “Has the tournament started?”

Bishop Dyfrig kept his eyes on Arthur, wondering why Merlin hadn’t answered his question. He said, “No, but it is about to. Are you planning to go?”

"Yes, but we'll only be there for a short while. We'll be back soon." Merlin and the king walked out of the church and crossed to the stone that held Caliburn. Merlin took a vial out of his bag and poured the contents of nano robots around the sword.

The king watched Merlin as he worked. "What are you pouring onto the stone?"

"Nano robots to loosen the rock around it. This way Arthur can remove the sword."

King Arthur moved up next to the stone and placed both hands on the hilt of the sword. Merlin's eyes opened and his jaw dropped. King Arthur II looked up with a sly smile. "Hmm. Arthur, the Once and Future King. You know, I just love this period of history."

Merlin placed his hand over King Arthur's. "Don't even think about it."

The king laughed and moved his hand away from the sword. "Lighten up, Merlin. But you must admit it would be interesting."

Merlin shook his head, thinking about what the king said. He looked at Arthur. "I'm in no mood to joke around. Let's get to the tournament and have a look around."

They worked their way through the crowd at the tournament until Merlin spotted King Cadwellon. He motioned for the ever-amazed King Arthur II to follow him and the two wove their way to where King Cadwellon, Sir Thomas, and General Ambrosius were standing.

General Ambrosius was the first to notice Merlin. "My friend, it's so good to see you. I have my army here as you requested. But what's up? Why did you need it here?"

King Arthur II wondered who these friends of Merlin were. As he looked over at General Ambrosius dressed like a

Roman military leader, he was on the mark in assuming this man to be the great General Merlin had talked about so often.

Merlin pushed his hood back; the temperature had risen with the afternoon sun. "Today is the day, my friends. You are about to have a new High-King."

The three men looked at Merlin and King Cadwellon said, "Is that so? And is this to be our new king?" King Cadwellon looked at King Arthur II, trying to determine what made Arthur so special.

Merlin looked back at Arthur before saying, "No. No, he is not to be your king. He's a friend from my homeland. He's here to witness the event. Ambrosius, are your men ready should they be needed?"

The great Ambrosius wrinkled his brow as he looked at Merlin. "They're ready, but why do you think there will be trouble?"

"When they see who the rightful heir to the throne is, I'm afraid they'll think they've found a weakness. They'll be wrong. Unfortunately, many good Britons will die from the news," Merlin said as he strained to find the young Arthur. "Has King Ector's son taken his turn in the tournament as of yet?"

Sir Thomas said, "No. Is he to be our new High-King?"

"No. King Ector is a friend. I was just wondering–" Merlin stopped, suddenly realizing the level of curiosity he had wrought with his announcement to his friends.

King Cadwellon strained his neck looking at the participants lined up for their turn. "I believe he's next. Yes, that's him," King Cadwellon said, pointing toward Sir Kay.

Merlin looked in the direction King Cadwellon was pointing and saw the young Arthur holding a sword and standing next to Sir Kay. Sir Kay mounted his horse and Arthur handed him the sword as Merlin said, "I must go now. I would appreciate it if the three of you would meet me back at the church in a few moments. The Sword of Briton will soon be drawn from the stone and I may need your help. I'll see you there."

Merlin waved to his friends and pulled King Arthur II with him and made his way through the crowd.

Returning to the church, the two men walked through it to a small window, which contained a view of the sword and the stone below. Suddenly, as in the legend, a young, well-built boy of about fifteen with sandy-blond hair appeared and grabbed the hilt of Caliburn. Bishop Dyfrig had seen Merlin return and joined him at the window just as Arthur withdrew the sword.

"Is he our new king? That young boy?"

"Yes. But it's not over yet," Merlin said.

The three men watched the boy run off. Merlin, King Arthur II, and Bishop Dyfrig returned to the bishop's office where they talked about what this would mean to the country when suddenly a young page appeared at the door. He pointed at the stone and urged the men to follow him. They reached the stone and found that a large group of men had gathered around it.

Merlin saw that his friends had made it as he had requested and cried out, "King Cadwellon, over here."

King Cadwellon nudged Sir Thomas and General Ambrosius and the three of them pushed their way through the crowd to Merlin. Once they'd made it to his side, Ambrosius asked, "What's going on here?"

"Sir Kay's squire removed the Sword of Briton from the stone," Bishop Dyfrig told them.

Merlin looked at Sir Thomas, who was looking on silently with a knowing smile. Suddenly the young squire was pulled through the crowd and told to replace the sword. Upon seeing this, Merlin raised his arms and calls out to the crowd, "Calm yourselves."

The crowd grew silent waiting for the imposing wizard's

next words. Merlin slowly turned to gaze at the silent mob. Then, speaking very slowly, he said, "The boy has removed the sword. Bishop Dyfrig and I witnessed this. Should anyone dare challenge us, please step forward." The crowd remained silent as Merlin and Bishop Dyfrig looked over the crowd. Merlin said, "Then the lad shall forever be recognized as the new Riothomus. The true High-King of the Island of the Mighty. This selection has been made through the grace and power of almighty God." Merlin moved up beside the lad. "Don't worry Arthur, it's time for you to take hold of your destiny. Are you ready?"

"I do not know, my lord. But what I do know is that you never told me you are Merlin the Sorcerer."

"True. But I never said I wasn't, either." Merlin laughed a hearty laugh as the new king smiled. "Now, when I tell you, I want you to put the sword back and remove it again. After removing it, I will place my hand on your shoulder. When I do this, I want you to hold your father's sword high above your head."

Arthur stared at his mentor for a moment before saying, "My father's sword? What do you mean?"

"You are the son of King Uther and Queen Ygerna."

Feeling his knees grow weak for a moment and not knowing what he should be feeling from the news, Arthur said, "You've known this all along and did not tell me. Why?"

"You have a great destiny before you. But you have many enemies who would have killed you to take the crown. Had you or anyone else known the truth, you may not have been alive for this moment. You would have also put you foster father's life in jeopardy. Would you have wanted that?"

"Did you know the truth?"

"Yes, but only I knew."

Arthur turned in silence and put the sword back into the stone before saying, "No. You're right. What shall I do next?"

Merlin placed his hand on Arthur's shoulder. "Withdraw the sword and prepare yourself to become king."

Arthur placed his faith in the magnificent Merlin's hands, a legend in his own time. Once again Arthur put both his hands on Caliburn's hilt and pulled the sword from the stone. He then held it high above his head while the crowd looked on. Bishop Dyfrig moved through the crowd and stood next to Arthur as the crowd kneeled in front of their king.

Bishop Dyfrig of Londinium called out, "Long live Arthur. Long live the High-King of the Island of the Mighty."

The spectators cheered and joined in the chant and soon the entire town cried out, "Long live the king. Long live Arthur. Hail Riothomus."

Merlin looked through the crowd and saw King Arthur II. Tears formed in Merlin's eyes, knowing he had just witnessed and been part of one of the most potent parts of the King Arthur legend. Merlin looked at Arthur I and told the boy to join him in Bishop Dyfrig's office. Merlin saw King Ector and Sir Kay and asked them and his other friends to join him in the bishop's office, too. King Ector stared silently at Merlin for a moment.

"You knew this day was to come at the time you first brought Arthur to me, didn't you?"

"Yes. But were it not for you, this day would not have arrived." Merlin placed his hand on his friend's shoulder and smiled.

As King Arthur I and the noblemen entered the office, Merlin turned to face them. "Gentlemen, today is the beginning of a period of great turbulence, so it's time for you to be informed that Arthur's true father was King Uther Pendragon. I had the boy hidden to protect him. He'll soon be challenged by many of the kings gathered here today. Arthur, to meet the challenge, you must go to Brittany and meet with King Bohart and King Ban. You must ask for their help. General Ambrosius, Sir Thomas, and King Ector, you must gather all the forces you can who will swear loyalty to Arthur. Let them know that I am backing him. King Cadwellon, you must return to your castle. You must protect the women I have entrusted to your care. We will all meet at Glevum in four months. Any questions?"

There were many questions, but Merlin insisted his instructions be followed to the letter. They all felt Merlin knew what he was talking about based on their past experiences with him, so each man vowed to do his part. King Arthur I rode out with King Ector and Sir Kay, while King Arthur II and Merlin began their walk back to the area that would one day contain Windsor Castle.

They walked in silence most of the way as they each played the events over and over in their heads. Finally King Arthur II broke the silence as they neared the departure site. "Merlin, this has been one of the most interesting days I've ever spent in my life. I must admit to feeling a bit envious of you and your life."

"I assure you it's only because you haven't had to live it."

"I know you're angry with me because I insisted upon your taking me with you. But I shall never forget you for this. I will always be in your debt. If you ever need anything, anything at all, please do not hesitate to ask."

Merlin smiled. "I may have to take you up on that once Bill finds out about this."

"I don't believe Dr. Barnes is aware of the value you have brought to this mission and to the lives of the people of this era."

Looking straight ahead, Merlin said, "Other than Adrian and Annie, and now you, I don't think anyone truly understands what I do here in the past."

Chapter Twenty-Six

The two men entered the wormhole and suddenly appeared just outside the pool at Windsor Castle. The gray look of the surrounding area was in stark contrast to the sunny skies the two travelers had just left, perhaps an omen of things to come. Adrian was waiting for them and ran as fast as his big body would carry him when he saw them reappear. "Merlin," shouted the big man. "We've got a problem. Bill heard about what happened and he's on his way here."

Merlin glanced over to the king. "Oh hell. Didn't I tell you?"

The king smiled looking at Merlin's expression. "Don't worry about it. I'll take care of it."

"I don't know," Adrian said. "I think Bill's planning an inquiry. It doesn't look good."

Just as Adrian finished his sentence a car drove up and Bill got out, along with Annie and Vivian. Bill stormed up to Merlin. "Just what the hell did you think you were doing? You know how dangerous this work is. Are you nuts?"

King Arthur II moved between the two men. "Now wait a minute here. He only took me after I insisted on going. If there's anyone to blame, it's me."

"Oh, don't worry about that, I do blame you. Just what were you two thinking anyway?"

"I have no excuse to offer." Merlin considered the oddity of how just a few hours before he'd intimidated an entire nation and now here he was being browbeaten by a guy named Bill.

The contrast didn't escape Arthur, either. Not sure what to say in Merlin's defense, but absolutely sure he must, he said simply, "I take full responsibility for Merlin's actions. Had I not threatened to withdraw funding for the project, I doubt I could have persuaded Merlin to do this."

With his fists clenched and his face turning red, Bill said, "I don't give a damn who's funding this operation. The United States government and the Carnegie Institute control this program. If word gets out about this I'm sure they'll close us down. Merlin, I'm going to have to think about whether we send you back again. Am I making myself clear?"

Merlin fought the desire to stand at attention. "Yes sir. So what now?"

Shaking his head, Bill turned and, as he headed back to his car with Annie, said, "You go home. I'll let you know what I decide tomorrow. But you should be prepared to be sent Stateside."

Merlin's deflated ego was apparent for all to see. In all their years of working together, this was the first time Bill had ever spoken to Merlin in such a manner. For his part, Merlin knew he'd been wrong in taking the king with him, but Barnes' reaction seemed overdone.

King Arthur II walked over to Merlin to console him. He

thought for a moment about Merlin standing in front of the crowd in Londinium and everyone listening to the great sorcerer. "Merlin, I'm sorry. I had no right to use you. Please accept my apology and know that I will do all I can to keep you an active member of the project."

Adrian and Vivian joined the king in soothing Merlin's hurt feelings. Merlin fought the desire to lose himself in the past and just say to hell with it all. He decided to stash everything he needed for a trip back should Bill's ruling be against him.

Adrian pulled his car around to take Vivian and Merlin home. They said their goodbyes to the king and rode in silence to the cottage. Merlin was greeted by Shadow, his truest friend, as he entered the cottage. Merlin wasn't hungry, but managed to eat a sandwich Vivian fixed for him. This was one time he was not in the mood for sex despite not having seen Vivian for several months.

The next morning Merlin and Vivian rose early and headed out to the research center so Merlin could try to save his position. As they drove up, Vivian noticed the king's limousine driving away. Merlin hoped the king was successful in helping Merlin.

Sliding his employee card across the entry pad, Merlin was alarmed that his card didn't work. Vivian used hers and the two headed for Merlin's office where they found all his personal items packed in boxes. Merlin looked at Vivian. "Let's get out of here. Take me back to the cottage now."

Vivian was equally alarmed by what she saw but said, "Merlin, wait. Let's go see Bill first."

"No, I want to go now," Merlin said, running to the door.

Vivian hurried after him, feeling that whatever Merlin was

getting himself into was not going to work out well. They jumped into the car and, as they left, Vivian noticed Adrian running after them in her rearview mirror. She said, "Merlin, I think we should turn around. Adrian wouldn't be running for nothing."

"No. I want to get back now."

As soon as they reached the cottage, Merlin bolted from the car and ran to the house. He gathered up his things and changed clothes as Vivian looked on in disbelief. "You're not doing what I think you're doing, are you?" she asked, desperation plain in her voice.

"It depends on what you think I'm doing," Merlin said, putting a travel kit together.

Vivian took Merlin's hand and led him into her room. "I have a present for you." She walked to the closet and pulled out a long, cylinder-shaped device. "I've been worried by the danger you seem to attract, so I had my researchers build a sonic cannon for your protection."

"What am I suppose to do with it?"

"You can use it to knock down the enemy and their defenses without actually having to kill them." Vivian then showed Merlin how to use the device.

He packed the cannon with the rest of his gear in his cart; there were enough supplies to last for months if needed. Just as Merlin finished and was headed to the backyard, Vivian heard the doorbell ring. Merlin glanced toward the door. "Keep them here as long as possible."

"Fine, but what are you planning to do?" Vivian asked as the doorbell rang again.

Merlin dashed out the backdoor. "Don't worry about it, just keep them busy." Then he turned back. "You know what I'm planning." Merlin quickly set up the pool while Vivian stalled a couple of MPs at the door. Soon she heard the familiar sound of a wormhole opening, as did the MPs. They ran into the back yard just as Merlin followed his cart into the past.

One of the MPs looked at Vivian. "Where did he go?"

Chapter Twenty-Seven

Merlin staggered around for a moment trying to regain his footing after his jump, this time without the benefit of the patch. He looked around and saw he was not far from King Cadwellon's castle. He felt like a criminal, sneaking his way into the past on an unauthorized mission. If he wasn't fired before he surely was now, he thought.

Merlin realized this was another rare nice day as he struggled with his cart. Upon arriving at the castle, Merlin saw his protégé talking to a beautiful brown-haired girl several years older than Arthur. It was apparent that Arthur was drawn to Lady Morgause, Queen Rowena and King Vortigern's daughter. Merlin watched as Arthur seduced the young lady, who had matured nicely while the rest of the court looked on.

Arthur saw his mentor and left the young lady. Arthur had a bearing about himself that told Merlin the young man had changed since Merlin had last seen him. Arthur grinned. "I was wondering if I would ever see you again."

"I told you I would be back. I saw you talking with Morgause. What's happening here?"

"Nothing, really. We've just become friends. They're isn't anyone else here close to my age I can talk to."

Merlin looked at the two young people. His instinct told him there was more going on here than Arthur was telling him.

One night later, Merlin was walking in the garden when he heard what sounded like someone in distress. He moved toward the noise and realized the sounds were from laughter, not distress. He looked closely and saw the naked body of a youthful woman with creamy white skin partially covered by the strong, nude body of a boy. Upon closer examination, he found it to be Arthur and Morgause embraced in passionate lovemaking. Merlin boiled inside and burst through the bushes. "What are you two doing?" he screamed.

The embarrassed Morgause grabbed the blanket to cover herself. Arthur stood up. "I'm doing as any man would do, I should think."

"I have been your teacher since you were a child. I never taught you to do this. In fact, I taught you the opposite." Merlin thought back for a moment to King Uther and Ygerna and wondered if there was a genetic cause for the actions of father and son. He closed his eyes and shook his head. "You still have much to learn about being a king."

In an apparent attempt to maintain his position and dignity in front of Morgause, Arthur said, "And you, sir, have much to learn about being a subject."

"Arthur, get dressed. We must talk now," Merlin commanded, completely unmoved by Arthur's comment.

Arthur reluctantly relented to the powerful wizard's wishes. After he and Morgause dressed, they returned to the castle, where Merlin took the young Arthur to his room. Once in his room, Merlin directed King Arthur to have a seat. "Arthur, you are about to do battle for your crown. Rowena, Morgause's mother, is a Saxon. Do you understand the ramifications of your actions should you have a child with her?"

"No. I had no idea they were Saxon."

"If you have a child of mixed Saxon and Briton blood, he could return to Briton and claim the crown. He could accomplish for the Saxons and the Anglos what no army could. I must have King Cadwellon send Rowena and Morgause to Brittany. I will find you an appropriate wife soon. In the meantime, keep your pants on and your hormones in check." Arthur cocked his head in question. "Don't be bedding anybody. And as for my being your subject, I'm not your subject, or anyone else's subject. What I am is something you will learn about in the future."

"You have been of great counsel to me in the years past. I will do as you ask for now, but upon your next return we may need to further this discussion." Arthur rose from his seat and looked Merlin square in the eye. He then smiled and silently left the room.

Merlin shook his head as he watched Arthur leave. What had he wrought?

Early the next morning, Merlin met with Ambrosius and King Arthur. There was no mention of Arthur's behavior the night before. Merlin was given an overview of the situation before them. Arthur was greatly impressed by the accuracy of Merlin's prophesy and sought his advice on the battle plan he and Sir Ambrosius had drawn up.

Merlin looked over the plans and found no flaw in it, other than that the odds were against defeating an army so much larger than Arthur's. The only conflict was in the timing of the battle. Ambrosius preferred a night battle so he could use the terror tactics of flaming arrows. Arthur preferred to see his enemy's eyes. They struck a compromise: The battle would commence one hour before dawn.

Sir Thomas assumed command of the archers and had them prepare their fire pits. General Ambrosius and King Arthur would lead a cavalry assault through the middle while Sir Kay and Sir Ulfius engaged the enemy with their infantry forces. King Bohort would take a combined infantry and cavalry force around the left flank while King Ban would do the same around the right flank.

Merlin was saddened by the thought that many Britons from both sides would die in this battle. They would die at a time Briton needed to be united for protection against invaders. But, sadly, he knew that history would not be kind to the Britons in that their struggle would ultimately end with the defeat of the Britons by the German tribes, who themselves would ultimately be defeated by the Normans. But this mix, forged through battle, would make Britain one of the greatest empires of all time.

As the time approached, the men went to their positions for launching the attack just as a strong wind began to blow. Merlin broke away, carrying the sonic cannon Vivian had made for him. He climbed through the dark underbrush and tripped over a low-lying limb as he made his way up the small hill. He looked around to see if anyone heard him and then continued to the top. He found an area to secretly set up the sonic cannon, making as little noise as possible. Merlin looked up at the stars strung through the darkness of the night.

Just as Sir Thomas had his archers release their arrows, without flame, Merlin turned on his sonic cannon. The cannon's burst knocked down all the tents in the camp at once just as the arrows arrived; Merlin hoped that everyone would think it was the wind that blew down the tents, thus making it an act of God. Perhaps this would help lessen his pain from the deaths that were to follow, or shorten the battle so that there were fewer deaths altogether.

The enemy camp instantly became a hive of terror as the tents collapsed and the arrows fell. Sir Thomas had his men quickly reload, but this time with flaming arrows. As they released their rain, the sky lit up with fire. Merlin could hear the screams of the frightened, wounded, and dying below as wave after wave of fire swept over them.

The enemy commanders began barking orders trying to form their men into ranks to meet Arthur and his troops. This battle would pit the brave, courageous young men of Briton against each other in a civil war to cement the crown in the hands of young Arthur. Merlin's only consolation was that this one battle would determine the leader of Briton which was much more merciful than a long, drawn out affair as was the case in the American Civil War.

Seeing the movement below, King Arthur ordered Sir Kay and Sir Ulfius to begin to slowly advance their infantry, while King Bohort and King Ban began to move rapidly along the flanks. Sir Thomas stopped the flight of flaming arrows one hundred paces before the infantry met the enemy. Next, King Arthur and General Ambrosius began their cavalry attack. King Arthur had gathered all the trumpeterss together and placed them directly behind the center of his cavalry. He instructed them to begin their calls at one time, thus adding to the terror of the sound of hooves from hundreds of horses galloping toward the enemy.

Merlin was but an observer of the horror of the battle as the men clashed, metal on metal, but as the sun began to rise, smoke obscured his view; he moved closer to the front of the battle scene. The mutilated corpses of the enemy were strewn over the battlefield and slowed Merlin's approach. His boots began to stick to the ground as the blood began to congeal beneath them. He looked around and heard sporadic clanging of clashing swords and saw men fall as the attackers' blades found their mark. Soon he heard the yells of triumph as he worked his way toward King Arthur and his men.

Suddenly, before he could verify the reason for the sound of triumph, he felt an urge to turn to his side. There he saw the mangled body of a familiar form. Merlin knelt next to the body and gently removed the helmet. Under the helmet, he found the face of Sir Ulfius with his eyes staring into nothingness. Tears filled Merlin's eyes as he gently laid his friend out. Merlin stood up and once again began making his way toward the sound of the cheers.

Over the smoke and fire, over the smell of the dead and dying, stood King Arthur, outlined by the rays of the sun so as to appear to be a god, a gallant man in the body of a boy. Merlin looked at his protégé for a moment, then made his way to Arthur and immediately embraced him. On seeing this, another roar of approval was unleashed by King Arthur's troops and the two men raised their swords toward the sky. The battle had been won with few casualties in Arthur's forces, one of whom was Sir Ulfius, perhaps King Uther's closest friend.

After the battle, Merlin urged King Arthur to call a war council. At the meeting, Merlin suggested they prepare themselves for the task of pushing the Saxons off the Island of the Mighty, for they were once again feeling like the Mighty. King Ban suggested that Arthur send an emissary to King Hoel of Armorica to enlist his aid. Arthur agreed to this and asked King Ban and King Bohort to accomplish this in his name. General Ambrosius was assigned the task of integrating the surviving enemy soldiers, who swore allegiance to Arthur, into his army. He was also told to put to death all those who refused. This was a necessary task because of the lack of prisons for housing the defeated soldiers, but it still saddened Merlin. The lands and possessions of those rebel kings who had died from battle or from refusal to swear allegiance were consfiscated. Some of these would be awarded to King Ector, while most of the rest went into the hands of King Arthur.

Arthur asked Sir Kay to assemble an honor guard to accompany the body of Sir Ulfius back to his family. General Ambrosius and Sir Thomas were assigned the task of gathering intelligence on the German enemy while King Arthur and a strong escort accompanied Merlin back to Sir Cadwellon's castle.

But before anything else could move forward, King Arthur had to be crowned as the High-King of Briton. They decided to all head to Londinium and have Bishop Dyfrig handle the coronation ceremony. They soon reached Londinium and told the bishop of their plans. A small crowd gathered as word spread about the coronation and soon the cathedral was filled to capacity. King Arthur, still dirty and bloody from the battle, walked down the center isle as Merlin looked on, feeling like a proud father would feel. Soon Merlin's protégé was officially crowned High-King of Briton, with all his challengers already taken care of.

Now they had to take care of the possibility of an invasion as word of the other king's defeat spread. Merlin thought the Germans would think that King Arthur would be most vulnerable at this time. As time was of the essence, the men quickly went about their individual tasks. King Arthur and Merlin made their way to King Cadwellon's castle as fast as the crowds of supporters along the way would allow them. Merlin was drained from all of the activity and decided to rest a few days. He needed the time to tutor his friend on many subjects.

With Arthur firmly established on the throne, Merlin felt it was time to return and face the music with Bill Barnes. If Bill did decide to fire him, Merlin reasoned that he could always sneak back to the past and live out the rest of his days as King Arthur's advisor.

Merlin said goodbye to King Arthur and left him with explicit instructions to remain celibate while he was gone. Merlin said goodbye to King Cadwellon, who had turned ill while everyone was away at war. He walked through the gates and to the time lake for his return, thinking about how he had just left instructions for the High-King to follow and had made it through another major battle in which he'd played a major part in the outcome and in a few hours he would have to stand in front of a bureaucrat, a paper pusher, though a friend, to be reprimanded certainly, demoted probably, and possibly fired for doing something he had *not* been instructed to *not* do.

Chapter Twenty-Eight

As Merlin arrived in the dreary weather of the future, the team, excepting Quetzal, once again greeted him. The solution dripped from Merlin as he climbed the stairs from the pool. Vivian ran to Merlin and threw her arms around him while the rest of the team surrounded him. He smiled and Vivian told him that she was going to go to her office and asked Annie to call when things were set up. Vivian grabbed Merlin's hand and the two of them headed for Vivian's office. Merlin quickly changed his clothes. Vivian got a call from Annie asking them to go to the conference room. They hurried to the room and saw the rest of the team waiting for them except for Quetzal.

Everyone was concerned about Merlin's status, which had gotten worse as a result of Merlin disobeying Bill's order to stay put. Adrian said, "There has to be a way to make things work out. We can't afford to lose you."

Just as Adrian finished, Quetzal strolled into the room reading a book and eating an apple. He looked up at Merlin smugly. "I've found a rather interesting coincidence. I think it might save your job."

"And what might that be?" Chac asked.

"I believe that your King Arthur is Kukulkán," Quetzal said.

"Give me a break," Lance said.

"No. Go on," Merlin said. "Please explain."

"'Kukulkán' means flying serpent, if you didn't know that. He appeared to the Maya dressed like a Roman wearing a metal helmet with two flying serpents on it. Part of the legend of King Arthur describes how you, Merlin, saved the likes of a young lad named Ambrosius. The legend had it that you described a battle between two dragons that symbolized the coming of a great king. That king was Arthur. He wore a helmet with the two dragons on it."

"The part I played is no longer legend. It did, in fact, occur. However, what happens to Arthur is still a legend as far as I'm concerned, because I haven't witnessed it or seen proof of it as of yet."

"Well, there is more: Kukulkán united the Mayan kings under a government system similar to that of Briton at the time of King Arthur I."

Vivian had remained silent and bewildered up to this point. She looked up. "Wait a minute. He's making sense."

"You know, right now I'm more worried about King Arthur the First and how he handles his new responsibilities," Adrian said.

"We know how he handles it," Quetzal said. "Haven't you read the book?" They all laughed and it looked like Quetzal might have worked his way into acceptance by the team.

The next step was to talk with Dr. Barnes and attempt to convince him of the importance of keeping Merlin as the leader of the project. Annie and Adrian went to Bill's temporary office at the research center and asked him to meet with the team regarding Merlin's situation. Bill agreed, although he was not happy with Merlin's recent unauthorized trip into the past. He joined the others in the conference room. They carefully laid out their arguments for keeping Merlin, which Bill weighed along with the argument from King Arthur II. Bill asked to meet privately with Vivian before making his decision.

Vivian could tell from the beginning of her conversation with Bill that he'd already made his decision and it wasn't the one everyone wanted. He asked for her input and in an effort to keep Merlin as part of the project, she suggested that Bill make her the head of the project and keep Merlin on as a Time Travel Archeologist for the remainder of this project, then reinstate him to his former position once they began the Mayan project. Vivian knew this would probably put a wedge in their relationship, at least temporarily, but it might save Merlin's job.

Bill asked Vivian to wait outside and ask Merlin to come in. Vivian was hesitant to speak to Merlin. But, as she entered the hallway, she somehow managed to find the courage to tell Merlin that Bill wanted to speak to him. Merlin entered the conference room, where he immediately got the feeling that things were not going to go in the direction he was hoping.

Bill looked at Merlin and said, "Merlin, we are friends. We've been friends for a long time. This is what makes what I have to do one of the hardest things I've ever had to do. Effective today, you are no longer the director of this program. Because of the support you have from within the team, as well as that from the king, I will allow you to remain as our primary Time Travel Archeologist for this project. As to where you will go after the completion of this project, that will have to be determined at that time."

Merlin had a choice. He could leave the project or he could stay and accept the demotion. His emotions and ego were pushing him to just walk away, but he felt an obligation to King Arthur I to help him. So the legendary advisor to the kings of old accepted his fate and punishment for doing as King Arthur II had wished. Merlin understood that, despite every argument to the contrary, Bill really had no choice.

The team was called back into the conference room so Bill could announce his decision, though it was clear from Merlin's expression that the decision wasn't one they wanted to hear. Bill stood, unable to look Merlin in the eye. "After careful consideration, it is with deep regret that I must tell you that Dr. Lakin is no longer the director of this program. He will remain as our primary Time Travel Archeologist for the time being, but you now have a new director. The new director for our projects is Dr. Vivian Weatherall."

The announcement wasn't a great surprise to the team, though it created a bit of resentment in those who'd expected Adrian to get the top spot. The team gave Vivian a grudging applause as she rose to stand beside Bill. Silence befell the room as Vivian glanced around. She said, "For the time being I anticipate few changes in the way we operate, other than I expect to be going on many of the jumps myself in the future. We are near the end of this mission and I fully expect to have it wrapped up soon. At its conclusion, we will be going to Mexico for the mission that has been of greatest interest to the members of this team." She looked at Merlin. "Merlin, you're special to everyone involved with this program, as well as to many of the legendary people of old Briton. I will understand if you should decide not to jump back in time for a while. All we really need to know at this time is if Morgause had a baby, the name of the baby, and if the child is related to King Arthur II. Both Adrian and Annie are acquainted with some of the people from the period and can get the information without you. So, I will leave it up to you. What do you want to do?"

The room was quiet as Merlin contemplated his answer. Finally, he leaned back in his chair and said, "To not accept my current situation would be to say that I'm somehow more important or superior in some manner to the rest of you. I wish to assure each of you that none of those feelings are in my heart. I believe Arthur still needs my help to bring peace and prosperity to his land. I, therefore, accept the position and wish to complete the mission. That is, if it's okay with Vivian." Merlin turned his head to observe Vivian and noticed a strange look in her eyes.

The meeting broke up with everyone giving Merlin their condolences, along with assurances that he'd be back where he'd been in no time. Merlin still had an odd feeling about Vivian that he couldn't shake.

Vivian asked Merlin to follow her to her office, where she showed him the results of her work on the homing device. Vivian and her team had made a beautiful sword for Merlin that contained a device in the hilt that would bring help, should he ever need it. All he needed to do was turn the pommel at the end of the hilt and throw it into any pond, lake, well, or anything else that contained enough solution and the sword would return to the present and give the researchers the time, date, and location where help was needed. The sword was made of Spanish steel, had a gold-plated handle and strong, mirrored, sharp blade with perfect balance. There was still some aesthetic work that needed to be done on the sword, but it would be ready by the time Merlin returned from his next trip.

Merlin packed his equipment as he prepared for his return journey. Vivian accompanied him to his office and helped him. Much of what he needed was in the boxes packed by researchers on Bill's orders. Vivian could tell there was sadness behind Merlin's somber expression as he went through the boxes. Vivian promised to get the balance of the boxes unpacked while Merlin was gone and to bring the supplies he left at the cottage back to his office. She also surprised Merlin with a new outfit for him to wear on his trip. Merlin truly appreciated Vivian as he looked at his new boss and watched as she twirled her hair on her finger.

Vivian was a bit watery-eyed as she walked with Merlin to the time pool. She pulled him toward her and gave him a long, deep kiss before saying, "That's to remember me by."

Merlin laughed. "There's no way I will ever forget you." He gave her another quick kiss and climbed the stairs to the top of the pool. The wormhole opened and soon Merlin found himself in the past.

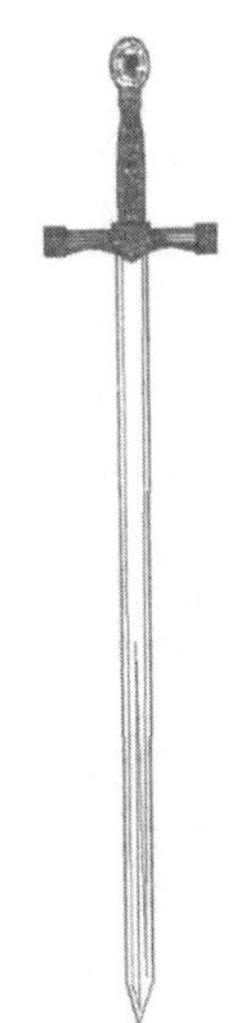

Chapter Twenty-Nine

Merlin felt this would be a quick trip, so he wanted to make every moment count. He looked around and noticed that the clouds were gray, signaling a dreary day ahead. He went directly to King Cadwellon's castle where he came upon Sir Thomas looking very distressed.

"Sir Thomas, what's wrong?"

"Although you've been gone but for a short while, much has happened in your absence."

"Yes? What?"

"King Cadwellon has died."

"What!" Merlin cried, falling to his knees in shock. Merlin had known the old king was ill, but he'd never suspected it was this bad or he would have been tempted to do something about it.

"I'm very sorry. We couldn't wait for your return before we buried him. I hope that you'll forgive us."

"Of course. How are you holding up?"

"I will miss the king. I don't remember life without him."

"And Arthur. Is he okay?"

"Yes. He returned to Londinium to meet with General Ambrosius. Arthur wanted to tell Ambrosius of his father's death face to face. There is also a problem with Rowena and Morgause. They went to Brittany as you requested, but later departed for Saxon lands. Morgause gave birth to a child who she claims is Arthur's. She named him Cerdac."

Merlin wanted to return to the future with his amazing story, but the burden on his heart was too great. He knew he had to get to Londinium as fast as he could. He would need to comfort his great friend General Ambrosius. Merlin knew that with this news, there might not be any more trips to visit Arthur, Ambrosius, and the rest of his friends of this time period. He almost felt guilty for feeling excited about moving to Mexico and beginning a new adventure.

Ambrosius had grown into a great General as a man. His life had changed dramatically since Merlin rescued him from certain death at the hands of King Vortigern. The open relationship with King Cadwellon after Merlin's involvement gave Ambrosius an anchor that spanned time. He was one of the participants who actually was recorded in history. His deeds and military strategies were so great that many of the people in the future thought him to be the King Arthur of legend or perhaps the legendary Merlin. But Merlin knew the truth. Ambrosius was a great man, and now this great man's anchor was gone.

Merlin, Sir Thomas, and an escort of six soldiers rode hard to the palace of the late King Uther. Upon their arrival, they quickly dismounted and ran into the great hall. There were a lot of men meandering about as they made their way to one of the pages. Merlin asked for King Arthur and was directed to the former chamber of King Uther. Inside, Merlin saw the king preparing for war. "Arthur," he called out. "Where is General Ambrosius?"

"Merlin. I've been waiting for you. General Ambrosius is with his unit commanders preparing for war."

"How is he handling the death of his father?"

"He grieved heavily for a while. But the coming war keeps his mind occupied."

"I must see him and add my condolences."

"That will have to wait. We have a war to fight and I need your views of the battle plan."

"Is everything ready?"

"Yes," Arthur replied, without any hesitancy in his voice. "Come, I'll show you." Arthur pulled out some hand-drawn maps showing the layout of Briton, including the forts, cities, and old Roman roads. Arthur then laid out the strategy for the ensuing battles. Pointing to a location on the map, he said, "We will begin our assault here. Sir Thomas' archers will fire four salvos into the enemy. He will then move his men to the next enemy encampment and repeat the process. Sir Kay will lead his infantry in a charge, directly at the enemy's front. His troops will stop three hundred feet short of the enemy's lines. General Ambrosius will lead his cavalry on a charge into the ranks of the enemy. King Ban will be stationed with his men to the rear of the enemy, thus herding them westward as they retreat. I will take General Ambrosius' position at the second battle site with King Bohort in King Ban's position and King Hoel in Sir Kay's position. We will continue this at four of the five main Saxon encampments and will make additional attacks along the way as they stop to regroup. We'll be herding them to a final battle at this location."

Merlin looked at the map and saw "Mount Badon" and

knew he was soon to witness a momentous event. He also took note that his protégé had designed the battle plan to make maximum use of the old Roman roads for the rapid movement of troops. The battle plan was drawn in a manner that should reduce casualties while maximizing the effectiveness of his army. Merlin felt a tingle of pride move up his spine as he thought of how well Arthur was doing as a leader.

"Merlin, for this war I have a gift for you." Arthur went to a corner of the room and produced a beautiful white shield with gold trim, emblazoned with the figure of a red dragon. Merlin held the shield as Arthur handed it to him and admired the workmanship. Merlin remembered how only a short time before he'd been demoted because of doing what King Arthur II had asked him to do; now he was being honored and rewarded as a great man. Merlin also remembered how he had talked about the battle of dragons to King Vortigern and how his story had become a mainstay of the future kings. Each king wanted to be the king Merlin had prophesized, but only now was the true red dragon present in the form of Arthur. "You have rarely asked for anything while in Briton's service. You must accept this shield from a grateful king."

Merlin looked at the king and saw the man that Briton, history, and the entire world would forever hold in a special place in their hearts, The Red Dragon of Briton, King Arthur I.

Merlin left King Arthur with his battle plan and found General Ambrosius. "My heart goes out to you, my friend."

"And mine to yours," replied General Ambrosius. "I know how close you were to my father. Right now my mind is on this war. I feel fortunate that my father died at a time when I would be too deep in war to grieve as I otherwise might."

"I sadly agree." With tears running down his face, Merlin embraced General Ambrosius and the two men left to join the march of war.

***

The spectacular army moved toward the enemy, King Arthur and Merlin at its lead, followed by General Ambrosius, King Hoel, King Ban, King Bohort, Sir Kay, King Ector, and Sir Thomas. All banners were flying as the men continue their march in the clear, cool air until they reached a crossroads. King Arthur led his half of the army toward their destination while General Ambrosius led the second group to the first battle site. Merlin waited at the crossroads and watched his two protégés lead their separate armies toward their deployment areas. He stretched high in the saddle, observing a sight that any archeologist would practically kill for.

The men under Sir Thomas' command were the first to see action. The former caretaker led his men to the top of a small hill overlooking the enemy's encampment. There would be no surprise attack this time as the enemy lined up for battle. As soon as the troops were in position, Sir Thomas unleashed his salvos, which reminded Merlin of the modern-day "scorched earth" policies the Air Force and Navy used to weaken the enemy before the final attack by the armor and infantry units. However, no matter how effective the archers, or artillery in modern warfare, might be, no battle could be won without the infantry physically taking the ground. Merlin continued to watch as the last arrow left for its destination.

Sir Kay began his charge while Sir Thomas gathered his men and began the march to King Arthur's location. The men under Sir Kay ran as fast as their legs would carry them, yelling war cries along the way. Sir Kay halted his attack three hundred yards short of the trembling enemy lines. His men reformed their ranks and stood with their swords, shields, and spears facing the enemy as General Ambrosius' cavalry prepared their assault.

The trumpets sounded and Ambrosius signaled the charge. The gallant cavalry spurred their horses to a gallop in a mad dash toward the enemy. Clouds formed as the grass was turned to dirt and the dirt to dust from the hooves of the attacking horses. The cavalrymen held their shields close and their spears straight ahead as they neared Sir Kay's lines. Sir Kay gave the order and the trumpets blared to signal the infantry to drop to the ground. Just as Sir Kay's men hit the dirt, General Ambrosius' cavalry reached Sir Kay's line and jumped over the infantrymen and burst upon the enemy. The Saxons' front lines were hit hard and immediately began to fall apart. Sir Kay's infantry joined with the cavalry as the Saxons tried to figure out exactly what was going on. The bewildered men on the enemy lines quickly faltered and routed despite both threats and encouragement from their leaders. The Saxons ran away from General Ambrosius and Sir Kay's forces and headed toward King Ban's troops. King Ban had his trumpeters sound a charge, but held his men back. The startled enemy broke into a panic and ran in the direction Arthur intended. The first battle of the day was a success, but there was still more to come.

Sir Thomas reached his destination in short order thanks to the old Roman roads. Once again his men lined up facing a prepared enemy. Once again Sir Thomas' archers unleashed salvo upon salvo of arrows. Merlin looked out upon the lines of the enemy and watched how heroically they stood their ground despite the accumulating death in their lines as the arrows found their mark. Sir Thomas finally ordered the trumpets to sound the cease-fire and he pulled his men back. The unsuspecting enemy soldiers began to cheer in the mistaken belief that they had somehow won the battle. Merlin shook his head at the idea of the Britons backing down.

King Ector rode up beside Merlin and stretched out over

his saddle. He pointed to where King Hoel's infantry stood and the two men watched King Hoel's men move forward as the trumpets sounded. In the distance, behind the enemy lines, they saw dead and wounded Saxons being pulled from the lines. King Hoel's men began a mad dash toward the waiting Saxons and began their war cries in earnest. As with Sir Kay, King Hoel had his men stop and reform their lines three hundred yards from the enemy lines. Just as they were completing their task, panicked Saxons from the first battle began reaching the Saxon lines in front of King Hoel. The retreating Saxons began yelling for an attack because they knew what was soon to follow.

The Saxon warriors raised their shields and swords just as the trumpets announced the charge of King Arthur's cavalry. Merlin leaned over in his saddle toward King Ector. "It appears that there will be no surprise in this charge."

King Hoel's troops hit the dirt just as King Arthur's cavalry reached them and just as the Saxons began to charge. The two armies met head on at high speeds with devastating effects on both sides. King Hoel commanded his troops to rise quickly and charge in support of King Arthur's cavalry. The cavalry quickly dropped their spears and unsheathed their swords and began hacking away at the barbarians. The Germans countered by pulling the cavalrymen from their horses and soon even King Arthur was on the ground. Merlin and King Ector watched as the slaughter turned the deep green grass crimson.

Merlin looked at King Ector and the two men spurred their horses forward toward the melee. Merlin watched the enemy cavalry begin their charge and saw out of the corner of his eye cavalrymen from General Ambrosius arriving on the scene. The enemy's cavalry turned to face Ambrosius' onslaught just as the German infantry lines began to break apart. Merlin saw Arthur wielding Caliburn as he hacked away at the enemy. Merlin and King Ector made their way toward King Arthur just as the frightened German cavalry turned and join the routing German infantry in retreat.

Within a few days the entire countryside was flooded with terrified Saxons fleeing the two armies.

Merlin reached down to his protégé and pulled the king onto his horse. Scouting nearby, Arthur saw his horse and they headed for it.

As the Saxons retreated, King Arthur called his captains into council to prepare for the final phase of the war. Orders were given to herd the enemy toward Mount Badon and the leaders rejoined their men, except for King Arthur and Merlin. These two mounted their horses and headed to the late King Cadwellon's castle.

As Merlin and Arthur rode toward the castle, Merlin looked over at King Arthur. "I want you to remember that you will need to crown General Ambrosius as soon as things settle down. He is the rightful heir to King Cadwellon's estate and title."

"Why would you think I would forget something like that? Briton owes so much to the General that it can probably never be repaid. Though I do have a concern about all the lands given King Cadwellon by King Vortigern, King Amris, and King Uther. It seems that he has been given land by every king of Briton except for me. It may be time for some of those lands to be returned to the crown."

Merlin had a strange look in his eyes. He looked at his protégé. "When I first met Ambrosius he was just a young lad about the same age as you. He was about to be killed by King Vortigern because of lies his mother had been forced to tell. With my help, he raised a great army that defeated King

Vortigern, something that the combined armies of the Germans, Picts, and Irish hadn't been able to do. Then, although the crown was in his hands, he turned it over to your uncle, King Amris, without any expectation of anything in return. He then secured the kingdom for your uncle and, after his death, held it together for your father, King Uther. In fact, had it not been for General Ambrosius coming to your aid after you pulled the sword from the stone, you might not be alive today. If I understand you correctly, this hero of your family and of Briton is the person you wish to take land from. Is that correct?"

Arthur laughed. "You know, I thought I could get you going on that." Arthur spurred his horse as Merlin faked being mad at Arthur and took off after the king.

While the two warriors were having fun with each other, a Saxon leader jumped from a high tree limb, knocking Arthur from his horse. Merlin pulled up on the reins of his horse as the Saxon jumped to his feet. The Saxon immediately struck Merlin in the leg, whereby Merlin fell from his horse. Another blow from the Saxon sent the unprepared Merlin in pain to the ground. Arthur pulled out the Sword of Briton and began beating back the huge warrior. Suddenly the enemy's axe blade struck Caliburn dead center and broke the Sword of Briton in half. Merlin had just pulled himself up and saw the stunned look in Arthur's eyes. As the Saxon swung his mighty axe again, Arthur deflected the blow with his shield. Priwen–Arthur's name for his shield–absorbed the blow, but the force pushed Arthur to the ground. Merlin held out his laser and released its power onto the Saxon warrior. The Saxon turned toward Merlin with a stunned look in his eyes and then fell to the ground.

Merlin helped Arthur to his feet and Arthur looked at his friend's wound. "We're getting near General Ambrosius' castle.

We must hurry and have your wound attended to," Arthur said.

"No. Take me to the lake."

King Arthur protested as the two men rode toward Merlin's time lake. The blood from Merlin's wound was soaking into his new pants. The loss of blood from the axe wound was too great for Merlin to take much longer, so he finally agreed to rest for a moment and allow the king to dress his wound. A group of King Arthur's soldiers happen by and commented on how impressed they were that the king would actually bandage a wounded comrade.

As soon as the king had finished, the two men continued their ride. Along the way they passed many of Arthur's troops who were trying to keep up with the fleeing Saxons. The pursuit was going good, with many dead Saxons lining the roads the men were following. Merlin looked at the dead along the way and told Arthur that he should set aside a detachment of soldiers to clean up the dead by either burying them or burning them. Otherwise Briton would have a health issue that could kill more Britons than the war. The young king hadn't given this much thought and agreed to have it taken care of immediately.

As they approached the lake, they come upon General Ambrosius and some of his captains. "Sire," Ambrosius said, "we have been looking for you. King Hoel has taken ill. He's at my castle."

"Arthur, you must go to him," Merlin said. "I'll return shortly." Merlin left the men and got to the lake alone. Once he arrived, he set his laser for the return home and his life as a follower in contrast to a leader.

Chapter Thirty

Adrian and Annie greeted Merlin as he emerged from the time pool. His leg had begun to bleed again as he hobbled onto the platform. "Adrian, please call Vivian and ask her to come here. Annie, I need to see you in my office." The ancient warrior returned to the mode of the scientist as he limped to his office. The hard part was to remember that he wasn't the boss any longer. Removing his sword and setting down his shield, Merlin sat down in his high-backed office chair.

"Merlin, don't you think you should shower before sitting down?" Adrian asked as he entered the office.

"Why? Are you trying to say I'm dirty?" Merlin laughed as he looked at the dirt and blood covering his chain mail and white tunic.

Annie said, "No, I'm saying you stink. In fact, I've found skunks more appealing than you. And what's wrong with your leg?"

"My leg?" Merlin looked down at his wounded leg and the pain began to return. "Oh damn. I forgot about my leg.

Could you get one of the doctors to come here and take a look at it?"

Merlin was taking off some of his soiled clothing when Annie, Adrian, a doctor, and a nurse entered his office. Merlin was unsuccessfully trying to remove his boot as Annie said, "Here, let me help you with that."

"Did you get a hold of Vivian?"

"Yeah, she'll be right over. What the hell happened to your leg?"

Adrian looked at the blood-splattered shield Merlin had brought back with him and noticed the damage it had sustained. "This is a well-made shield you have here, my boy. Where did you get it?"

The doctor started looking at the wound as Merlin said, "It was a gift from Arthur."

The doctor looked at Merlin, eavesdropping on the conversation.

Merlin looked at Adrian. "I need the sword Vivian and the team made. Would you get it and bring it here?"

"Sure, but I'm not coming back in here until you shower." Adrian looked at Merlin's wound. "You're getting full of scars from this project. At this rate there's not going to be enough left of you to do another one."

The doctor looked at Merlin. "You need stitches. And I agree with Adrian on that shower. We have a bandage that will wrap around your leg while you shower. But when you finish, I'll need to sew it up."

"Fine. Fine. Why don't y'all get out of here and let me get cleaned up and I'll call you in about a half hour?" Merlin smiled as he rose and began removing the remainder of his clothes. The doctor handed Merlin the bandage to cover the wound while he showered and left with Annie. Merlin cleaned around the wound the best he could and covered it with the bandage. He quickly showered and called the doctor while he put on his robe.

The doctor came in, along with Annie, Adrian, and Vivian. Vivian looked at the gash on Merlin's leg and screamed. "You said you wouldn't get hurt."

"It's not that big a deal. Sorry about the new clothes. They seem to have been torn up a bit," Merlin said as the doctor sewed up his wound. Merlin looked at the team. "Adrian, did you get the sword?"

"Sorry about that, we'll go get it now," said Adrian. Vivian and Adrian got the sword, which Vivian had just finished putting the finishing touches to. They took several pictures of the beautiful sword, which had a steel hilt, pommel and hand-guard plated in gold. The steel blade was razor-sharp with a mirror-like finish. No shield, axe, or sword in King Arthur's era would be able to stand up to it. Embedded in the hilt was the retrieval device which, when the pommel on the end of the hilt was turned and the sword thrust into the time lake, would return the sword to the future with a reading of the time and date from where it was sent. Therefore, should Merlin ever be in need of help and be near the time lake or any other area containing enough of the solution for time travel, he could throw the sword in and help could be sent to him.

Once the sword was ready, Merlin dressed himself in his armor for the return trip. Annie had brought him some clean clothes to replace the damaged ones, as well as a change, should he need it later. He leaned down to kiss Vivian goodbye when it dawned on him that he couldn't take the sword back with him. He grabbed Vivian and took her to her office and commanded, "Take your clothes off."

Vivian smiled. "Do we have time?"

"I wish we did. I have to get you something to change into."

"What?"

"Wait here. I'll be right back." Merlin left his beautiful new boss as she began removing her clothes. He went into the wardrobe room and emerged with a white cotton full-length gown. He brought it to her. "Here. Put this on."

Vivian looked at the gown. "Oh Merlin, it's beautiful." Vivian pulled the gown over her naked body as Merlin looked on and then she moved over to stand next to him in front of a full-length mirror. "Now wouldn't we be the hit of a costume ball?"

"Come on. We've gotta go."

"Go where?"

"Arthur needs our help."

"What? Are you suggesting what I think you're suggesting?"

Vivian had always been a bit jealous of Merlin's trips back in time but was resolved to staying behind. Now, as the project director, she was the one who should be making the decision as to who went back and when. She was a bit put off by Merlin telling her what to do. After all, she was the boss now, not Merlin. But the thought of seeing the world he'd been living in was just too much for her to harbor anger. She told herself that she'd deal with Merlin later.

Merlin grabbed Vivian's hand and half pulled her to the time pool. As they hurried to it, they passed Adrian and Annie, who stared for a moment at the sight of Vivian in the white gown. Adrian leaned over. "She is a beauty, isn't she?"

Merlin grabbed another laser wand and handed it to Vivian as he held onto the sword, his laser wand, and some snacks in a waterproof pouch. "It's time to go."

***

Vivian opened her eyes and looked around at the bright colors of the past. "Merlin, is this it?" she asked with a smile.

Merlin carried the sword as they walked from the lake. Each of them carried a laser wand in the shape of a walking stick. They walked to a nearby tree, which had a small wooden bench under it. Merlin looked at Vivian as the sun's rays penetrated her cotton gown and found himself aroused by the sight. He forced himself to put the thought out of his mind. "I must go to Arthur. You wait here while I'm gone. I have a sandwich, some chips, and a Dr. Pepper for you in this bag—be careful not to let anyone see you with those as none of them existed during this time period. Also, be sure to take the can and wrappers back with you when you leave." He handed the sword and bag to Vivian. "Remember the story of the lady of the lake? It's your story."

Vivian thought about that for a minute as the realization of Merlin's words hit her. The sword she'd made for Merlin was going to become Arthur's sword. She was responsible for making Excalibur! She could barely speak as she uttered, "When will you be back?"

"I'll return soon. Take care of the sword. You must give it to Arthur when he asks for it."

"I love you."

"I love you, too." The sorcerer kissed the Lady of the Lake and mounted his horse for the ride to retrieve Arthur. This was the first time Vivian had expressed any love for him since he'd been demoted. In fact, this was the first time she had ever actually told Merlin that she loved him. Merlin spurred his horse as he thought about the words that had just danced from the lips of the woman he loved.

Vivian waved to Merlin as her handsome wizard rode off. She then glanced down at the beautiful sword he'd left with her. Her thoughts turned to the legend of the Lady of the Lake and her heart began to race at the thought of meeting King Arthur. She looked around at the landscape as she sat down on the bench. She took out the sandwich and chips and began munching as she awaited Merlin's return.

Merlin found General Ambrosius and King Arthur in deep discussion at Ambrosius' castle about the upcoming battle at Mount Badon. Merlin walked to the two men. "Arthur, I need you to come with me."

"Merlin. What's wrong?" King Arthur asked, concern evident in his voice. "It must be pretty serious for you to not even acknowledge your long-time friend here."

"I'm sorry Ambrosius. I didn't mean to slight you. I'm just in a hurry. Arthur, I have someone you must meet. We need to leave right away."

"As you wish," King Arthur replied, turning to follow Merlin. Arthur knew from Merlin's voice that, whatever he was up to, it had to be important.

The two men rode to the time lake where they saw Vivian sitting under the tree where Merlin had left her. The two men dismounted and Merlin took the reins of the horses and said softly, "Arthur. Go to her. She has a gift of great importance for you."

"Who is she?"

"Her name is Vivian. She's the Lady of the Lake. She'll watch over you should I not be able to. Go. Go receive your gift." He pushed Arthur toward Vivian.

Arthur hesitantly walked toward Vivian, constantly looking over his shoulder at Merlin. He wondered who this woman was and what kind of gift she had for him. He looked at the beautiful lady. "Madam, I am King Arthur. I understand you have a gift for me."

Vivian stood before the legendary King Arthur and raised the sword with both hands as she walked the short distance between them. Arthur looked in amazement at the sword, glimmering in the sunlight. He slowly raised his hands to accept it, "What is the name of your sword, O Lady of the Lake?"

Vivian looked at Arthur, astonished by what she saw. This young, handsome king with hair the color of sand protruding from his helmet with a dragon emblazoned on each side was real. Tears formed in her eyes as she replied, "Excalibur. This sword is for you. Its name is Excalibur. It was made to protect you. It must only be used for good."

Merlin walked up behind Arthur and placed his hand on the young man's shoulder. "It's time. Meet me at the horses." Merlin turned to Vivian as Arthur walked away, still holding the sword before him with both hands as if mesmerized by it. Merlin leaned down and kissed Vivian, knowing the affect the meeting had on her. He took her hand and led her to the lake. He gently took her wand and set it with the return setting and again kissed her as he held her tight. "It's time for you to go back. I will join you soon."

Vivian began to move into the water but suddenly stopped and turned. Looking at Merlin she said, "Take care of Arthur." With that she vanished into the wormhole.

Merlin smiled to himself at what Vivian had said while he walked back to Arthur and the awaiting horses.

"She is something special to you," the king said.

Merlin silently nodded. "Arthur, there is something very magical about this sword."

"I can see that."

"No. It's more magical than anything you might imagine. Should you ever become injured and need me or Vivian to help you, simply turn the pommel on the end of the sword and toss it into the lake here and Vivian and I will come to your rescue. Do you understand what I'm telling you?"

"I believe so. If I get hurt I can call you by turning the pommel and throwing Excalibur into the lake. Yes, I understand."

"Good. Tell no one about what I have just told you."

The two men mounted their horses and rode out to rejoin the troops. At the castle, Merlin saw that the army was ready for their march on Mount Badon. Without entering the castle, Merlin and Arthur pulled to the lead position, and the march began with banners waving and trumpets blaring.

Chapter Thirty-One

The forces continued to move forward until they were within a short distance of Mount Badon. Arthur had his camp set up in a clearing, which was soon buzzing with activity. Tents were erected, a defense perimeter was set up, and the wagons and horses were cared for. One of the pages had been assigned to Merlin and came to find him after a short period of time to tell him that his tent had been prepared.

Just as he was getting settled in, another page entered the tent to let Merlin know that King Arthur would like him to join the king for the evening's repast. Merlin followed the young page to Arthur's tent, where a large table had been set up and servants were busy preparing to serve the meal. Merlin saw that Ambrosius was already there, so the sorcerer made his way over to where his friend was seated and sat beside him. Soon all the other seats were filled, except for one next to Merlin, which was soon occupied by High-King Arthur. Various kinds of breads, meats and other delicacies were served as the leaders dug into their food. Merlin had grown accustomed to the table manners of the era, but for some reason it struck him as odd, the difference between how people ate in the fifth century and the twenty-first century. The conversations were loud and boisterous as the battle captains downed mug after mug of good ale. Merlin nudged the king and suggested that if he was going to meet with his battle leaders this night, he better do it quickly or they'd all be too drunk to be able to contribute, much less remember.

King Arthur looked around the table and agreed that now was the time. He stood and called for a meeting of his war chiefs to be held in his tent. Merlin and Ambrosius walked together to the meeting and saw a large, red-and-white-striped tent, with several guards stationed around it. He looked around and saw some of the noblemen standing around a large, makeshift table that consisted of a large board held up by four large, flat-topped rocks. Merlin moved to the table and watched as King Arthur and General Ambrosius laid out the plan for the ensuing battle.

Once again, General Ambrosius was going to use his favorite battle plan by having Sir Thomas rain arrows of fire upon the enemy while Sir Kay attacked with his infantry right at the heart of the enemy. King Ban was to take a combined force of infantry and cavalry along the right flank while King Bohort did the same along the left flank. General Ambrosius was to take a large infantry force with a small cavalry unit around the rear of the enemy to stop their retreat. The main cavalry charge was to be commanded by King Arthur, with Merlin and King Ector by his side. King Hoel had become terribly ill and stayed behind at General Ambrosius' castle.

At midnight, the rain of terror began as wave after wave of flaming arrows were sent into the enemy camp. This time, the enemy seemed better prepared–the flames were quickly extinguished. The enemy archers formed their lines and opened up with their own salvos as they returned fire in the direction of King Arthur's camp. Wave after wave of fire passed each other as they lit up the sky while the men of both sides began to question why they were there.

Just before the first light of dawn, Arthur received word that all the infantry and cavalry forces were in position. Merlin looked at his friend, who stood out with his spectacular gold-plated helmet with two flying dragons on it. Arthur gave the command for Sir Kay to begin the infantry assault. The men moved forward, trumpets sounding off behind them. They yelled at the top of their lungs, charging into the early dawn toward the enemy lines. King Bohart moved his men into position with little resistance, while General Ambrosius waited for the Saxons' retreat. King Ban found the going to be much tougher on his end; the Saxon lines were longer than Arthur had anticipated.

Just as the first rays of light broke through to reveal the bloodied scene, Arthur lowered his lance, which he had named Ron, and held high Priwen, painted with the likeness of the Holy Virgin. He spurred his horse and began the cavalry charge while yelling, "In the name of the Virgin Mary!"

King Ector looked at Merlin. "We've watched over him up to now. I guess we better get going."

Merlin held his shield up and pulled out his sword. The two old warriors spurred their horses and were soon next to Arthur.

The hooves of thousands of horses beat down upon the earth as the dust flew to cover the assault. War cries added to the noise and it sounded like the God of Thunder was beating down upon the pagan Saxons.

Merlin and King Ector were beside Arthur, as the three men hit the Saxon front line. Sir Kay's men were fighting hard, but making little progress against the Saxon hordes. Merlin turned his head and saw a scene he'd become all too familiar with. He wondered if these men would be fighting so strongly if they knew that their future generations would eventually melt into one people. His attention was being diverted to thoughts an archeologist would have, not a warrior. He suddenly felt a pain in his wounded leg.

Arthur looked up just as two Saxon warriors tried to drag Merlin from his saddle. Arthur nudged his horse toward Merlin and ran his lance, Ron, through the two Saxons. He then drew out his sword, Excalibur, and began to beat a path through the enemy lines. Saxon upon Saxon fell to Excalibur's deadly blade.

Merlin was too engaged in his own fight to observe the flying arms and heads of the soldiers of both sides as the battle continued. With aching muscles, the men fought on as dawn turned to dusk and returned to dawn again. For two days the mighty armies met, with firm resistance and bravery on both sides. But slowly, inch-by-inch, Arthur's troops began to win the day.

Merlin's replacement white tunic was again turning red from the blood of Saxons killed by his hand. Merlin no longer fought as the sorcerer, but as a highly experienced warrior. He barely thought about it as he slashed away at the arms, heads and torsos of the men he killed.

Finally, the Saxons were pushed toward Ambrosius' waiting blades. Now from two sides the Saxons died. King Bohort turned the flank and the Saxons were almost boxed in. They began to fight even more fiercely, more like caged lions, as they became aware of the trap they were in. King Ban struggled to close the door of the cage as the Saxons began to squeeze through and run toward their waiting ships. Both sides lost good men in this battle, but the Saxons would never again set foot on the shores of Briton while King Arthur breathed the air of the Island of The Mighty.

King Arthur stood at the crest of Mount Badon with his war chiefs, watching the last of the Saxon ships sail off. He turned and looked across the battlefield where many good men had died.

Merlin looked up at Arthur, outlined by the rays of the sun, holding Excalibur, with his red cape blowing in the wind. The soldiers of the Army of Briton had become more than the protectors of Briton; they had pride in calling themselves the Army of King Arthur, Riothomus of the Island of the Mighty.

Merlin moved beside Arthur. "You have done well here. It is now time to go to Cameliard. Your reward awaits you. Have your men clean up this mess and we will leave at first light. I will select thirty-two of your best knights to accompany us along with your war chiefs."

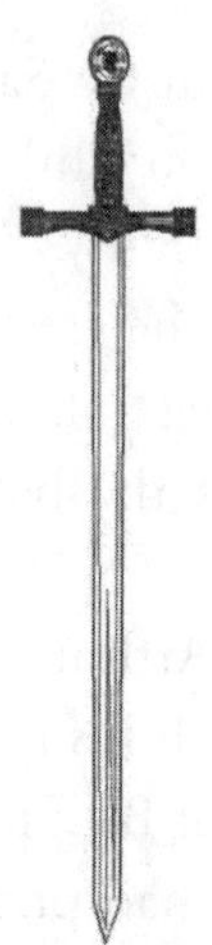

Chapter Thirty-Two

Arthur didn't know what to think of Merlin's instructions, but thus far Merlin had been on target. Merlin made his selections and early the next morning the forty men took off. Upon reaching Cameliard, the knights found the castle surrounded on three sides by soldiers of King Ryence of Ireland. The noblemen made their way through the lines of the Scots and into Cameliard Castle. Merlin thought for a moment about how the future would bring the Scots into control of the lands now dominated by the Picts north of Briton while the Anglos and Saxons would eventually control Briton. One day these warring factions would be united as a single people and, for quite a while, be the most powerful force on earth.

Merlin, speaking for the group, offered their services to the besieged King Laodegan under the condition they not be made to reveal their identity until a time of their choosing. The agreement was made and the men were shown to their accommodations.

King Laodegan was a strong forty-something-year-old man with a black beard peppered with gray and matching hair. He introduced his daughter, Princess Guenevere, to Merlin, the supposed leader of the band of knights. Guenevere was a beautiful, petite woman near Arthur's age, with cream-white skin, long brown hair, and a small button nose. The young princess was dressed in a beautiful white dress with a sky-blue apron. With one look, Merlin knew that what he'd heard about this lady was true and she was the correct choice for Arthur. Guenevere noticed Arthur on their arrival, but she dared not talk to him.

Ryence and Laodegan enjoyed a temporary truce, but Ryence finally received the last of his troops and decided to surprise the city by attacking early one morning. Sir Cleodalis, the commander of King Laodegan's forces, quickly assembled his men to defend the castle. The enemy sent salvo after salvo of flaming arrows at the castle. The men and women inside ran in all directions attempting to put out the fires as King Laodegan looked on. After much time the arrows stopped and loud war cries were heard outside the castle walls. Merlin, Arthur, Ector, and Ambrosius watched as the Scots rushed the walls.

Laodegan didn't have many archers and those he had were running low on arrows. The archers fired blindly into the air, knowing that the Scots were so thick that, wherever their arrows landed, they would strike someone. The Scots began placing ladders against the wall at a rate that was too fast for the soldiers along the ramparts to do much about it. The Scots entered the ramparts and the defenders were obviously being defeated.

Arthur nudged Merlin. "Let's go show them how to fight a battle."

Merlin looked at his protégé and smiled. He signaled for the rest of the knights to follow.

Just as things began to look their bleakest, the small band of knights with Merlin at the lead burst through the gates and attacked head on into the two thousand Scots. The Scots were momentarily stunned by the sight and fell back. It wasn't long, however, before they regained their composure and began a counterattack. But the citizens, soldiers, and King Laodegan saw the knights' bravery and had already left the walls of the castle to join them.

Guenevere, watching the battle from the walls of the city, spied the young knight she had admired most as he slashed through the enemy with the most handsome sword she'd ever seen. She imagined briefly being rescued by the handsome young hero as he continued his efforts to save the castle. The Britons were beating back the Scots at every turn, when suddenly Guenevere felt the urge to look in another direction. To her horror, she saw that the forces with her father were being surrounded. She called over the walls to the young knight and pointed in her father's direction. The Scots had just pulled King Laodegan from his horse and were beginning to carry him away.

King Arthur saw the beautiful Guenevere motion toward her father, just as her father was pulled from his saddle. A huge man had pulled the king across his saddle and was beginning to ride off with him. Arthur attacked with one purpose in mind: Save the king. He pulled back Excalibur as he neared the big man and with one swift movement of his arm, he cut the man's head halfway off. Arthur then pulled the king onto his horse and watched as the Scots began to flee at the sight of the giant riding nearly headless toward them. The battle was won. King Laodegan had his men form ranks and pushed the enemy to the sea.

Upon the return of King Laodegan, there was much celebration over the victory. Guenevere let it be known that she desired the young knight who had saved her father. Merlin and King Laodegan discussed the matter of Arthur's betrothal while the young man himself courted the princess in the gardens of the castle. Merlin had not as yet allowed anyone to know the identity of the men he supposedly led, other than that they were all men of quality.

The brave knight still had blood smeared over his tunic as he gently handed a full rose to Guenevere. Only moments before, Arthur had been killing and maiming men without a thought and now he appeared as a gentle and noble knight before the island's most valuable treasure, Guenevere.

Arthur was looking deep into the eyes of this beautiful princess when she asked, "Please tell me, my love, who are you? I care not whether you are a blacksmith or farmer, for I shall follow wherever you lead."

"My Princess, I can tell you nothing as my master has sworn us to secrecy. But, if it be in my power, I shall make you the Queen of Briton. My love for you is deeper than the sea." Arthur pulled the young princess to him and they embraced as Arthur gave Guenevere a deep, passionate kiss.

"Arthur. Come with me," Merlin said, moving to interrupt the two lovers. "It is time."

"You said we were to keep our identities secret, Merlin," said Arthur with a sly smile.

"Arthur. Merlin. I know these names," said an astonished Guenevere.

"If you wish to marry this lovely lady, it is time we make ourselves known. And you, young princess, you must not say a word of this to anyone," said a happy Merlin.

The astonished princess complied with Merlin's wishes and the three returned to the castle. Guenevere felt her stomach begin to churn at the thought that she had not only met the great King Arthur, but she was going to marry him and become the High-Queen of the Island of the Mighty.

Without revealing the names of Merlin's band of knights, the wedding ceremony began. Merlin stood at the end of the hall next to the local priest and King Laodegan. Facing the king was his daughter, Princess Guenevere. Facing Merlin was his band of knights with the lowest-ranking one nearest him and King Arthur at the end of the line. Merlin had each man step forward and give his name and bow to King Laodegan and kiss the hand of the bride. Soon it was Sir Thomas' turn, followed by Sir Kay, King Ector, and General Ambrosius. Then it was King Ban of Brittany, King Bohort of Brittany, and finally King Hoel of Armorica. As Arthur approached, Merlin stepped forward and the good King Laodegan asked, "As leader of this distinguished band of knights, may I know your name?"

Arthur stepped forward with a smile. "It is with the greatest of honor that I introduce you to my friend, Merlin. Merlin the Sorcerer."

King Laodegan's expression changed for a moment to one of horror for before him stood the man he had tried to avoid ever since King Uther had given him the Round Table. King Laodegan momentarily wondered if this were a trick. Was Merlin out to seek revenge? King Laodegan stopped his destructive thoughts. "Then you must be–" he started before Merlin stopped him.

"Yes, he must," Merlin said. Then in a loud, booming voice, he announced, "I am pleased to present your soon-to-be son-in-law, the Riothomus of Briton, the Island of the Mighty, High-King Arthur Pendragon."

With the announcement the entire audience, including those who were standing outside, as well as King Laodegan and Princess Guenevere, bowed to the great King Arthur.

Guenevere and Arthur married that day in a grand ceremony. In a gesture of friendship, and perhaps to keep Merlin from becoming angry and seeking vengeance upon him, King Laodegan announced he would give the Round Table that King Uther had given him to King Arthur.

Merlin accompanied King Arthur and his bride on their way back to Arthur's palace in Londinium. They all stopped at General Ambrosius' castle so King Arthur could give Ambrosius his birthright by making him an Early-King.

Upon completion of the coronation, Merlin asked King Arthur to speak with him for a moment. The king and Merlin went to a nearby drawing room and Merlin said, "Arthur, you have done well and I am proud of you."

Arthur looked at his mentor with a curious smile before saying, "Merlin, I am thankful and fortunate for your counsel. But I detect in your voice a tone I have not heard before."

Merlin looked at the proud king and a tear formed in his eye as he embraced his protégé. Merlin turned his back to the king. "You have grown quite perceptive, my young friend. On this joyous occasion I must tell you that I am to leave your land and we may never see each other again."

The news took Arthur by surprise. Everything had gone well for the young king thus far, but now here was his anchor and friend about to leave him all alone and he might never see Merlin again. The shocked king, who had fought so bravely in battle, felt his knees grow weak. "Merlin," began the young king, "how can you leave me at this time? This will be a period where I will need you even more that I have in the past."

Merlin looked silently at his protégé for a moment before saying, "You will do fine, Arthur. In my place, Vivian, the Lady of the Lake, will look over you. Listen to her and you will do well."

Merlin left the distraught king so he might say goodbye to his friends. He had spent much time with King Ambrosius and Sir Thomas, two who would remember Merlin well. And then there was King Ector, the man who raised Arthur, and Ector's son, the gallant Sir Kay. These men would miss Merlin, as there was much remaining to be done within the legend of Arthur, but it might have to be done without Merlin.

Merlin turned and left the castle for the last time. His journey to the time lake was one he was making alone, giving him time to contemplate his future as well as that of his many friends in old Briton. Merlin arrived at the time lake with the reflection of the moon shining across it.

The great Merlin the Sorcerer glanced back at the road he had just taken and in his mind said goodbye to King Ector, Sir Kay, Sir Thomas, King Ambrosius, and the great, legendary King Arthur. He took notice of the bright sun and thought how this might be a change for good, after all. He took one last look around at old Briton before creating a wormhole for his journey home.

Author's Notes
The Truth Behind the Series

The legend of King Arthur is one of the world's most enduring legends. Of late, there has been a great deal of research into the truth behind the legend. The Battle of Dragons series is based on extensive research into several intriguing links between the legend of King Arthur and the equally fascinating legend of Kukulkán and the Mayan Empire. When you compare the two legends using only what is historically accurate, and the parts of the legends that are yet to be disproved but could have occurred with the right set of circumstances, it makes you wonder.

This story was based on the question: What would a time traveler discover if he visited the past? What makes this a science fiction story is the use of time travel and nanotechnology. Nanotechnology is real and the advances within that field will be far beyond what is predicted here. That leaves us with time travel. The fact is that the first people to conduct research into time travel were the Maya. They *did* build a research center where each Maya kingdom sent scientists, though the research center has never been located. (Using satellite photographing, NASA has found over 50,000 Mayan ruins that have yet to be excavated.) Their leaders were called to a meeting, some believe at the research center, and all but three disappeared (this time corresponds with the beginning of the decline of the Mayan Empire) and they did write a book that described future events, along with dates, which have proven through time to be completely accurate. How did they know the future? Were they successful in their research into time travel? (The Maya have not disappeared; they live today in an area from southern Mexico south through Belize, in South America.)

I said there were similarities between the two legends. King Arthur was said to have worn a helmet with two dragons on it. Kukulkán also wore an identical helmet which is why he was called Kukulkán–which means, in English, "Flying Serpent." Both carried a sword whose blade and brass hilt had a reflective shine. Celtic drawing would have adorned the handle of Arthur's sword; strange writing adorned Kukulkán's. Both men were white, wore beards, and had long, sandy-blond hair. Kukulkán dressed in a long robe. If King Arthur was real, he would have had to have lived in the 5th to 6th century AD, and would have dressed as a Roman–he could have easily worn long robes. (In later writings, the King Arthur legend became one of romance and chivalry with dashing knights in Middle Age armor, and living in stone and turreted castles.) Briton, in the 5th and 6th centuries, was a nation of sub-kingdoms, each with a king. The sub-kings elected one of their own to be the High-King or *Riothomus*, in Latin. Kukulkán persuaded the leaders of the government of the Maya to change their system of government to one almost identical to that of Briton. He was even asked to be the High-King, but declined.

As for Merlin and Lakin, they both carried staffs that shot beams of light. Lakin used his to defend the city of Ucyabnal. His success brought about a change in the city's name to"Sorcerer of the Well," or Chichén Itzá, and Merlin used it on many occasions. Both men were white, of similar appearance and build. Merlin was an advisor to King Arthur while Lakin was an advisor to Kukulkán.

All the battles depicted concerning Merlin and Lakin are either part of legend or recorded in history. Most of the characters within this story were real people; only a few have not been confirmed by historians. The only characters that are totally made up are Adrian Dupré, Annie Stewart, Sir Thomas, and Bill Barnes.

Bibliography

MAYAN

Alonzo, Profr. Gualberto Zapata; *An Overview Of The Mayan World*; Libros, Revistas y Folletos de Yucata'n; 1995

Fagen, Brian; *From Black Land To Fifth Sun*; Addison-Wesley; 1998

Stuart, Gene S. and Stuart, George E.; *Lost Kingdom Of The Maya*; The National Geographic Society; 1993

UNITED STATES

Varhola, Michael J.; *Everyday Life During The Civil War;* Writer's Digest Books; 1999

ROMAN

Hintzen-Bohlen, Brigitte; *Art & Architecture Rome And The Vatican City*; Barnes & Noble Books; 2001

BRITON & BRITAIN

Ashe, Geoffrey; *The Quest For Arthur's Britain*; Hunter Publishing; 1987

Castleden, Rodney; *King Arthur The Truth Behind The Legend*; Routledge; 2000

Coghlan, Ronan; *The Illustrated Encyclopaedia Of Arthurian Legends*; Barnes & Noble Books; 1993

Hartt, Frederick; *Art A History Of Painting, Sculpture, Architecture*; Harry N, Abrams, Inc.; 1989

Knauth, Percy; *The Metalsmiths*; Time-Life Books; 1974
Kostof, Spiro; *A History Of Architecture*; Oxford University Press; 1985

Moore, Richard (Editor); *Fodor's London*; Fodor's Travel Guides; 1985

Norton-Taylor, Duncan; *The Celts*; Time Life Books; 1974

SCIENCE

Nahin, Paul J.; *Time Travel (A Writer's Guide To The Real Science Of Plausible Time Travel)*; Writer's Digest Books, 1997

Time-Life Editorial Staff, *Volcano*; Time-Life Books, 1982

Walker, Bryce; *Plant Earth Earthquake*; Time-Life Books; 1982

Weyland, Jack; *Megapowers: Science Fact Vs. Science Fiction*; Kids Can Press. Limited; 1992

Bibliography-Websites

MAYAN

http://www.indians.org/welker/may.htm; Mayan Civilization

http://www.learner.org/exhibits/collapse/mayans.html; the Collapse Of The Maya

http://www.questia.com/Index.jsp?CRID=mayan_civilization&OFFID=se1; Mayan Resource Library

UNITED STATES

http://sunsite.utk.edu/civil-war/warweb.html; The American Civil War

ROMAN

http://www.unc.edu/courses/rometech/public/frames/art_set.html; Ancient Roman Technology

http://www.roman-empire.net/index.html; Illustrated History Of The Roman Empire

http://www.teacheroz.com/romans.htm#republic; The Roman Republic

http://www.vroma.org/~bmcmanus/clothing.html; Roman Clothing

BRITON & BRITAIN

http://www.mystical-www.co.uk/king_arthur/ King Arthur Fact, Semi-Legend, Or Myth

http://www.rook.org/heritage/celt/briton.html; Our Briton Heritage

http://www.legends.dm.net/; Legends

http://www.roman-britain.org/main.htm#; Roman Britain

http://www.britannia.com/history/h12.html; King Arthur and the Early British Kingdoms

http://www.kingarthursknights.com/structures/tintagel.asp; King Arthur And The Knights Of The Round Table

http://www.lib.rochester.edu/camelot/geofhkb.htm; The History of The Kings of Britain by Geoffrey of Monmouth

http://www.royal.gov.uk/output/Page6.asp; The Monarchy Today http://www.clas.demon.co.uk/html/sounds.htm; Celtic Phrases

http://www.s-gabriel.org/names/tangwystyl/cornishwomen.html; Table of Cornish and other Celtic Names

http://www.francenet.fr/–perrot/breizh/dicoen.html; English to Celtic Dictionary

http://www.users.comlab.ox.ac.uk/geraint.jones/about.welsh/; History and Status of the Welsh Language

http://britannia.com/celtic/wales/index.html; All About Wales

SCIENCE

http://science.howstuffworks.com/framed.htm?parent=laser.htm&url=http://www.repairfaq.org/sam/lasersam.htm; Solid State Lasers

http://www.pbs.org/wgbh/nova/time/; Nova Time Travel

http://www.timetravelinstitute.com/; Time Travel Institute

http://www.zyvex.com/nano/; Nano Technology

http://www.nano.org.uk/; Institute Of Nano Technology

http://www.foresight.org/; Foresight Institute Nano Technology